The 7th Victim

Mary Burton is the critically acclaimed author of *I'm Watching You*, *Dead Ringer*, *Dying Scream*, *Senseless*, *Merciless*, *Before She Dies* and *The 7th Victim*. She lives in Central Virginia with her family.

For more information about Mary, please visit her website:
www.maryburton.com.

The 7th Victim

MARY BURTON

PENGUIN BOOKS

PENGUIN BOOKS

Published by the Penguin Group
Penguin Books Ltd, 80 Strand, London WC2R ORL, England
Penguin Group (USA) Inc., 375 Hudson Street, New York, New York 10014, USA
Penguin Group (Canada), 90 Eglinton Avenue East, Suite 700, Toronto, Ontario, Canada M4P 2Y3
(a division of Pearson Penguin Canada Inc.)
Penguin Ireland, 25 St Stephen's Green, Dublin 2, Ireland (a division of Penguin Books Ltd)
Penguin Group (Australia), 707 Collins Street, Melbourne, Victoria 3008, Australia
(a division of Pearson Australia Group Pty Ltd)
Penguin Books India Pvt Ltd, 11 Community Centre, Panchsheel Park, New Delhi – 110017, India
Penguin Group (NZ), 67 Apollo Drive, Rosedale, Auckland 0632, New Zealand
(a division of Pearson New Zealand Ltd)
Penguin Books (South Africa) (Pty) Ltd, Block D, Rosebank Office Park,
181 Jan Smuts Avenue, Parktown North, Gauteng 2193, South Africa

Penguin Books Ltd, Registered Offices: 80 Strand, London WC2R ORL, England

www.penguin.com

First published in the United States of America by Kensington Publishing Corp., 2013
First published in Great Britain in Penguin Books 2013
002

Copyright © Mary Burton 2013
All rights reserved

The moral right of the author has been asserted

Set in 12.5/14.75pt Garamond MT Std
Typeset by Jouve (UK), Milton Keynes
Printed in Great Britain by Clays Ltd, St Ives plc

A CIP catalogue record for this book is available from the British Library

ISBN: 978-0-718-17714-0

www.greenpenguin.co.uk

MIX
Paper from
responsible sources
FSC
www.fsc.org   FSC™ C018179

Penguin Books is committed to a sustainable
future for our business, our readers and our planet.
This book is made from Forest Stewardship
Council™ certified paper.

ALWAYS LEARNING   **PEARSON**

Prologue

Seattle
Seven years ago

The man crouched by the unconscious woman lying on the dewy grass by the interstate and tilted her pale, still face toward the moon. He laid calloused fingertips over the pulse point on her throat. The *thump, thump* of her steady heartbeat drummed against his skin.

Relief collided with excitement.

Thank God. She wasn't dead. He'd hit her so hard hours ago that he'd feared there'd be no coaxing her awake. And he needed her to open her eyes. To see his face.

Gently, the man stroked her blonde hair as a chilling, wet breeze blew over the lush landscape. Stars twinkled between thickening pockets of rain-soaked clouds, which hid a waning moon. Twenty yards behind him, cars buzzed past on Route 10.

'Wake up!'

Several minutes passed as he patted her face, each touch growing increasingly harder. 'Open your eyes. Look at me. You need to know what is about to happen.'

He needed fear. Her terror.

The woman's eyes moved under her lids, but they did not open. Damn. He'd hit her too hard.

In the distance, cars rushed by. He should carry her deeper into the woods to avoid detection, but he was more worried about waking her up than discovery. He'd not anticipated heavy traffic. A horn honked. Shit.

Frustrated, angry, and worried, he slapped the woman's face hard. This time her eyes fluttered open as she raised a trembling hand to the red-purple bruising on her pale cheek. The bluest of blue gazes stared up at him with sightless confusion.

She did not see *him*.

He struck her with his backhand.

Her gaze cleared, and the fear he'd so craved blossomed and radiated.

'Where am I?' The woman's dry throat and mouth had roughened her voice.

'With me,' he whispered. 'Look at me.'

'I hurt.' Her flickering panic, like flint to tinder, ignited a fire in him that quickly raged bright and strong. Yes, this is what he needed. Her pain. Her fear. Saliva pooled at the corners of his mouth. His heart raced.

In one swift move, he straddled her and grabbed her slender neck in his strong hands. His erection throbbed painfully in jeans that scraped against the gauzy white dress straining over her belly. He had already taken her twice and still he craved more sex.

He tightened his hold around her slender neck. 'Do you know who is going to kill you?'

The woman could barely keep her vacant eyes open, but the pressures against her neck fuelled a primal need to survive. Blindly, she dug her fingernails into his hands.

She screamed, but the wind paired with the rush of traffic drowned out her cries.

Yes. This is what he wanted. Fear. 'Open your eyes. Look! See me!'

The first time he'd seen her years ago, the beast in him had wanted him to drag her into the woods. However, logic demanded caution. And so he'd tracked her every move. Photographed her. Kept a detailed account. Nothing violent. Nothing alarming. Simple. Easy. Thrilling.

It had gone on this way for years, until two nights ago when he'd scraped together his courage to implement what he'd planned for so long. She'd had too many drinks. Celebrating. Relaxed. Unaware. And he had taken her easily.

Memories of what he'd done replayed in his mind. He squeezed his thighs against her midsection compressing her ribs and shoving the air from her lungs. She arched, kicked, and twisted her neck as more traffic roared past. A streak of lightning cut across the sky. Thunder rumbled. But he barely noticed, his focus fixed on the erotic play of energy between master and victim.

'Look at me!'

As the woman grasped his fingers encircling her neck, tears pooled in her unseeing eyes and trickled down the side of her cheeks. Her nails dug into his flesh, as desperation oozed from her pores. He squeezed harder, his excitement growing as her fingernails clawed his hands.

'Do you see me?' he said. All this planning would be fruitless if she didn't know who had brought her to death.

She wasn't listening, but channeling her energy into the last moments of her struggle. She clung to life.

She kicked and arched, pushing her belly into his erection. A strangled cry croaked from her lips, but she did not have the air in her lungs to scream or the strength to break his hold. Her eyes closed.

In mere moments, it would all be over. She would die. But she would never know who had dominated her in the last moments of her life.

A car horn honked. The frantic shouts of men grew louder as the glare of approaching flashlights glared brighter. His capture loomed; seconds separated him from ending her life. Seconds. *Tick-tock.*

His grip slackened. What would be the point of her death if she didn't see her killer's face? Angry and frustrated, he released his grip and stumbled off her limp body, and ran into the night, knowing one day he'd see her again.

Chapter One

Stop and smell the roses.

Texas Ranger James Beck's captain had spoken those last glib words seconds after he'd put Beck on paid administrative leave three weeks ago.

The words rattled in Beck's head as he parked his black Bronco at a murder scene located twenty miles south of Austin off Interstate 35's access road. The day's new sun glowed red over the haze of heat, rising over rolling, dusty western lands blanketed with rocks, brush, and scrubby trees. On the road's shoulder sat a sidelined truck hauling lumber, a half dozen county sheriff's cars, and a forensics van. Already early-morning commuter rubberneckers had snarled morning traffic.

Oddly, the controlled chaos eased the tightness bunching the muscles in Beck's lower back. He was officially back in the saddle and free of the oppressive slower pace of a forced 'vacation.'

The seeds of Beck's trouble began six months ago when Misty Gray, a ten-year-old girl, had vanished. The last person to see Misty had been her mother's live-in boyfriend,

Matt Dial, who reported to police that the girl had left to play with friends and then vanished.

After three days and no sign of the child, local authorities had summoned the Texas Rangers and Beck had been assigned to the case. The Rangers, often relegated to tales of the old west, were in fact a modern, elite part of the Texas Department of Public Safety, known as DPS.

Twenty minutes into Beck's interview with Dial, he knew the construction worker was lying. But the more questions Beck fired, the faster Dial shot back denials.

Finding Misty became Beck's personal mission, and he stayed on Dial long after media stories shifted from rescue to recovery. When Dial, who turned out to be the black sheep of a well-connected family, complained about Beck's dogged trailing, Beck's boss ordered the ranger to stand down until the political winds eased. Beck disobeyed, using personal time to trail Dial. Two weeks went by before the out-of-work construction worker made a midnight run to a deserted farm. Beck, trailing close, watched Dial unlock an old shed and drag out a large plastic bag that could easily hold a child's body. Weapon drawn, Beck called out to Dial, who raised a .45 and fired. Dial's shot trailed high, but Beck's shots struck Dial in the chest, dropping him instantly. Misty's decomposing body was in the bag.

Forensic investigators found childlike messages scratched on the shed walls, scattered food wrappers and empty water jugs. They theorized the girl has lasted three weeks in the shed before she'd died of dehydration.

When Dial family attorneys attacked the child's character during the ensuing investigation, Beck's temper had blown. He'd spoken words a politically aware man would have avoided and in the end, Beck's commander had saddled him with paid leave.

'Enjoy the next three weeks. Lay low. Stop and smell the roses.'

Shit.

Beck's downtime had been spent at his grandfather's garage getting his hands dirty under the hood of a '67 Mustang. Never once had Beck been plagued by his own actions or his razor-sharp candour to the attorneys. When asked during mandatory counselling sessions if he had any misgivings about the shooting, he'd honestly said he had none. His regrets were for the little girl who'd suffered alone for three weeks. The little girl he didn't save.

Beck rubbed a calloused hand over tense neck muscles as police lights bounced off the freshly waxed hood of his car and yellow crime scene tape brushed brittle, brown grass skirting the access road. He grabbed his white Stetson, standard gear for a Texas Ranger, and got out of the car.

His exile had officially ended.

Gravel crunched under his polished cowboy boots and bone-dry dirt dusted the hem of his khakis as he moved down the side of the access road past the truck and the line of cop cars.

At thirty-five he moved with the quick stride of a younger man. When teased about his fast pace he joked too many hits playing high school quarterback had left him edgy and ready to dodge.

Beck nodded to the local deputies, paused to talk to some, shook hands with others. All offered best wishes and hearty welcomes.

One hundred feet off the road he spotted fellow Texas Ranger Rick Santos. Tall, and lean as gristle, Santos pulled off his own Stetson and wiped a red bandana over his damp brow. As the thirty-something Santos glanced toward the morning sky, Beck could almost hear him curse the temperature, which was expected to kick up over one hundred degrees. Texans often said the state had two seasons: winter and summer.

The sun had etched lines around Santos's eyes, tanned his skin golden, and left blue-black highlights in already dark hair. Santos's uniform was similar to Beck's, though he favoured string ties over Beck's traditional.

Beck glanced toward the forensics van, which blocked the view of the body. The 5 AM call from Beck's captain in Austin hadn't supplied Beck with many case details: female, young, and found midway between the seventy-mile stretch between Austin and San Antonio. This crime scene fell smack in the heart of the Texas Rangers' largest division, Company F, which spanned counties south of San Antonio to several north of Austin.

As Beck approached, the San Antonio-based Santos extended his hand. 'Looks like we both were invited to the party.'

Santos clasped his hand, squeezed hard. 'I hear the captain's call pulled you out from under a car engine early this morning. Still working on the piece of crap you call a car?'

Too restless to sleep, too early for the first-day-back arrival, he'd gone to his grandfather's garage at 3 AM and tinkered with the Mustang. 'Keeps me out of trouble.'

A muscle twitched once, twice in the side of Santos's jaw. 'No one liked seeing you off the streets.'

Anger, he thought, conquered, clawed beneath the surface even as he reminded himself that dwelling wouldn't help him catch the next monster. 'Penance is good for the soul.'

Santos looked as if he wanted to say more, but he let it pass. 'You know Deputy Eli Stiles, right?'

'Sure. We worked a couple of car theft cases.'

'Good. I'll let him fill you in on the details.'

They found Eli standing just outside the crime scene tape watching his technicians work. He was a tall man with a neatly shaved head and a wide salt-and-pepper moustache. Though he'd been well muscled in his youth, thirty years in a patrol car had thickened his belly.

Deputy Stiles gripped Beck's hand in an iron hold. 'Good to see you back in action, boy.'

His intent was to avoid all inquiries, even the well-meaning ones, about the last three weeks. Time to move forward. 'I know this isn't a social call.'

Deputy Stiles tugged his hat forward a fraction. 'No, sir, it is not. I have a Jane Doe I want you to see.'

Beck nodded. 'What's special about this one?'

'This whole setup is off, which is why I called in the Rangers.'

Beck rested his hands on his hips. 'Why off?'

The deputy shook his head. 'You tell me.'

'Have a look at her, Beck,' Santos said. 'You'll see.'

The trio ducked under the yellow crime scene tape and came up behind the forensic technician, who for a moment blocked the view of the body. When the tech shifted her stance Beck got his first real look at the victim.

The woman lay on her back, her hands folded over her chest. Blonde hair splayed out onto the ground mirroring a fully fanned skirt. She looked like some grim angel.

'Minute I saw her, I thought about the dead woman they found in San Antonio three weeks ago,' Deputy Stiles said.

Benched at the time, Beck's information on the San Antonio murder had come from the newspaper. There'd been three articles about the San Antonio victim, and to his recollection, her picture had not been released. 'Why do you say that?'

'Not a whole lot left of her after weeks, maybe months outside. What the sun and rain didn't get, the animals dragged off. No identification found on her, but local law determined that she'd been wearing a white dress.'

'A white dress,' Santos said. 'Common enough, isn't it?'

Deep worry lines were etched into Stiles's forehead and at his temples. 'On one victim it might be. On two, well, call me jaded, but I don't think so,' he said.

Seeing this victim struck a chord deep in Beck's memory that went farther back than a month. But the harder he tried to wrangle the memory the faster it pranced out of reach.

The three men stared at the body, the air around them pulsing.

Finally, Santos broke the silence. 'When Stiles mentioned the San Antonio murder, I pulled up my computer files on the case.' He shifted his stance. 'According to the report the local sheriff used approximate characteristics from the medical examiner and matched their victim to a missing persons report. Long story short, her name was Lou Ellen Fisk, age twenty-two. She lived just north of San Antonio.'

Deputy Stiles hooked his thumbs in his belt. 'Local boys figured the boyfriend killed her. Fisk and her man had had their share of fights.'

Santos nodded. 'He didn't much like the idea that she was graduating from college and moving to Chicago. They haven't pinned the murder on him, but the cops think it's a matter of time.'

'He got an alibi?' Beck said.

'Pack of his buddies swore he was drinking with them most of the night.'

'So what does Lou Ellen Fisk have to do with this victim?'

'White dress, young, blonde,' Stiles said. 'Can't speak to the Fisk case, but whoever killed this little gal, planned it all out.'

Beck pulled rubber gloves from his back pocket and moved toward the technician working the site. The cast of his shadow caught the technician's attention. She rose and turned, and he recognized her immediately. 'Melinda Ashburn.'

She'd worked the murder of Misty Gray. He'd watched her open the bag and tenderly examine and record what remained of the little girl's body. In her late twenties, Melinda wore dark sunglasses and a wide-brimmed hat that protected a stock of red hair and pale freckled skin. 'Good to see you back, Sergeant Beck.'

'Good to be back. What did you find, ma'am?'

'Still taking pictures and sketching. As you can see she's got a good bit of bruising around her neck. My guess is strangulation.'

'Yes, ma'am, I do see that.' The rising heat of the day beat down on Beck. The body had yet to take on the coiling smells of decay, but that would soon change. Night-time temperatures had bumped close to eighty and faint dark patches, the first signs of decomposition, had started to appear on her cheeks. Soon the body would bloat and then split. By sunset she'd barely be recognizable. If left out here a couple of days, she'd quickly go the way of Lou Ellen Fisk.

He crouched and studied the details: neatly trimmed nails, delicate hands that didn't look like they'd seen hard labour and smooth skin unmarked by the hard Texas sun. 'She can't be much more than twenty.'

'That's my guess,' Melinda said.

'Any identification?'

'None that I've found. But we'll roll her prints as soon as she gets to the medical examiner's office.'

Prints were no guarantee of identification. If she wasn't in the Automated Fingerprints System known as AFIS, they'd start digging through missing persons reports. 'Any signs of bruising or wounds on her face or arms?'

A warm wind skidded across the grass, teasing the hem of the victim's white skirt. Her almost peaceful features mocked what had to have been terrifying last minutes.

Beck flexed his gloved fingers as he stared at the woman. 'Is she clenching something in her right hand?'

'I think so,' Melinda said. 'I'll be getting to it soon enough.'

'I don't want to rush your process, but when you open that hand let me know what you find.' Again a vague memory pestered.

Beck rose, thanked Melinda, and turned to Santos. A muscle in the back of Beck's neck tensed as it did when he grabbed for a memory out of his reach. 'Why does this case feel familiar?'

'Bugging the hell out of me, too,' Santos said.

Beck rested hands on hips as he mentally shuffled through old case files. Strangulation. White dresses. Blonde females. And then the memory hit. 'Remember the Seattle murders six or seven years ago?'

Santos rubbed his chin. 'I do. I was still with DPS then. The press called him the . . . Seattle Strangler.'

As mental gates opened, the memories flooded. 'Six women were strangled and all were wearing white. Each had a penny in her hand. The penny detail had never been released to the public but Beck had heard about it through police channels.'

Santos nodded. 'Good memory.'

'He caused a panic in Seattle. I read about it in some report, but when the case went cold, it was pushed to the back burner.'

'The guy ever caught?'

'From what I remember, no. His last victim survived. The killer went dark, and I heard all kinds of theories. He was jailed. Died. Moved on. Lost his nerve.'

'What happened to the last victim?' Santos said.

'A passing motorist interrupted the attack.' Beck dug

deeper. 'The surviving victim claimed no memory of the assault.'

Santos glanced toward the victim splayed in the dirt. 'San Antonio victim's bones were bleached white and scattered by the animals. We don't know how she died. And a penny didn't turn up during the search.'

'No one was looking for it.'

'True. And if the killer left a penny, we had a hell of a storm last month that likely washed it away.'

As Santos turned to respond to a question from a DPS officer, Beck shoved out a breath and turned back toward the body. 'Melinda, would you do me a favour and have a look inside that gal's hand? Mighty important.'

She nodded and squatted by the clenched hand. Carefully, she peeled back fingers stiffening with rigor mortis. As she raised her camera to photograph her discovery, she said, 'There's a penny.'

Beck leaned closer. 'You sure about that?'

'Very.' She snapped dozens more pictures.

Beck called Santos over and pointed to the victim's hand.

Santos took one look at the penny and swore. 'This nut might have resurfaced in Texas?'

'Or a copycat.' Beck rubbed the back of his neck with his hand. He'd need all the information San Antonio had on the first victim and an identity on this victim quickly.

'These cases could stir up a hornet's nest,' Santos said.

'I believe you are right.'

Melinda bagged the penny in a small zip-top evidence bag. 'Beck, I'll pass it on to the medical examiner in Austin.'

'Thanks, Melinda. Appreciate that.' Beck turned to Santos. 'I've got to get situated in the office, and then I'll swing by the medical examiner's office. I want to be there for the autopsy.' He'd not seen his desk in three weeks, but he welcomed the waiting chaos.

'Sounds good, Sergeant.'

Beck turned back toward the road and caught sight of the big rig. The massive black cab hauled a trailer loaded with lumber. 'You said a trucker called in this murder?'

'Yeah.'

'He still in his rig?'

'Yep, and getting more pissed by the minute. He's squawking about schedules.'

'Let me talk to him.' Beck moved toward the truck cab and knocked on the driver's-side door window. No one was in the cab, but these big rigs came with a rear sleep compartment. Beck's grandfather, Henry Beck, had been a long-haul trucker in his younger days before opening his garage and often said that during his trucking days, he'd have traded a year's worth of steak and sex for a solid twelve hours of sleep.

Beck pounded his fist on the side of the cab. Finally, a gruff, 'Just a damn minute.'

Beck stepped back, squinting north over the median into the oncoming interstate traffic, now moving slower and slower as motorists tried to glimpse the crime scene. Soon there'd be a hell of a backup on I-35.

After some shuffling, cussing, and more shuffling the cab door opened and a tall bear of a man appeared. He wore jeans, a Dallas Cowboys black T-shirt, and a belt buckle shaped like Texas. He grabbed his hat from the cab, smoothing back thick grey hair before settling the cap on his head. 'You here to tell me I can go?'

'In just a minute or two. Right now I'd like a rundown.'

The trucker pulled a can of dip from his back pocket and tucked a pinch of tobacco in his cheek. 'I already told the other cops.'

Beck shoved aside irritation. 'And I do appreciate that. I do. But mind running it by me one more time, Mister . . . ?'

'Raynor. Billie Raynor.'

He pulled a small notebook and pen from his back pocket. 'You're from?'

'El Paso.'

'So how'd you find the body? Can't be seen from the road.'

''Cause I had to pee like a damn race horse. Fucking prostate. Thought I could make it to the next stop but was about to bust so I pulled over. Figured I'd drain the well and get back on the road. Then I saw the buzzards flying overhead. I couldn't see what they saw, but thought I'd take a look. Twenty steps and I saw her. At first I thought she might be sick or asleep, but as I got closer I saw the flies.' He shuddered. 'Looked like she was covered in wax.'

'Did you see anything or anyone else?'

'No. Just the woman and the buzzards.' He jabbed his thumb toward his cab. 'Hightailed it back here and called the cops.'

'Appreciate that.'

He spit. 'Enough to let me get going? That damn deputy has held me up for two hours.'

16

'I suppose you should be grateful he's not hauling you to the station for questioning.'

The trucker's gaze hardened. 'Why the hell would you do that?'

Beck grinned. 'Killers have called in their own work before.'

'Well, not me.' He lifted his hat and smoothed his palm over his damp brow before replacing it. 'Shit. I should have just kept driving.'

'You drive all over the state?'

'Sure, I do. What of it?'

'Been down to San Antonio lately?'

Chapter Two

Beck got caught in the tangle of northbound traffic into Austin and arrived at the office an hour later than he'd have liked. He passed through the main lobby and paused at reception to show his badge.

A middle-aged woman with ink black hair, a barrel-shaped body, and thick-rimmed glasses grinned up at Beck. 'Well, look what the damned cat dragged in.'

He removed his hat, grinning. 'Susie. You're looking mighty fine today.'

A hint of colour rose in her cheeks. 'Glad to have you back, baby doll.'

'Glad to be back, darlin.' He'd never admit to Susie or another soul alive how much he'd missed the job.

'So what you been doing with yourself these last weeks?'

'Stirring up trouble. Stirring up trouble.'

As she chuckled, he winked and headed toward the stairs, climbing to the third floor. He pushed through the door and wove his way through the cubicles, finding comfort in the hum of ringing phones, muted conversations, the buzz of the fluorescents, and the scent of the worst coffee ever made. He was anxious to get back to the business of being a Ranger.

He flipped on his office lights and for a moment stood in his office door, silent and still, his gaze roaming over what had been so familiar twenty-one days ago.

Desk piled high with papers. Shelves crammed full of books and scattered awards. Texas A&M diploma on the wall. A print of Galveston Island at sunset. Beck standing in front of his grandfather's garage with his mother and brother.

His return from leave barely two hours old, he stared at the picture of his family, remembering no matter how much a man wished, hoped, or loved, nothing lasted forever. He'd learned that fact the day his father had walked out. Beck had been three. His brother two. His mother nineteen.

His mother, Elaina Beck, terrified and desperate, had turned to the very man who had condemned her marriage: her father-in-law, Henry Beck. Beck remembered the fear and rage thundering through his body as he'd stared at his mother's tear-streaked face and his grandfather's stoic, grizzled features. As much as he'd wanted to cry, he'd squeezed his mother's hand and snuggled close to her.

Beck shrugged off his suit jacket, carefully hung it up on a hanger dangling from the hook on his office door, and then placed his hat on the edge of his desk.

A glance at his overflowing in-box told him a Ranger's work went on regardless of his or anyone else's troubles. Flexing his fingers, he sat behind his desk and flipped on his computer.

'I figured you'd slither back in here like a rattlesnake.'

The deep baritone belonged to Captain Ryder Penn. In his late fifties, the captain had been with the Rangers for over twenty-five years. Tall, lean with tanned, sun-etched skin, Penn looked as if he'd been plucked out of the American West. At his last twenty-fifth anniversary party there'd been jokes circulating that Stephen Austin himself had recruited him. Jokes aside, Penn was a crackerjack investigator.

Beck rose, kept his tone even. 'Giving it my best effort. With luck I'll slide back into the old routine without anyone noticing.'

Penn extended his hand to Beck. 'Not likely.'

Beck accepted his hand and shook, burying the heated exchange they'd had when Penn pulled Beck off the job. 'I just want to get back to work.'

Penn stepped back, casting his gaze over the in-box. 'Hope you're willing to hit the ground running.'

'Fast as I can.'

Penn paused as if wrangling with unspoken thoughts and maybe an apology. 'Santos said you've seen the crime scene on I-35.'

'The victim was a woman, dressed in white, blonde. She appears to have been strangled and posed. Sheriff Stiles suspects the victim is connected to one found in San Antonio about four weeks ago. There wasn't much left of the first victim after a month in the open, so it's too early to tell.'

Penn's gaze narrowed. 'How did the first victim die?'

'Cause of death was inconclusive.'

'So what's the connection?'

'The first victim appeared to have been wearing a white dress.'

'A white dress.' Penn shook his head. 'Slim. And you got a mighty full plate, Beck.'

This case had already sunk its teeth into him. 'I'll make room. The medical examiner is going to be doing the autopsy this afternoon. I'd like to be there.'

Penn stared at him hard. 'Sure. I'll give you this one. But look at your backlog before you dive in and no more lone-wolf shit.'

'Will do.'

Penn studied Beck an extra beat and then left him alone with his overflowing in-box and an unshakeable curiosity for two murders that might or might not be related.

He spent the better part of the morning digging through his in-box and getting a handle on the active cases he'd been forced to put aside.

Several hours passed before he tore away from his backlogged files to do an Internet search. In the search engine he typed: *strangulation, white dress, female.* Several unrelated hits appeared, but halfway down the page a reference to the Seattle case popped up. He clicked the link to an article that had been written five years after the last attack. The anniversary perspective outlined the history of the six murder victims – all young women who'd been strangled and dressed in white. A seventh victim had survived her attack, but police had never revealed the woman's identity. The article also discussed the fact that police had never found the Seattle Strangler.

The hinges of his chair squeaked as he continued

searching the Seattle Strangler case and reading through old online references to the case.

Six Women Dead.
One Survivor.
A Missing Killer.

Beck absently tapped his fingers on the keys to his computer, and then checked his watch. Seattle would be two hours behind, making it about 12 AM West Coast time.

He picked up his phone and dialed Seattle Police. When he was finally connected to the homicide department and got a Detective Steve Cannon on the phone, he introduced himself.

'Well, sir,' Beck explained. 'We have two murders that remind me a bit of a few cases you had some years back.' He recapped the details of what he knew about his two victims.

Detective Cannon hesitated. 'I've had calls like yours over the years. Cops like you who think a strangled blonde woman is linked to the Seattle Strangler.'

'Your victims have a penny in their hands?'

A heavy silence radiated through the lines. 'No one has ever mentioned the penny.' Cannon hesitated. 'We kept that detail close to the vest.'

Beck doodled a box around *Seattle* on his desk pad. 'The guy was never caught.'

'No, he was not.' Defensiveness sharpened the words.

Beck understood that Cannon had to have been frustrated. No cop liked losing one of the bad guys. 'Sounds like you were pretty involved in the case?'

'Spent a lot of hours working with my partner on it. I hated that we couldn't crack the case.'

'Your partner couldn't have been pleased.'

'Royally pissed to put it mildly. Mike was real disappointed.'

'Mike?'

'Mike Raines. He retired six years ago. Opened his own detective agency here in Seattle. I can tell you that Raines just about drove himself insane trying to find the killer. Shit, we all did.'

Beck understood that kind of drive. That kind of obsession. He wrote *Raines Detective Agency* on a yellow notepad and circled it. 'What about the surviving victim? She still in Seattle?'

'I lost track of her, but I'd bet Raines might know her whereabouts. Like I said, he fixated on the case. He wanted this guy in the worst way.'

'Why'd this case get under his skin?'

Cannon sighed. 'You telling me you haven't had a case that got under your skin?'

Beck shoved aside images of Misty Gray's dead body. 'Point taken. Do you remember the name of the survivor?'

Cannon exhaled. 'That I do remember. Lara Church. We never released the name publicly to protect her privacy.'

The name meant nothing to him as he jotted it on the notepad. 'I'll keep that in mind.' He glanced at Raines's name, his in-box, and then his watch. 'Thanks.'

'I'd have said your guy wasn't the Seattle Strangler, if not for the penny. Shit, I can't believe he'd resurface after all this time.' Cannon sounded weary. 'Keep me posted?'

'Will do, and if I have more questions, I'll give you a call?'

'I'd be mad if you didn't. It's been seven years, but I still want this guy caught. I know Mike would feel the same.'

'I'll keep you in the loop.'

'Appreciate it.'

Beck hung up and checked his watch. The medical examiner's autopsy was scheduled in a couple of more hours. Hopefully, he'd know if he had a connection to Seattle or not.

He glanced down at his pad where he'd written *Seattle Strangler . . . Lara Church*.

Beck's early afternoon skidded through a haze of case files, welcome backs, meetings, and phone calls. He was knee-deep in securing a warrant when Penn appeared in his doorway cradling a mug of coffee. 'Thought you'd be at the medical examiner's office now.'

Beck checked his watch. 'Delays in the ME's office. Said he'd be starting the autopsy in a half hour or so.'

'And you still plan to observe?'

'As soon as I get this warrant.'

'Let me worry about the warrant. You get to the ME's office.' The uncharacteristic offer no doubt doubled as the only apology Beck would get from Penn on the Gray case.

'I've just about got it.'

'I know. But go on and get. Let me get it taken care of for you.'

Beck rose, noting the stiffness in his back. 'I'll keep you posted.'

A wall of heat hit Beck as he moved out of the air-conditioning of the Rangers' offices and moved across the parking lot to his car. Even late in the day, heat thickened the interior and the leather seats scorched his back as he slid behind the wheel and fired up the engine. Soon the air-conditioning hummed, and he was on his way to the ME's office.

Out of his car, heat rose off the asphalt as he crossed to the medical examiner's building. The thick smell of ammonia and death greeted him as he signed in and strode toward the medical examiner's office.

A reed-thin man with a dark mustache stood behind a desk covered in stacks of files, journals, and papers. He wore scrubs and a surgical cap, which covered a stock of dark hair. 'Heard you might be joining me.'

'Doc.'

Dr Hank Watterson was in his late thirties and had joined the medical examiner's office just months ago. From Colorado, he'd served in the Air Force after graduating from medical school. 'Beck. Santos called. He'll be here in ten minutes. Traffic delay.'

A Ranger spent a good bit of his time in the car covering his territory and understood stalled traffic, storms, and a dozen other delays could slow him down. After more pleasantries, Beck donned a surgical gown and gloves and followed Watterson into the autopsy room. The victim lay on a stainless steel gurney. A white sheet covered her slight frame except for the shock of blonde hair, which peeked out by her shoulder.

'I did a quick look at the body this morning. The bruising around her neck is consistent with strangulation, but I'll make the official call once I've done a full exam.'

Dr Watterson's assistant, Fran, a slight woman with mousy brown hair, nodded to Beck as she clicked on the overhead light and double-checked the instruments. 'Ready Doc,' she said.

The doors pushed open, and Santos appeared unruffled and ready to work. 'Give me a minute, and I'll be good to go.' He removed his hat and, like Beck, donned surgical gear.

Santos stood shoulder to shoulder with Beck as the doctor began the external examination of the body.

She'd been a pretty little lady: petite, delicate frame, high slash of cheekbones. She had no signs of drug use and sported a yellow rose on her right ankle.

The doctor did a full set of X-rays including her neck, which he put on the viewing screen. The hyoid, a horseshoe-shaped bone in the center of the neck, had been snapped.

'She was strangled,' Dr Watterson said. 'The snapped hyoid is consistent with strangulation.'

The internal exam showed no stress to internal organs. This woman had lived a clean life. What had attracted the killer? Her beauty and youth could have been factors. And her small stature would have made her an easier target.

When Beck stepped out of the autopsy room two hours later, the digital clock read 7:02 PM. His stomach growled and he realized, except for a pack of nabs, he'd not eaten since a bagel at the garage. Coffee and a steak would tank up his reserves and keep him moving for hours.

Dr Watterson emerged from the exam room. 'Here are her personal belongings.'

Beck and Santos tossed their scrubs in the hamper and took the plastic bag filled only with a white dress. The simple dress was made of white cotton and brushed. Lace trimmed a scooped collar and a hem long enough to brush her ankles.

'There's no label,' Beck said as he inspected the inside collar.

'It looks handmade,' Santos said.

Beck rolled a length of lace between his calloused fingers. 'I called Seattle this morning about their Strangler case.'

'Kind of premature.'

'Maybe. But the killer took his time and Seattle never caught their Strangler.'

Santos shrugged stiff shoulders. 'What do you know about the survivor?'

'Only a name. Lara Church. The lead investigator has retired but is still in Seattle. A private detective now.'

'So you gonna call him?'

'I want to dig more on our end. See if there are more connections.'

'What's that in the evidence bag?'

Beck dug out a small plastic bag containing a penny. He studied the coin through the plastic. 'The penny is dated 1943. A heavy patina suggests extensive circulation, but there is nothing remarkable about it.'

'So why put a penny in her hand?'

'Why dress her in white and why lay her on the side of the road? Crazy's got its own set of answers.'

Beck didn't have to wait long before he got identification on his Jane Doe. He'd been back at his desk less than an hour when a detective in Austin's Missing Persons division called.

'Jim Beck,' he said cradling the phone under his chin.

'Detective Walter Cass, with Austin Police Missing Persons.'

Beck leaned forward in his chair. 'Detective Cass, what can I do for you?'

'I think I might have a hit on your Jane Doe.'

'Really?'

'We started a file yesterday on a Gretchen Hart, age twenty-two. She'd been a waitress at a diner near the university. Her boss got worried when she didn't show up to work three days ago. He sent one of the other waitresses to her apartment, and when she didn't answer, the gal got the manager to open up Hart's place. No signs of trouble, but no Gretchen.'

'She could have just taken off.'

'Not her style according to the boss. Punctual and hardworking. She was a student studying English at the university and using the waitress gig to pay bills.' Paper rustled through the phone. 'I'm looking at your autopsy picture, and it matches the pictures I have.'

Beck scribbled the woman's name on a pad. 'The victim's prints have no hits in AFIS.'

'I doubt this gal would be in the system. Seems squeaky clean. What happened to your victim?'

'Strangled. Body found this morning on the side of I-35.'

Cass released a sigh. 'Sorry to hear that.'

'What can you tell me about her?'

'I don't have much else other than a DOB, height, and weight. But I can give you her boss's name. Mack Rivers of the River Diner.'

'Can you send me her picture?'

'I'll upload it now.'

'Thanks.' Beck hung up and checked his watch. Ten-fifteen. Minutes later the picture arrived in his email. A quick look and he knew he had his victim. The image featured a bright-eyed young girl who stared directly into the camera. Long, full blonde hair framed a face with skin as smooth as porcelain. His thoughts flashed to the crime scene and what the killer had done to this young woman. 'Damn.'

A quick phone call to the River Diner told him he had two hours before closing. Standing, he stretched the knots from his back and crossed to his door where he retrieved his coat. He grabbed his hat and headed out.

The diner was less than a ten-minute drive from his office and within twenty minutes he sat in a booth scanning a menu. The place was nice enough. Fairly new, but built to resemble a classic fifties diner. The waitresses were young and wore matching pink T-shirts that said THE RIVER DINER.

Beck ordered a burger, fries, and a soda and asked for the owner. The waitress hesitated and eyed him carefully for a moment and then left.

Minutes later a man approached him. Early forties with dark black hair and olive skin, he wore the same T-shirt as the waitstaff, but grease and flour stains covered his. 'I hear you wanted to see me.'

Beck rose. 'Sergeant Jim Beck with the Texas Rangers.'

'Mack Rivers.' He wiped his hands on his kitchen apron. 'Does this have to do with Gretchen?'

'It does.' Beck nodded toward the booth seat across from him and waited until Rivers sat.

'Did you find her?'

'I believe we have.'

Rivers shoved out a breath. 'This isn't good news.'

'No, sir. We found her body early this morning.'

Rivers sat back as if the wind had been knocked out of him. 'What happened?'

'She was strangled.'

'What?' He shook his head. 'That doesn't make sense.'

'No, sir, news like this never does.' He pulled a pad from his breast pocket. 'She have any boyfriends or family that you know of?'

Mack's face paled as he fully absorbed Beck's news. 'No. Said she didn't have time for a boyfriend. She was either working here or going to school.'

'What about patrons or any guy that might've been giving her a hard time?'

'Everybody liked Gretchen. Sweet kid.' Mack rubbed the back of his neck as if trying to distract himself from strong emotions.

'Where'd she go to school?'

'UT here in Austin.'

'She have close friends?'

Rivers pinched the bridge of his nose as if fighting tears. 'Everybody liked Gretchen. She was a good, hardworking kid. Are you sure it's her?'

'The picture you sent to Austin Missing Persons matches the victim we have at the morgue. We'll match fingerprints and dental records to seal the deal, but I don't anticipate surprises.'

He dug his fingers through his hair. 'Good lord.'

'Did she have family?'

'Came from back east. Family in Maryland, I think. Living in Texas on her own and paying her own way.'

Beck glanced around the diner, which even at this late hour maintained a lively pace. 'There been anyone hanging around here that might have shown a special interest in Gretchen?'

He cleared his throat, drawing Beck's attention to a large snake tattoo that coiled around the guy's neck. 'Like I said, not that I know.'

'Would you have known? The place is busy and there's a lot to keep up with.'

His gaze sharpened. 'I look after my girls. If there is a problem, I hear about it.' He shook his head. 'Shit.'

'Can you give me her home address?'

'Yeah, sure. I've got to look it up.' Rivers rose and walked away, his shoulders hunched.

The waitress appeared again. 'Your order is almost up.'

'Can you make it to-go?'

'Sure.' Small, pale hands clenched at her sides. Her name badge read DANNI. 'This is about Gretchen, isn't it?'

'It is.' Heavy eyeliner couldn't hide the blonde waitress's youth. She couldn't be more than seventeen.

'I'm the one that went by her place and got the manager. She's not the type to blow off work.'

'I'm surprised your boss sent you.'

A dark brow arched. 'Why? Because I'm young?'

'Exactly.'

She shrugged. 'None of us figured we'd find real trouble.'

'But you did.'

'There were a couple of newspapers in front of her door and a notice from a delivery company. She'd been waiting on a new exercise video and wouldn't have just left the sticker on the door and not gotten the package.'

'There anyone out there with reason to hurt her?'

'She is like the ultimate Goody Two-shoes. She never made anyone mad.'

'Danni, how long have you known her?'

'Not super long. A couple of months. She was nice.'

'No one gave her trouble?'

'No one. The customers loved her.'

'You get lots of regulars?'

'Eighty percent of the business is repeats. Our cook

32

makes good food, and it's cheap, so people keep coming back.'

Rivers appeared with a notecard that he handed to Beck with a hand that slightly trembled. 'Here you go.'

'Thanks.' He glanced at the address. Apartments near the campus.

It was late, but Beck wanted to visit Hart's apartment. 'Thanks. If I've got more questions, I'll give you a call.'

Danni and Rivers promised to answer whatever questions he had, and after leaving them both his card, he left. He called Santos. 'It's Beck. I spoke to the owner of the River Diner. He's given me Hart's address.' He repeated the address to Santos.

'I'll meet you there.'

'How long will it take you to get up to Austin?'

'I'm halfway. A half hour.' Rangers worked until the job was done. Didn't matter how long, they just kept working. 'The diner people give you any idea who might have done this?'

'As far as they were concerned she was an angel.'

Chapter Three

Beck pulled up to the large apartment complex just after eleven. He'd called ahead to the manager, who now waited for Beck outside the three-floor apartment building. As he got out of his car, Santos rolled up in his Bronco.

Santos slid out of his car, a file in his hand. 'I brought this for you. It's the Lou Ellen Fisk case file.'

Beck accepted the thin file. 'Have you had a chance to read it?'

'Yeah. When you read it, we'll compare notes.'

'Right.' He locked the file in his car, and the two men went to the front desk, where the apartment manager met them. Beck and Santos showed her their badges.

Yawning, the manager, a heavyset woman in her late twenties, grabbed her master key and walked toward the steps. Over faded low-riding jeans she wore a king-size, orange Austin Music Festival T-shirt.

The sounds of music and laughter rumbled through the building as they climbed to the third floor. A short walk down an industrial carpeted hallway led them to apartment 306. As the manager opened the door, two girls, giggling and dressed for a party, burst out of the

34

apartment next door. The girls took one look at Beck and Santos and their grins faded.

'Hey, what's going on?' The question came from the taller of the two girls. She had ebony hair that swept over her shoulders and the straps of a red halter. Short jean shorts and heels completed her look. 'Is Gretchen okay?'

Beck glanced between the tall brunette and her friend, a tall, sturdy blonde girl who wore dark blue eye shadow and a pink sundress. 'Did you two know Gretchen?'

The brunette and blonde nodded. 'Yeah,' the blonde said. 'I mean we didn't know her super well, but we saw her in the hallway and elevator, and last month she came to the mixer hosted by the apartment management.'

'And your names?' Beck said.

'I'm Janice Davis,' the brunette said. 'And this is Lindsay Michaels.'

'When is the last time you saw Gretchen?' Santos said.

The girls glanced at each other as if stumped by the question before nodding. 'At the mixer last Thursday,' Lindsay said. 'She was drinking a margarita and talking to Sam.'

'Who's Sam?' Santos said.

The manager answered. 'Sam Perkins. He lives on the third floor. They often talked to each other at property-sponsored events.'

Beck wrote the name down. 'They were dating?'

The girls shook their heads. 'No,' Janice said. 'They just kinda flirted a lot. Sam knows that after graduation Gretchen is going to move to New York.'

'She was planning to leave,' Beck said.

'Yeah,' Lindsay said. 'She was going to work for some

PR firm. She was super thrilled to be going and couldn't wait. But don't think Sam had a problem with that, 'cause he didn't. They were just good friends. Fact, I don't think they ever even hooked up.'

'She date anyone?' Beck said.

'No. She was all about the job and getting to New York,' Janice said. 'She even started wearing lots of black because she said everyone in New York wears black.'

'She's not had any trouble? And I mean anything?' Beck said.

'No.' Janice fingered a dangling silver earring.

Lindsay chewed her bottom lip. 'She got along with everyone.'

Not everyone, Beck thought. 'Thanks, ladies. We do appreciate your time.' He took down their contact information and gave them his card, instructing them to contact him if anything new came to mind.

Lindsay stared at Beck's card. 'Texas Rangers. What happened to Gretchen?'

'We're just asking questions right now. Nothing to report.'

The girls frowned, clearly worried by his presence. But neither pressed the issue and they hurried down the hallway.

When the manager opened the door, she stood back, all traces of annoyance replaced with curiosity and worry. 'So what is going on?'

Beck smiled. 'Did she have a roommate?'

'Each room is rented individually. The other gal in the apartment gave up her room in February when she dropped out of school. It being mid-semester, she was still on the hook for rent so we've not bothered to re-rent it. I heard she was trying a sublease, but it never happened.'

'So Gretchen lived alone.'

'For the last ten weeks or so, yes.'

'I'm going to need all of Gretchen's contact information. Parents, family, emergency contact.'

The manager didn't like having her question dodged, but she nodded. 'Sure. Stop by the desk on your way out.'

'Appreciate it,' Beck said.

When the manager started to the elevator each Ranger pulled on rubber gloves. Beck snapped on the front entry light.

The apartment was basic, but as college apartments went it was suitable. The foyer opened into a small kitchen, which led into a small living room furnished with a leather sofa and a chair. A collection of boxes was stacked high in the corner of the living room by an old television.

'Looks like she was getting ready to pack,' Santos said.

Beck glanced down at an open calendar on the counter. Notes were scribbled in the thirty-one blocks of May. He flipped to June and saw that the fourth was circled and in bold red ink Gretchen had scribbled *Move!* She'd been weeks away from starting a new chapter in her life.

Down a short hallway were two bedrooms on the left and a bathroom on the right. The first bedroom was stripped bare, and furnished only with the stock bed and desk supplied by the apartment building. The next bedroom was a riot of purple bedding, pillows, and sheer curtains. Neatly laundered and folded clothes were piled high in a laundry basket by a desk that was covered with books and papers. Above the desk hung a collage picture frame with an assortment of black-and-white photos. Some shots appeared to have been taken in Austin, others at the beach, and others in New York. Gretchen was smiling in them all.

Beck rubbed the back of his neck as he stared at the neatly made bed and the high-heeled shoes lined up beneath it. 'She was organized.'

'Hell of a sight better than my college dorm room.'

Beck had lived at Henry's when he'd gone to UT. It hadn't been the fun ride lots of his friends had had, but he'd never been able to justify the extra rent. Plus, being at home, he'd been able to work in the garage during his spare hours. 'I'll have a check run on her financials. According to Missing Persons, she has no police record in Texas.'

Santos leaned into a picture of Gretchen hugging a woman who could have been her mother. 'Kid seemed to be doing everything right. Played by the rules.'

Beck opened her closet. It was crammed full of clothes that came in every colour but white. 'She doesn't seem partial to white.'

Santos glanced over his shoulder. 'The whole room is colour.'

Beck captured a red coat sleeve between his fingertips. 'Nice material. The dress we found her in was homemade.'

'So the killer put her in it?'

'In Seattle, the killer did redress his victims.'

'You actually think we have the Seattle Strangler?'

'Shit, I don't know.' Fatigue hung heavily on his shoulders. He'd had two hours of sleep last night, and the adrenaline from this morning had waned.

They spent the next hour searching the apartment, going through her mail, her notes, her schoolbooks, and even the kitchen drawers. No evidence suggested she'd been threatened, hassled, or stalked.

'How the hell did she catch his attention?' Beck muttered.

They'd have to dig and peel away the layers of her life before they could hope to find that answer. Most folks who stayed on the straight and narrow didn't find themselves murdered. Generally it was the folks who strayed to the dark side – drugs, alcohol, or prostitution – who got tagged.

But there were exceptions. And after two hours of mining information and finding nothing, he wondered if Gretchen Hart hadn't been one of those who'd just attracted the attention of a nut with his own twisted agenda.

Gently, he closed *The Book of Gretchen* and placed it on the shelf in his office. The slim red book resembled several others he'd shelved, and like the others, was filled with a collection of notes, photos, musings, surveillance notes, and of course his dark plans.

Keeping and creating the books for his girls was such a part of his process now he didn't think he could just kill anyone without knowing them. His books created an intimacy. A connection. A bond.

He'd been watching Gretchen since Christmas. He'd seen her crossing the university campus. It had been a cool, brisk day, and she'd been wearing a black turtleneck, jeans, and boots. She'd stopped for coffee – a nonfat latte. She'd been talking to a friend. Laughing. Her eyes had danced with excitement. And she'd spoken of moving to New York. *'I'm counting the days,' she'd said.*

He'd kept his gaze on his newspaper, but he'd not seen a single word after she'd come into the shop. She had consumed him. Overtaken him. And that exact day, he'd gone out and purchased one blank red leather-bound book and had her name engraved in gold raised lettering on the cover: *Gretchen Hart.*

He skimmed his fingertips over the other books and settled on the thickest. *The Book of Lara.*

He'd been keeping this book for twelve years. He'd kept so many notes on Lara that he'd had to buy another book, which he realized was now almost filled. She was the one that got away.

After Seattle, he'd lost track of her. He'd felt lost. Empty. But then circumstance had brought her back to him. The instant he'd seen her, he'd begun taking more notes on her. He dreamed of her. Of having his fingers around her neck again.

It would have been easy to kill her outright. She was his for the picking. But where was the fun in rushing? She wasn't going anywhere, and he had time.

Carefully, he pulled the book from the shelf and

thumbed through the full pages stuffed with pictures and more notes. He flipped to one of the first pages, dated June 1, twelve years ago.

> When I saw her I just about tripped over my own feet. She looked so sweet, so lovely and so sad. I couldn't find the right words to speak when she said hello, so I fumbled a quick awkward greeting. Immediately, a keen stirring inside made me sit a little straighter. I stretched my arms as if awaking from a slumber.
>
> When I slept, it was not a restful time. I dreamed more than I had in years, and all my dreams focused completely on Lara.

He ran his hand down the page. He was no longer a stumbling fool as he had been twelve years ago. He was a man in control of himself.

Lara was the one whom he craved when he'd strangled Lou Ellen and Gretchen. She was the one. And soon he'd let his beast out to play with Lara.

For now, watching was enough.

Chapter Four

Lara's German shepherd, Lincoln, barked behind the house, a clear sign he'd found another rabbit to chase.

While the dog woofed, she watched the sun rise over the horizon as she'd done dozens of times over the last eight months.

Daybreak never failed to awe and calm. A new sunrise. A new day. A gift. A victory.

Most folks missed moments like this. Too busy, still sleeping, or just not interested, many people never paused to watch the sun rise. Not Lara. She watched every one she could.

Lincoln barked louder, prompting her to rise from her chair and walk around the one-level rancher to the backyard. The lush, now overgrown gardens had been her grandmother's pride and joy. They'd grown wild during the last years of her grandmother's life. Though she'd tilled the soil with her grandmother as a child, she'd neglected the beds. She'd claimed lack of time, but in all honesty she wanted to avoid the memories of a loving grandmother whom she still missed.

To appease her grandmother's spirit she'd bought a collection of annuals and put them in scattered pots on the porch. But so far she'd not been great about watering them. For the last six years, she'd dedicated herself to photography, and the rest of life just got done when it got done.

Lincoln dug deep next to a rosebush, and though she enjoyed watching the dog joyfully burrow, her grandmother's unquestionable concern for her roses had her saying, 'Let it go, boy.'

Lincoln looked up, his brown nose snorting.

'Go on. Eat the breakfast I set out for you.' She took the dog by the collar and led him to the large dented bowl by the back sliding door. He sniffed his dry food, which she'd laced with a bit of chicken broth. He started to eat.

She sat on the stoop beside him and sipped her juice.

For the last seven years, Lara had lived a gypsy's life, travelling from west to east and back again. Fear of settling had kept her moving from town to town.

And then eight months ago her grandmother had passed in her sleep and had willed Lara her one-storey limestone house set on ten acres of wooded land accessible by a winding gravel road. Her grandmother, Edna Bower, had not been an easy woman. She and Lara had had their share of disagreements. Lara had been a bit of a know-it-all in her teens and her grandmother rigid. But despite their differences she'd given Lara all her summers and finally the home they'd shared.

Lara had been in Maine when Edna had passed, and she had not received word in time to return for the funeral. When she had come back to Austin, she'd had no intention of staying. She'd settle the estate and move on. But this place, her summer home as a kid, had had a pull she'd not expected.

The house, more than simple shelter, had come with a collection of comforting memories that had seduced her to defy better judgment and give up her nomad life 'for just a few days.'

Days soon turned into a few weeks, and when she'd been here a month, she'd set up a darkroom in her grandmother's old potting shed. She'd cleared out the collection of clay pots, swept the dirt off the floor, and covered the windows with black plastic. The shed came equipped with electricity and water, so it was little time before her equipment was out of the back of her truck and installed in her first official darkroom.

And almost immediately, Lincoln had fallen in love with his morning walks, digging in the yard, and chasing rabbits. Despite their recent gypsy life, the idea of putting him in the truck and hitting the open road made her feel selfish.

Without constant travel, she'd had so much more time to pull out the glass negatives she'd created over the last six years with her antique bellows camera and carefully go through them. No longer developing on the back tailgate of a truck but in a real space, her art had taken on a sharpness she'd never experienced before.

Seeing her work in print and on the walls of her studio and in her home had fostered a satisfaction that ran deep.

So much motivated her to make Austin her home. So much.

And yet offsetting the many was the one important reason why remaining so endangered her life.

Her neck muscles tensed as she raised a tentative hand to her throat's tender skin. She could still remember the moment seven years ago when her eyes had sprung open, and she'd gasped for air. Terrified, a hoarse scream had strained her bruised vocal cords as she'd stared widely around a hospital room at the dangling IVs pulling at her arms. As the heat in her throat burned hotter, her panic heightened. She'd screamed. Nurses and orderlies had come rushing. There'd been swift assurances that she was safe.

'Shh, shh, Lara. No one will hurt you again.'

No one would hurt her again.

What made matters worse was that she could not remember what had happened or what her attacker looked like. The horrific attack that had left her battered inside and out had been wiped from her memory. Doctors had said she'd suffered a concussion. Her memory of the two days leading up to the attack may or may not return. The nurses again assured her she was safe. But as the days passed and her memory didn't return, her anxiety swelled.

Just relax. Heal. It will come back to you.

But the memories had not returned. There'd not even been nightmares to offer glimpses of her attacker.

The police had been careful to keep her name from the press, which had been clamouring for an interview with the Seattle Strangler's lone survivor. Reporters had guessed at what might have happened to Lara. They'd done piece after piece on amnesia. Experts had said how lucky she was that she could not remember such an appalling attack.

But she didn't feel the least bit lucky. She wanted to

remember. She *wanted* to know who had raped, beaten, and strangled her so that she could look him in the eye when police slapped on cuffs. She *wanted* to see him locked away behind bars, his whole future taken away.

Police had theorized her attacker would strike again. And when he did attack, they'd catch him, they had said. But the Seattle Strangler had never struck again. He had vanished, leaving Lara to wonder if he was dead, in prison, or simply passing by her on the street.

Realizing he could be so close and she'd never know it had started to play on her mind. And as the days and weeks passed, she'd freaked out at the oddest sounds at night, the lingering look of a stranger, wrong numbers on her cell or the odd email.

No one could reason with her. Not, her grandmother, not her cousin, not even her friend from Texas who'd come to take care of her. None had the magic words to ease her fears. Two months after the attack she'd dyed her blonde hair brown, packed her bags, and left Seattle forever. The last seven years had been a collection of odd jobs, endless new towns, and a sea of faces that all left her rattled and questioning.

Through that entire time the one constant had been her photography. It had been her home, her sanctuary, and it had kept her sane.

Her grandmother's neighbour to the east had heard she might be staying and had offered her a job at the university teaching photography. He'd explained she'd be an adjunct and wouldn't make a fortune, but it was a start. Her gut had told her to keep her ties to a minimum. A real job meant roots, even responsibility. But she'd gone against grain and agreed to teach a class this semester.

So these days, her time was split between her photography and the university classroom where she taught an intro class. The move to teaching had been happenstance, but so far it worked.

This week marked yet another milestone. She was introducing her photography to the world in an Austin gallery. The show opened in five days, this Friday, and she was . . . excited, not only for the show but the future.

Lincoln's barking pulled her back to the moment and she glanced over her juice glass toward her one-year-old German shepherd. She'd found the large black and tan dog in an animal shelter when he was eight weeks old. According to the shelter owner, the dog had been left behind because of a bent ear and a crooked tail. Such imperfections had rendered him poor breeding stock and therefore worthless. In her mind the imperfections made him perfect. She'd taken him immediately, and they'd been inseparable ever since.

Lincoln ran up to her and dropped a large stick at her feet. Wagging his tail, he barked. She picked up the stick and heaved it across the back lawn. Lincoln ran, pounced, and immediately brought the stick back to her. He could play this game for hours. She tossed the stick a second time.

'Catch it quick, boy. We've got to get to our morning hike, so I can get into town and check on the displays.'

Restlessness stirred in her bones as she finished off her juice. There were papers to be graded and prints to be made, but those were jobs for the heat of the day. Now she'd enjoy the precious cool morning. She grabbed her grandmother's well-oiled rifle and locked up the house. 'Ready to go for a walk?'

Lincoln barked and wagged his tail, dashing toward the trails that led into the foothills.

As she followed behind him, she dared to smile. She had a home. A car. A job. A show opening. Had her life finally turned normal?

Beck could get by on a couple of hours of sleep a night for weeks on end. The trait, which had confounded his mother when he was a kid, served him well now.

Last night, still jazzed from returning to work, Beck read the Lou Ellen Fisk file. The San Antonio woman had also been a student, working two jobs on top of fifteen credit hours. Liked by friends and other students, no one, according to the statements, could believe anyone would want to hurt Lou Ellen. There'd been mention of her boyfriend, but local police had cleared him. She'd been scheduled to leave Texas at the end of the semester.

So far the two victims had more in common than he'd have liked. Young. Blonde. Leaving Texas. White dress. He still didn't know enough about Fisk to draw a firm link between the two cases, but the connecting threads were weaving together faster than he'd have imagined.

Now as he crossed the lot toward his office, balancing a cup of coffee and the Fisk case file, his cell phone rang. 'Beck.'

'I hear you're looking for me.'

48

He squinted against the sun, already bright and hot. 'And who might you be?'

'I'm Mike Raines. I was the investigating officer into the Seattle Strangler cases.'

Beck had never placed a second call to Seattle. But no surprise that Detective Cannon had called his former partner and given him the heads-up. He'd have done the same. 'Who said I was looking for you?'

Raines chuckled, accepting Beck's test with grace. 'Steve Cannon. He was the officer you spoke with yesterday.'

He paused outside the front door of the Rangers' offices, preferring privacy to the cooler inside temperatures. 'What else did he say?'

'Steve and I went to the academy together. He was there when my kid was baptized, and I was there for all his six kids' christenings. We were partners for eight years. When you called he thought I'd like to know. He told me you've got a case reminiscent of the Seattle Strangler.'

'Right now I can't say for certain what I have.'

'There are a couple of red flags you need to watch out for.'

'Such as?'

'Cannon said there was a penny.'

Beck turned from the building's front entrance, but didn't acknowledge the statement, not knowing if he actually had Mike Raines on the phone.

'Was the year 1983?' Raines prompted.

He could have been speaking to the Almighty himself and Beck wouldn't have given case details away.

'I can appreciate you not wanting to talk. Shoe on the

other foot, and I wouldn't be talking to you. The first six victims in Seattle had pennies dated 1983. All the victims died except the last.'

'I'm listening.'

'Her name is Lara Church.'

And according to Cannon only a handful of cops knew the name of the survivor.

'I spent many a long hour trying to crack this case. More sleepless nights than I could count.' He hesitated for a moment. 'In the end it was too much. I retired from the force.'

'Yes.'

After a pause, Raines said, 'I'm a private detective now, and I make my own hours. I'd like to come down to Texas and help you with this case. Unofficially, of course. Before I die, I want to see this guy caught.'

'That's mighty generous of you, Mr Raines, and if I need you I'll be sure to call. But we got the resources here in Texas to catch this guy.'

'He's a smart one, Sergeant Beck. I can help you.'

'Well, sir, no disrespect, but you had a couple of years to catch this guy, and you didn't. Now it's my turn.'

Another hesitation. 'I've got information that might help.'

'Such as?'

'Count me in, and I'll tell you.'

Laughter rumbled in Beck's chest. 'Why don't you let me have a crack at the case, and I'll be sure to call if I need you.'

'I want to help.'

'I'll call if I have a question.' He hung up. Raines could be a resource, or he could be a liability. And until Beck got to know his cases and the Seattle cases he had no intention of reaching out blind to Raines.

As Beck reached for the front door he heard, 'Sergeant Beck.'

Beck turned to see a lean, muscular man walking toward him. The guy was in his mid-forties and had blonde short-cropped hair, a strong jaw, and a straight-backed posture that suggested a stint in the Marines or Army.

The man tucked a cell phone in his breast pocket before he extended his hand. 'Sergeant Beck, I'm Mike Raines.'

Beck took his hand, not sure if should smile or have the guy escorted to the nearest airport. 'When did you arrive in Austin?'

'A half hour ago. I booked the red-eye as soon as Cannon called me.'

Beck didn't like been hoodwinked. 'You might as well turn around and head on back to Seattle. I got this covered.'

Dark circles smudged the skin under his eyes. 'I'm here to stay until this killer is caught.'

He shook his head annoyed that this guy was pushing. 'No, sir.'

'I can help.'

'You got information, then give it to me. Otherwise, move along, or I'll find an officer to help you.'

A faint smile tipped the edge of Raines's mouth as if the threat amused him. 'Did you know the Strangler's lone survivor lives here in Austin?'

That caught Beck short. He'd given Lara Church more than one or two fleeting thoughts since he'd first heard her name, but had dreaded the search to find her. 'What?'

Raines grinned. 'That's right. She lives in town. Has for the last eight months.'

Beck's gaze narrowed. 'And how do you know that?'

'I've kept tabs on her. She was my only witness, my only link to a killer, and I wasn't going to let her slip through my fingers.'

'Where is she?'

Raines scowled. 'I want in on this case, Beck. I want this guy caught.'

He paused, letting the air hum with anger. 'I want him caught too. But this is my case now.'

Raines muttered an oath. 'You've never had a case that dogged you or got under your skin?'

Misty Gray. Beck didn't answer.

'So you do understand.' Raines nodded. 'If you were me,' Raines said, 'what would you do?'

A smile tugged at the edge of his lip. He'd have gone to the ends of the earth to catch Dial. 'I'd be here dogging your ass.'

Raines shoved out a breath. 'I don't want to get in the way, and I don't want credit. I want this guy caught. Then I'll go back to my life.'

'Tell me where I can find Lara Church, Mr Raines. She might have been your witness in Seattle, but in Austin she's mine.'

He shoved his hands into his pockets and rattled change. Finally, he said, 'She lives outside of Austin. In a small place she inherited from her grandmother.' He supplied the address. 'She wasn't much help after the killings in Seattle. She didn't remember her attack or her attacker.'

Beck set his coffee on a ledge, pulled a notebook from his pocket, and scribbled down the address. 'You think she was telling the truth?'

'At first, no. I thought she was scared and might have even known her attacker. But as the weeks went on and she still had no memory, she agreed to hypnosis, hoping it would help.'

'Did it help?'

'No. We kept coming up empty handed. I had an army of forensic psychologists who worked with her. Toward the end she was pretty sick of dealing with cops and doctors.'

Beck checked his watch. He could clock in and be at Church's place within the hour. 'She's gonna have to deal with another cop.'

'I'd tag along, but I think you'll get more out of her if you see her alone. She was pretty angry with me toward the end. I'm not good at letting go.'

'Really? Never would have thought it.' Beck shifted his stance toward Raines. 'Let me make myself clear, Mr Raines. She is my witness now, and I want you to stay away from her.'

Raines smiled. 'I'll stay clear for now. You have my word.'

'What does "for now" mean?'

'You get the job done, and we won't have an issue.'

Beck didn't like threats, even sugarcoated ones. 'You don't lift a finger on this case, period, while you are in Texas.'

'If you were to ask my former commanding officer, mother, or wife, they'd tell you I could be stubborn.'

'I intend to place a call to your commander.' He tucked his notebook in his side pocket.

'I would too. Like I said, you don't know me from Adam.' He opened a small briefcase and removed a thick, weathered file. 'My case notes on the Strangler case. I'm giving you what I have because this guy needs to get caught. I don't give a shit about my ego anymore.'

The file, now pressed against the Fisk file, felt heavy in Beck's hand. 'Thanks.'

Raines smiled. 'I suspect we'll get to be good friends before this is over.' He removed a card from his breast pocket. 'Call me any time. I'm in town for a while.'

Beck glanced at the card made of a nice thick white stock. Embossed in black and gold was RAINES SECURITY and below it a P. O. box and a phone number. 'Stay out of my case, Raines.'

The first call Beck made when he got to his desk was to Seattle. Cannon was not on duty this early, but after fifteen minutes of introducing and reintroducing himself, he got Captain Ron Grayson.

'What can I do for you, Sergeant Beck?' Grayson, who'd be ending his night shift soon, sounded tired and annoyed.

'I got a visit from one of your former detectives this morning. Mike Raines is in Austin, Texas.'

After a moment's hesitation, Grayson sighed into the phone. 'He called in yesterday out of the blue and asked me and Cannon to lunch. We said yes and your call came up during the meal.' A chair squeaked in the background.

'Him showing up in Texas ... that's classic Mike. He always was like a dog with a bone.'

'It's one hell of a bone for him to get on a plane and fly down here to see me.'

'That case got to him. Hell, it got to us all. Six women strangled in six months. The press ate us alive and the public was furious. But no matter what we did, we couldn't catch the guy. Drove Mike nuts more than any of us.'

'Why'd he leave the force?'

'The job had drained him, and yet it still wanted more. He just didn't have more to give. And he'd pissed off too many higher-ups. He was offered early retirement and he took it. His security business is one of the best in our area, and he's done real well for himself. I was kidding him yesterday that he didn't look like a beat cop no more. Mr Fancy Pants, I called him.'

Beck tried to picture himself if he'd not cracked the Misty Gray case. Would he still be parked outside Dial's apartment? Yes. Would he have been driven to retire?

'He wants in on my case.'

'He could be a resource. He was one hell of a cop.'

'Is he going to be a problem for me? Is he going to start stirring shit up?'

Grayson choose his words carefully. 'He'll give you some rope, but if you don't deliver he won't remain on the sidelines.'

If Raines had still been with Seattle Police, Beck would have demanded Grayson bring his man home. But Raines was a private citizen, and until he broke a law there wasn't much he could do.

Beck thanked the man and hung up. He found his commanding officer and gave him the rundown.

'Go see this Lara Church,' Captain Penn said. 'This Raines guy has given you a real nugget.'

'I'd bet my last dollar Raines doesn't give much. And he'll expect payback.'

'You don't owe him squat. This is your case. Look, it's been seven years since the attack. Something might have jogged free in Lara Church's mind. Plus your second murder is going to hit the media outlets soon. I don't want her reading about strangled women, connecting dots, and bolting.'

'I'll head out there now.'

'Keep me posted.'

Chapter Five

Tuesday, May 21, 9:00 am

Beck's black truck kicked up dust and heat wafted on the horizon as he wound his way up the back road toward Lara Church's home. Without Raines, it would have been a bitch to find Lara Church, who resided in a house still under her grandmother's name. Raines got points for the tip.

Raines.

Raines shared a single-minded dedication with Beck. Firsthand experience had taught Beck that the trait was as valuable as it was volatile.

Beck slowed at the entrance of the driveway and noted the name on the mailbox. Bower. The Bower name tickled his memory, and for a moment he paused, staring at the scratched lettering on the rusted box.

The more he mined for the memory the more elusive it became so he tabled the search and drove down the winding gravel driveway. He shut off the engine, got out of the car, and surveyed the house.

Made of stone, the one-storey house had to have been a hundred years old. Rustic with a bit of weather-beaten charm, the house had a low, wide front porch furnished with a couple of bright blue rockers and a scattering of painted planters filled with flowers. Lara Church didn't know much about Texas summers if she thought keeping those flowers alive was going to be an easy task. Last summer's heat had cracked foundations and dried out wells. One missed day of watering, and the heat would burn up those pretty little flowers.

A rustic wind chime dangling from the porch jingled gently in a breeze. Twin sets of windows decorated with faded red curtains flanked the front door. A new stained-glass oval hung above the door.

Before he'd headed up here, he'd run a check on Lara. There'd been no priors in the system, but a quick Internet search led him to the 101 Gallery located on Congress Street in Austin. According to the gallery site, Lara Church was having her first photographic exhibit opening this Friday. It was entitled *Mark of Death*. It didn't take a shrink to figure out what lurked behind her subject matter. The gallery site included several of Lara's black-and-white images, but there'd been no picture of the artist herself.

In the distance he heard a dog bark. Judging by the animal's deep timbre, it was big and running in Beck's direction. Absently, he moved his hand to the gun on his hip. Nice places like this could turn nasty or even deadly in the blink of an eye.

The dog's barking grew louder. Tightening his hand on the gun's grip, he scanned the wooded area around the cabin until his gaze settled on a path that cut into the woods. In a flash, a large black and tan shepherd emerged from the woods, its hair standing on end. The animal glared at Beck, barking and growling. The animal was a beauty, but he'd shoot if it attacked.

Seconds later a woman emerged from the woods. She carried a shotgun in her hands and the instant she saw Beck she raised the barrel.

Beck didn't hesitate. He drew his gun and pointed it directly at the women. 'Texas Ranger. Drop the gun now!'

The woman stared at him, her gaze a blend of surprise and wariness.

'Put. The. Gun. Down.' Each word was sharpened to a fine point.

She lowered the tip of the barrel a fraction but didn't release the gun. 'How do I know you're a Texas Ranger?'

The Texas Ranger uniform was easily recognizable to anyone who'd been in Texas more than five minutes. But that discussion came after she released the weapon. 'Put the gun down, now.' He all but shouted the command over the dog's barking. 'Now!'

Carefully, she laid the barrel down and took a step back as if she was ready to bolt into the woods. The dog bared its teeth, but she made no move to calm the animal. She might have surrendered the gun, but the dog remained a threat.

He braced his feet. 'If your dog lunges at me, I will shoot him.'

Her gaze flickered quickly between the dog and his gun. She understood he'd meant it. 'Okay.' She looped her fingers through the dog's collar and ordered him to heel close at her side.

'You and the dog step back.'

'Why?'

'Do it!' He glanced at the shotgun, knowing he'd not breathe a sigh of relief until he had it in hand.

'I am not turning around.' Her raspy voice stutter-stepped with panic. 'I want to see your badge.'

He studied her. If this was Lara Church and she'd survived the Strangler, fear would be a logical response. 'Step away from the gun.'

She drew in a breath and moved back with the dog. He picked up the shotgun and holstered his gun. Slowly, he pulled his badge from his breast pocket and held it up to her.

'Sergeant James Beck,' he said.

'Okay, Sergeant.'

He opened the break-action shotgun and found two shells in the double-barreled chamber. The safety was off. He removed the shells. 'You always greet people with a shotgun?' He glanced from her to the growling dog.

'When I'm alone, yes. And it is registered, and I am on my land, so I'm well within my rights to carry a weapon.'

As he held her rifle, he glared at her and the barking shepherd. 'You know how to shoot it?'

Blue eyes held his. 'I sure do.'

As the adrenaline ebbed from his veins, his brain processed the details he'd only skimmed over moments ago when she'd been holding the gun. She was a slight woman, not much more than five feet tall. Long light brown hair gathered in a loose ponytail that left strands of hair free to frame a narrow face. Peaches-and-cream skin, a high slash of cheekbones, and blue eyes combined to create a face that would have made any man look twice.

'Why are you here?' Her raspy voice, seductive in quieter tones, was powerful when rising above the dog's barking.

'Quiet that dog.'

She tugged gently on the shepherd's collar, and he stopped barking. 'What can I do for you, Sergeant Beck?'

'You are Ms Lara Church?'

Her slim frame tensed, as she released the dog's collar and scratched him between the ears. 'That is correct. Can I have my gun back?'

He ignored the question. 'I came to ask you a few questions.'

Her lips flattened as if she already sensed where this conversation was headed. 'About?'

'We had a murder outside of Austin yesterday. A woman was strangled to death.'

She stopped stroking the dog between its ears. 'What does that have to do with me?'

He snapped the shotgun barrel closed with a firm click. 'I think you know why, ma'am.'

Her jaw tensed, but as if the words refused to be voiced.

'You were attacked in Seattle about seven years ago. Strangled nearly to death by a man police believe was the Seattle Strangler. And you are the lone survivor.'

Lips compressed into a fine line. 'Seattle's over two thousand miles from here. And seven years is a long time ago.'

He took a step toward her. The dog growled. Beck met the animal's gaze and held it until the dog looked away. 'This woman was wearing a white dress, and there was a penny in her hand.'

Absently, she curled the fingers of her right hand closed. Drawing in a careful breath, she released it slowly. 'I still don't know how I can help you.'

He wondered what shrink had taught her the self-calming trick. 'Tell me what you know about the man that attacked you.'

The involuntary shake of her head told him she did not want to revisit the past even for a second. 'If you found me here then you know people in the Seattle Police Department. Did they also tell you that I don't remember my attack?'

'It's been seven years, ma'am. Something's got to have stirred up over that time.'

She cocked a brow. 'Yeah, you'd think, wouldn't you? But I've remembered nothing.' Reading his doubt, she added, 'I know you don't believe this, but I'd actually want to remember . . . even the dark and scary stuff. At least if I remembered this guy I'd know if he was standing in front of me. Maybe then I could take a walk in the woods without a shotgun.'

'You always carry it?'

'I walk with it. It's close by when I eat, and it sits by my bed when I sleep.'

'You said yourself you are two thousand miles and seven years away from Seattle.'

'I think I don't want to be a victim ever again. So I've learned to take care of myself.'

He handed the shotgun back to her. 'Would you be willing to come into town and talk to our forensic psychologist? She's sharp and might do you some good.'

She crossed her arms. 'How did you find me?'

'I spoke to the Seattle Police.'

Her expression showed her distrust. 'They don't know where I am.'

'Mike Raines does.'

Her gaze narrowed. 'Detective Raines. How?'

Beck rattled the shells in his hands. 'He's kept tabs on you.'

She tightened her fingers around the gun barrel. 'If you talked to Raines then you know he had me speak to every doctor he could find.'

What Raines had done was of no interest to him now. 'My doctor is top notch.'

A cynical smile curved the edge of full lips. 'This doctor might be good, and she might think she's different and smarter than the rest, but she's not. I've seen more doctors than I can count, and I've talked to countless cops. I suffered a concussion during the attack and don't have memories to share; otherwise I'd have shared them years ago.'

A dozen questions condensed to one. 'What's the last image you do remember before the attack?'

She slowly shook her head from side to side. 'I don't want to answer your questions. Now get off my property, Sergeant Beck.'

The abrasive clip in her voice thinned his patience. Deliberately, he kept his voice even and precise. 'I came all this way to see you.'

'You've wasted a trip, Sergeant Beck.'

He managed a smile that didn't feel the least bit friendly. 'This visit was a courtesy because I did not want to put you out, ma'am. But I have come here for answers.'

Her hand tightened around the gun barrel. 'You have come to the wrong place. I can't give you what I don't have.'

'I could detain you and drive you into Austin, where we could have a more formal chat.'

'Cops . . . so predictable,' she muttered as she rubbed her temple with her fingertips. 'You've no cause to take me anywhere.'

'Ma'am, you are a material witness in an active murder case, and I have every right to take you in to Austin.'

'I don't remember.' She sounded weary.

'Appears to me you haven't even tried that hard.'

She tipped her head back as if struggling for patience and control. 'If I had any detail I would tell you. I really would. But I don't.'

'It's in this morning's paper.'

'I haven't had the chance to read it.'

'Then I suppose you haven't read about the woman in San Antonio?'

'The paper never said how she died.' And at his questioning look she added, 'I do read the papers, Sergeant.'

The Austin paper and television stations had spent several days covering the unknown San Antonio body, trailing the story through the discovery and the identification. When the leads had run dry, the articles had stopped. 'We don't know how she died, but believe she was dressed in white.' He rested his hands on his belt, the heavy leather creaking. 'She'd been exposed to the elements. Sun and animals took most of her away.'

Tension flattened her lips. 'There was no mention of any of that in the paper.'

'That was deliberate on the part of the local police. They don't want to show their cards until they have to.'

The pink he'd seen in her cheeks when she'd come out of the woods had faded. 'The first woman's name was Lou Ellen Fisk. Mean anything to you?'

'No.'

'What about Gretchen Hart? She's the one that died yesterday morning.'

'No.'

Her clipped, almost defiant answers shortened his temper to breaking. She wanted to stay out of this game. Wanted him to walk away. Not happening. 'You remember having that man's hands around your neck? Remember what it's like to have your wind slowly cut off?'

Her eyes widened. Fear and then anger shot back. 'Is that supposed to shock a memory from me? Or make me go rushing to your doctor? Because if it is you'll have to do better than that.'

'I got two dead women and I expect a little help from you.'

She sighed her frustration. 'All I *remember* is waking up in a hospital room. My throat burned, and I could barely talk. I *remember* my face and neck were bruised and my eyes were so bloodshot it was hard to see my pupils when I looked in the mirror. The doctors said the Strangler just about crushed my windpipe. My voice is still hoarse today because of the attack.'

Imagining her face battered and bruised cooled the fire in his belly. 'Any idea how you got away?'

'I was told someone passed by and saw what was

happening. I must have blacked out by then, but I'm told the guy and his girlfriend called the cops and my attacker ran away.'

'Where were you attacked?'

'If you've spoken to Mike Raines then you have more details than me.' Impatience nipped at each word.

When he had a spare moment he'd read the Raines files cover to cover. 'I want to hear what you have to say, ma'am.' His tone remained cool, even.

'There'd been a party, and I'd had too many drinks. I took a cab to my apartment, and I remember putting my key in the lock. And then my next memory starts in the hospital.'

'The other Seattle victims were killed by the highway.'

'It was in all the papers at the time. All women, including me, were thinking twice before heading out on Route 10. It never occurred to me that he'd be in my apartment building.'

He dug into his own memories of the crime. 'The other victims had police records.'

She rubbed the side of her neck with her hand. 'And I did not. Yes, I know. Some of the cops were certain I was lying and went to great lengths to dig into my past. In the end, they found out what I told them they'd find: one speeding ticket, which I got when I was sixteen. What I know is in Detective Raines's files.'

'Except who attacked you. That detail is locked in your head, Ms Church.'

She wiped a bead of sweat from her forehead with the back of her hand. 'The key is gone, sir. There is no way to reach the memories. Now I need to ask you to leave. I've got to be in town in less than an hour.'

'You have a show opening, don't you?'

'That's right.'

'Photographs?'

'Yes.'

He dropped the shells in his jacket pocket and pulled out a couple of Polaroids taken of the body at yesterday's crime scene. 'They look like this?'

She took the pictures and glanced at crime scene images of Gretchen Hart. Immediately her face paled and she swayed before she handed him back the images. 'You're full of nasty questions and tricks.'

He suffered no remorse. 'Thought if you could see firsthand what I'm dealing with you might be more open to helping me.'

'Get off my land, Ranger. I have no more to say to you.'

He slowly tucked the pictures back in his breast pocket. 'I'll leave for now, Ms Church, but you are gonna see me again. That I do promise you.'

Gripping the shotgun by the stock, she turned toward the house, her dog following.

As she reached for the front door, he said, 'If the Seattle Strangler is active again, don't you find it a bit odd that he'd take up his work only twenty or thirty miles from where his last victim lives? I don't know about you, but I've never put much stock in coincidence.'

She turned partway toward him, unwittingly giving him a view of her slim neck. 'You're assuming it is the Seattle Strangler. I am not.'

Tension rippled through his body. 'It's a solid assumption.'

She hesitated as if a blast of frigid air cut up her spine and then vanished with her dog into her house.

Lara Church wasn't the timid artsy type he'd expected. She had steel running down her spine. Getting her help wouldn't be as easy as he'd hoped. But in the end he would get it.

Raines had been on Texas soil not more than four hours, and he already hated the heat and the dry dust. He blotted a handkerchief on the back of his neck as he pulled up in front of the hotel. He'd been working a surveillance gig in Washington for five days straight. The case, a woman cheating on her husband, had been a lucrative gig. Ferreting out adultery paid the light bill, but it didn't offer the same rush of police work.

Raines glanced at his watch. It would take Beck several hours to check his story out, and to track down Lara Church. That would give him time to scrounge up a gun dealer open to a cash sale, and find a criminal attorney willing to defend. Sleep would have to come later.

He crossed the parking lot quickly, hating the heat beating down on his back and head. He pushed through the front glass doors and moved to the front desk. A twenty-something girl wearing a maroon vest, white shirt, and black skirt smiled up at him. 'Welcome.'

The genuine energy behind the word softened his mood. 'Thanks. Hoping you got a room to spare.'

'We sure do. How long will you be staying?'

'Can't say but at least a week.' He fished out his wallet and credit card.

She tapped in information into her computer keyboard, swiped his credit card, before handing over the card and a room key. 'I've got a nice room facing the pool. Top floor. Quiet.'

His slid his credit card into his wallet. 'I appreciate that.'

'And we offer breakfast every morning from six to nine. It's good, hearty fare.'

He smiled. 'Stick to my ribs, as you Texans say?'

A faint blush rose in her cheeks. 'That's right, sir. So where are you from, if you don't mind me asking?'

'Seattle, Washington.'

'And what brings you to Austin?'

'Just thought I'd have a look around.'

'Well, we've got any kind of brochure you'd ever need on the rack by the elevators. Lots to see in town.'

'What do you recommend?'

'Well, if you don't mind a bit of a drive, the Alamo is a sight to see. It's down by San Antonio. Though if you're driving down I-35 don't go during rush hour. There's always a backup.'

He winked. 'I'll be sure to grab some brochures.'

After collecting pamphlets he'd never read, he made his way to the elevators. Less than a minute later he'd stepped off the elevator and found his room. It was neat, tidy, and efficient. Not fancy, but it would serve his needs well. He moved to the curtains and pushed them back. As promised, his room overlooked the pool, which now hosted a young couple with two small children splashing around the shallow end.

Seeing the kids tugged at the knots in his back. He thought about his own wife and daughter. God, but he missed them.

Raines flipped open his phone, checked messages, and played a message from his wife.

'Hey, baby, happy birthday.' From the background his daughter's giggling rose up like a blooming flower. She started to sing 'Happy Birthday' and his wife, laughing, joined in. He closed his eyes and listened as they danced through the song. 'We miss you,' they said. 'Come home soon.'

He closed the phone and pressed it to his temple. He should be with them. Only an insane man would fly across the country and chase a killer that no one else remembered but him. But if anyone understood his need to catch this guy, it was his wife, Susan. She understood he'd always be a cop and that being a cop was more than a job.

'It's not your nature to give up,' she'd said so often. 'It's why I married you, after all.'

He checked his watch and subtracted two hours. Susan would be getting Tara off to school now. She'd be rushed. Distracted. Tara would be sitting at the kitchen table nibbling on her toast and taking far too long to eat. He smiled. Now wasn't the best time to call.

He'd give anything to be there.

'I'll catch this guy, Susan. I'll catch him and then it will be over just like I promised.'

Chapter Six

Lara sat on the stone hearth next to the cold fireplace and buried her face in her hands. Her heart drummed so loudly she was certain it would crack through her ribs.

She'd told Beck she read the papers. What she hadn't told him was that these last seven years she read the local papers from cover to cover searching for signs that the Strangler had resurfaced. She'd read about dozens of murdered women over the years, and each time she'd paused to pray for the soul wrenched from this earth.

She closed her eyes and whispered, 'Lou Ellen and Gretchen, God bless you.'

After several moments of silence, Lincoln nuzzled her hand with his nose and looked up at her as if he was worried. She summoned a smile and scratched him between his ears. 'It's okay, boy. I'm just fine. Only a little rattled by that guy.'

That *guy* was a Texas Ranger. She didn't know a lot about Texas or even being Texan, but she'd gleaned enough to know that the Texas Rangers tackled some of the nastiest and toughest cases in the state. They weren't people to go against. The fact that Sergeant Beck had shown up on her land suggested that this case, and especially that Ranger, weren't going away.

Even without the hat and the badge, Beck would have put her on edge. A six-foot-six frame coupled with broad shoulders and a lean, muscled body intimidated without a single word spoken. Cutting ice green eyes combined with steel under his Texas drawl had had her struggling not to lock herself inside her cabin.

She shoved out a breath and straightened. Just because two women had been murdered within thirty miles of her didn't mean the Strangler had returned. Those two women, like most, probably had known their attackers. She'd read all the statistics. Random acts of violence, as she'd suffered, were indeed rare. Most women were killed by men they knew or, worse, loved.

The man who'd attacked her was not in Texas because the odds that he had come to Austin were astronomical.

Beck's extremely male appraisal had her smoothing nervous hands over her jeans. Worse still, a deep, deep part of her had been intrigued and pleased.

There'd been a time when she'd loved the scent and feel of a man. Confident and self-assured, she'd never been afraid to ask a man to dance or to join her for a cup of coffee. But for the last seven years, she walked wide circles around males. And most who showed interest were easily dissuaded by anger, sarcasm, and humour. Her shields. God, she wanted to love, wanted to be held, but behind each new man lurked the fear that he was her attacker.

The lingering unknowns and lost memories no longer sent her into hiding as they had after the attack. These days they drove her to her camera.

Though she needed to finalize details for her gallery opening, the need to create overrode practicalities.

Lara's upcoming show, *Mark of Death,* featured murder scenes from around the country that she'd photographed with her one-hundred-and-fifty-year-old bellows camera. Since only a handful of people knew about her attack, many considered such subject matter odd and more than a little quirky in one so young. But it didn't take a shrink for her to know why she took the pictures she took. In each new image she searched for the spark that would trigger her memory.

'Come on, Lincoln, let's get our lunches packed so we can hit the trail and shoot some pictures before class this afternoon.' She thought about yesterday's murder scene. As it was only twenty-four hours old, the cops would still have it roped off. She'd not get close for days.

But the first crime scene that Beck had mentioned was well over a month old. That scene would be open now. She made herself a cup of coffee and toast and headed to her computer.

Lincoln followed and lay down at her side, keeping a careful eye on her toast, just in case crumbs should fall to the ground. Since he was a small puppy she'd never been able to eat in front of the dog without sharing. He'd had her number since day one. She tossed a piece of buttered bread his way, grabbed her reading glasses, and searched *San Antonio, Woman's body found, April.*

She got a hit almost immediately. The woman Beck had mentioned had been in her twenties. She'd worked in a bar and, according to the articles, been liked by friends. She'd been a student. She'd been months shy of graduation.

The murder scene was off I-35 north of San Antonio. The articles did not mention that she'd been wearing a white dress or that she'd had a penny in her hand. But then the Seattle cops had not released many details at first. They'd been guarded about giving specifics until the fourth victim had been discovered. That's when they'd mentioned the white dress. There was no label in those dresses, but the hope had been that someone might come forward with a description of the man who'd commissioned the dresses. But the tips, from what the media had reported, had led nowhere. The fifth and sixth victims had been wearing the same dress and when she'd been found, she'd been wearing the same dress.

She ran her hands over her arms, remembering the feel of the dress's cotton sleeve. She couldn't recall wearing the dress during the attack, but one of the shrinks had convinced her to put on the dress, hoping she'd remember. The dress had smelled of sweat and the backside of it had been stained with grass. She'd stood in the doctor's office for over an hour willing her brain to release one single detail that would help catch this killer. Nothing had come that day or the next or the next.

Inwardly, she'd begun to crumble under police questions and the constant talk in the media about The Unidentified Victim. Who was she? How had she crossed paths with the killer? One reporter had offered a bounty to anyone who could identify her.

Fear of discovery coupled with not knowing her

attacker had simmered to boiling until finally she'd fled Seattle.

She'd not had a plan when she'd left the West Coast. All she'd wanted was to get away. And so she'd bounced around aimlessly for months, working odd jobs that kept her gas tank filled and food in her belly. She'd been aimless. Lost. And about nine months after Seattle she'd wandered into a pawnshop and spotted a digital camera. On a whim she had spent what little savings she'd had and bought the camera. That precise day she'd started snapping pictures and almost immediately a sense of peace had eased the tension gripping her body. The world made a little more sense when she saw it through the lens of a camera.

Her subject matter had been varied and scattered until she'd read an article in the Baltimore paper about a murder scene. A woman had been stabbed near the Inner Harbor. Pulled by forces she could not articulate, she'd gone to the murder scene and started snapping pictures. Later when she loaded the images onto her computer, she'd studied them so carefully, hoping to see just one element that would explain the violence that had claimed a woman's life.

No answers had surfaced that night, or the next. But the need to keep shooting remained. Her cameras got fancier, more sophisticated, but none gave her the feel she needed. And then she'd visited a Chicago auction house selling old photographic equipment. The trip had been more of a curiosity than a mission until she'd seen the hundred-and-fifty-year-old bellows camera. Instantly drawn to the camera, she'd bid high enough to win the camera and drain her savings.

The digital camera had forgiven her amateur photographic skills, but the bellows camera had no patience for novices. She'd found a photographer in Pennsylvania who taught her how to prepare her glass negatives, shoot her images, and develop the smoky, moody pictures that so suited her subject matter.

Lara scribbled down the address of the murder scene and grabbed her keys. 'Ride in the car?'

The dog perked up immediately and bounded out the front door to her black truck. He sat by the driver's-side door barking and wagging his tail while she fired up the engine and the car's air-conditioning. She loaded her camera equipment into the back of the Bronco along with a cooler of water in the backseat.

She slid behind the wheel, shifted into drive, and headed toward the main road.

Travelling to the murder scene took forty-five minutes and by the time she arrived the sun was high in the sky and the air hot.

Lara pulled off the highway. A glance at the rolling landscape told her the light was not right. The sun was too high. But later, maybe at sunset.

Still sitting behind the wheel, she snapped digital pictures of the road, her truck, and the area around it as she tried to get a feel for the area. In the distance she spotted a slight flap of yellow, which she guessed was crime scene tape left behind by the police.

Shutting off the engine, she locked the car and with Lincoln headed toward the hint of yellow. Gravel crunched under her boots as Lincoln dashed ahead. She stopped ten feet short of the yellow tape. The tape looked fresh, as if the cops had returned to the area to renew their search. Made sense if they were looking for a connection between the two murders.

Pulling off her sunglasses, she stared at the low-lying grass in the centre of the tape; it still appeared to be matted down. She squatted and set her sunglasses on a rock.

Was that the impression of a body? She started to snap pictures moving in a counter clockwise fashion around the site. Later she'd load the images on her computer and then determine which angle would work best for the bellows camera and tripod.

When she'd snapped over one hundred images she lowered the camera and without the lens' protection stared at the ground. A woman had lain here, perhaps dead, perhaps dying, as someone had knelt over her and wrapped strong fingers around her neck.

She closed her eyes as she'd done a hundred times before and tried to imagine her attacker. The cops had said that she'd had no defensive wounds, but there'd been skin under her nails. She'd fought.

The strangler had brought her to the wooded location off Route 10 and had laid her on the ground. What had happened next? Had he straddled her before he wrapped fingers around her neck? Had he been in a rush or had he enjoyed slowly watching her fade away? She glanced at her hands, wondering where she'd scratched him. She prayed it had hurt him like hell.

Lara could not remember.

A honking horn from the highway snapped her back to the present. Sweat dampened her brow and the sun had left her pale skin pink. 'Lincoln!'

The dog appeared over the ridge and ran toward her. The two hurried to her truck, where she replaced her camera in its bag and then filled a water bowl for Lincoln. Her hands trembled slightly as she held her own bottle to her lips and drank. The liquid cooled her body temperature but did little to ease her nerves. She did not like this place, though at dusk she would return to shoot the same scene in the fading light.

And so here she was, trying to put down roots, let go of the past, and live. She glanced toward the yellow tape and the grass that looked a little matted.

Here she was.

But where was he?

Beck spent the better part of the day reading the Raines file on the Seattle Strangler. The case files were detailed and precise. The observations were thoughtful. Raines had not taken any shortcuts. There was no doubt that Raines had been one hell of a cop.

As he'd sipped a fresh cup of coffee, he studied a seven-year-old picture of Lara that had been taken right after the attack. It was rough. Not only was her neck black and blue, but also her eyes were so bloodshot their vivid blue was lost. Notes indicated that an internal examination confirmed rape, though no semen had been found in or on her body. There was DNA under her fingernails, but the sample didn't match any known DNA on file.

Anger twisting his gut, Beck closed his eyes and rubbed calloused fingers over a brow. He willed memories of the gun-toting Lara Church to elbow aside images of the sad, broken woman in these police photos. Seeing any woman hurt bothered him. Seeing Lara Church bruised and battered cut deep.

His phone rang, pulling his thoughts back. 'Beck.'

It was the officer at the front desk. 'There's a guy named Raines out here to see you.'

Beck pinched the bridge of his nose. He did not have time for this guy. However, to ignore him invited trouble. 'I'll be right down.'

He rose, rolled down the sleeves of his white shirt and fastened the cuffs, and slid on his coat. He took the elevator down to the lobby and found Raines talking to the officer on duty.

Raines was relaxed as he and the duty officer shared a joke.

'Raines,' Beck said.

The detective looked up, wished the officer behind the desk a good day, and moved toward Beck with a confident stride. He'd showered and shaved and was alert.

Beck extended his hand toward a bank of chairs in the lobby. 'Raines, caught any sleep?'

He eased into a chair as if he owned the place. 'You get caught up on your rest while you were on leave?'

Beck sat down, irritation snapping. 'Been doing a little homework.'

Raines grinned. 'For what it's worth, I'd have done the same if I were in your shoes. You shouldn't have been benched. I'd have kept trailing Dial.'

Beck didn't need Raines's approval. 'Others didn't see it that way.'

Raines was relaxed as if they were old friends. 'Fuck the rest. You got justice for that kid and put that piece of garbage in the ground. That's what counts, not the shit the media spins.'

'You've had your issues with the media.' The statement didn't require research. If he'd been lead investigator on a serial murder case, the press would have been all over him.

'I have.' He shook his head. 'And if you end up with more strangled bodies, you'll learn how hellish the press can make your life.'

'What's the point of this chitchat?'

Raines chuckled. 'Direct. Good. Saves time. Did you go and see Lara Church?' His voice sounded crisper, stronger and all business.

'I did.'

'And?' Raines spoke to him as if they were partners.

'And nothing I can discuss.'

'Ah, come on, Beck. I gave you Lara. I didn't have to, but I did. At least tell me if she remembers?' When Beck didn't answer right away, he added, 'I'd ask her myself, but I'm afraid she'd shoot me on sight. I made her life tough in Seattle. In fact, I blame myself for her leaving town. I pushed too hard, and she couldn't take it.'

'She's no wilting flower now. She's grown some steel in her back.'

Raines cocked a brow and nodded. 'Good. I'm glad. She's gonna need it if the Strangler is back. She might not believe it, but I liked her. She's talented and didn't deserve what happened to her.'

'No.'

'Was she of help to you?'

Same question asked differently, just like a good homicide detective. 'She told me to get lost.'

Raines shrugged. 'She was anti-cop by the time she left Seattle.'

'That hasn't changed.'

'If you keep at her, she'll come around. Not remembering plagued her. I'll bet that her curiosity will get the better of her, and she's going to want to figure this out.'

'I've every intention of visiting her again. If she's got any memory locked in that head of hers, then I want at it.'

'Go easy, or she'll spook.'

Beck shook his head. 'I did a little reading up on her. She's put down roots in Austin. She's teaching photography at the university, and she's got an art show opening this Friday.'

'I saw the notice in the morning paper. The show's called *Mark of Death*. Interesting topic.' Raines tugged at a loose thread on his cuff. 'She might not remember Seattle, but it made an impression.'

Beck leaned forward. 'Stay away from her. I don't need you mucking up this investigation.'

'I'm not making that promise. If the Strangler is back, and you can't make headway with her, I will be paying her a visit.'

Beck bristled. 'Stay away.'

'Find the Strangler, and I will.' Raines rose. 'I hear you've got good food here in Austin. Looking forward to trying it. See you soon, Beck.'

'Stay out of my case, Raines.'

'Solve it, and I will.'

Raines couldn't hunt this killer if he didn't understand the hunting grounds. Austin, like all towns, had its quirks with streets and traffic. After reading a collection of street maps, he got in his rental car and drove around the city.

When he saw the off-ramp to Interstate 35 he took it, knowing that the killer had left the two bodies near the southbound side of I-35. He barely noticed much of the landscape. Instead his gaze was searching for signs of a crime scene: yellow tape, burned flares, a stray cone.

Finally, thirty-five minutes outside of Austin, he found the spot where the San Antonio paper had reported the first murder. He'd been getting both the San Antonio and Austin papers since Lara had settled in town.

Though tempted to walk over to the scene, he didn't. His vehicle would stick out here, and he didn't need to explain himself to a highway patrolman. Spotting the access road, he drove a little farther south until he found the exit that gave him access to the secondary road that ran parallel to the interstate. Backtracking, he searched for the signs of a crime scene. Years of stringing yellow tape made it easy to spot the tattered strip left behind by the technicians.

He parked and got out, cursing the heat as he moved

over the rough terrain toward the site. He reached the site, wiped the sweat from his brow, and then turned his attention to the land around him. He could see why the killer had chosen it. Isolated, quiet, it would be easy to leave a body here in the middle of the night without being seen. And this kind of heat would quickly decimate a body in days.

He glanced at the highway. 'But you don't want them to vanish and go unnoticed, do you, sport?' he said. 'You want them found. That's why you take the time to dress them and leave them out in the open. Probably why the second body was closer to the road. The initial one took too damn long to be noticed.' When he'd read about the first woman, he'd not given her much thought. The papers had said scattered bones and mentioned the boyfriend was a person of interest. Now with this latest victim, he needed to take a real look at the forgotten first.

The first six Seattle killings had been different. Yes, the women had been dressed, but they'd been left in a remote section of woods. In those days, the Strangler had not wanted to be caught. And then there'd been the sloppy attack on Lara Church. The killer appeared to have acted impulsively. He'd introduced sexual assault to his new MO. He'd strayed too close to the road. So what had changed?

Lara.

Seven years ago, the notion that Lara was the key burrowed into his bones. And though not everyone in his department believed him, he'd not wavered. It was why he'd kept tabs on her the last seven years.

What was it about Lara?

Frustrated by the taunting lack of answers, he caught the glint of metal in the corner of his eye and moved toward the shiny object. He reached down and picked up the sunglasses. They looked clean and pristine. They'd not been out here long and likely did not belong to the first crime scene unit. And, judging by the size, they'd belonged to a woman. What woman would come out here to see a strangler crime scene?

He grinned. It made sense Lara would come out here with her camera after Beck's visit. This place, like all the murder scenes she'd photographed, potentially could unlock the answers trapped in her mind.

'Lara Church.'

She still wanted to remember. Good. He pocketed the glasses, knowing he'd see her soon.

The glaring sun prompted Lara to reach up on her head for her sunglasses. When she didn't feel them she remembered setting them down by the crime scene. Twenty miles back. 'Damn.'

She considered going back for the glasses, but she was already a half hour late for her appointment at the gallery. She balanced the value of dime-store glasses against the cost of gas and her lack of time. The glasses lost.

Lara, with Lincoln in the front seat of her pickup truck, rode into Austin. Her show was opening in just a couple of days, and she'd promised the gallery owner and her cousin Cassidy Roberts that she'd swing by to discuss last-minute show essentials.

Cassidy's 101 Gallery was located on South Congress

84

Street in a bustling, albeit quirky, section of Austin. The three-storey brick building, rimmed by glass high-rises on neighbouring streets, dated back to the 1930s. It had belonged to their grandmother, who'd snapped up land in the seventies when it was cheap and converted it into a dress shop. When her grandmother had gotten ill two years ago, she'd gifted the building to Cassidy. Her cousin had painted the brick building white with three red horizontal stripes and expanded the first-floor windows so that passers-by could see the art inside the studio. Gallery 101 blinked bright in blue neon above the main door.

Lara parked in the small lot behind the building, and she and Lincoln made their way through the back entrance. Dwindling renovation dollars had left the back entrance area much as it had been when their grandmother was alive, with dim lighting, old cracked linoleum floors, and a rickety shelving system.

'I can smell that mutt a mile off!' Cassidy's clear, young voice shot down the hallway that led to the main gallery.

'He doesn't smell.' Lara dropped her car keys in her backpack. 'You saw my truck pass in front of the gallery.'

Cassidy emerged from a small office. She wore a peasant blouse, a black ruffled skirt, and a thick belt that matched a pair of cowboy boots. Dark hair was swept into a topknot and held in place by hair sticks. No makeup enhanced her smooth olive skin and high cheekbones. Silver and turquoise bracelets jangled from her wrist.

Cassidy tossed a wary glance at Lincoln, who settled on the cool wood floor. 'God, he gets bigger every time I see him. Are you sure he's not part wolf?'

Lara rubbed Lincoln between the ears. 'He's just a big puppy.'

'With big fangs.' Despite Cassidy's protests she looked as if she had no problem with the dog. Though she groused about his smell and his hair, she never once said he wasn't welcome in her gallery.

Cassidy had been twelve when her mother had died, and she'd gone to live with their grandmother. Lara, however, had only lived in the Austin home during the summers, a time when her own mother needed a break from the demands of motherhood. The start of her summers with Cassidy always began with tension as each wondered how much the other had changed over the year. But by end of summer the girls cried when Lara's mother appeared and took Lara away.

Cassidy studied Lara. 'Looks like you got some sun today.'

'I did some preliminary shooting.'

'You should wear a hat. The Texas sun chews you up.' Cassidy arched a brow just as their grandmother had. 'Where did you shoot?'

'A site out off of I-35 north of San Antonio.'

'Odd choice.'

'I don't pick the places. They pick me.'

'Not another murder scene.' The words rushed out in a sigh.

'Yep.'

Cassidy was silent for a moment. 'Don't get me wrong, I adore the pieces you've taken. But every time I look at them I realize how dangerous it is for you to take those pictures. And the side of a highway can't be the most secure location.'

'I'm always careful.'

Cassidy clasped her hands together. 'Please, for my sake, would you not take any major risks between now and the opening? I need my artist looking radiant and wonderful and not dead on the side of a highway.'

Logic demanded Lara lock her doors every night and carry a shotgun when she walked and was out in the field. However, deeply buried emotions overruled logic, at times sending her to tenuous places to take pictures. The irony was not lost on her. 'I'll be fine. Now show me what you have so far.'

Cassidy grabbed a ring of keys and unlocked the door that separated the front of the gallery from the back. 'Are you nervous about this show?'

A casual shrug hid a flurry of nerves. 'No. Why would I be nervous?'

'It is a big step.'

'It's a show.' *It's a show. It's just a show.*

Green eyes narrowed. 'Then why do I smell your unease?'

Lara smiled. 'Maybe you just smell Lincoln.'

Cassidy wasn't put off by the joke. 'No, you've been different since you got back to Austin. You travel to crazy places for your pictures and yet treat strangers with caution.'

'You have an imagination.'

'You weren't like this as a kid. You were the brave one. The one never afraid to talk to anyone.'

'I've grown up.'

'You have an obsession with death.'

'I do not.' And that was the truth. 'I'm compelled to understand death and the mark it leaves behind, but I have no desire to meet up with it for at least another fifty or sixty years.'

Cassidy smiled but didn't appear amused. 'Maybe the time has come to understand life.'

Lara arched a brow. 'You sound like a shrink.'

'Maybe you need a shrink.'

The offhand comment struck a painful nerve, but she grinned. 'Don't all artists?'

Cassidy's head tilted as if she picked up the dark vibrations under the words. 'What happened to you?'

'What do you mean?'

'Like I said. You've changed since we were kids.'

'Life is change.'

Cassidy shook her head. 'You're not going to tell me what happened.'

'Cassidy, I'm here to look at the show, not talk about me.'

Cassidy opened the door to the gallery. 'Follow me.'

The front side of the building had been completely refurbished, the old linoleum replaced with polished wood floors, whitewashed walls, and bright lights.

Relieved to be off the topic of Lara Church, she told Lincoln to stay in the back.

Cassidy's boots clicked as she made her way down a side hallway. Many had questioned Cassidy's business sense when she'd announced she wanted to own an art gallery, but so far she was doing more than just keep her head above water. She was also making a name for herself in art circles.

'This opening is going to be good for you, Lara. Your pieces are stunning, and you are going to end up on the map.'

On the map. She'd done her best to stay off the map for the last seven years. 'Be nice to sell a piece or two and put some money away in the bank. The idea of not living hand-to-mouth is refreshing.'

'With luck we will both make money. There is so much I want to do with this place.'

'You've done well for yourself, Cass. You've much to be proud of.'

She grinned. 'And everyone thought the former cheer-leader would piss away her inheritance.'

'I can only imagine what everyone says when my name comes up in conversation.' Mimicking a Central Texas drawl, she added, 'Used to be so normal. Now wanders the country taking pictures of death scenes. Odd little lady.'

Both women laughed.

'Now I want you to close your eyes,' Cassidy said before they rounded the corner into the main gallery. 'I want you get the full effect when you see your work on the walls.'

Lara smiled even as butterflies chewed at her stomach. 'Do I need to close my eyes? Kinda dramatic, don't you think?'

'This show is dramatic,' she said, her tone growing serious. 'This show is going to put you on the map in the art world.'

'How far on the map? I kinda like being the unknown.'

'Right smack dab in the middle of the map. Now close your eyes!'

Lara grinned but did as she was told. Cassidy took Lara by the hand.

'By the way,' Cassidy said, 'get a manicure before Friday. Those photo chemicals you use, which create such magic on film, make your hands look as if they belong to a sharecropper. Don't want customers distracted by the nails.'

'I'm an artist,' Lara said, opening one eye. 'People expect me to be quirky.'

'Quirky with nice nails, if you please.'

Lara glanced at her nails, darkened by photo chemicals, and then slid her hands in her pockets. 'I've not had a manicure in so long I don't even know where to go.' Closing her eyes, she moved slowly down the hallway, worried she'd trip.

Cassidy laid her hands on Lara's shoulders and turned her toward the right. 'I'll set up an appointment for you with my girl.'

A protest danced on the tip of Lara's lips, but Cassidy cut her off. 'Open your eyes.'

Lara drew in a breath and then opened her eyes. Every bit of wall space in the large whitewashed room sported a Lara Church original. The black-and-whites, all taken with her bellows camera, were of murder scenes she'd seen over the last five years.

Drawing in a breath, she moved into the room, studying each picture with care. There was the triple homicide in the Atlanta back alley. In that case the killer had used Molotov cocktails to incinerate three rival gang members.

There was the stabbing in the Memphis playground. The shooting on Main Street in the small Utah town. All the places had seen death and in her view were changed by the violence. The Atlanta back alley still bore the scorch marks of the flames. A local women's group had totally refurbished the playground save for one old swing as a memorial to the dead. And the business on Main Street in the small Utah town had added bars to its windows.

She'd photographed the sites at the times of the victims' deaths. At night. Dusk. Noon before a rainstorm. The images had been powerful when she'd seen them developed in the darkroom, but seeing them collected and presented together took her breath away.

Lara's throat tightened. 'You've done a great job, Cassidy.'

Cassidy smiled. 'No, you've done a great job. I just hung the pictures on the walls.'

'It's more than that. You had a vision to put all this together. I'm not sure I'd have been brave enough to do it.'

'Sure you would, honey. I could tell when I first drove out to Grandma's house that there was a hunger in your eyes. And as I remember, it didn't take too much arm twisting to get you to say yes.'

She rescanned the images a second time. 'I love the way you arranged them. I would have expected chronological.'

'I tried it that way, but it didn't feel right. I opted to arrange by mood. From light to dark back to the light.'

Indeed the last print in the collection had been taken at sunset as the sun had cut through clouds and shone down on a tiny cross left at the site of a New York murder.

'I sent out press releases again today and followed up with calls. There's a good bit of buzz, and I think we're going to get some decent coverage.'

Yesterday those words would have given her pause, but today they sent a cold shiver down her spine. There was a strangler in the area. Was it the man who'd attacked her? And did he know that she was in town? Beck had said coincidences were bull.

'Why are you frowning?' Cassidy said.

She shook her head and smiled. 'I guess I'm a little nervous about being in the spotlight.'

Even in the worst days after the attack in Seattle the cops had mercifully kept her name from the public. Not even Cassidy knew what had happened to her in Seattle. So, it would be impossible for a reporter to connect this show to that past. Right?

Cassidy laughed and hugged her. 'Cuz, you better get used to the spotlight because it's gonna be on you for years to come.'

Chapter Seven

Beck sat at his desk, staring at the notes he'd made on Lara Church. As soon as he'd gotten back to his office he'd run any check he could on her. From the Seattle files he had her Social Security number and date of birth, so he'd plugged both into the database. He'd discovered she'd had driver's licences in three states in the last seven years: Maine, Florida, and, most recently, Texas. There were no outstanding warrants against her, and she owned her black ten-year-old truck outright. He'd even visited a website set up for students to rate their professors. She'd received comments like 'Tough but fair,' 'Likes pop quizzes,' and 'Hot!'

Looking locally, he searched the name Bower and found that she'd inherited her house from her grandmother, Edna Bower, eight months ago. Edna Bower had lived in Austin all her life and had had two daughters, Barbara and Leslie. Barbara had been Lara's mother and according to records, she had died eleven years ago of a drug overdose. Her sister, Leslie, was also deceased. Leslie had shot herself in the head in a local motel sixteen years ago.

Seattle wasn't the first time Lara had seen trouble.

He tapped his finger on the side of the notes he'd written on a pad by his blotter. His phone buzzed and he snapped it up. 'Beck.'

'Sergeant,' the receptionist said. 'I've got Gretchen Hart's uncle on the phone. Line two.'

He pinched the bridge of his nose and nodded. 'Thanks, Susie.' After a moment's hesitation, he punched line two. 'Mr Hart, this is Sergeant James Beck.'

A grim silence. 'Sergeant, you called me this morning about my niece, Gretchen.' His voice was tight, tense.

'Yes, sir,' he said, softening his voice. 'I'm sorry this has to be done over the phone, but I've got some bad news.' He remembered when he'd faced Misty Gray's mother and told the woman her daughter was dead. For the next three nights, the woman's cries had echoed continuously in his head. 'Gretchen was murdered.'

An anguished sob cut through the lines. 'Jesus. What happened?'

'We are still putting the pieces together, but she was strangled to death.'

The man started to sob. 'Are you sure it was Gretchen?'

'Yes, sir. We are sure.'

The next ten minutes was a painful loop of Beck repeating the news and Mr Hart searching for some kind of way that the news could be wrong.

When Beck finally hung up the line, tight bands of muscles gripped his lower back. He rose and stretched, hoping he could ease the muscles and the heaviness weighting his shoulders.

He glanced down at his blotter and zeroed in on Lara

Church's name. 'If you think I'm letting you off the hook, you are a damn fool.'

Raines had been in Texas less than twelve hours, and he could safely say he hated it. The heat was brutal, the air dry, and the coffee sucked. He glanced down into the dark mud that the River Diner called coffee and wished he still had the power to arrest.

But he wasn't here for the coffee. He was here to find out what he could about the second victim, Gretchen Hart, whose identity had been released this afternoon. It wasn't lost on him that the two Texas victims had been students, like Lara had been.

Setting the cup down on the café table he leaned back in the metal chair and surveyed the busy diner located blocks from the university campus. College students huddled at tables, chattering to each other, talking on their cell phones, or listening to music. There was a lot of activity and noise, but he wondered how much they were truly getting done.

Shit, half of them looked like they couldn't be more than twelve. And he wondered if he had ever been that young or if there'd been a time when he wasn't worried. He'd known from a young age that he'd wanted to be a cop and had been focused on getting a spot on the force. Initially there'd been the entrance exam and then the academy. He'd had to work his ass off for both, but the struggle had been worth it when the chief had pinned his first badge on his chest. He'd been settled in a patrol car less than two months when he'd realized a college degree would take him farther on the force. So he'd set his sights on college and the homicide division. It had taken another twelve years of hard work, but he'd managed both.

He checked his watch. According to the online class schedule, Lara Church was slated to hold her class from seven to nine today. Monday and Wednesday were lab days, and Thursday was another classroom day.

God, how many times had he dragged himself into a night class after a twelve-hour shift? He'd drunk gallons of coffee and eaten candy bars to juice up his system for the ninety-minute classes. He'd made straight A's in college, and he was damn glad he had done the work. However, life had given him new goals and another advanced degree no longer made the list.

His number-one goal now was to see Lara Church. He understood speaking to her wouldn't help matters, but it wouldn't hurt to get a visual.

'You gonna drink that coffee, or you just gonna swirl it around and stare at the kids?'

The crisp feminine voice had him raising his gaze to a petite young woman who wore a red RIVER DINER STAFF T-shirt, jeans and a nametag that read: DANNI. She had ice-blonde hair, gold hoop earrings, and black nail polish. Her attire was strictly punk rocker, but the tough choice of clothes did not jibe with the young face and clear green eyes. She couldn't be more than sixteen or seventeen.

He glanced down at his cup. 'I was thinking I'd swirl it around a couple hundred more times. I like the way the sludge moves.'

A half smile tweaked the edge of her lips. 'It does have

its own ballet, doesn't it? I just brewed a fresh pot. Care to give it a try?'

He pushed the cup away from him. 'I'm not sure how much more Texas coffee I can stomach.'

'I made this latest batch. It will be good.'

'Good coffee in Texas? I don't think so.'

She cocked a brow. 'Be right back.'

Before he could answer, Danni vanished behind the counter. She grabbed a new cup and carefully poured coffee into a mug. She moved toward him with quick, purposeful steps and then set the mug in front of him. 'That's good coffee.'

'Really?'

'I can't write legibly, and I can't cook a lick, but I can make coffee.'

He took a sip and found he was pleasantly surprised. 'Good.'

'Puhleez. It's the best.'

'I'm from Seattle. We are ground zero for coffee.'

'As long as I'm on duty the coffee will be good.' She took the half-full cup and set it on her tray. 'Enjoy.'

'Thanks, Danni.' As she turned he said, 'Hey, didn't that girl that was killed work here?'

Danni's eyes grew suspicious. 'Yeah. You a reporter?'

Raines shook his head. 'God, no.'

'Cop.'

'Do I look like a cop?'

Danni arched a brow. 'Yeah.'

'Nice to see I haven't lost that.' At her confusion he

added, 'I used to be a cop. Long time ago. I guess the case caught my eye. Hard not to ask questions. Sorry.'

His honesty appeared to disarm her. 'No harm. And for the record, I didn't like what they said about her in the news today.'

'Straightforward enough.'

'I guess I just didn't like the way they boiled her life down to bare facts. She was so much more than that.' Anger hardened her face, but there was no hint of tears. 'Her uncle is flying in tomorrow to claim her.'

'I feel for them. I wouldn't wish losing a child on my worst enemy.'

'Yeah, well.'

'What can you tell me about her, so I'll remember more than the basic newscast?'

Danni's voice grew softer. 'She was kind of corny. Liked pink and singing Lady Gaga in the kitchen. She was moving to New York. I was kinda jealous of her.'

'You've got nothing to be jealous of, Danni. You strike me as a sharp kid.'

She snorted a laugh.

'Was there anybody who might have wanted to hurt her?'

'Mack and I were talking about it, and none of us can think of anyone. Like we told the Rangers, we're all thinking it was some random guy.' A customer at another table caught her attention. 'I've got to go.'

He watched as she moved toward another table and began to gather up plates. Danni was a tough nut and no wilting flower. Just like his daughter.

He could almost hear his wife now. 'That girl of ours is going to be a general one day.'

He sipped his coffee, thought of his wife, Susan, and how much he missed her, their daughter, and home. Pushing aside a pang of guilt, he redirected his gaze to the patrons.

Within seconds he spotted a slight blonde woman enter the café. She wore jeans, a T-shirt, and sandals and had a backpack slung over her shoulder. She was as slight as a teenager, but she moved with a confidence that only came with maturity.

Lara Church.

Beck had been right. She wasn't the meek girl who'd fled Seattle seven years ago. As a man approached her, Raines noted slight stiffening in her back as she extended her hand. Her handshake was firm and her gaze direct.

She laughed as the graying gentleman in his fifties spoke. After what looked to be a question, she pulled out a notebook and made a note. They chatted another half minute and then she made her way to the diner register, where she ordered a coffee. Just as quickly as she came, she was gone.

Lara Church, the Seattle Strangler's last victim, had managed to rebuild her life.

But she would have to remember this time. Lives depended on it.

He might not be a cop now, but his cop's instincts burned strong. Two strangled women. Both dressed in white. One with a penny and the other's bones too scattered to be determined.

He'd spent a lifetime studying killers and their motivations. And the Seattle Strangler, like nearly all serial killers, enjoyed the ritual of death. He enjoyed the planning, the fantasizing, the hunt, and, of course, the kill.

'So why haven't you gone after Lara?' Raines whispered. 'I'll bet there were a dozen times you could have killed her by now. Why are you waiting? Why the new victims?' He traced the rim of his cup.

Raines would bet his left nut that the killer had attacked Lara last in Seattle for a reason. He'd likely been dreaming about killing her long before he wrapped his hands around her neck. He had an obsession with her.

The Seattle Strangler, who, many had come to believe, was either dead or in prison, was back.

'Keep playing your game, pal.'

Danni hadn't expected to like college. When her high school counsellor had suggested she try the college art class she'd thought the woman was mental. High school sucked so why would she want to take on more schoolwork? But the counsellor had pushed and knowing the class would keep her away from home more often, she said yes.

And then the unexpected happened. She'd been pleasantly surprised. The two-day-a-week class plus lab wasn't totally lame and her teacher, Lara Church, was pretty cool. When she was on the university campus, life didn't totally suck.

She hefted the tray of dirty dishes, pushed it in the industrial dishwasher of the River Diner, and hit start. As she reached for the strings of her apron, her boss called out from the kitchen door.

'You're gonna be late for class,' Mack said.

Mack River had offered her the job in February when she'd tried to pay for a coffee with spare pennies and had come up short. Mack liked to talk about high school and his days on the gridiron, and he wasn't so fond of the college crowd. Spoiled. Ungrateful. He used those adjectives plus a host of others all the time. His life had peaked during high school, and the once-muscled lean body of a high school receiver had turned doughy and a little ugly.

She glanced up at the large clock positioned above the stainless steel sinks. Five-forty-five. Class started in fifteen minutes. 'I've still got the glasses to run through. And we're shorthanded since Gretchen . . . left.'

He wiped his hand on his white apron. 'I'll do the glasses. Don't be late for class.'

'You sure? I can be a little late.' She didn't want to lose this job. She'd be eighteen soon. Her father would stop paying child support and there'd be no reason for her mother and stepfather to keep her around.

He nudged her away from the dishwasher. 'Go or you are fired.'

She grinned as she untied her apron and hung it up. 'You're the best.'

Chuckling, he loaded glasses into the next tray to go into the dishwasher. 'That's what I keep telling everyone.'

'I'll be back tomorrow right after school.'

'Can't wait.'

Danni grabbed her backpack from Mack's office, hoisted

it on her shoulder, and hurried across campus toward the brick building that housed the art department. She'd not stopped to analyze why she liked the class. Likely it had more to do with its unstructured nature. Adjunct Professor Lara Church expected her students to work hard, but she had no desire to babysit. Art was subjective, she'd say, but it was also time consuming and hard. If you put the work into her class, you'd do well. If not, your grade would suffer.

Lara's speech had hardly put the fear of God in Danni. She'd seen enough shit in her life not to be intimidated by Lara Church. But in Lara she'd seen another wounded soul whom she happened to like.

The photography classroom was large with long, wide windows that allowed lots of sunlight. It was furnished with ten big wooden worktables that each could seat four students. There were twenty-five students in the class, which often meant she could claim an entire table for herself. She liked working alone. Other than a couple of other kids, most were jerk-offs. Jocks, cheerleaders, deadheads looking for that easy A from the school's greenest professor.

So far most of the kids were just getting by and would be hard-pressed to finish their portfolios in the next week and a half. Danni had had to pawn several bracelets to get the money for her digital camera, but she'd more than gotten her money's worth. She'd snapped thousands of pictures over the semester and was kinda pleased at the way her own portfolio was coming along. Who'd have thought Danni Smith, the kid who hated high school, would ever be thriving in college?

The kids ambled into the classroom and took their seats. The jocks tended to stick together, and they always sat close to the cheerleaders' table. Everybody was always looking to score.

At exactly seven o'clock Lara Church breezed into the classroom, a coffee in one hand, backpack on her shoulder, and her dog, Lincoln, in tow. Danni was pretty sure that dogs weren't allowed in the classroom, but Lara had not cared about rules. Lincoln stayed with her. Period.

'Today in the darkroom I'll be looking at edging and burning techniques.' She set her coffee on her lectern and her backpack on the floor beside her. Lincoln stretched out and went to sleep. 'But before we head into the darkroom I wanted to toss out a word of caution. I was having a look at the photos some of you downloaded to the class site, and I see you're having a little trouble with mood. Too much light. Flat photos. Washed-out images. Many of the photos will need to be redone, but I'm on hand as always to answer questions.'

A bit of sniggering from the cheerleaders had Lara tensing. 'You all are adults and can use your time this evening as you wish, but I'll expect you to upload your pictures to me by eight tomorrow night. No photos means an F. And, please, no photos taken earlier in the semester. This last portfolio is about applying what you've learned.'

A tall jock named Tim yawned and checked his watch.

'If you need to leave, Mr Gregory, go right ahead. But I should remind you that you've got a lot of work to do.'

Tim winked at a cheerleader. 'Whatever.'

'Your failing grade. Not mine.'

The football jock leaned back in his chair, narrowed eyes glaring at Lara, who appeared unconcerned by his angry stare. Instead of backing down, she tossed out one or two more instructions and dismissed the group to the photo lab.

Danni grinned, not sure if Lara's dismissal of Tim was super brave or just crazy.

Beck arrived down in San Antonio just after seven, parked at the Ranger offices, and climbed the steps to Santos's office. He found Santos at his desk, leaning forward and frowning over paperwork.

'That bad?' Beck said.

Santos glanced up and shrugged. 'I hate paperwork. Hate. It.'

Beck laughed. 'What cop doesn't?'

'You'd think it would get easier with time.'

He eased into the chair in front of Santos's desk.

'I had an interesting visitor,' Beck said. He updated Santos on Raines's arrival and his own visit to Lara Church.

Santos leaned back in his chair. 'What's Lara Church like?'

'She's wound a little tight when she's approached by a stranger. She held a shotgun on me.'

Santos raised a brow. 'And?'

'I convinced her to put it down.'

'And you didn't arrest her?'

'Having read her file I'm not surprised by her reaction. The Strangler left her in bad shape.' He listed key details related to the seven-year-old attack. 'The Texas victims fit a profile that is more like Lara than the Seattle victims. Students. Ready to move out of state.'

Santos nodded. 'The killer's tastes changed.'

'Seems so.' He flexed his fingers. 'Did you go back to the first victim's site and look for the penny?'

'We looked. Took metal detectors. But we didn't find it.' He tapped his index finger on his desk. 'But we got a lot of rain last month. Gulley washers. Could have washed away.'

'Send more officers out there. Work the area like an archeological dig. I need to know if the first murder is connected to the second.'

Santos nodded. 'I'll have another team out there tomorrow.'

'Good.'

'So what is the deal with Raines?'

'First stab, I'd say he's a lot like us. A cop with a case that got under his skin that he can't forget.'

'He came a long way to follow up.'

'How far would you go to track down a killer?'

'A guy who kills women.' Santos's expression turned pensive. 'Damn far.'

'He's not the kind of guy that will sit and wait for my report. He believes this is his case.' Beck flexed his fingers.

'Escort him to the border.'

Beck rubbed the back of his neck. 'He might be of help.'

'Odds are he's going to be more trouble than he's worth.'

*

Lara nodded to the students as they filed out of the class-room and back through the corridor. Danni, the girl who usually sat alone in the back, hefted her backpack on her shoulder, eyes downcast, left the room without a word.

The kid was a bit of an odd duck, but perhaps that was just being a high school kid in a college setting. She didn't say much, could get hostile if approached by other students, and had disaster written all over her. Yet, she was brilliant when it came to photography. She had an eye for setting and detail that none of her other students had. Sure, some had the techniques mastered, but they failed to inject emotion into their work like Danni.

And considering the girl had not even known how to use her camera when she'd arrived ten weeks ago, her progress amazed Lara. Teachers at the university often talked about students. There were always a handful that made the grades without effort, and then there were the kids who didn't quite care. But the kids who kept the teachers returning to the classroom were the rare ones who worked hard and wanted to learn. Danni was one of those students.

A knock on her door had her lifting her head to a friendly face. 'Jonathan.'

Jonathan Matthews's family had lived on the land that adjoined her grandmother's. There was an eight-year age difference between them, but he'd always been kind. The summer before her senior year of high school they'd become friends when he'd hired her to work part-time in his woodworking shop. After her attack, her grandmother, too ill to travel, had sent Jonathan to check on Lara.

When he'd arrived at the Seattle hospital, she'd been sitting up in her bed, stiff and so afraid. She could still remember him lingering in her doorway as if he just didn't know what to do, his large hands gripping the umbrella in his hands. She'd held out her arms to him and he'd gone to her immediately, holding her close and enveloping her in his scent, a combination of fresh pine and linseed oil.

'Lara, I'm so sorry,' he whispered in her ear. 'I should have been there for you.'

Her voice caught in her ragged throat. 'Jonathan. How did you know?'

'Your grandmother called me.'

She wept, letting loose of the grief and hurt. 'Thank you.'

'Who did this to you?' His breath brushed hot against her cheek.

She pulled back. 'I can't remember.'

'You don't remember?'

Tears streamed down her face as she shook her head. 'Nothing.'

He'd been patient and loving and attended to her every need, taking leave from work in his woodworking business for weeks. He'd told her over and over again that he'd protect her and care for her, but the spectre of not knowing had lingered over her like Damocles's sword. After eight weeks of police questions, sleepless nights, and jumping at every shadow, she'd left Jonathan and Seattle behind.

When she'd returned to Austin, he'd been thrilled to see her and had offered to take her to dinner. To her relief he'd not brought up Seattle, and when he'd told her about the teaching job, she'd gladly accepted.

'So how were the kids today?' he asked. Jonathan had a long lean body accentuated by loose-fitting jeans and the V-neck sweaters that he favored. He wore his light brown hair long and tied back at the nape of his neck.

'Just like you warned me. Some love it, most tolerate it, and some hate it. How are your kids?'

'Mine aren't kids. It's a master's class, but like you I've got some that don't love it. Some even think they know more than me and they can be real . . . challenging.'

She shut off her computer. 'Nice to know it's not just me.'

'I've been at this for ten years. Believe me, most teachers share the same frustrations.' He shifted his stance from side to side. 'Any pieces you think will work for the student art show?'

'As a matter of fact, yes. I've got one student who's doing some amazing work. I'll be sure to talk to her on Thursday and ask her if I can use one of her pieces. What about you?'

'A stunning cherry chest and an ornate desk. Both students outdid themselves.'

'Great.'

'The president of the university plans to attend the opening reception, and he's bringing board members. Rumours are again flying about budget cuts, so we've got to put on a show to hold on to what we have. You are going to submit a piece, aren't you?'

A faint smile tugged at the edge of her lips. 'Are you sure you want my work? Kinda dark.'

He laughed. 'Maybe avoid the murder scenes and use the images of the Alamo. The Alamo is always a hit in these parts.'

In recent months, she hadn't limited her work to just crime scenes but had also started shooting pictures of battlegrounds where death had also left its mark. Though the Alamo was a scene of great bloodshed, it was also a source of pride for Texans. 'I'm not so lost in my art that I don't understand the practical side of life. I'll print and mount the Alamo series.'

'You've come a long way.'

'Really?'

'In Seattle, you were all about career and goals and doing only what you thought was best.'

That was the first time he'd mentioned Seattle since she'd arrived in Austin. 'A taste of real life tempered me.'

He frowned. 'Lara, you've been back eight months, and we've not talked about Seattle.'

She stiffened. 'I appreciate that you've not gone there.'

He dragged long fingers through his hair. 'Maybe we should talk about it.'

She shoved her laptop in her backpack. 'You were great to me while we were in Seattle. I wish I could have held my act together, but I don't want to talk about it.'

He nodded. 'Deal.'

Relief washed over her.

He kissed her on the cheek. 'Friends?'

'Yes. And you'll come to my opening this Friday?'

He winked. 'Wouldn't miss it for the world.'

It was past ten and his coffee sat cold and virtually untouched as he leafed through the pages of the newspaper one more time. He'd started with the crime section and found a small article.

Of course he understood why his first victim had gotten so little play. He'd left her too far off the road, so it had been over a month before she was discovered. There'd been little to find, thanks to the elements and animals. It made sense that no one would realize who had arrived in town.

But the second victim was different. He'd left her close to the road, and she'd been found quickly. He'd seen the cops and the crime scene roped off with yellow tape as he'd driven by on the interstate.

Didn't the cops see that this murder was different from most? No crime of passion, it had been a cold, calculated staging to get their attention.

Frustration gnawed at his gut as he drummed his fingers over the newspaper. Where was the coverage?

How many bodies would it take for the cops to connect the dots? Two wasn't enough? He shoved out a sigh and sat back in the chair.

In the Entertainment section there'd been an ad placed by the gallery featuring Lara's show. It was a small ad, just two-by-two, but he reread the details a half dozen times. The opening would be a fun affair, and he looked forward to it.

Anticipation had the tips of his fingers burning as he

reached for the red book embossed with the gold letters, *The Book of Blair.*

After Lincoln's late-night walk, Lara locked up the house and moved into the bathroom to brush her teeth. Her limbs ached with fatigue, and she was ready to sleep. After she rinsed her mouth and raised her head, she stared at her face, wondering for the millionth time what he'd seen in her all those years ago that made him want to kill her. She ran long fingers through her light brown hair and drew in a breath.

'*He didn't see you as a person.*' She repeated the words Seattle's forensic psychologist had told her over and over again. '*You were just an object. A means to one of his sick ends. For him, it wasn't personal.*'

'Well, it felt pretty damn personal.' After brushing her hair she stripped off her clothes, hauled on an oversized T-shirt, and then climbed into bed. Lincoln jumped on the bed and curled up at the edge.

She shut off the light and closed her eyes, listening for any kind of sound that might make her jump. Outside a breeze blew, and the branches from a tree by the house scraped against the windows. She pulled her blankets up close to her chin.

She thought about the front door lock and wondered if she should recheck it. Damn. It had been years since she'd been hung up on locks and outdoor sounds. And she knew she worried tonight because of James Beck's visit.

He was doing his best to drag her back into that old,

dark world of shrinks and crime scene photos that had nearly driven her insane.

Lara had barely gotten out of that world with her sanity. It had taken nearly seven years in exile, but she was finally healthy and whole again, and she'd be damned if she'd go back. Beck would not take her back to hell.

Healthy and whole.

Her laughter echoed in the darkroom. Lincoln perked up his ears and grunted in response. 'And what are you doing, Ms Lara Church, at the crack of dawn in the morning?' She hesitated and then answered herself, 'You're taking pictures of a murder scene.'

She rolled on her side and curled her body around her pillow. 'Yeah, that's healthy.'

Chapter Eight

Wednesday, May 22, 4:45 am

Lincoln glanced up from the passenger seat of the truck, yawned, and laid his head back down as Lara climbed out of the front seat of her truck cab. Eyes heavy with sleep and joints stiff after a restless night's sleep, she stretched her arms and glanced at the night sky perched on the edge of dawn.

When her alarm had sounded at three-thirty she'd been so tempted to roll back over and go to sleep. She'd tossed and turned too much last night and had not gotten more than a full hour of sleep at any one given time.

But as much as she craved the warmth and security of her bed, she needed to get up and photograph this spot. Her art wasn't a job. It was a compulsion, a jealous mistress that required her attention and kept her from straying too long.

She'd exited the interstate onto the access road and then, spotting a flat stretch, drove off the side road onto the dry, cracked land. The truck bumped and rocked as she crossed to the murder scene. She'd parked as close as she could to the site, knowing she'd have to move quickly to prepare her negatives and catch the rising sun.

'Stay put, boy. See you in a bit.' As the dog relaxed

against the seat, she shut the cab door, moved to the back, and opened the lid of the camper top.

Between the cobbled sections of clouds stars winked clear and bright. The scent of rain hung in the air.

Switching on her flashlight she did one last inspection of her equipment and then studied the path ahead.

A hundred yards behind her, a truck blew past on the interstate, sending a rush of energy, air, and sound cutting through the quiet night.

She hefted her large bellows camera on her shoulder and, with her flashlight in hand, followed the matted path until she spotted the billow of the yellow crime scene tape. She set up the tripod facing east and checked her watch. It was 5 AM and the sun would rise in about forty-five minutes. Thunder rumbled in the distance.

She hurried back to her truck and from a wooden storage box retrieved a ten-by eight glass plate that she'd pre-cut and cleaned last night. After wiping down the plate one last time, she uncorked a glass bottle filled with the chemical collodion, poured the syrupy liquid on the glass, and gently tipped her wrist back and forth. The trick was to evenly coat the glass. The masters of this process, known as 'flowing the plate,' strove for no streaks or runs, but she'd found the occasional imperfection added depth and interest to her final prints.

When she'd coated the plate to her satisfaction, she poured the excess collodion back into the bottle and opened what looked like a black slim file box. She slid the glass negative into the box, which was filled with silver nitrate, and waited five minutes. Tenting her work area under a large black blanket that blocked out all light, she removed the tacky, light-sensitive glass negative and loaded it into a plate holder. She hurried back at her camera, knowing her negative needed to be used while still damp.

Under another black drape, she inserted the first negative into the camera just as the initial bits of light appeared on the horizon. Through the viewfinder the image appeared upside down, but when she processed the negative it would right itself.

The sun inched up to the edge of the horizon, and she reached around and pulled the cap off the lens. She counted to thirty and then replaced the cap. With the morning heat already rising, she hurried back to her truck with the exposed negative, ducked under her blanket again, and poured developer evenly over the glass plate. As she counted to fifteen she gently agitated the glass and watched for her image to appear.

More thunder rumbled in the distance and the rising winds whooshed over the tall dry grass. When the image emerged, she poured water over it, halting the development process. She set the negative aside to dry and prepared a second.

With thunderclouds looming, she shot and developed two more negatives before the threat of rain forced her to load up her equipment.

By six-thirty, as the morning traffic on the interstate built, she was angling her camera gently into the back of the truck.

The pleasure of her morning's work ended abruptly

when flashing blue police lights reflected in her side mirror. 'Damn.'

She'd been through this before, cops spotting her at a crime scene and stopping to ask what she was doing. Logically it made sense. What person in their right mind would do this? But logic didn't temper her irritation.

The officer, in his mid-forties, short with dark hair, got out of his car and approached her, one hand on his gun. 'Ma'am, what are you doing out here?'

Turning, she kept her hands, palms open at her side. 'I'm a photographer. I was taking pictures of the sunrise. In the back of my truck, you'll see my camera and equipment.'

He moved to the back of the truck, touched her back tailgate with his palm, and glanced inside. 'Are you alone?'

'Yes, sir.'

Eyes narrowed, he pulled a flashlight from his belt and shined it inside. The light swept over the camera, the chemicals, and the box of negatives.

'My name is Lara Church. I teach at the university, and I have an art show opening this Friday in Austin.'

He glanced at her and then at the equipment. 'What is there to photograph out here?'

'I've been known to pick some random places at odd times.'

'What kind of camera is that?'

'It's a bellows camera. The kind photographers used during the Civil War. Ansel Adams took his pictures out west with a bellows camera.' She'd found the better she explained herself the less time she would be detained.

He stared at her as if he wasn't sure if she was crazy or just stupid. She could have told him maybe a little of both.

'Can I see your driver's licence and registration?'

'Sure.' She moved toward the front of the truck and paused. 'I have a dog in the front seat. He's pretty big but harmless.'

The officer nodded and held back as she moved to the front of the cab and grabbed her purse. She fished her driver's license out of her wallet and handed it to the officer.

He glanced at the license. 'Texas.'

'I just changed it to Texas from Florida a couple of weeks ago.' She'd had the Florida license for two years but hadn't lived in the state for over two years. After Florida there'd been Vermont and then Maine. Out-of-date identification was another red flag she was careful to avoid.

'I'll be right back. And do me a favour. Get back in your truck.'

The order made her bristle. 'Sure.'

She slid behind the wheel of the car, scratched a curious Lincoln on the head, and waited, irritated. If she'd been just a minute faster she'd have been gone and well on her way home. This delay meant she'd get caught in early-morning commuter traffic.

After a ten-minute wait the officer returned and handed her back her papers. 'Looks like you're clear.'

She swallowed a smart-ass response. 'Right.'

'It's not safe out here by yourself, Ms Church. We've had trouble in this stretch of road.'

I know. A woman was murdered, and I just photographed the spot where they found her body. 'I'll be more careful.'

'It's not about being careful, it's about staying away from places that leave you vulnerable.'

Seven years of careful had landed her in a half-living kind of existence. 'Thanks, I'll keep that in mind.'

The drive back to her house took forty-five minutes, and by the time she arrived, she'd driven through a heavy but brief thunderstorm. She let Lincoln out of the car, reached over the backseat to grab her box of negatives. A barking Lincoln waited for her on the front porch.

'Okay, okay, I hear you. Breakfast. Pronto.'

She set her negatives down on the dining room table, moved into the kitchen, and pulled out his bag of food, which she dumped into a bowl. She filled his water bowl with fresh water and then placed a chew stick by his bowl.

Her stomach grumbled, but instead of taking the time to eat, she grabbed a piece of cheese from the refrigerator and her negatives. She'd eat a real meal later.

She closed the shed door and moved to the table where she had her chemical trays and light source set up.

As soon as Lara opened the box of glass negatives she lost track of time. When she worked with the negatives and the images, the outside world melted away, along with worries and fears.

When Lincoln started barking, she glanced at her wristwatch and realized that five hours had passed. Knowing she had to wrap for the day, she still took one last glance at the images she'd created. She was pleased. On one negative the chemicals had not reached the edges of the glass so when the image developed, her imperfect technique created a jagged frame that wrapped around thunderous clouds backlit by a rising sun and the strip of crime scene tape that flapped in the wind.

She held the image up. At first she stared at it with an artist's critical eye, but as the seconds ticked, she found herself searching beyond the physical elements to the dark mind of the killer. *Why did you kill her?*

Lincoln barked louder, dragging her from her unanswered questions. 'I'm sorry, Lincoln. I didn't mean to lose track of the time.'

She opened the shed door and found herself face to face with Sergeant James Beck. Lincoln barked from the kitchen window, clearly frustrated that he wasn't free.

As the dog barked, she took a step back. 'What are you doing here?'

He glared at her and then back at the dog. 'Your dog needs to be let out.'

Torn between arguing and Lincoln's needs, she brushed past him as she dug the key from her pocket. Seconds after she opened the door, the dog bounded up to Beck, who stared at the animal until it lowered its gaze.

'What are you doing here?' she repeated.

His gaze held the darkness of an angry man. 'What were doing at my crime scene this morning?'

She teetered between flustered and annoyed. 'How did you know where I was this morning?'

'The DPS trooper who took your identification called my office and mentioned your name.'

She folded her arms over her chest. 'Big state, small world.'

He raised his brow. 'I put the word out that if your name came up I wanted to hear about it.'

Annoyance snapped. 'You've had people spying on me?'

'Not spying, just on the lookout.' He towered over her by nearly a foot. 'Why were you there?'

His commanding tone had her muscles bristling. 'I wasn't aware that it belonged to you.'

His jaw tightened. 'What were you doing there?'

She danced with the devil. 'I didn't see any "No Trespassing" signs.'

He leaned so close she smelled hints of his soap. 'Do you really want to get into a pissing match with me, Ms Church? *Do you?*'

Anger pushed aside the fear pounding in her throat. 'Sure, why not? I haven't had a good workout this morning.'

His gaze narrowed. 'You can tell me what you were doing this morning now or downtown in my office. I've got time to kill and it would give me great pleasure to drag you into headquarters and waste your day.'

Beck didn't make idle threats, of that she was certain. She could dig in her heels and win a trip into Austin. Or she could talk, and get on with her day. 'Detective Raines was like you. He didn't think twice about screwing with my day if he didn't like the answers I gave him.'

Beck's brows knotted. 'What were you doing at my crime scene?'

She folded her arms over her chest, wondering why he drove her to be so childish. 'I was taking pictures. I am a photographer.'

'What's out there worth photographing? It's the side of the interstate.'

'It's a crime scene. That's what I photograph.'

He shook his head, his disapproval evident. 'Does the world need to see more violence?'

She brushed her bangs out of her face with the back of her hand. 'Good art makes people think.'

Beck glanced at her fingertips darkened by chemicals. 'What were you doing in the shed?'

'It's my darkroom. I was developing the prints I took this morning.'

'You must have been pretty absorbed. You didn't hear me call. Hell, the damn dog was about to bark its head off.'

'I get lost when I'm working. I never heard you, but I did hear Lincoln barking.'

Absently, he rested a hand on his hip. The butt of a gun peeked out from under his jacket. 'Mind showing me those pictures?'

At this stage the work remained too raw to show. The idea that anyone, especially Beck, would scrutinize her work left her feeling vulnerable. 'Come to my show on Friday. It will give you a good idea of what my work is about.'

His smile held no hint of humour or warmth. 'I'm interested in the pictures you took at my crime scene. Today.'

My crime scene. He was a dog with a bone. 'The work isn't finished.'

'I'll keep that in mind. Show me.'

An order. Not a request. 'Will you arrest me if I don't?'

'Yes, ma'am.'

A promise. Not a threat. Demanding a search warrant would likely translate into a lot of lost time for her. 'Sure. Follow me.'

She opened the shed's screened door. Lincoln scrambled past Beck to be by her side. Beck fell in step behind them. His purposeful steps sounded annoyed and angry against the cobblestone path.

She pushed open the door to her darkroom.

The heavy smell of chemicals hung in the air. Above the developing table hung a clothesline where a half dozen prints hung.

'You painted the walls black,' he said.

'Better for the negatives.'

She clicked on the overhead light and moved toward the worktable where the prints dangled. The chemical scents grew more cloying the deeper she moved into the room. If she didn't keep the A/C window unit running, the smell could leave her lightheaded.

She gestured toward the pictures. 'See? Just photographs.'

He pulled off his hat, leaned in, and with a narrowed gaze studied the prints. 'They look old.'

This close, the restrained power in his body made her skin tingle. 'I use a bellows camera. It's well over a hundred years old.'

He kept his gaze on the photographs. 'Why do murder scenes interest you so much?'

'Probably because I almost had my own personal murder scene.'

'Seven years ago.'

She shifted her stance. 'You're not the first person to tell me to get over it. I know I should be back to normal after all this time, but, well, I don't think that I am.'

His intense gaze soaked up the images' details. 'Why'd you shoot at sunrise?'

'I don't know. Normally I shoot at sunset.'

'The end of a day. The end of a life.'

'Yeah.'

'But you chose sunrise.'

The beginning of a day. The beginning of life. 'Yeah.'

'Someone like you – a survivor – should go out of your way to avoid murder and violence. Someone like you should take colour pictures of flowers and clouds. Kittens and puppies.'

A laugh startled from her. 'You think? Those subjects don't feel exactly real to me.'

As he straightened, his gaze settled on her. 'It's because you can't remember your attacker.'

She cocked her head. 'You think you've got me all figured out.'

'You're not so complicated. You were attacked, nearly died, and you are using your camera to jog your memory.'

Annoyed, she brushed a stray hair out of her eyes. 'Fill in the memory, and I'll be all better?'

'You cannot cure a problem that you do not acknowledge, Ms Church.'

She cocked a slim brow. 'Is that my five-cent shrink evaluation?'

'Common sense, Ms Church. Until you can put all the pieces together you aren't going to feel whole.'

Silence, as heavy as death itself, settled before she broke it. 'I don't want your advice, Sergeant.'

'Stay away from my crime scenes, and I'll keep my thoughts to myself.'

She wasn't sure if she could stay away.

When she didn't answer, he said, 'Like it or not, you are involved in this case.'

'I'm not involved in this case. I am not.' The words rang hollow.

'When it comes to my case your opinion doesn't mean much.' He flicked the edge of a dangling print with his finger. 'I don't want you close to any evidence.'

She shoved her hands in her pockets. 'I never go near an active scene. I wait until the police are finished with the area.'

'Don't care, ma'am. While you're in my district you stay away from all murder scenes.'

'You can't tell me where I can or cannot go.'

'I can when it comes to crime scenes.'

'So what are you gonna do, arrest me?'

'That's about right, Ms Church. That is about right.' He swapped the smile for a sneer. 'And if you'd care to test me, and see if I am a man of my word, go right ahead.'

Resolve radiated from him, raw and intense, triggering

a sudden shakiness that permeated her muscles. She attributed the unsteadiness to her early-morning wakeup call, an empty belly, and too much time in the darkroom. 'Fine, I've been warned. If that's all, you can leave now.'

He took another step toward her. Close enough to bump, but not violate, her personal space. 'Ms. Church, we have not seen the last of each other.'

'I bet you we have.' Grinning, he replaced his hat. 'I'll take that bet.'

Chapter Nine

Wednesday, May 22, 1 pm

Lara drove into Austin shortly after Beck left. She told herself she was not skittish or restless because of Beck. Her sudden lack of concentration and frayed, restless nerves were rooted in hunger. Not Beck. She just needed to eat and then she'd be fine.

She had no groceries in the house, and she hadn't eaten a real meal in twenty-four hours. Lab wasn't until four so she had time to treat herself to a hot meal at the River Diner near campus.

When she sat at the café's corner table her stomach grumbled, and she was suddenly anxious to eat. As she glanced at the menu she noticed her nails remained chipped and stained from work. Cassidy had called her this morning and told her she'd scheduled an appointment for Friday morning.

Lara studied her chewed and chemically darkened fingernails. She used to care about makeup, manicured nails, and pretty clothes when she'd lived in Seattle. She'd been in fashion, and appearance mattered. Clothing stores, shoes, and accessories had driven her days. It had been her eye for structure and assembling quirky combinations that had won her the job with the Seattle-based fashion company Forward. She'd gone for an interview with the company's marketing department, not sincerely believing she had a shot at the job. But the director had liked her mix of vintage and modern and suggested a second interview. A week before the holiday break she'd been offered a job to start after graduation. It was entry level and paid little, but it had been a first huge step toward the rest of her life.

Her life had all been blue skies in those days. Danger and death were reserved for movies and novels. She'd been such a different person then.

'What can I get you, Ms Church?' Danni said.

Lara glanced up at her student. 'Danni, I didn't know you worked here.'

'Almost four months now.'

'Aren't you supposed to be in school this morning?'

'I get out at eleven on Wednesdays. That gives me time to work the lunch rush here.'

'When do you graduate?'

'A couple of weeks.'

'And what's after that?'

She shrugged. 'I'll know when I get there.'

Patrons at other tables were already vying for Danni's attention, and the diner's owner was watching them.

As Lara stared at Danni she saw her younger self and couldn't help but remember her high school days. Transient. Uncertain. Lonely. She'd make a point to talk to the kid more in the coming days and see if she could find out more. 'What's the vegetarian special today?'

Danni shook her head. 'If you weren't in Austin you'd get laughed out of any self-respecting Texas eatery.'

Lara grinned. 'You might be right. Does that mean there's no special today?'

'Nope, Mack has done a black beans and rice. He's also stuffed zucchini with white beans. And it's decent.'

'I'll have the beans and rice, a side of bread, and a tossed salad.'

'That's a lot of food.'

'I've been working in the darkroom and haven't had time to stop and eat. I didn't realize I was starving until about an hour ago.'

'Well, I'll get that bread and salad right up.'

'Thanks.'

Danni returned minutes later with a side of hot bread and a garden salad with dressing on the side. 'Anything else I can get you?'

She picked up a chunk of bread and tore it. 'I've been meaning to tell you how much I've enjoyed your work this semester. You've got a great eye for light and composition.'

Danni's gaze brightened. 'Thanks.'

'You said on your student survey form that you'd never taken photography before.'

'Nope.'

'You must have dabbled in it.'

'No. Didn't pick up a camera until I bought the one I have in class.'

'Amazing.'

'What can I say?' Her attention drifted as a man at another table flagged her. 'Got to go. See you soon.'

Lara had eaten her bread and salad when Danni

returned with the plate of black beans and rice. To her amazement, she was still hungry. 'Thanks.'

'Hey, Ms Church, if you ever go out into the field with that crazy camera you showed the class I'd love to tag along.'

She'd never taken anyone along before. But she liked Danni and wanted to encourage her. 'How old are you?'

Without blinking Danni said, 'Eighteen.'

Lara smiled. 'I've got access to my student's birthdates.'

Danni shrugged. 'So I'm weeks away from eighteen.'

'Can you get written permission from your mother to work with me in the field?'

'Sure,' Danni said easily. 'Mom loves that I'm taking the class.'

Lara searched her gaze wondering if she should take the kid with her. 'I'm working on a series of photographs.' An image of Beck's grim face flashed in her mind. He'd be pissed if he knew she planned to return to the site. 'The set I took this morning were good, but I wanted to shoot it at sunset.'

Danni shrugged, but there was a spark of interest in her eyes. 'Where?'

'It's a site off the interstate. If we leave after lab today and make a quick stop at my house for the equipment, we could get the shot.' If caught, Beck would hang her out to dry, but she was certain he'd leave Danni alone.

'Sure. See you then.'

'Great. But you've got to get a note from your mother.'

'No worries. I'll see her right after my shift today.'

The pictures Lara had taken this morning had turned

out better than she'd expected. There was no need to return to the site. So why return? Maybe she wanted to encourage a bright student. Maybe it was because Beck had told her to stay clear. Or maybe, just maybe there was a key that could unlock her memory.

The drive to San Antonio took Beck just over an hour. He arrived at the small rancher-style house that Lou Ellen Fisk had rented the last six months of her life. The front yard was mostly dried weeds, and last summer's heat had cracked the cement sidewalk in a couple of places. Yellow crime scene tape still sealed the front door.

Beck had requested financial information from Fisk's and Hart's banks but didn't expect a report until later today or tomorrow. When he'd called Santos and asked to see Lou Ellen Fisk's place he'd learned that the local cops had kept the apartment sealed. He still didn't have a solid link between the two victims, but the more he learned about them the more he hoped to learn about their killer.

Minutes later Deputy Santos pulled up behind his vehicle. He slid out of his black SUV, squinting against the afternoon sun as he put on his hat. The men nodded a greeting, as both moved toward the front door.

Santos fished keys out of his pockets. 'The locals went over the Fisk site with a fine-tooth comb and didn't find anything.'

'No penny?'

'Nothing. Though it was clear someone had been to the site. Footprints everywhere.'

'Lara Church was there early this morning.' Irritation rumbled under the words.

'Really?'

'DPS officer spotted her parked by the murder scene and called me. She was loading up camera equipment.'

'Got a sixteen-year-old sister who's into art. She was talking about Lara Church's show this morning. Mark of Death. Hell of a theme. I said no.'

'You don't want to go to an art exhibit?' Beck teased.

'No way in hell, and I'm sure not letting Maria drive up to Austin alone to see the show.'

'Good call.'

Santos searched the ring of keys. 'A part of me hopes the cases aren't linked.'

'A serial killer opens a whole new can of worms.' Beck pulled down the crime scene tape. 'Let's see what we can learn about Ms Fisk.'

Santos nodded toward the house. 'Ms. Fisk moved in here about four months ago.'

'Did she have roommates?'

'There was a gal scheduled to move in this month, but when Fisk was found dead she changed her mind. In fact, she moved back to Oklahoma.'

When the door swung open, Beck and Santos pulled on rubber gloves. He found the light switch controlled an overhead bulb that spit out enough light to illuminate the main room. From what he could see, the place was a mess. Clothes, blankets, pizza boxes, and magazines littered the floor. A couch in the centre of the ten-by-fifteen room was stained and covered in more junk. To the left was a small kitchenette and to the right a small bathroom.

'This place reminds me a lot of the first apartment I shared with a couple of guys after Basic,' Santos said. 'Hell of a mess.'

Beck moved into the kitchen and glanced at the dirty dishes piled in the sink. He opened the refrigerator, winced at the smell, and discovered ten beers, a couple of yogurts, and a half-eaten pizza.

'I read the Seattle case files,' Beck said. 'The Seattle victim profiles were different than Fisk and Hart. None were in college. In fact several never graduated high school and a couple had arrest records for prostitution. They didn't have much in the way of a future.'

'Lara Church had a future.'

'That changed after the attack.' Violence had stripped away her dreams.

Beck turned his attention to a round table covered with papers and bills. 'From what Lara's police file says, she wasn't the ghoul she is today. Before her attack she wasn't obsessed with death. She was in fashion design and had plans to work with a Seattle design firm. After the attack she gave up fashion and turned to photography. Left the Pacific Northwest for good.'

'Understandable.'

He picked up an envelope marked OVERDUE. 'Raines's initial notes theorize Lara faked amnesia. Later his notes are less sure.'

'What do you think?'

'I don't know. She's done a good job over the last seven years of running. She's been all but invisible.'

'Running from shadows or a real man?'

'She says shadows.' Beck frowned. 'Now she's coming back into the spotlight and there are more murders. That can't be a coincidence.'

Beck foraged through the papers on the table. They looked like a collection of work sheets from class. 'She was taking a biology class.'

Santos nodded as he checked his notes scribbled on a pad. 'She was also taking accounting. Had an A in both classes. Both her teachers considered her a solid student.'

Buried under the papers was a laptop. Beck opened it and hit the power button. Seconds later the screen popped up. The screen saver was a photo snapped of Lou Ellen and several other smiling young girls. Crystal blue skies. Fall leaves covering the University grounds. The girls wearing sweatshirts.

She was Lara Church at the time of her attack.

After a call from forensics, Beck and Santos returned to the Department of Public Safety's Austin offices to meet with Melinda Ashburn, the forensics technician who'd worked the Gretchen Hart crime scene.

Beck and Santos entered the lab. The large white room had a single window on the far side and five grey lab tables, each manned by a forensic technician. Some technicians stared into microscopes while others sat at computer screens. They found Melinda hunched over a computer typing notes. She wore khakis, a green polo, and a white lab coat and had her red hair tied back. She looked pale. Tired.

Beck cleared his throat. 'Ms. Ashburn?'

Melinda Ashburn peered over the edge of dark framed glasses. 'Sergeant Beck and Santos. Glad you could make it.'

'You said you had an update for us.'

She rose, stretched the kinks from her neck. 'Let's go to the conference room.' She snatched a file from her workstation and led the two Rangers down the hall to a small meeting room. The three sat at a mid-sized round conference table.

'I don't have much, but I do have one or two titbits.'

'We'll take whatever you got,' Beck said.

'Let's start with the coin,' she said. 'It was the one piece of evidence not released to the Seattle press and then repeated at the Hart crime scene.'

Melinda opened her file and removed front and back pictures of the penny. 'A 1943 wheat penny made of steel.'

Santos pulled a notebook and pen from his jacket breast pocket. 'What does that mean?'

'According to a coin collector I spoke to it means the coin is worth about fifty cents. If it had been made of copper and imprinted with an S, which means it was minted in San Francisco, then it could have been worth sixty thousand dollars. There were many counterfeits made of this coin and this is one of them.' She shook her head. 'As you can tell, my coin collector is passionate about his work and kept me on the phone too long.'

A hint of a smile tugged the corner of Beck's mouth. 'I

want a tight lid kept on the source of the penny. The cops in Seattle kept the same detail from the press, which was the primary reason Lara Church's strangulation was pegged on the Seattle Strangler.'

'The dealer I spoke to is in Boston. I gave him no case particulars, just a verbal description of the coin. He told me to hold a magnet to it and test for the steel-versus-copper issue.' Her gaze sharpened. 'I made no mention of the Strangler and asked him to be discreet.'

'And he will be?'

Melinda arched a brow. 'Sergeant, I did not just fall off the turnip truck. Times like this everybody who knows you work for the cops wants the inside scoop. If I can keep it from nosey dates and my own mom I can keep it from the press.'

'Good. Everyone needs to guard that detail carefully.'

She scanned her notes. 'These days the Internet is the go-to place for coins like this one. The possible dealers are too vast to count. But my pal did offer a bit of lore about coins and death.'

'The significance of a coin placed in the hand of the departed?'

Melinda pulled off her glasses and wiped them with the edge of her coat. 'In some cultures a coin is placed in the hand or on the eyes of the dead to pay Charon, the ferryman on the river Styx.'

'Who?'

'Charon. In Greek mythology he is the one that transports the departed souls across the river Styx, which separates earth from Hell.'

'Even the dead got to pay a tax,' Santos said.

'If you don't pay Charon, it's said the departed soul wanders the earth forever.'

Beck stared at the photo of the penny. 'So placing the coins on the body is a sign of kindness.'

'Yes, I would say so. The killer cared for the well-being of the dead person's soul.'

Beck rubbed the back of his neck. 'Hell of a way to show that he cares.'

Beck drew in a breath. 'Melinda, what else do you have?'

She glanced at her notes. 'No traces of blood. No defensive wounds. The dress isn't remarkable. It appears handmade. It's cotton with machine-made lace. It hit the victim below the knees and fit her well, as if made for her. I went over it millimetre by millimetre. I pulled blonde hair samples that belonged to the victim and a couple of dark hair samples that could belong to the killer. I'm testing DNA, but it will take weeks to get results.'

'Seattle pulled DNA from Lara. A match would tell us if the Strangler came south.' Beck rarely had the puzzle pieces of a crime fit together so neatly. 'What about DNA under her nail beds or vaginal area?'

'None in either location. She didn't fight, and he wore a condom when he raped her.' She scanned her notes. 'I did find several footprints at the crime scene that do not match any of the people I know that walked the area. The truck driver who found her has a size-thirteen shoe whereas the unknown print is a ten. Appears to be a work boot, and I'm working to identify it.'

'Where were the prints?' Santos said.

'One partial at the top of the body and one full at the foot of the body.'

'He was admiring his handiwork,' Beck said.

'I did take samples of the dirt so if you find him get me all his shoes,' Melinda said. 'I can analyze his boots, and if there are any trace soil samples on it I can put him at the scene.'

'That's the trick, isn't it? Finding the killer.'

During lab, while the students worked at stations equipped with enlargers, Lara moved behind them offering advice and words of encouragement. Burn in. Edge. Exposure. This was her chance not to just talk about theories but to put them into action. In the classroom awkwardness and discomfort still shadowed her, but in the darkroom all doubts vanished.

The session wrapped by five-fifteen. Danni gave Lara a note from her mother, and they got in the truck and headed toward her house, where Lincoln waited, barking inside. While he took a quick break, Lara and Danni hauled out her equipment from the house and loaded the truck.

Danni studied Lara's house. 'So how did you end up here?'

'The place belonged to my grandmother,' Lara said. 'I spent a lot of my summers with her when I was a kid.'

'I can think of a lot better places to be during the summer than Texas.'

Lara smiled as she closed the camper top. 'I loved it

here. Would have loved to have lived here.' She opened her passenger door and Lincoln hopped up on the front seat.

When the two had slid into the front cab of the truck Danni snapped her seat belt as she glanced down at the dog already drifting off to sleep. 'Where did you live?'

'All over. My mother got married several times when I was a kid so we were either moving in with a new stepfather or running away from one.'

Danni fiddled with the silver and bead bangles dangling from her wrist. 'We moved here for my stepfather.'

Lara backed up the truck and drove down the gravel driveway toward the road. 'How's that going?'

'He's a douche, but he's manageable.'

The faintest hitch in her voice caught Lara's attention. 'Has he hurt you?'

Danni's exaggerated laugh rang false. 'No. He's just a blowhard.'

Lara sensed a retreat in the girl and suspected if she pushed, she'd sever whatever fragile communication the two might build. 'You've got my number if you ever need anything.'

'Please, I'm fine.' Danni shifted her gaze out the passenger-side door. 'So what are we taking a picture of?'

Lara glanced at the sleeping dog between them. 'A crime scene. My work lately focuses on crime and death and the land.'

Danni nodded. 'You don't look like the dark and scary type.'

Lara smiled. 'Really?'

Absently, Danni scratched Lincoln's head. 'Yeah. I see you photographing babies and puppies.'

Lara laughed. 'I've gotten a lot of that lately.'

'No worries. We all have the dark and creepy best left in the past.'

Lara glanced at the girl again, tempted to ask questions. But having been on the receiving end of too many personal questions, she understood curiosity could breed anger. *Why did he choose you? What did you do to attract him? If you'd been a little smarter, do you think it would have happened?*

'So you aren't from Texas, are you?' Lara already knew the answer.

The silver bracelets jangled on Danni's wrist as she smoothed her hand over her faded jeans. 'Did the accent give me away?'

'Or lack thereof.'

'I'm from the Washington, D. C., area. I moved here about a year ago when my mom married my stepdad.'

'Long way from family and friends.'

She shrugged. 'I Skype my friends when I can.'

'What about family?' Lara glanced in her rearview mirror and noticed a car coming up behind her fast. She moved to the right lane.

'Dad works a lot. He's good for the monthly child support payment, and he bought me my car, but that's about it.'

As the speeding car passed, Lara mulled Danni's statement. 'I didn't know my Dad growing up. Mom never would talk about him.'

Danni's gaze shifted to Lara and lingered a moment

before she said, 'I think my Dad was a little relieved when Mom told him she and I were moving to Texas. We never got along great. I guess I drive him nuts.'

'You're a teenager. I think it's written in your job description to drive your parents nuts. That doesn't mean he doesn't love you.'

A heavy silence hung between them as Danni stared ahead, her fingers still rubbing Lincoln's head. Lara liked the kid and wanted her to feel like they could talk, but Lara's people skills were rusty at best.

'So you move around a lot?' Danni said.

'Yeah. You'd think after a childhood of being on the move, I'd find a place to settle, but I've been a rolling stone since college.'

Shifting the focus back on Lara relaxed the lines furrowing kid's forehead. 'Should I ask why?'

'I just couldn't stay still.'

Danni grinned. 'And maybe one day you'll tell me why, and I'll share my sordid story.' She hesitated. 'Or maybe we won't.'

Lara tightened her grip on the steering wheel. 'Being closed off is safe, but it can be lonely.'

'I've always opted for safe.'

Lara nodded. 'Me too.'

Traffic slowed, and they didn't reach the right mile-marker until about a quarter to seven.

Lara checked her watch. 'We've got a half hour before sunset. We're gonna have to hustle to get set up in time.'

'I am here to serve.'

The two got out of the car. Danni hauled the developing table and Lara carried the camera along with the chemicals in a backpack. As they approached the scene Lara noticed that fresh yellow tape had been strung. The cops had been back to this location today. Was it because she'd been here today, or were they searching for new evidence?

'A crime scene, Lara?' Danni said. 'Where's the art?'

'I know it's different. I shoot crime scenes.'

She blew a stray strand of hair from her eyes.

Danni stilled. 'You shoot what?'

Her truthful answers put most on edge. 'I shoot places where people have been murdered.'

Interest, not fear, sparked in Danni's gaze. 'So did someone get murdered here?'

'A woman. Just over that rise, about a month ago.'

Danni glanced around as if trying to find the spot. 'How did she die?'

'Strangled.'

She shook her head. 'What a way to go.'

'Yeah. It's bad.' She offered a smile to Danni. 'Are you still up for helping? If you feel weird about it, I understand.'

'It takes a lot to rattle me, Ms Church,' Danni said. 'This is low on my weird-o-meter.'

Relieved, Lara lowered her backpack to the ground and kicked out the three legs of the camera tripod, holding firmly onto the camera until the legs were firm and rooted into the ground.

Danni's gaze scanned the horizon. 'So why are you re-shooting? Did the photos not work out?'

'No, they were great. I shot them at sunrise and now I want to see sunset. Death is an ending, not a beginning.' Plus, James Beck had told her not to return, so a repeat trip bumped up to the top of her priority list.

Danni shaded her gaze with her hand as she stared into the sun, which hovered above the horizon. 'Light changes perspective.'

Lara grinned. 'It does my heart good to know someone is listening in class. There are days when I feel like I'm talking to myself.'

'Most of the kids are about the easy A in art. They were expecting to snap a dozen pictures and be done. No one figured the teacher would be a ball buster.'

Lara laughed. 'I've never been called a ball buster.'

Danni's eyes twinkled with a humour Lara had never seen before. 'I meant it in the nicest way.'

'Oh, I'm taking it as a compliment. Maybe I'll have new cards made. *Lara Church, Photographer, Teacher, Ball Buster.*'

Both had a good laugh as they pulled out the four legs from under the table and together they set it up. She pulled the chemicals from her backpack and as she went along she explained the process to Danni.

When the table was set Danni shook her head. 'God, and I thought thirty-five millimeter was a pain in the ass.'

'All a matter of degree, I guess. This was cutting-edge one hundred and fifty years ago.'

Danni watched as Lara prepared the glass negative.

In the next several minutes Lara and Danni barely spoke as she treated the negatives and then exposed them to light. By the time Lara replaced the cap on the last shot the sun was all but gone. The remaining ten minutes of light allowed them to pack up and get back to the car.

They hauled the equipment to the car, and she closed the back hatch. All the while she kept her gaze on the highway, searching for a DPS car.

'So why do you keep looking in the rearview mirror?' Danni said.

'I'm not.'

'You are.' Challenge underscored the two words. 'You think the killer might come back.'

Lara shrugged, knowing she'd never win the girl's trust if she wasn't honest. 'There's a Texas Ranger who doesn't appreciate me hovering around his crime scene. He's threatened to arrest me. And I am prepared to take all responsibility, so you won't get in trouble.'

Dark eyes sparked with interest. 'Then why did you still come here?'

Lara shook her head. 'I suppose I'm just a little hardheaded.

'Join the club.'

Pasty Kline's '*Crazy*' crooned from a CD player, greeting Beck as he walked into the service bay of his grandfather's garage just after eight. The place smelled of oil and gasoline, two scents that reminded him of home.

He'd been working all afternoon and planned to return to the office after this quick visit to check in on his grandfather, Henry, who he found under the engine of a late-model red Honda cussing as he struggled to release a stubborn bolt. Tall, as wiry as rawhide, Henry Beck had skin leathered and lined by the sun and a stock of white hair still as thick as Beck's. His grey coveralls were covered in grease stains no amount of washing could erase.

When Beck had been a kid, Henry had been a force larger than life. Big, bold, strong as an ox, and loyal to his grandsons, Henry could've tackled any challenge, Beck believed. In those days, hell, even five years ago, Henry would have loosened that bolt without breaking a sweat.

Beck considered helping the old man but understood his pride went bone deep. 'Kinda late to be working.'

'Couldn't stand to watch another minute of television,' Henry said.

Henry gave the stubborn bolt one last jerk before turning away in frustration. He swiped the sweat from his brow with the back of his hand. 'What the hell are you doing here? Doesn't a guy like you got better things to do than visit an old man?'

Beck wasn't put off by Henry's gruffness. The old man took pride that his oldest grandson was a Texas Ranger. 'Just thought I'd check in.'

'I don't need a babysitter.' The statement wasn't friendly but didn't bite.

When Beck had been on mandatory leave he'd spent most of his time here working on the infrequent repair job that still trickled into Beck's Garage. And his presence had allowed Henry to kick back and rest more. Technically, Henry was retired and working only part-time, but the old man was having trouble adjusting to the slower pace that his ageing heart demanded. Now that Beck was back with the Rangers, Henry was back under cars. Despite part-time, Henry didn't appear to be faring well. He looked pale and drawn, and was sweating more than he should.

'Not here to babysit.' One whiff of patronizing and Henry would shut down. 'Just wanted an ear to chew.'

The old man set the wrench clenched in his hands on the workbench. 'The boss giving you more shit?'

Despite the checkup nature of the visit, Beck valued Henry's open ears, sparse but sage advice, and discretion. 'Penn and I both put the work before the personal.'

'It's that murdered woman case.'

'The case is chewing on me.'

'Girl strangled, the papers said.' Henry, for as long as Beck could remember, had read the paper from cover to cover every day.

Beck sat on a stool by the workbench, hitched the heel of his boot on a rung, and removed his hat. 'There might be a second victim, but we haven't made a solid connection yet.'

Henry set his wrench on the bench. Instinctively he understood Beck had more to say, so he waited.

Beck's hat dangled from his forefinger as he toyed with a Concho on his leather hatband. 'Got a woman who survived a brutal attack a while back. I think it's the same killer. She says she doesn't remember her attacker.'

Henry wiped grease from his hands with an old rag. 'And you don't believe her?'

'Says she wants to but can't.'

'Can't or won't?'

'I think whatever's locked in her head is so bad she just can't bring herself to retrieve it.'

'They got fancy doctors to help with that.'

'She says she's seen 'em all. Nobody helped.'

Challenge glistened from grey eyes. 'Since when do you take no for an answer?'

Beck smiled. 'Since never.'

Chapter Ten

Most women relaxed when they walked into a beauty salon. It was their time to sit back and enjoy. But for reasons Lara could not explain, the shop set her nerves on edge. She wasn't sure if it was the smell of the polishes, the searching eyes of the technicians, or the simple fact that this was a reminder of a world she'd left behind.

In Seattle, she'd adored being fussed over. She'd worried about her hair, her makeup, and her nails. She had looked good in those days and known men always gave her a second look, which had stoked her feminine pride. Maybe that was at the heart of her unease today. She didn't want to be noticed by anyone, especially men, and primping would make her more noticeable.

Cassidy came through the door seconds after her and laid her hands on her shoulders. 'You look ready to bolt.'

Lara glanced into the line of chairs and mirrors in the salon. 'I am.'

'Good, Lord, Lara,' Cassidy said, laughing. 'This is supposed to be fun. You look like you are about to be shot.'

Lara dragged fingers through her hair. 'It's been a long time since I came to a salon.'

Cassidy arched a brow. 'My point exactly. You need a cleanup before tonight.'

Lara huffed out a breath. 'It's not about me. It's about the art.'

Cassidy laughed as she rolled her eyes. 'You are the art. You are the brand. You need to be someone that people remember.'

'Please. You make me sound like a pair of jeans or a car.'

'Marketing is marketing.' Cassidy spoke to a redheaded receptionist wearing cat glasses and a sleek asymmetrical haircut and turned back to Lara. 'They'll take us in five minutes.' When Lara opened her mouth to argue, Cassidy shook her head. 'Baby, just shut up, and let the ladies here do their magic.'

'Magic?'

Wooden bracelets jangled on Cassidy's wrist as she adjusted her purse on her shoulder. 'You know photography, and these girls know colour and cut. And they are artists.'

Lara glanced toward the exit. 'Will there be time for me to visit my studio before the show opening tonight?'

'No. If you go to that studio, you will pull out the nasty chemicals and mess up all the good work we are doing here today.' She grabbed a strand of Lara's hair. 'Maybe they can brighten up your hair as well. It still is a bit drab from that terrible dye job you attempted. Why you'd go brown is beyond me. It's almost as if you didn't want people to see you.'

That had been exactly the plan. 'That's not so bad.'

Cassidy cocked a brow. 'You were such a show-off when we were kids and well into college. You craved attention and everyone knew your name. I'd get so sick of people asking me, "When is Lara coming home?" or "Too bad Lara had to leave again." Everyone noticed when you were in town.'

'That's not true.'

The light in Cassidy's eyes never dimmed. 'Of course it was. The house came alive when you arrived for your summer visit. I thought by now you'd be a fashion super star, but then you dropped off the face of the earth.'

'I started travelling and taking pictures.' Which was true.

Cassidy caught the attention of her stylist and smiled. 'I've never understood why. What changed? And do not tell me nothing.'

The truth danced on the tip of her tongue, but she couldn't find the right words. 'We're here now. My show is about to open. Does it matter?'

Cassidy softened her voice. 'Yeah, it matters. I always thought something pretty drastic must have happened to you.'

Lara glanced around at the receptionist, who was trying to get their attention. 'It doesn't matter anymore.'

Cassidy frowned. 'It does if it's still driving your life.'

'It's not. It is not.' The conviction behind the words almost convinced Lara that she was just fine.

Cassidy hesitated. 'Was it about your mom dying? I know when my mom died I didn't feel like myself for a long time.'

'That was a little different. You were twelve when your mom died.' To the shock of everyone, Cassidy's mom had committed suicide. 'And I've long forgiven my mother for the demons that drove her to uproot us almost yearly.'

'Before Mom died, I used to be so jealous of you and all the cool places you lived. San Francisco. New York. Chicago. And then I was jealous because I couldn't get out of Austin away from the sadness.'

Lara glanced at her chipped nails. 'San Francisco was a one-room efficiency that always smelled of garbage. The Chicago place was on the south side full of warring gangs. And New York, I think was a motel room. If anyone should be jealous, it was me who was envious of you and your mother.'

The light in Cassidy's gaze dimmed for a moment. 'Your mother left you for summers, my mother shot herself in the head and left me forever.'

For a moment neither woman spoke before Lara broke the silence. 'How did this get so serious?'

Cassidy arched a brow. 'Memory lane not the smooth ride, is it?'

Lara shrugged. 'The past is a done deal. It's over. Time to move on.'

Cassidy leaned in closer and lowered her voice. 'How can you move on when you're not at peace with the past?'

Unease nibbled at the back of her neck. 'What makes you think I'm not?'

Cassidy dug her BlackBerry out of her purse. 'I know you. I know when you're happy and when you are not. A dozen summers burned your moods into my brain. What's eating you?'

Lara swallowed. 'Maybe I'm just nervous about the

opening. Maybe once I get that behind me I'll be my old charming self.'

Cassidy looked as if she wanted to say more, but instead said, 'After our morning of beauty, we have got an appointment at a dress shop and then a makeup artist.'

A groan rumbled in Lara's throat. 'Cassidy, does it have to be this involved?'

'Baby, your ass is mine until after the event.'

James Beck had never been to an art opening. Truth be told, he didn't have much use for art. He appreciated the talent it took to create a painting, but art was about as interesting to him as watching paint dry.

The 101 Gallery wasn't a good-sized piece of property in Austin. Three storeys, the building had been around for sixty years, but it hadn't always been a gallery. There'd been a time when it was a dress shop and before that a butcher shop. Henry said when he was a kid he and his dad had shopped here for steaks. And later when it was a dress shop his mother had shopped here, though he suspected she'd done more looking than buying in the high-end shop.

And now it was all cleaned up and painted white. Hanging in the window was a sign that read MARK OF DEATH.

The invitation had said the reception ran from six to nine, but he'd made a point to show up early, hoping to get a glimpse of the show and Ms Church before the crowds started to appear.

He removed his hat as he stepped into the gallery. Soft harp music greeted him. Small candles lined the centre of a long rectangular table in the centre of the room. The table was filled with displays of dainty, well-garnished finger foods too pretty to eat. He supposed that was the kind of food the fans of art ate. Delicate and not nearly enough to stick to your ribs. Beyond the food were Ms Church's photographic images.

One more step into the gallery caught the attention of a woman at the food table. She had dark hair, lots of makeup, and she wore a blue ruffled dress that reminded him of a cartoon character. A plucked brow arched as she moved toward him.

'Now what brings a Texas Ranger to my doorstep? Are you a fan of the arts?'

'I met Ms Church earlier this week. Thought I'd stop by and have a look. She here?'

The woman had assessed him in a blink. She'd be polite, but knowing he'd not buy one of the pieces shifted him into a different, less important category. 'And your name?'

'James Beck. And you?'

A slightly pointed chin tilted up. 'Cassidy Roberts. This is my gallery.'

'I don't plan to stay too long. Mind telling me where Ms Church can be found?' Though formed as a question, the words sounded like an order.

Ms. Roberts studied him, as if considering whether tangling with him was worth the trouble. 'She's in the back of the gallery getting herself centred before the show.'

Centred. Wasn't the kind of word a gun-toting woman used. 'Thank you, ma'am.'

As he started to move past her, she blocked his path.

'This is not the best time. She's got to be *on* tonight, all smiles, if you know what I mean. It would be nice if she's not distracted in any way.'

'I've no intention of distracting her.' Though in fact that was exactly his plan. He wanted her to know he'd not forgotten about her or his need for her to remember.

Her gaze narrowed. 'See that you don't.'

When he entered the backroom he was looking for a jean-clad gal who was wearing a worn T-shirt and had her hair twisted on top of her head. Instead, he found a woman who could have stepped off a fashion magazine page.

Lara's hair, restored to natural blonde, was down, gently curled and skimming the middle of her back. She wore heels that added several inches to her height and a sleek black dress that hugged her curves, which had been almost hidden days earlier with loose jeans and boxy T-shirt. Four slim gold bracelets dangled from her right wrist. *Damn.*

'Ms. Church.'

She turned and immediately her quizzical look became suspicious. 'Ranger Beck. What brings you here?'

His gaze held hers. 'Thought I'd come by and have a look.'

She arched a brow. 'Why?'

'You interest me.' He moved close to her, knowing his height would invade the space around her. He'd half expected her to take a step back, but she held her ground in her high heels.

'I'm fairly unexciting.'

'I'd never say that.' He caught the scent of a perfume.

A bit too spicy. But he liked the dress and hair. 'Show me what you got.'

Gold bracelets jangled from her wrists, and he suspected the bling and the whole look had been Ms Roberts's doing.

'What?'

'Your pictures. Show me what you got.'

She glanced past him, half hoping there'd be someone else to rescue her, but an empty studio was the reason he'd come early. He'd wanted her to himself. 'Sure.'

Those high heels gave her legs a long, lean look that he liked. They also caused her hips to sway just a bit back and forth when she walked. Perfume aside, he gave Ms Roberts big points for the new Ms Church.

Lara stopped at the first black-and-white photograph. It was an interior shot of an old warehouse, and like the pictures he'd seen in the darkroom these images had sharp detail, high contrast, and frayed edges that added a moodiness to the piece. 'This was taken in the Washington, D. C., area. This is a warehouse that overlooks the Potomac. I was able to get to the top floor, where the body was found, and take this image.'

The chalk outline of the body remained, as did a couple of discarded plastic evidence bags. A full moon shone through a large window and caught the lingering flecks of dust dancing in the air. He spotted holes in the ground. 'I remember that case. The killer thought his victims were witches. He staked their bodies to the floor.'

'I'm surprised you'd know. Virginia is a couple of thousand miles away.'

'I remember the worst cases.' Like Seattle.

She didn't speak for a moment and then moved to another scene. This one, she explained, had been taken in Boston. He didn't know the section of town, but it didn't take a local to recognize twilight in a back alley.

He traced the rim of his hat with his fingertip. 'You've been to some dangerous places. Do you always go alone?'

'Sometimes. I had a friend who worked with me at the art store go with me to this site. Even I know when to take precautions.'

Even when she was dressed down, no man would miss the fact that Lara Church was a beautiful woman with a stunning figure. He hated the idea of her going to any of these murder scenes alone or with some work acquaintance. 'Not smart, Ms Church. Not smart at all.'

Her smile looked brittle. 'I suppose you've got your opinions and I've got mine.'

Tension rippled through his muscles. He wondered if her hair was as soft as it looked. 'How'd you come across your first murder scene?'

She shifted her stance, uncomfortable with the heels or the question. 'By accident. I was in a small town in Utah, and there'd been a brawl. A man was killed. The yellow tape caught my eye and I stopped. Before I realized it, I snapped a picture with my cell phone camera. That night in the motel I was fascinated by the image. It had secrets to tell.'

He leaned closer. 'The scene needed to talk to you.'

'Yeah.' Fire flashed in her eyes. 'Sounds crazy. I know that. But after Seattle I didn't care so much about people's opinions.'

'Why?'

'After touching death, life's smaller details can be petty.'

That he did understand. 'So just like that you became a photographer.'

'More like a waitress who worked the odd shifts, so I could shoot when the light was right. I moved around, studied with different people.'

'Where'd you get the old camera?'

'An auction in Chicago. I didn't know what to do with it and had to travel to a photo shop in Pennsylvania to get a photographer to show me how it worked.'

'And now you have a show, and you're teaching.'

'That's right.'

He leaned into a photo taken on a sandy bank by a river. 'Want to know what I think?'

Her gaze trailed his. 'I suspect you'll tell me either way.'

'I think your memories are stowed away in a dark, shadowy corner of your mind.'

She shook her head. 'You think too much.'

'That's what I'm paid to do, ma'am.' He leaned in, nudging her personal space. 'Do you remember the coin in your hand?'

Her face paled and without realizing she curled the fingers of her right hand into a fist. 'I don't remember it. Raines told me about it. A penny.'

He studied her gaze searching for hints of a lie. He was good at reading body language, and all he was reading off her now was fear and nerves. 'What are you afraid of?'

A delicate chin lifted. 'I'm not afraid.'

'You are.' Seeing her fear fuelled his protective instincts.

She gestured toward the wall of photos. 'The show. It has my nerves on end. I'm not used to so much attention.'

'This is your first time out of hiding since Seattle?'

'Yes.' Sorrow lurked behind the word, but she smiled as if forcibly embracing joy. 'But it had to happen. I can't live a gypsy's life forever.'

'Have you ever considered going public about what happened in Seattle?'

She stiffened and in a half second he glimpsed fear in her eyes. 'No.'

'If the killer is out there, he can find you.'

'I don't need to paint a bull's-eye on my head.'

'Lara!' Cassidy called to Ms Church from across the room. She had two folks in tow. One was a spindly woman who wore all black and had a short dark bob and the other was a short man with tight jeans and a crisp white shirt. 'I have two people I'd adore for you to meet.'

Beck straightened, frustration clawing at him. Given more time, he thought he might have reached her. Now, Ms Roberts would sweep her away into the glitter of the evening.

Lara's smile was bright, but he imagined her visibly bracing. 'If you will excuse me, Ranger Beck.'

'Looks like you're headed to a firing squad.'

Her smile softened. 'Close. Art critics.'

He didn't need more time with her, but he wanted it. He had no business wanting her. The case always took priority. He was a Texas Ranger. But for the first time, he almost resented the silver star's weight. 'Been a pleasure, Ms Church.'

Without responding, she moved across the room toward the art critics.

She extended her hand, demonstrating a poise that reflected the life she'd lived before the attack.

Cassidy moved toward him, a look of irritation flashing in her green eyes. 'You were nice to Lara, I trust.'

'No reason not to be.' He had the sense they were burning time. As much as he wanted to play nice, he knew in his gut he didn't have the luxury.

Lara had trouble concentrating as she talked to Ms Vera Jones, a writer for the *Austin Chronicle*. Ms Jones was expounding on her theories of modern photography.

She'd not seen Beck in a half hour, but she sensed his presence and at times his gaze burrowing into her back. Tonight he'd set her off balance. When she'd seen him, she'd expected him to be pissed off. She'd expected him to be frustrated. Instead, he'd been almost charming. He was a chameleon, able to adapt, be what the situation dictated. And that made him dangerous.

'Why does such a lovely young woman choose such a dark subject?' Vera's question pulled Lara's attention back to the slim woman standing in front of her.

'Darkness brings conflict and conflict is interesting.' She swirled the untouched glass of wine in her hand.

'Frankly, you look like the flowers and butterflies kind of photographer.'

Lara raised her wineglass to her lips and pretended to drink. 'I get that a lot.'

Vera leaned in closer to Lara, as if they were co-conspirators. 'What drives your work? This attraction to death doesn't come from a place of butterflies and puppies.'

Anxiety clutched Lara's stomach. 'No.'

Vera's eyes narrowed. 'Then where? What drives your art?'

Later she'd wonder over and over what prompted her candid answer. Beck's presence. Guilt. Need. Anger. She'd never peg what prompted her to say, 'I was attacked seven years ago. I survived, but it left its mark.'

Vera's expression softened, but her eyes gleamed with excitement. 'What happened?'

'I was nearly strangled to death. Several women before me were killed by this man, but I survived.' She'd never spoken the words out loud, and there was a freedom that came with the truth.'

'Here in Austin?'

'No. Seattle. Seven years ago.'

Vera's eyes gleamed. 'I remember reading about the case. What did they call him? Ah, the Seattle Strangler.'

She nodded, her body now numb. 'Yes.'

'That case got national attention.'

'It did.'

'I never heard your name mentioned.'

'I was the seventh victim, the one that survived. The police never released my name.'

Vera sipped her wine and Lara could almost hear gears

turning in her brain. 'There was a woman strangled in Austin recently.'

Her throat tightened. 'I know.'

Vera's attention was finely honed. 'That's got to make you uncomfortable.'

'It makes me very sad.'

Vera glanced around the room. 'I would think death scenes wouldn't interest you.'

She swirled her wineglass, staring at the golden depths. 'There are gaps I don't remember. I keep thinking I will remember with each photograph.'

Vera released a breath she'd been holding. 'Remarkable. Fascinating.'

She didn't feel remarkable or fascinating, only vulnerable and afraid and sorry she'd been so candid.

Vera laid a hand on Lara's chilled hand. 'I'd like to talk to you more about this.'

'Perhaps another time.'

Before Vera formed a new question, Cassidy came up beside her and hooked her arm around Lara. 'Vera, do you not love Lara?'

The slim woman's smile was calculating. 'She's charming. And her work is as excellent as she is fascinating.'

'Violent death is not easy.' Cassidy, sensing Lara's stress, said, 'Ms. Jones, let's get a fresh glass of wine and have another pass around the gallery. There is a picture that I must show you.'

Lara eased a sigh from her lungs as the two walked away. In the moments she'd been talking to Ms Jones the gallery had filled with several dozen people enjoying the wine and food as much as the art. She wished she could just get outside for a moment and get fresh air.

'You look like you could use this.'

The sound, a familiar and friendly voice, made her smile. Jonathan Matthews grinned down at her as she exchanged her warm wine for a cool fresh glass. 'My hero.'

'I do try.' His smile deepened the lines around his eyes.

As much as she craved a cool liquid sliding down her throat, she didn't take a drink.

'So how is the show going?' Jonathan said.

'Well. Really well, I think. Everyone is definitely talking about the photographs.'

'I knew you'd be a success.'

'Did you? I could use an extra compliment or two right now.'

'You? Oh come on. You are the bravest person I know.'

She smiled. 'Feet of clay my friend. Feet of clay. But you are the only person I'd dare admit that too.'

His gaze softened. 'I'm glad you feel like you can talk to me. I have your back.'

'I know. And thanks.'

Cassidy cut through the crowd, her smile bright and eager. She nudged Lara gently with her elbow. 'You are a hit, my girl. I've heard whispers of sales.'

Heat rose in Lara's face. 'I wasn't sure how well my work would be taken.'

'Taken tremendously well.'

Cassidy glanced at Jonathan. 'Jonathan, I don't think I've seen you in several years.'

Jonathan smiled. 'I've been busy. You've been busy.'

'That's nice of you to support her.' A chill iced the words. Cassidy and Jonathan had never been friends, for reasons Lara could not explain.

Jonathan winked at Lara. 'She's the best.'

'And now I must steal her away from you,' Cassidy said.

Lara tossed a fleeting glance to Jonathan, who smiled back, and allowed Cassidy to introduce her to more people.

Lara let their conversation trickle over her head as she scanned the room, not so much looking at the crowds as looking for James Beck. For reasons she couldn't explain she wanted to talk to him again. Tell him what she'd told Vera. When she didn't spot his huge frame standing above the crowds, disappointment nagged her. Odd. Yesterday she couldn't wait to get rid of the guy.

Beck's warnings and his concerns replayed in her head. Anxiety churned in her belly before she made a conscious effort to still the chaos. Good or bad, Vera would write up her interview with Lara and the residents of Austin would know about her past.

Raines had intentionally arrived late to the gallery opening because he'd wanted to blend into the crowd and see Lara in action without being noticed. As he glanced toward the gallery's large picture window, he spotted the petite blonde staring into the gallery's display window. He recognized the girl instantly from the diner. Danni.

Most would have hustled right past the kid, but he couldn't. Her fear and anxiety blinked bright like the gallery's neon sign. 'You heading inside?'

Shocked that someone had spoken to her, she hesitated. 'I know you from the diner. Mr Pancakes.'

'My friends call me Mike Raines, but for you, kid, I'd answer to Mr Pancakes.'

A smile teased tense lips. 'Raines suits you better.'

'And you're Danni, right?'

'Good memory.'

'I do try.' He glanced through the window at the nicely dressed people milling around the framed photographs.

'So are you going inside?'

'I'm considering it.' Her black shirt and jeans made her blonde hair and pale skin look almost translucent.

'What's to consider? It looks like a great party.'

Her chin lifted a fraction, as she did her best to look disinterested when he would have guessed she was actually the opposite. 'It looks a little stuffy.'

For whatever reason he liked the girl. She'd been friendly to him from the moment she'd poured him fresh coffee. She was in her late teens at most, and her attempt to look so self-assured made him wonder what had toughened her veneer.

'I'm about to head inside. Why don't you come with me?'

She arched a brow. 'Are you hitting on me?'

His laugh was genuine and clear. 'You're young enough to be my kid.'

She folded slim arms over her chest, her eyebrow arched. 'And your point is?'

He shook his head, genuinely amused. 'Kid,' he said

adding emphasis to the word, 'I want to look at some art and have a beer. Underage kids are not on the menu.'

'I'm not underage.'

'If you're not now, you were last week.'

His laughter eased her anxiety and he stayed clear of her personal space, knowing a violation would fortify her defenses.

She pushed back her hair with an agitated hand. Her fingernails were painted black. 'So why do you want to see this exhibit? No offense, but you don't look like the artsy type.'

'I'm not. But I know the artist, and I'm just being supportive.'

'You know Lara Church?'

His slid his hands into his pockets. 'From the days we both lived in Seattle. And you?'

'I'm one of her students.'

'I'll bet she's a good teacher.'

'Yeah. Takes no crap, but can make the most complicated technique sound easy.'

'That's a gift.'

'I guess.'

He held out his hand. 'Danni, you got a last name?'

She glanced down at his hand and then took it. 'Danni Rome.'

His grip was firm, but he released her hand quickly. She was looking for an excuse to bolt, and he didn't want to be the one to give it to her. 'So are you coming inside, Ms Danni Rome? Or are you gonna stand out her and dream and wish?'

164

She straightened. 'Dreaming and wishing are for saps.'

'I couldn't agree more, and you don't strike me as a sap. So what do you say? You want to come inside with me?'

'Okay, Mike Raines, let's go inside.'

'That a girl.' He opened the door for her and waited until she passed before he followed. 'Let's hit the bar. Easier to break the ice with a drink in hand.'

'Sounds like a plan.'

He followed behind her and, though tempted to place his hand in the small of her back and guide her, he did not. At the bar, he glanced down at her. 'What would you like, Ms Danni Rome?'

'Beer.'

The bartender raised a brow.

Mike grinned. 'She meant to say soda. I get the beer.'

The bartender nodded. 'Right away.'

Colour rose in her face, but she didn't speak. 'You still act like a cop.'

Mike leaned toward Danni. 'I'll take that as a compliment.'

The bartender popped the top on a beer and handed it to Mike. Both with drinks in hand, they faced the crowd.

Danni took a long sip. 'Thanks.'

'Sure.' Raines glanced at the artsy crowd. They lived in an insulated dream world. He worked back alleys and dark streets. 'So what can you tell me about this art, Danni Rome? I'm helpless in places like that.'

'You, helpless?' Laughter twinkled in her gaze.

'What can I say? The artsy types aren't for me.' He glanced down at her. 'Present company excluded.'

'Thanks.' She took another sip. 'Lara uses a one-hundred-and-fifty-year-old bellows camera.'

He listened as she explained the photography process to him. 'Sounds like you know what you're talking about.'

'As of yesterday. She asked me to help her with a shoot, and I got a chance to prepare a glass negative and shoot a picture.'

'Nice. So what did you shoot?' He knew the answer but wanted to hear it from her.

'What she always shoots. A crime scene.'

'A crime scene.' Tension rippled up his spine. 'I'm surprised she'd take an underage kid.'

Danni sipped her drink. 'I gave her a note from my mother saying it was okay.'

So she was as young as he thought. 'Did your mother write the note?'

Danni sipped her drink, her lips wide in a grin.

'Thought so. When do you hit the big one-eight?'

'Nine days.'

Raines let out a sigh. 'Kid, you are far too old for seventeen.'

'Technically eighteen.'

'In nine days.' He raised a brow. 'So where did you go?'

'A clump of land off of Interstate 35. Not much to look at, but she was determined to get the shot.'

'When did you go?'

'About dusk. She'd been there earlier in the day at sunrise. And she wanted to get a different perspective on the site.'

He thought about the woman's sunglasses in his breast pocket. 'And did you?'

'I'll know tomorrow. We'll be developing the negatives.'

He spotted Lara across the room and for a moment was taken aback. When he'd first met her she'd been traumatized and so afraid. And during their subsequent interviews she'd drawn deeper into herself. The harder he pushed the deeper she'd burrowed.

However, this Lara wasn't like the woman he'd interviewed countless times. This Lara was hot. Her blonde hair draped over her shoulders, and her black dress hugged her curves in all the right places. Her smile was radiant and her gaze sharp.

'So do you know who died at that spot?' Mike said.

'Some woman was strangled there. Apparently she was pretty decomposed when a utility worker found her body.'

'You two should be careful,' Mike said. 'Killers have been known to return to the crime scene.'

She cocked a brow. 'So that line you gave me about being a cop was true?'

'You don't believe me?'

'I don't know you. You could have been feeding me a line.'

He winked. 'Smart girl.' He sipped his beer. 'Yeah, I was a cop. Best twenty years of my life.'

'Was?'

Regret always mingled with these words. 'Gave it up about six years ago. Time to expand my horizons.'

'And the new horizon is?'

'I own a security firm. We aren't huge, but we get by and do well enough.'

'So do you follow or find people?' She tapped a finger against her glass.

He sensed the deep curiosity behind her questions. She wasn't just making small talk but was intrigued. 'So Danni Rome, do you need me to follow or find someone?'

She offered a whatever shrug. 'Just making conversation.'

'I hear interest. There a boss, neighbour, or boyfriend out there giving you a hard time?'

'No,' she said quickly. 'No one.'

His cop radar said differently, but he let it pass. Not only did he like her, but she was close to Lara and that connection might prove beneficial. 'Danni Rome, let's have a look around this place.'

She stopped tapping her glass. 'Sounds like a plan.'

Chapter Eleven

By the time the evening ended, Lara's feet ached from the heels, and her face hurt from so much smiling. Cassidy waved goodbye to the last guest and locked the front door behind her. A wide grin softened her face. 'You, my dear, were a huge hit tonight. Huge! This is just the beginning.'

Lara shrugged, trying to shake loose the knot between her shoulder blades. 'It's been a long time since I've talked to so many people.'

Cassidy walked to the bar and poured them each a glass of wine. She handed one to Lara as she took a sip from the other. 'You were great. A natural. And you looked stunning.'

'Thanks.'

'It's almost as if I was looking at a different person tonight. The first time I proposed the show, you looked as if you wanted to run and hide.'

Lara swirled her wine in her glass. 'That's not too far from the truth.'

Cassidy tipped her glass toward Lara. 'But you did not run. You were like your old self tonight.'

Lara recognized seeds of change growing. 'You're right.'

Cassidy sipped her wine, her eyes keen and sharp. 'Why didn't you run? What made you say yes?'

Lara stared into the gold depths of her wine, wishing she could drink, knowing she wouldn't. 'I was tired of hiding.'

Cassidy cocked her head to the side. 'And what were you hiding from?'

Lara's secrets rose up again begging to be spoken. 'You need to know this because I shared it with Vera tonight.'

Cassidy stilled her entire attention and fixated on Lara.

'I had a trauma in Seattle about seven years ago. It sent me inward.'

Cassidy's glass paused inches from her lips. 'What kind of trauma?' Her cousin always drove straight to the heart of the matter.

'I was sexually assaulted and nearly strangled to death by an attacker.'

Cassidy's grip on her glass tightened. 'What?'

'I don't remember what happened.' She recapped what she did remember.

Cassidy set down her glass. 'So you don't remember who did this to you?'

Fatigue rushed over her. 'No. I have no memory of the attack.'

'How can that be?'

'Doctors said it was the trauma of the concussion. Some even thought I was lying so that I could avoid the police investigation.'

'You weren't lying.' She shook her head as if pieces of a puzzle fell together. 'Grandma was upset around that time. I thought it was because she was sick and couldn't attend your graduation.'

'I called her and told her what had happened. I begged her not to tell anyone, but she asked Jonathan to come and be with me.'

Cassidy's lips thinned. 'I would have come.'

'You were in New York. Life was going so well for you. I wouldn't have wanted to drag you into my mess.'

'I would have come,' she said softly.

'I know.'

After a heavy silence, Cassidy said, 'Jonathan always liked you.'

'He was great after the attack and so good to me, but I couldn't stand being in a town where my attacker lived. I've been on the move until eight months ago.'

'And that explains why you take pictures of so many crime scenes.'

Lara set her glass down. 'I told Vera because I know she'll write about it, and I'm tired of hiding.'

Cassidy raised a brow. 'Oh, she will. It will be an eye-catcher for her readers when it runs in Sunday's paper. That kind of news could take the exhibit national.'

'That wasn't my intent.'

Cassidy tugged off a clip-on earring and rubbed her earlobe. 'Then why talk to Vera?'

'I've been hiding for seven years. And I'm tired of it. I want my life back.'

Cassidy nodded with approval. 'Well, after that article hits you will have a different and, I hope, a very lucrative, life.' She took one last sip and set her glass down. 'You want to stay the night here?'

'No, no, I'm fine. But do you need help cleaning up?'

Cassidy laughed. 'Lara, you must be more of a diva. Artists do not clean up.'

A chuckle rumbled in her throat. 'I'll remember that when I'm walking Lincoln and bagging his business.'

'No, I do not need help. I was offering a bed so you don't have the long drive home.'

'I can't leave Lincoln.'

'The wolf will survive a night.'

'Likely. But I'd worry. I better get home.'

'If you must.'

Cassidy hugged Lara. 'I'm proud of you. Tonight was a big step for you.'

An understatement. Lara thanked Cassidy again and then headed outside. The night air was cool and crisp and a welcome break from the day's heat and the gallery crowds. Her heels clicked on the sidewalk as she crossed the street to the parking lot where her truck remained. She dug her keys out of her purse and shoved the key in the lock.

'You had an impressive crowd there tonight.' Beck's rough voice startled her.

She turned, surprised to see him stepping out of the shadows. 'What are you doing here?'

'Working late at the office. Thought I'd swing back by and see how the show was going.'

'It's over.'

'I can see that.' He moved closer, his steps purposeful. 'You should have had your keys in your hand when you came out of the gallery.'

'The street is well lit, and this is a good part of town.'

A wry smile lifted the edge of his mouth. 'You, more

than anyone, should know that the safe part of town is never really safe.'

She bristled, annoyed because he was right. 'Is this some kind of safety lecture?'

His white hat shadowed his face, making it hard for her to read his expression. 'Friendly advice.'

'Duly noted. Is that all?'

'See anyone in there tonight that might have set off alarm bells? Not so much in your memory but your gut?'

Fear slithered down her spine as she imagined the Strangler close and watching. 'No. Why?'

'Bit of a coming-out party for you tonight. If I were the Strangler and I were back in Austin, I'd have made a point to be at that opening.'

Beck's observations ratcheted up her worries about Vera's coming article. 'Someone like that would stick out in the crowd.'

'Don't you believe it for one minute, Ms Church. Those kinds of killers can blend in real well. Can be as charming as the best. Fact is their charm can be as smooth as a magician's sleight of hand.'

'I don't understand.'

'When a magician wants you to look away from his hand while he makes a switch, he'll move his other hand to distract your attention. A killer is all nice and charming, and that's all you see until he attacks.'

Had her attacker been a charming guy who'd simply fooled her before he'd placed the rag over her face? 'Sergeant, I have the chance to really rebuild my life and start fresh. Stop digging up all the dark and scary.'

'I didn't go looking for the dark and scary. It found me and now you.' Menace lurked behind the words.

Her heartbeat quickened despite her mind's demand for calm. 'I am tired of living in fear. I won't live in fear.'

'I don't expect you to live in fear,' he said clearly. 'I want you to remember, so we can put his guy away forever.'

'I have no memories to give.' The words sounded defeated even to her ears. 'And you might as well hear this from me. I told Vera about my past.'

The subtle tightening of his jaw coupled with a slowly drawn-in breath had her anticipating a sharp response. 'You told her about Seattle?'

'Yes.'

Beck stood silent as he stared at her.

'I'm tired of being afraid. If he knows I'm in Austin there's no point in hiding.'

His eyes narrowed.

'Your timing is fortunate. You and your show will get a lot of publicity.'

Frustration had her taking a step back. 'That's not why I did it.'

'That so?'

Her fingers clenched into fists. 'That is so.'

He took one step, reclaiming the distance she'd tried to put between them and more. 'You shouldn't be talking to reporters but to a psychologist.'

'I don't want any more shrinks poking in my head.'

'Talk to my gal once. If it doesn't work, I'll back off.'

That made her smile. 'You would really back off completely if the doc and I came up empty handed? Really?'

He frowned.

She shook her head. 'Don't kid yourself, and don't kid me. Once would not be enough. You'll hound me until this case is closed.'

He didn't address her statement. 'An article like that is going to bring a lot of nuts out of the woodwork.'

In the rush of emotions, she hadn't thought beyond the telling. 'There's only one nut I fear right now.'

Beck rubbed the back of his neck. 'I'm going to have DPS step up patrols near your house.'

'I don't regret what I said.' A half-truth.

He shook his head. 'Not going to get into it with you tonight.'

'But tomorrow.'

A smile tugged at the edge of his lips. 'Like you said, I don't give up easy.'

Stunned by his clear-cut honesty, she got into her car and started the engine. He waited, watching as she backed out of her space and drove down the block. At the stop sign she paused and glanced in her rearview mirror to find Beck watching her.

Her life wasn't going to come close to normal until Sergeant Beck had his killer.

Blair Silver was irritated.

She lit up a cigarette and slid into the front seat of her Bronco just before midnight. She was bone tired, and she'd spent the better part of her Friday night studying. With exams just over a week away, she had been studying nonstop for three days so she could pass her econ exam.

Her grade hovered between a C and a D, and she needed a C to graduate and leave Austin.

On top of school pressures, her mom had called three times today, nagging her about her AA meetings. Blair had been polite the first time her mother had called, promising that she'd attend and that, yes, she was still clean and sober. Four hundred and ninety days sober. She'd told her mother to stop worrying. But her mother had called a second time while Blair had been in the middle of a class. Her phone had vibrated loudly and caught the attention of the teacher. A call back to her mom had been a replay of the earlier conversation.

Are you going to AA*? Are you all right?*

Yes.

Are you sure?

Shit.

She loved her mother, was trying to be patient, but the woman was smothering her.

Smoke swirled around her head as she pulled in a long drag, held the smoke in her lungs for a moment, and then slowly released it. 'I am going to pass econ and Mom is going to chill. I can do this. I can do this.'

It had been a long road for Blair the last couple of years. And she could acknowledge that she'd created her own problems. No one had forced her to start drinking or using. Her shitty choices had not only jeopardized school, but they'd nearly killed her.

Her hands trembled as she dug a slender hand through her blonde hair. *Don't go there. You screwed up, but you've fixed it. Life is better. Even Mom is more chill than she was six months ago.*

She started the engine and prepared to back out of her space when there was a knock on her driver's-side window. She jumped. 'Shit!'

Her heart racing, she turned to see a guy standing there smiling in an embarrassed sort of way. 'You scared the shit out of me.'

'Sorry,' he said loud enough to penetrate the glass. 'I was hoping you had a cell phone I could use. My battery is dead, and so is my car engine. I just need to call my wife so she can come and get me.'

Blair glanced at his left hand holding the cell and noted the wedding ring. He had an easy smile, looked nice enough, and she could have sworn she'd seen him on campus. 'Sure, why not?'

Holding her cigarette between her teeth, she fished her phone off the bottom of her purse and then lowered her window halfway and handed it to him. 'Here ya go.'

'I won't be more than a couple of seconds. And the call is local.'

'Sure whatever.' She drew on her cigarette and watched as he dialled, waited as the phone rang.

'Hey, baby, it's me,' he said turning away. 'The car is doing that thing again. It won't start.' He nodded, listened. 'Yeah, I'm near the econ building, but just pick me up at the River Diner.' He grinned. 'Thanks, baby.' He ended the call. 'Hey, thanks a lot. You saved me from a long walk.'

She accepted the phone. 'Sure. No worries. So your wife is on her way?'

'Yeah. It'll take her about an hour, so I'm going to hoof it over to the café. Hey, thanks again. I'm Bill by the way.'

'Blair.'

'Aren't you in Roger's econ class?'

'Yeah.'

'He can be tough. How's it going?'

She smiled. 'He's killing me.'

'He's littered the halls of the econ building with lots of failed students.'

She stubbed her cigarette in the ashtray. 'Grr. Don't say that. I need to pass so I can graduate.'

'You look like a smart cookie.'

'Let's hope.'

He shoved his hands in his pockets. 'Well, take care, Blair, and I'll be pulling for you and a passing grade.'

'Thanks, Bill.'

She put the car in reverse and started to back up as he walked across the parking lot. A part of her wanted to give the guy a lift and another chided her for being reckless. Yeah, she'd seen him around campus, but that didn't mean much. He could be trouble.

But he'd been nice. He'd called his wife baby. And he wasn't asking for favours. If he'd wanted to cause trouble he'd have stirred it up by now.

She pulled up beside him and rolled down the passenger window. 'Hey, isn't the River Diner about a mile or two from here?'

He slowed his pace. 'Thereabouts.'

'That's a long walk.'

'Good for me. Builds character.'

She stopped. 'Hop in. I'll give you a lift.'

He shook his head. 'That's nice, but you don't have to.'

Okay, he had to be a nice guy. He didn't pounce on her offer like a crazed guy would. 'No, really. I'm going that way, and it'll save you a few steps.'

He cocked his head. 'Sure?'

'Yes.' She unlocked the automatic door locks.

He opened the door and slid into the seat. Inside the car he appeared much bigger. His smile didn't fade, but this close he had an odd vibe. One mile or two, and he'd be out of her life for good. 'The River Diner, next stop.'

Bill grinned the devil's grin, and before she could blink he pulled a long butcher's knife from his pocket and poked it in her side hard enough to make her flinch. 'I have a better idea.'

'What the hell,' she said.

He poked the knife tip harder into her side. 'I've been watching you.' He inhaled the remains of her cigarette smoke. 'Light me up one.'

When she didn't move, the knife tip cut through her blouse and into her side. Tears of fear burned her eyes as she frantically dug the cigarettes out of her bag, lit one, and handed it to him.

He inhaled deeply. 'Start driving.'

'Where?'

'A place where we won't be disturbed or rushed.'

Five hours later Blair huddled naked in the corner of the dank dark room and stared at the man who'd held and brutalized her for hours. When he'd first brought her here, she'd feared he'd rape her. And then after she'd lain under him, she'd sensed deep in her bones that she'd never leave this room alive.

He held up a simple white dress trimmed with a hint of lace at the cuffs and collar. 'I want you to put this on.'

She pushed back a lock of hair, wincing when she touched the bruise on her cheekbone. Though craving the protection of clothing, she understood his offer had nothing to do with kindness. Mustering strength and defiance, she lifted her chin a fraction. 'Why?'

A smile twitched the edge of his mouth. 'I can make you hurt more.'

Blair's chin dipped and quivered. The things he'd done to her. She'd not known pain be so intense.

'You don't want me to make you hurt more, do you?

'No.'

He held out the dress.

She accepted it. Without rising, she lifted the garment over her head and slid it on. Oddly, it felt soft and warm against her skin. Carefully, she tugged the hem over her naked legs, craving coverage. 'I won't tell. I won't.'

He nodded. 'I know you won't tell, Blair. I know.'

Fresh tears filled her eyes. 'Then you'll let me go?'

He held out his hand to her and waited for her to accept it. Wrapping gentle fingers around her hand, he pulled her into a standing position. She winced as she straightened, trying to ignore the pain and cling to the hope that he just might let her go.

His hand trailed up her arm, over the cotton sleeve, and rested in the hollow of her throat. 'Your heart is beating so fast.'

'I'm scared.'

'You've no reason to be scared, Blair. The worst is over.'

His other hand joined the first at the base of her throat. 'You remind me so much of her. A fighter. I like that.'

'Her?'

His warm, rough fingers closed around her windpipe and he started to squeeze. She clutched his fingers, trying to pry them free, but they were as fixed as iron. Her heart beat faster as her body demanded air. Her fingers dug into his hands as she stared into dark eyes filled with such hate and anger. Soon spots formed in front of her eyes and her eyelids closed as her body's systems shut down. Her knees crumpled, increasing the tension on her neck.

As the last tethers to the world frayed and snapped, he said, 'You remind me of Lara.'

Blair's body weighed heavily in his arms as he carried her across the grasslands. Little moonlight lit the way, but he didn't need it. He knew every rock, crevice, and blade of grass in this area.

In the distance behind him, the traffic on the interstate whooshed as he knelt and laid her body on the dry, cracked earth. Carefully he arranged her hair and then fanned her skirt like a butterfly's wings. He dug two pennies from his pocket and dared a glance at her half-open eyes. No matter how hard he'd squeezed her throat, her eyes had not closed. He laid the pennies on her lids, knowing the weight would end her death glare.

Blair had been good. Better than the last.

But she'd never be as good as Lara.

And she would soon be his.

Chapter Twelve

Nearly a week of eighteen-hour days had dug into Beck's reserves, and by rights he should have slept like the dead last night. After he'd left Henry's for a quick dinner of takeout, he'd gone to his apartment and fallen into bed just after midnight. But instead of drifting off, he had tossed for hours until three in the morning when a light, fitful sleep had taken hold.

During those brief moments of slumber, he'd dreamed of Lara, standing before him in her black dress. She'd been smiling as she'd cupped his face with her hands and kissed him. The kiss hadn't been tentative or light, but fierce and demanding. He'd pressed his hand to the small of her back, urging her silk-covered body against his. He'd deepened the kiss. Run his hands over her shoulders and down to breasts barely contained by the sleek material.

He'd awoken at five o'clock in the morning, hard and primed. He wanted a woman who likely would end up hating him before this investigation closed.

A cold shower had done little to take the edge off, so he'd dressed. As the coffee gurgled in the machine, the apartment walls closed in, smacking of his paid-leave days.

Coffee in hand, he'd headed out, picked up the Sunday paper, and by seven was sitting at his desk.

He flipped to the entertainment section and found a striking picture of Lara standing in front of one of her photographs. Her sleek black dress hugged her curves and accentuated her blonde hair. Diamond stud earrings sparkled and a lariat necklace dipped down her neck into the V of her dress. Her smile was radiant. Her eyes looked bright.

Absently he traced her jawline and wondered if her skin was as smooth as it looked. Shaking off the thought, he shifted his attention to the article and stopped dead.

Art Imitates Life

Local artist Lara Church opened her exhibition Friday night at 101 Gallery. The show, Mark of Death, featured landscapes that had all witnessed murders. The images were stark and striking and caught the attention of many who attended the opening Friday night.

When I first met the radiant artist I could not help but wonder why such a bright young woman would tap into such a dark subject.

And then Ms Church disclosed that she had been nearly murdered herself seven years ago. She'd been a young fashion merchandising student in Seattle when she was viciously attacked and left for dead. Police believed her attacker was the Seattle Strangler, the mysterious serial killer who vanished after the failed attack on Church.

Beck sat back in his chair, continuing to read. The article went on to praise Ms Church's work and draw parallels between her attack and her art.

With nearly a day and a half to ease the euphoria of her opening, he wondered if she'd be so pleased with her decision to reveal her past for all to see.

The muscles in his shoulders and neck stiffened as he thought about someone watching Lara. Until now, isolated by her secrets, she'd been the killer's own personal toy. Now that everyone knew about Lara's past, there'd be lots of eyes on her.

His phone rang and he snapped it up. 'Beck.'

'Bill Fields here with DPS. We got another body on the side of Interstate 35. Another woman strangled. White dress. Pennies.'

Beck tensed and glanced down at the article and Lara's shining face. 'Do you have an ID on the woman?'

'What I just gave you is all I've got now.'

'Where are you?' Beck took note of the location. 'Thanks.'

'Got more information on the Fisk case.'

The ominous tone of the officer's voice tightened his muscles. 'What?'

'Officers found a penny at the Fisk murder site. 1947. Found it about fifteen feet from the body site and under an inch of silt. They reckon it washed away after the rains in April.'

Beck sat back in his chair. 'Thanks.'

Shit.

Three Austin murders were now linked. The killer that had hunted in Seattle seven years ago was in Austin. And

Lara had put herself in the crosshairs. He dialled her home number and cursed when he got the answering machine.

He was out the door in seconds, praying like hell Lara wasn't the latest victim.

Thirty minutes later, he arrived at the crime scene, roped off by hundreds of yards of tape. The traffic leading up to the crime scene had been slow on the interstate, and as he got closer he could see that DPS had closed two lanes of traffic.

At the scene, a half dozen squad cars, lights flashing, were parked on the side of the highway. The forensics van had arrived, as had the medical examiner. In the distance he could see a tent had been erected over what must be the body. Two officers with canines were searching the area around the body.

Beck parked his car, donned his hat, and moved down the shoulder of the road past the squad cars without stopping to speak to Santos or any of the DPS officers as he normally did. He followed the access path to the crime scene, his boots crunching on the uneven bone-dry terrain.

Thoughts of Lara stabbed at Beck as he made his way to the body. Hands clenched at his side, he studied the swollen, bloated body, dressed in white and ravaged by the Texas heat. As bad as the body looked, he'd learned one critical fact. It wasn't Lara.

Relief washed over him, taking with it the gnawing worry that had hunted him since the DPS phone call less than an hour ago.

As Santos approached, Beck sensed the other Ranger's

honed eye for detail had shifted to him. It wasn't like Beck to rush into a crime scene as a loved one of a victim might.

Santos tipped his hat back. 'Pull you away from anything interesting?'

'Paperwork.'

If Santos had questions about Beck's behaviour he didn't air them, and Beck was glad of it. At this point he didn't understand it himself.

'There'll be a mountain of paperwork on this one,' Santos said.

Beck turned from the body. 'She's like the others.'

'Yeah.' He rested his hands on his hips. 'No identification yet, but if she's like the other two she'll be a student. You heard about Fisk.'

'Found the penny.'

'Yeah.'

They watched as Melinda snapped pictures of the entire scene and Eliza Rio, a medical examiner technician, examined the victim's neck.

Without glancing up, the olive skinned Rio said, 'She appears to have been strangled. Her body dumped at least twenty-four hours ago.' No good morning. No how's it going. 'Bruising around the neck suggests that he may have strangled her several times.'

The killer had been playing with his victim. 'Other injuries? Sexual assault?'

'No visible bruising on her body, and I'll need to get her back to the lab to determine sexual assault.'

Beck stared at the blonde woman dressed in the white

186

dress made of soft cotton and lace. 'What about the pennies?'

'One on each eye,' Melinda said.

Santos glanced at Beck. 'That Raines fellow still in town?'

'I think so.'

Santos looked like a man about to swallow a bitter pill. 'As much as I hate to say this, might be time to call him. Bring him into this.'

Beck hesitated, his first instinct to handle this case internally. And then the image of Misty Gray's decomposed body flashed in his mind. Yes, he'd caught Dial, but the kid had died. A hollow victory.

He nodded. 'I'll call him.'

Raines read the article on Lara Church three times. Seven years of silence had ended and now the world knew the secret he'd worked so hard to guard in Seattle. He never would have guessed Lara Church would tell the media.

He sat back and sipped his coffee. Its bitter taste said that Danni wasn't working today. He liked seeing Danni. She was a good kid, and he was a creature of habit. When he found a restaurant, a clothing item, even a style of car, he stuck with it. His wife joked often enough that they'd go on vacation to get away from it all and within twenty-four hours he'd create a brand-new rut.

'Mix things up, for God's sake,' his wife would say to him.

This article on Lara was certainly going to change the dynamics. No more hiding. No more running. 'Time to remember, Lara.'

An unknown waitress brought him a stack of pancakes and a fresh pot of coffee.

'Thanks.'

She refilled his cup. 'Hope you like the coffee. Danni says you like a fresh cup, not too bitter.'

He smiled, gratified the kid had remembered him. He held up his cup. 'Thanks. To both of you.'

As he sipped the still-too-bitter coffee, his phone rang. He recognized the number instantly – Ranger James Beck. Wiping his hands, he wondered if Beck had seen the article as he picked up the phone. 'Ranger Beck.'

'Detective Raines. Do you have a minute this morning?'

Liking the sound of *Detective*, he relaxed back in the booth. 'For what?'

'To visit a crime scene.'

Raines pulled off his glasses. 'Another woman?'

'Why don't you meet me?' He rattled off directions and exits. 'Do you know where that is?'

This nightmare scenario was playing out as he'd predicted, but he experienced no joy. 'That's close to the first two sites.'

'Correct.'

Raines checked his watch. 'I'm leaving now.'

'Where are you?'

'The River Diner. Austin.'

'See you in twenty minutes.'

'If not sooner.' Raines paid his tab and hurried out to his car. Excitement pumped through his veins. For seven years he'd waited for the Strangler to make a move. But the killer had remained dormant. And now, the son of a bitch had at least two and possibly three killings to his credit in this area.

He didn't care why the killer had awoken after seven years of slumber. Theories about the killer being hurt, jailed, or dead never had meant much to him. All that mattered was that he was active again. 'Keep it up, you son of a bitch. Keep it up, and I will nail your ass.'

Manoeuvring out of town proved to be more frustrating than he'd expected, but he soon found access to the interstate and within minutes parked behind a parade of cop cars with flashing lights.

He moved toward a uniform. 'I'm Mike Raines. Sergeant James Beck called me.'

'May I see your ID?'

For twenty years he had been the insider. The Seattle cops had looked on him with respect. When he entered a crime scene, people got out of his way. Now, he was nobody, accountable to a uniform who looked twelve years old.

Raines shoved aside irritation and pulled out his Seattle driver's licence, conscious of the fact that it didn't carry the weight of a badge.

The DPS officer inspected the licence and then Raines a couple of times. He handed the ID back. 'Thank you, sir. Sergeant Beck is just over the rise. I'll show you the way.'

Beck inhaled pride and a renewed sense of purpose. He'd convinced himself over the last six years that money and regular hours could take the place of the Job, but he'd been kidding himself. He'd fucking missed the Job.

'Not necessary. I see Sergeant Beck. Should I follow the path marked by the tape?'

'Yes, sir.'

Sir. He liked that.

Dust and dirt kicked up on shoes that he'd had polished in Denver's airport nearly a week ago while waiting for his connection. He almost laughed at his blunder. He had lost his touch. No smart cop wore his good shoes to a crime scene.

As he moved closer to Beck, he gave the Ranger credit. He wasn't sure if he'd have put his ego aside and relied on a cop from the outside.

'Sergeant Beck.'

Beck turned and extended his hand. 'Mr Raines, I appreciate you coming down here.'

He wouldn't have missed it for the world. 'Glad to help.'

'I'd like you to meet fellow Ranger Sergeant Rick Santos from the San Antonio office. These crimes have fallen right between our jurisdictions.'

Santos's ice-blue eyes projected distrust. 'Mr Raines.'

Raines didn't miss the tension ripping through Santos. 'I would have been pissed if I had to deal with an outsider at my crime scene.'

Santos offered no apology. 'I'll do what it takes to solve this crime, but understand that I do not trust you.'

'I'd worry if you did.' Raines glanced at the white-hot sun. 'I swear I'll never bitch about the rain in Seattle again.'

Santos's expression remained neutral.

So much for humour. 'Can I see the body?'

Beck held out his hand. 'This way. We kept her here so you could see the positioning, but we're going have to move her soon. The heat's not helping.'

Raines stared out across the grassy field. 'Let's get to it.' He accepted rubber gloves from Beck, donning them as he had thousands of times in the past. Death's sick sweet scent trailed out toward him even before he reached the body. Automatically, he blocked out the stench.

The woman lay on her back, her hands crossed over her chest. She wore a white dress and no shoes, and her blonde hair was strewn out on the ground behind her. There were blue and purple fingerprint marks around her neck. 'Take away this damn heat, and I could be back in Seattle at one of my old crime scenes.'

He squatted by the body. The skin under the victim's arms and the back of her legs had darkened. Once the heart stopped pumping, the blood settled to the lowest points of the body. In her case it would be the backside of her body.

'You have any theories on your killer?' Beck said.

'You've read my files.' He studied the marks on the woman's neck.

'I did. Twice. But I'm looking for the ideas you had in your head but never wrote down.'

All cops had theories that they weren't willing to make a matter of record. 'I wrote down all my theories until Lara Church was attacked. After her attack and survival I suspected a shift in the killer.'

'Elaborate,' Santos said.

'She was not only raped,' Raines said. 'But she was

beaten. And she survived. No other victim was assaulted or left alive.'

'Killers change,' Santos said.

'I know. They have stressors just like we do. But this guy was one hundred percent consistent. He didn't rape the first six women, and he didn't make a mistake. Suddenly, he rapes and nearly gets caught. I'd have said he was a copycat if not for the penny.'

'Lara could have been his target all along,' Beck said. 'The first six could have been a warm-up.'

'That was my thought. I kept thinking this guy must know her. But I couldn't prove it, and of course she could not remember.'

'What about the men in her life?' A hard edge sharpened Beck's words.

'I checked them all out. Her boss at the department store where she worked was clean, as was her landlord. Her professors. The men she'd dated casually. All had alibis the night of her attack.'

'Tell me about the men she dated,' Beck said.

'As you know from the files, there were three. I leaned on them hard, but all three had alibis for Lara's attack and the first six murders.' He glanced toward the highway and then at the body. 'He's playing his game all over again, practicing and playing with others before he goes after Lara.'

Tension clawed at the muscles in Beck's back. 'He's playing before he strikes.'

'It's my theory.' Raines stood. 'You behind Lara talking to the press?'

Santos's gaze shifted to Beck.

'No,' Beck said. 'She did that one all on her own.'

'Got to give her credit,' Raines said nodding his approval. 'She's not hiding this time. Taking the bull by the horns, so to speak.'

Beck shook his head, wishing he'd never suggested she go public.

Chapter Thirteen

Sunday, May 26, 4 pm

Beck, Santos, and Raines spent the afternoon in the autopsy room with the medical examiner. The exam had been eerily similar to the last. Bruising around the neck. Signs of sexual assault. When the exam had concluded the three had tossed their scrub gowns in a hamper and convened in Dr Watterson's office.

The doctor kept his space neat and organized. Books on the shelves were in alphabetical order, and the stacks on the desk were precise. Dr Watterson was obsessive about all the details of an autopsy and his life.

The medical examiner eased into a chair behind his desk. Santos and Raines took the seats on the opposite side of the desk, while Beck remained standing by the door.

Raines removed a clean handkerchief from his coat pocket and dabbed the sweat on his forehead. 'These killings are more violent than Seattle. Time has made him more brutal.'

For a moment the air hung heavy with tension.

'I'd be willing to bet that the killer lives or works near the exit on I-35,' Raines said. 'I always thought he knew that stretch of Route 10 in Washington well.'

'Why do you say that?' the doctor said.

'Most of us are creatures of habit, and we stick to the same routines.'

Beck had stuck to what he'd known in the Misty Gray case. Long hours and dogged determination had added up to failure.

Santos stared at the tip of his scuffed cowboy boot. 'Insane habits make sense to the insane.'

Raines nodded. 'Exactly. Just like you and I tend to shop for food, shoes, or clothes at the same stores, this nut shops for his victims in the same way.'

'So how do we find him?' Santos said. 'We know he likes blonde students, but that's a wide description with so many schools around here.'

'We're looking for someone who lived in Seattle or nearby. He's familiar with Washington's Route 10 and I-35 in Texas. Likely knows Lara Church even if it's a passing acquaintance, though I would guess he's built up an elaborate fantasy life about her.'

Dr Watterson leaned forward, his gaze intent on the conversation. 'Today's victim showed more trauma than the last.'

'Lara Church,' Beck said. 'We start with her. Raines gave us a good history on her life in Seattle, but I want to know what she did between then and now. I also want to know about the summers she spent in town when she lived with her grandmother.'

'I kept tabs on her over the years,' Raines said. 'I can give you my logs.'

'You kept tabs on her for seven years?' Beck said.

Raines remained relaxed as if his brand of intensity

was normal. 'I tracked her through her Social, DMV, and the one credit card she carried.'

'Did you follow her?'

Raines nodded. 'Not always. But I checked in on her from time to time. I also monitored crime stats wherever she lived. No Strangler-like cases until Austin.'

Beck studied the former detective, wondering if he was capable of such obsession. 'Your notes would be helpful.' He shifted his attention to Santos. 'Can you dig into her past in Texas? Her grandmother's name is Bower.'

'Be glad too.'

'You had her talk to Dr Granger?' Dr Watterson said.

'She won't consider it,' Beck said.

'She saw an army of shrinks in Seattle.' Raines's deep voice held no censure. 'The lady developed an intense dislike for psychologists.'

Beck would keep stoking the fire until the heat forced her to cooperate. 'Remind DPS again that if any report comes up with her name on it, I want to know about it.'

Santos rose. 'Will do.'

Until this was over, Lara was a marked woman.

After Lara glanced at her watch and realized how long she'd left Lincoln alone, guilt chased her the last mile home. She'd not intended to stay in town for so long, but a visit to the grocer had turned into a marathon of questions and answers from strangers and acquaintances. Everyone had read the article. And questions ranged from kind to downright rude. Her stand had cost her privacy.

She'd only read the article through once. Vera had

quoted her several times and clearly she'd done some digging on the Seattle cases. But Lara had no desire to read it again or to dissect her past.

Hopefully, her fifteen minutes of fame would pass quickly.

Gravel crunched under the tyres of her car as she pulled in front of the house. Keys jangling in her hand, she got out expecting to hear Lincoln's welcoming bark. The dog had a deep woof that could carry for miles.

But Lincoln didn't greet her with his barks. Instead there was only silence, coupled with the hissing and rattling of her truck engine as it cooled. Worry rippled up her back, tightening around the back of her head.

Beck and this morning's story forgotten, she hurried up the front steps and fumbled with her keys. In her haste, she dropped the keys. 'Lincoln! I got chew sticks at the store!'

She scraped the keys off the porch floor, found her house key, and shoved it in the lock. The lock turned and the front door swung open. 'Lincoln! Where are you, boy?'

An eerie stillness confronted her the instant she stepped into the house. Immediately, anxiety prickled her skin. Everything was in its place, and yet everything was wrong.

Clutching her keys, she shouted, 'Lincoln!'

As the silence grew louder and louder, her worry simmered hotter and hotter. She moved from room to room, calling the dog's name. But there was no sign of him in the house. What had happened to him?

She rattled the knob on the back door and found it secure. With today's heat forecasts she had been adamant about keeping him inside even as he whined to go back out. Could he have slipped out as she was locking up this morning? She closed her eyes replaying each moment of the morning step by step. Lincoln had been on the living room sofa when she'd left, giving her his best doe-eyed, don't-leave-me look.

Where was he?

She moved out of the air-conditioned house into the dry heat. She stood on the small brick patio and called the dog's name again and again. Nothing. She glanced back at the door. No sign of break-in there or on the front door.

And then beyond the potted herb planters and flower-pots she spotted a tuft of hair in the brush. She raced across the yard to the woods, her heart thundering and her stomach tightening with spasms. Her worst fears were realized when she saw Lincoln lying in the dried shrubs.

She dropped to her knees and carefully ran trembling hands over his head. 'Lincoln.'

He didn't respond to her voice. Dear God, he was dead. Tears welled and spilled down her cheeks. And then she noted the slight rise and fall of his belly. 'Lincoln!'

She touched his warm nose panting out jagged breaths. In and out. In and out. The cadence was sluggish, but he was breathing. His tongue and gums were pink, a sign that he was getting enough oxygen, but she wondered for how long.

She inspected every inch of his body and found no signs of blood, wounds or broken bones. Fearing he might have been poisoned, she knew she had to get him to an emergency vet as soon as possible. For a heart-stopping moment she panicked. Who should she call? It was a Sunday afternoon.

'Shit. Think, Lara. Think!' Quickly, she raced back into the house and opened her laptop. Her hands trembled so that she mistyped *Emergency* and *Veterinarian* so badly she wasn't sure if the search engine would turn up anything. However it spit out the name of a twenty-four-hour service in northwest Austin.

She grabbed her keys and hustled through the house to her truck. She fired up the engine and drove the truck around the side of the house, unmindful of the wilting flowerbeds her grandmother planted years ago. She parked her truck right next to Lincoln. The dog weighed seventy pounds and, unconscious, his body would be unwieldy.

Later she'd never know how she got Lincoln in the bed of the truck, but she'd managed it.

She covered the shepherd with a quilt from her living room couch and kissed him on the muzzle. 'Hang on, boy.'

Lara slid behind the wheel, ground the gear into reverse, and backed out the path she'd just dug in the yard. A quick spin of the wheel and a gear change, and she was headed down the dirt road back toward town. The twisty winding roads didn't allow for top speeds, and she did not want to jostle Lincoln too much, but she kept the pace faster than reason dictated. When she hit the main road, she floored it.

The speedometer nudged ninety more than a couple of times as she wove in and out of traffic. As she skidded around Austin and headed north, the stress and panic that had first gripped her melted to a laser-sharp resolve. Just get him to the doctor.

As she took her last exit, she glanced in her rearview mirror and saw the flashing lights of a police vehicle. 'You're gonna have to wait, pal.'

She didn't break speed, and the cop stayed on her tail. Up ahead she spotted the vet hospital and slowed to make her final right turn. Breaks squealed to a halt as she stopped in front of the main door.

She slid out the door and ran inside the vet before the cop could react. She dashed to the receptionist desk. 'I've got my dog in the car. I think he's been poisoned. He's a shepherd and he weighs at least seventy pounds.'

The girl nodded and reached for the intercom just as the cop burst into the vet hospital. His hand was on his gun grip, his dark eyes sparked with adrenaline and anger.

Lara held up her hands in front. 'Let me get my dog to the doctor, and then I'll do whatever you want.'

Mid-sized with dark hair, grey eyes, and a thick black moustache, the cop shook his head. 'Outside now.'

Lara glanced back at the startled receptionist. 'Are you going to help my dog?'

The young girl nodded. 'Someone is coming up to get him right now.'

Lara nodded and followed the cop outside. 'He's in the back of the truck. My dog. Lincoln.' She'd been so focussed on the trip her, but now her brain unravelled with emotion and fear.

The cop directed her to the back of the truck and glanced inside at Lincoln. The dog was still breathing but painfully still. 'What is wrong with him?'

'I think he was poisoned.'

'Do you know how fast you were going?'

She kept her gaze on Lincoln. 'I didn't care. Too fast. I don't know.'

'I need for you to sit in the front of your truck.'

'Can't I stay with Lincoln?'

The front door of the hospital burst open, and two young men appeared with a gurney. 'There's nothing you can do for him now. They've got him.' The sharp edges of the cop's voice eased. 'I need to see your driver's licence.'

She slid behind the wheel and dug her wallet out of her purse. She handed it to the officer and watched in the rearview mirror as the technicians loaded Lincoln onto the gurney and took him inside.

Lara leaned her head against the steering wheel. Tears rolled down her cheeks.

'Ma'am? Ms Church?' the officer said.

Surprised to hear her name, she sat up and swiped the tears from her cheeks. 'Yes?'

The name Brown glistened from a gold nameplate on his chest. 'I'm writing you a ticket for going eighty-nine in a seventy, that's a mile short of reckless driving. And I'm not going to cite you for failure to pull over when I flashed my lights. I got a couple of dogs myself and, well, I get it.'

'Thanks.' She watched as he scribbled information on his form and turned it around for her to sign. Her signature was shaky at best.

He handed her back her driver's licence, insurance card, and a copy of the ticket. 'Any idea who might have poisoned your dog?'

The image of him lying in the backyard flashed and tore at her. 'No. None.'

He hooked his fingers into his gun belt. 'Think it might have anything to do with the article written about you this morning?'

She stiffened. 'Has everyone read that?'

'By now, I'd say just about.'

She'd accepted that she'd catch heat for the article, but it had never occurred to her that Lincoln might be a target. 'I don't know.'

He nodded. 'Go ahead and park your truck. I suspect they'll have paperwork inside.'

'Thanks.' Minutes later she sat alone in the tiled waiting room filling out papers fastened to a clipboard. The receptionist had assured her that Lincoln was being looked after and that a technician was caring for him. While she waited, another family rushed in a small mixed breed hit by a car and another couple brought in an old cat that was seizing. The animals were taken in the back and the distressed owners were left to wait with her.

When the front door to the hospital opened the third time she didn't even bother to glance up, but kept her focus on the papers.

'Lara.' Beck's deep baritone voice startled her.

She found him standing there, his hat in his hand. Stiffening, she rose. 'Sergeant? What are you doing here?'

'DPS tells me you racked up one hell of a speeding ticket.'

Worry for Lincoln kept her temper in check. 'You're keeping an eye on me.'

'That's right.' He nodded toward the chair as he removed his hat. 'Have a seat. You look wrung out.'

'I'd rather stand.' Nervous energy snapped and popped under her skin.

'Sit.'

Another order.

If she'd had an ounce of fight, she'd have stood her ground. But she had no attitude to rally. She sat down, and he took the seat beside her.

His hat balanced on long, lean, calloused hands. 'Want to tell me what happened?'

She tipped back her head, willing fresh tears to stop. 'Don't be nice to me. I'm not up for mind games right now.'

His gaze roamed over her from head to toe. 'I don't have an angle.'

A bitter smile twisted her lips even as she fought back tears. 'Of course you do.'

'I want to know.'

Despite genuine empathy underscoring the words, this visit wasn't about her. It was about the case. Always the case. For reasons she couldn't explain, that hurt.

She centred the papers on her clipboard, hoping her thoughts would do the same. 'I don't know what happened. I came home and found him in the backyard. He wasn't moving.' She scribbled her name, but the ink went dry. Shaking the pen, she resisted more tears.

Beck removed a pen from his pocket and handed it to her. Without looking up, she nodded her thanks but didn't speak as she filled in the vitals.

His presence gave her an odd quiet strength that

softened the edges of her nerves. Only when she'd finished the forms and turned the clipboard back into the receptionist did he speak.

'Did you leave him outside?'

She shook her head. 'That's the thing. I left him on the couch in my house. I clearly remember that.'

'You're sure?'

'That part of my memory is crystal clear.'

'And you locked the house?'

'Yes. I am obsessive about security for obvious reasons. Whoever got to Lincoln broke into my house and got to him.'

The staff door opened and a young woman in surgical scrubs said, 'Lincoln.'

Lara rose. 'Yes. How is he?'

Beck stood, his head at least twelve inches above her.

The woman at the door was small. Dark hair brushed her shoulders, and she wore rimless glasses and no makeup. 'I'm Dr O'Neil. And he's doing just fine. He's starting to wake up now.'

Lara studied the woman's face for any signs of stress or deception. Finding none, the ribbons of fear binding her chest eased. 'Wake up?'

'You can come back and see him.'

Lara hurried to follow. She didn't invite Beck back, but he followed as if he had every right to be there. The doctor pushed through a swinging door, which led to an exam room. Lincoln lay on the stainless table. His eyes were half open, and he was panting a little. An IV ran from his front leg to a clear bag. When she lowered her face to his and spoke his name, his tail thumped awkwardly against the table.

'I think he was drugged, not poisoned,' Dr O'Neil said.

'Drugged with what?' Beck said.

'I don't know. But because he's such a big dog he was able to metabolize the drug. If he'd been ten pounds lighter it might have been too much for him.'

She stroked Lincoln's head. 'Is he going to be all right?'

'I believe he'll be just fine. The heat did not do him any favours, but I'm pushing liquids now. I'd like to hold on to him for a couple of hours and make sure he's fully awake and hydrated, but he should be good to go. And when you get him home let him drink lots of water. He'll want it.'

A wave of relief washed over her, and the tears she'd been holding back spilled down her cheeks. 'Thanks, Dr O'Neil.'

The doctor smiled. 'It's nice to have a happy ending today.'

She swiped away the tear, mindful of Beck's gaze on her. 'Can I stay with him?'

The doctor frowned. 'I'd like to put him in a crate. He'll be safer and can wake up at his own pace.'

'Okay. I can wait out front. And when he's ready I'll take him home.'

Dr O'Neil glanced at Beck. 'It's going to be a couple of hours. Maybe you'd like to run an errand.'

'I'll wait,' Lara said.

Beck shook his head. 'We'll go out and have an early dinner.'

Lara stiffened. 'I'm not leaving.'

Beck met the doctor's concerned gaze. 'Doc, is Ms Church gonna do Lincoln a bit of good sitting here making herself sick with worry?'

'Not a bit of good. Get some fresh air, Ms Church. We'll take good care of your baby.'

Lara finally conceded and allowed Beck to lead her outside. The heat of the day proved a welcome relief to the chill in her bones.

Not sure what to do, Lara glanced around. It would be too hot to sit in her truck, but there had to be a mall or a fast-food place around here somewhere.

Beck made the decision. 'My car is right here. I know a place that makes the best enchiladas.'

'I'm not hungry.'

His muscles bunched. 'You are pale and the circles under your eyes look like bruises. A meal will do you good.'

'This is my fault,' she whispered. 'If I hadn't talked to Vera . . .'

He frowned. 'You did not cause this, so do not blame yourself.'

'Who would do this to an animal?' More tears threatened.

The furrows in his brow deepened. 'I just hope I can get my hands on 'em.'

Gratitude washed over her. 'Thanks.'

His expression softened a fraction. 'Now you must eat.'

'Really, I'm fine.' The rush of adrenaline had ebbed, leaving a clear path for exhaustion to take over.

He cupped her elbow in his hand and walked with her toward a black SUV. 'When's the last time you ate?'

Her skin warmed at his touch. 'I ate lunch yesterday, but then I went into the darkroom and I meant to eat again but forgot. And then I went into town and bought groceries.' She thought about the bags on the floorboard of her truck and the cold items she stowed in the cooler. 'God, my groceries are still in the truck. Even in the cooler the cold items won't last.'

He opened the passenger side door to his car. 'Wait here and give me your keys.'

She complied and slumped back. Her mind raced as she replayed the scene over and over. Who could have done this?

Beck returned, startling her. He opened the driver's-side door to his car and slid into the seat. 'The vet has a refrigerator and they are stowing your cold goods.'

'Thanks.'

'And you need food.'

He started the engine and they were blending into traffic. His car reminded her more of a command centre with its computer between their seats, a printer, maps jammed in the side door, and a GPS that he quickly shut off when it started issuing orders.

The restaurant he chose was a small adobe-style place on the side of the road. If she'd been driving she'd have gone right past it, never dreaming that it would be a place to eat. Beck parked his SUV in the front of the restaurant and got out. She quickly unfastened her seat belt and got out, not expecting him to open her door.

He met her at her side of the car and closed her door. 'It's not much to look at, but the food is good.'

She'd always liked Mexican food, but it wasn't until she moved to Texas as an adult that she'd experienced authentic Mexican fare.

They moved out of the heat into seventy-degree temps and up to a counter that had no menu posted.

A young wiry boy behind the register grinned at Beck. 'Mama is gonna be sorry that she missed you. She says you don't come by enough.'

'I got no good excuses for your mama. But I'll be sure to do better.' Beck nodded. 'Manny, this is Lara. And she's mighty hungry.'

The boy nodded. 'Should I get your usual times two?'

'Perfect.'

'I'll take the usual without meat,' Lara said.

Beck raised an amused brow. 'You don't eat meat?'

It was a concept that often didn't fly well in Texas. 'No. But I will eat cheese.'

He shook his head. 'Manny, you heard the lady.'

Lara didn't know what the usual entailed, but the place smelled of cumin, stewed tomatoes, and pepper. And if it didn't have meat she'd be fine. She reached in her purse for her wallet, expecting to split the tab.

Beck shook his head. 'Your money is no good here.'

She continued to count out bills. 'I can pay for myself.'

'I bet you can. But you won't be doing it here today with me standing at your side. Manny, if you take her money I'm gonna arrest you.'

Manny laughed. 'Yes, sir.'

Annoyed, Lara tried to hand her bills to Manny, who would not touch them. Finally, she tucked them back in her wallet. 'Don't you think that's a little old fashioned? People split the bills all the time.'

'And if you were a man I'd agree. But I've never split a bill with a lady, and I never will.'

'You have got to be kidding.' Lara adjusted her purse strap on her shoulder.

He handed the amused kid a twenty. 'There are three things I never kid about. The first two are food and good manners.' He shoved his wallet back in his back pocket. 'Keep what's left for yourself, Manny.'

'Thanks, Beck.'

He guided her to a table and they sat. Seconds later the boy brought them two glasses of fresh lemonade and a basket of freshly made chips and salsa.

Lara drank deeply from her lemonade; she hadn't realized how thirsty she was. 'That's good. Thank you.'

'Best in Texas. And you are welcome.'

She traced the line of condensation with her fingertip. 'So what's the third thing you never kid about?'

He grinned. 'Don't believe I know you well enough to tell you about that one.'

The sensuality lingering behind the words sent a rush of heat rising up her face. She sipped her drink. 'You come here often?'

'Been coming here since I was a kid. Manny's older brother and I used to run together when we were kids. We were hell on wheels.'

'I can't imagine you causing any trouble. I picture you born with that star on your chest.'

He laughed. 'Far from it. I was raised in east Austin.'

'Near the river?'

'Yes.' His eyes narrowed and then he nodded. 'You said you grew up in the area.'

'I visited Austin when I was a kid during the summer. The house I live in now belonged to my grandmother. She left it to me in her will.'

'Did you enjoy your Texas summers?'

'I did. Cassidy and I were like sisters, especially after her mom died.'

'How'd her mother pass?'

Lara released a slow breath. 'Suicide. She shot herself.'

His gaze sharpened. 'That had to have been rough.'

'It was awful. Cassidy and her mom were very close and she was devastated. I tried to help, but I wasn't so close to my own mother so it was hard for me to ever find the right words.'

Under his direct gaze, this close, she found her unease rising. 'You got that cop expression happening again.'

He sat back in his chair and made an effort to relax. 'Do I?'

'Yeah.'

A wry grin tipped the edge of his mouth. 'I suppose I never really leave the Job behind.'

She shifted in her seat. 'So what did you and Manny's brother do to stir up trouble?'

'Typical trouble teenaged boys find. General raising hell.'

'And what is that?'

He chuckled. 'Let's just say we gave our mamas a good bit of grey hair.'

He was just as unwilling to talk about himself as she was herself. 'So what changed you?'

He sipped his lemonade and carefully set his glass down. 'Finally grew up, I suppose.'

Manny arrived with two steaming plates of food. Tamales, rice, beans, avocadoes and fresh salsa filled the turquoise plate. The queso fresco cheese looked like melted velvet. 'This looks wonderful.'

Manny's chest puffed with pride. 'It'll taste better than it looks.'

'Thanks,' Beck said. 'And tell your mama I said hi.'

'Sure thing, Beck.'

Beck nodded. 'Dig in. Best food you'll ever eat.'

She took her first bite and savoured the warm blend of spices and fresh food. If she'd been alone she'd have closed her eyes and savoured the moment, but with Beck so close she did her best to keep her expression neutral. He might be all kind and nice, but she understood that under the *aw shucks* veneer he was driven steel. 'This is wonderful.'

He loaded his fork. 'I'd eat here every day if I could. I'm surprised you never heard about this place, seeing as you're part Texan.'

The jab had her smiling. 'My grandmother was a great cook, and we ate in almost all the time. As a kid I'd beg to go to a fast food joint, but she'd never allow it unless it was my birthday. Looking back I can see what a dope I was as a kid.'

'My mother was either working or going to school. Home-cooked fare was rare. But Manny's mom kept me well fed.'

The glimpse into his past tweaked her curiosity. Though tempted to dig deeper, she resisted. As nice as he might appear, he wasn't her friend.

They ate in silence for a time. The food was good and eased some of her tension. She was far hungrier than she'd realized and found her senses and nerves stabilizing with a full belly.

'So is the house the reason you came back to Austin?' Beck said.

'Pretty much.' She wiped her hands with a yellow paper napkin.

He sat back in his seat and regarded her closely. 'You like it here?'

'I did.' She frowned. 'I'd honestly thought the past was done, and I could truly start living again. I shouldn't have stirred up old news.'

A silence settled between them.

'There's a Dr Jo Granger who consults with DPS and the Rangers. She is good, Lara. She could help you remember.'

She shook her head. 'There are no memories.'

'You need to talk to her.' His clipped tone told her he didn't like hearing no.

Tough. She wasn't playing his game just because he could play nice. 'All I need to do is get my dog. Can we go now?'

He reached for his hat, but the furrow in his brow deepened. 'I'll ride out with you to your cabin and have a look around. Someone got into your place, and I'd sure like to know how.'

If it were just her, she'd have told him not to bother,

but she couldn't risk someone else hurting Lincoln again. 'Okay.'

He drove her back to the vet hospital, where she paid a hefty vet bill that maxed out her credit card and then collected her groceries and a groggy but tail-wagging shepherd. He walked out to her truck like a sailor who'd had too many cheap whiskies on shore leave. With a boost from Beck, the dog hopped into the front seat of her truck, licked her on the hand, and promptly fell back to sleep.

Beck touched the tip of his hat. 'Lead the way, Ms Church.'

'Okay.' She slid behind the wheel, patted Lincoln on the head, and headed back south. She barely remembered the harried ride north just hours ago. It had passed in a blink. The return trip took forever. Likely because she was so conscious of Beck's black SUV trailing behind her, moving in and out of traffic as she did.

It was as disconcerting to have Beck close as it was comforting. She might not like the guy, who could be a hard ass, but he'd projected genuine concern when he showed up at the vet clinic.

'You can stop right there, Lara Church.' She tightened her hands on the wheel. 'He is all about this case. You are a means to an end. So do not read into this what is not there.'

The sound of her voice had Lincoln raising his head and yawning.

She patted him on the head. 'We're almost home.'

A half hour later she parked in front of her cabin. By this time, Lincoln was awake, snorting and raising his head as she parked. Seeing home, he wagged his tail and barked.

She hurried around to the passenger side as Beck's SUV parked behind her. She opened the door and the shepherd jumped down. He wobbled a step or two and then took off toward the edge of the woods, where he promptly raised his leg and peed.

As the dog sniffed and rooted through the woods she moved to the front door.

Beck cut her off. 'Before you open that door, take a moment to look around the place and see if anything is out of place.'

She turned, key in hand, to find him standing at the base of the porch, his hand resting casually on his gun. The brim of his white hat angled just a bit. 'What should I look for?'

'Whatever doesn't fit or feel right. Come on down here and just look.'

She moved back down the stairs as he eased back a step. Her gaze travelled over her home. No broken windows. No overturned pots. No marks. 'It's the same.'

His sunglasses tossed back her reflection. 'Do you keep a spare key hidden around here?'

'I do.'

He frowned. 'Show me.'

Around the side of the house at the back patio she lifted an urn filled with withered flowers and removed a key. 'It's right where I left it.'

'Anybody know about that key?' The rough edge had returned to his voice.

She dropped the key in his outstretched palm. 'No. I mean, I never told anybody.'

A look filled with disapproval settled as he turned the key over in his hand. 'How long has it been there?'

'I don't know. My grandmother used to keep a key there.' She held the gold key in her hands. 'This key is new. I had the locks replaced when I moved in.'

'Why take the time to put in new locks when you leave a key outside?'

Colour warmed her cheeks. 'Because if I get locked out, which has been known to happen, I have no one to call. And seeing as Lincoln doesn't have pockets, I thought it wise to keep a key hidden.'

He rested his hands on his hips. 'Not smart.'

'You're right. Not so smart. But a necessary evil.'

'Pocket that key now.' His fingers brushed hers when he handed the key to her.

She clenched her fist over it. 'What if I get locked out?'

'Then call me. I'll get you inside.'

He said it as if he meant it. 'I'm not calling you if I get locked out. That's crazy.'

He leaned forward a fraction. 'What's crazy about it?'

'If you live in Austin then it means you're a good half hour away.'

He grinned. 'This is Texas, Ms Church. A half hour is just around the block for us.'

Dependence was a slippery slope. And dependence on a man who'd already stated his murder investigation trumped her wishes was foolish. 'Still.'

'Still nothing.' He looked around as if the matter had been decided. 'Let's have a look inside?'

It would have been nice to brush him off, but if someone

had gotten into her house before, they could have returned while she was at the hospital.

She unlocked the back door, but he moved in front of her and entered the house first. A flick of his thumb and the lights clicked on. His right hand rested on his gun.

She followed. The cool interior was a welcome change from the heat, but it did little to soothe the tightness in her belly.

He pocketed his sunglasses and let his gaze scan the room. As he searched for predators, she spotted a shirt she'd tossed on the floor, a nightgown she'd discarded when she dressed in the middle of the room yesterday morning, and a half dozen cups filled with varying levels of tea. She started to collect the cups and put them in the kitchen sink.

He checked windows, tested the front door lock with his hand, and then strolled down the hallway toward her bedroom. Images of her unmade bed had her wishing she cared more about house chores.

As Beck moved through the house he moved slowly, taking in every detail of the home's interior: a stack of magazines on a dusty coffee table, a casually tossed jean jacket on a cloth couch covered with a flowered quilt, hiking shoes covered in dust and mud. The walls had once been covered in photos, but the images were gone, leaving behind their shadowy outline on the wall.

'Why take the pictures down, Lara?'

Her name sounded rougher when he spoke it. 'Old family pictures of my mother and my aunt.' They'd been smiling, young and happy.

'That so bad?'

'The images were painful. My mother and aunt looked so much alike and yet were total opposites.'

'How so?'

'My mother was the difficult moody one, according to my grandmother, while my aunt was the light of her life. My aunt adored Cassidy. And in the end my aunt killed herself. My grandmother said once she always feared my mother would take her life. Never Aunt Leslie.'

'Your mother ever consider leaving you in Texas full time?'

'My grandmother asked her every year if she would. They often argued over it. But Mom always took me with her in September.' She shrugged. 'I always wondered why mom just didn't leave me in Texas. Motherly devotion wasn't her driving force. Maybe it was pride. Or maybe it was as simple as Grandmother wanted me.'

Beck didn't press her for details as he took a second glance at the shadowed outlines and then moved down the hallway. When he reappeared minutes later he said, 'All the windows are locked and secure. And there are no signs of a break-in, which is all the more reason for you to not hide that key outside anymore. Better, do you have someone in town you can bunk with for a while?'

'Not really.'

'What about that art lady?'

'Cassidy? She hates dogs, and I don't want to impose.' They got along well enough, and Cassidy would have taken her in, but asking her cousin for help went against the grain.

He frowned, clearly irritated. 'She's family. She wouldn't mind.'

'I would. I can take care of myself. I spent a dozen summers in the area with my grandmother. And I've got Lincoln.'

Frustrated by her stubbornness, he frowned. 'A dozen summers. That's a lot of time in the area.'

'Four months out of the year I was here between ages six and eighteen.'

'How were your summers here?'

'For the most part fine.'

He arched a brow. 'For the most part?'

'The first week I'd miss my mom. And then I'd start to get used to the place again, and then I'd have to leave. I hated leaving.'

'Where'd you and your mother live?'

'All over. Depended on where her husband at the time lived.'

'Anything memorable happen during those summers?'

'Memorable how?'

'Anything that sticks to mind.'

'Nothing out of the ordinary. Cassidy and I were either here at the house or helping our grandmother in town at her shop. It was a good time.' She frowned. 'Do you think someone from my past is the killer?'

'I don't know. I do know someone knew about that key and drugged your dog.'

Shock and adrenaline gave way to anger. 'Maybe some nut who read the morning paper broke into the house.'

'Maybe the article did unsettle someone. Maybe the article and Lincoln are unrelated. But I'd bet my last dollar that the two are connected.'

Fingers curled into fists. She had no answer to that puzzle. 'How can you know that?'

'I don't, and until we know, be careful, Ms Church. Keep the doors locked even when you are inside alone.'

Her defences rose. 'I do.'

A dark brow arched. 'I walked in on you in your studio the other day.'

Colour rushed up her cheeks. 'I was working and just got lost.'

'All it takes is once.'

Being spoken to as if she were a child grated. 'I can take care of myself. I almost shot you.'

Amusement lightened his gaze. 'Not even close.'

'I had my shotgun.'

He leaned forward just barely. 'If you'd not lowered it when I asked, we'd not be standing here having this conversation.'

A deadly intensity swirled around him. She could argue all she wanted, but she was no marksman and would have lost to an expert. Nodding, she dragged a hand through her hair. 'I get it. I will be careful.'

His gaze held hers an extra microsecond. 'I'm going to have DPS swing by every half hour. Someone out there is fixated on you.'

'That doesn't mean it's the Strangler.' She spoke the words hoping he'd agree. 'It could just be about the article.'

He touched the brim of his hat. 'Don't you bet on it for a minute. Not for a minute.'

Chapter Fourteen

Monday, May 27, 8 am

In the early hours of Monday, the third victim's finger-prints scored a hit in the AFIS. The victim's name was Blair Silver, age twenty-three years. She'd been arrested two years ago for possession of cocaine. The girl's well-to-do family had hired an expensive attorney, who'd arranged a plea agreement to a misdemeanour charge. Reports from Blair's parole officer, however, had been positive. She'd been clean and sober for eighteen months and was finally going places with her life. Beck tracked down the girl's mother and arranged a meeting at their home.

Adjusting his tie, he rang the bell as he stood at the front entrance to the big, beautiful house. Beck shifted his stance a couple of times. He didn't love big homes. Didn't have anything against them, just wondered why anyone would need this kind of space. And this house, judging by the clean, sterile looks, wasn't too old.

As footsteps sounded on a tile floor, he rubbed the back of his neck, dreading delivering his message to Mrs Silver.

The front door opened to a petite, mid-fifties woman, who stared up at him with a wary gaze. Her hair was done, her makeup styled, and she wore dark pants, a white blouse, and a pearl necklace with matching earrings. The outfit was simple and expensive.

He touched the brim of his hat. 'Mrs Silver?'

She nodded. 'You must be Sergeant Beck.'

'Yes, ma'am.'

'Won't you come in?'

'Thank you.'

She escorted him to a sunroom filled with plants, overstuffed couches, delicate tables, and gilded framed pictures. Drapes, with the shimmer of silk, pooled on the polished floors.

She sat on the sofa and motioned for him to take the seat across from her. 'Can I get you something to drink? Sweet tea or a cola?'

'No, ma'am, but thank you.'

She smoothed her hands over her pants. 'You said you had questions for me.'

His seat was fashioned out of bamboo and struck him as too delicate for a man his size. He was careful not to lean back or to the side on the armrest. 'Ma'am, I've not come with good news.'

Her lips flattened into a grim line. 'It's about my daughter, isn't it?'

'Yes, ma'am.' No easy way to say this. 'We found her body yesterday.'

Mrs Silver lifted her chin and curled manicured fingers into fists. 'I've been waiting for a visit like this for a long time.'

'Ma'am?'

'Blair has made some rather unfortunate choices in the

last five years. I knew she'd been in recovery for the last year or so, but each day I feared she'd slip again. I kept telling her that her wild lifestyle would come to a bad end, but she refused to worry.' She drummed manicured hands on her pants leg. 'We fought on Friday.'

'That when you talked to her last?'

'Yes. It was after eleven.' She drew in a breath. 'Can you tell me how she died?'

'She was strangled.'

The older woman's face pinched with surprise for just a brief moment, and then the expression vanished before she met his gaze again. 'Strangled? I was certain you were going to tell me it was a drug overdose or an accident.'

'No, ma'am.'

Mrs Silver sat so straight he thought her spine would snap. 'Where was she found?'

'Near the interstate.' Every death notice was different, many times unexpected reactions. Tears. Anger. Denial. Frustration. He usually got some kind of response. But Mrs Silver was completely flat. It was almost as if she'd not actually heard him.

He watched her closely. 'Ma'am, can you tell me if Blair had boyfriends or acquaintances that might have done her harm?'

'Truthfully, I don't know any of her friends anymore. The set of friends she had a couple of years ago were not good people. But she kept swearing to me she'd changed and her friends had changed. I just couldn't allow myself to hope. I called her often. Was always checking up on her.'

He couldn't imagine not dogging a child who was

headed toward trouble. 'She listed your address as her permanent address.'

'Well, I suppose you could say it was her last permanent address. She's been moving around a lot for the last couple of years.'

'What was she studying at the university?'

'English. History. Economics, of late. She could have done anything. She was brilliant. But she chose to have a good time rather than apply herself. She was about to graduate but just barely.'

'Mrs Silver, I've got two other victims who might have been killed by the same man.'

Her eyes widened as she struggled with unwanted emotions. 'Her death didn't have anything to do with her drinking or the drugs?'

'I don't think so.'

She swallowed. 'I don't know what to say.'

'I'm trying to retrace her last days.'

'I wish I could help. But Blair and I didn't communicate well. I called. We were polite, but our conversations had little depth and generally ended with us shouting at each other.'

'When was the last time she lived here?'

'She spent a night here about three months ago.' Mrs Silver leaned forward and from a silver box removed a cigarette and lighter. She lit the tip and inhaled deeply. 'It wasn't a good visit. We fought. I was worried she'd start drinking again and she was furious that I didn't trust her.'

'Could I have a look at her room?'

'Certainly.' Stiffly, she snubbed out her cigarette and rose. 'Follow me.'

He sensed beneath the ice, sadness and regret swirled in a destructive twister. 'Thank you.'

Mrs Silver led Beck up a cream-coloured carpeted staircase that wound by walls sporting neatly framed water-colours. In his grandfather's house the carpets had been worn and threadbare and the walls filled with pictures of Beck, his brother and his father as a child. There were images of Beck swinging a bat and posing with the foot-ball team. It was a chaotic mishmash of pictures. And he still found it warm and welcoming especially compared to the elegant sterility of the Silver house.

Mrs Silver led him down a centre hallway toward a door on the back left. She opened the door and stepped back as if entering hurt. 'Spend as much time as you'd like in the room. I'll be downstairs waiting.'

'Thank you, ma'am.'

'There is a computer in her room. She didn't take it with her but the last time she was here she spent time on it.'

'Thank you.' He waited until she'd turned to leave before entering the room. Painted in a pale pink, the room was dominated by a large canopy bed with a white eyelet coverlet. Twin nightstands sported crystal lamps and a chaise set by a large bay window. It was the perfect little girl's room.

He sat down at a delicate, girly-looking desk, hoping it would support his six-foot-six frame. The chair groaned a protest but held steady. He pressed the computer's power button. The screen saver was a collage of pictures taken of Blair and her friends over the last couple of years. In most of the images she was grinning, her arm wrapped casually around someone's neck, a drink and cigarette in the other. In several, Blair's hair was dark brown, in others she had dyed a streak purple, and finally she'd switched to blonde – the colour that had caught the killer's attention. She wore deeply cut blouses and heavy makeup. Lots of gold bangles dangled from her neck and wrists.

He shifted his attention to the men in the photos, wondering if any of them stood out. Many sported the ruddy cheeks and goofy expressions of a drunk and most appeared to be college age. Seven years ago, they'd have been in middle or high schools. Nothing caught his attention.

He opened her emails. Two hundred and twelve messages appeared. Most were ads for clothes, shoes, some even from an online university. Only a few appeared to be from actual people, but that wasn't surprising. Kids Blair's age communicated via text or cell. Email, Santos's youngest sister had once said, was for old people.

The majority of the personal emails were from men and their messages dealt with setting up a meeting. Nothing specific was discussed, and Blair's outgoing box showed no responses on her computer. He'd need to track down her cell phone records for that. He checked her browser history but found most of her stops were online stores and tarot reading sites.

Beck rose from the chair and unplugged the computer, hoping Mrs Silver would let him take it with him so his experts could search it. He could get a warrant but hoped she'd make this easy.

He checked dresser drawers, which were empty, and he checked her closet. The clothes that remained were for a younger girl, and many of the dresses still had the tags on them. He could picture Mrs Silver buying perfect clothes for a daughter who wasn't so perfect and would never wear what her mother had chosen.

He moved down the centre staircase, the computer in hand. He found Mrs Silver sitting in the living room where they'd first visited.

She'd lit another cigarette and with a trembling hand lifted it to her mouth. 'I never would have smoked in this house while my husband was alive. He hated the smell. I think that's why Blair started smoking. She wanted to make him angry.'

'Mrs Silver, would you mind if I took Blair's computer? I'd like my forensics experts to have a look at it.'

She nodded. 'Take whatever you want.'

'Thank you.'

She snubbed out the end of her cigarette in a crystal ashtray. 'I read about a woman in the Sunday paper. Lara Church. The photographer. The article said she had survived the Seattle Strangler. And you said my Blair was strangled.'

'Yes, ma'am.'

'Is the article about Ms Church true?'

'Yes, ma'am, it's true.'

'Do you think the Seattle Strangler is here?'

'I don't know.'

Her gaze narrowed. 'But you have suspicions.'

'Which I cannot discuss.'

'Can Ms Church give you a description of her attacker?'

'She has no memory of the attack.'

Dark eyes flashed with frustration. 'There's got to be a way to make her remember.'

'We're doing all we can.'

Mrs Silver shook her head. 'Are you?'

Her pain burrowed under his skin and grated against his nerves. 'Yes, ma'am, we are.'

'I made a lot of mistakes with Blair. Warning signs I shouldn't have ignored years ago. I should have trusted that she wanted to get sober, but I didn't. I failed her in so many ways, but there is one last thing I can do for her.'

'What's that?'

Grey eyes hardened. 'Make sure you find her killer.'

'I'm giving it my best.'

'You damn well better, Sergeant. You damn well better.'

Mrs Silver walked to the front door, each step controlled and brittle. 'Thank you for your kindness.'

He opened the door. 'I'll be in touch.'

A quick nod was all she managed as she opened the door and watched him step onto the porch. She closed the front door with a soft click. Seconds later he heard the soft muffled sounds of her weeping.

When Lara arrived in the lab with Lincoln, the room of students was unnaturally quiet. The students, who normally were chatting and texting and thinking about everything other than lab, sat tense and silent. As Lincoln lay down behind her desk, she set her backpack on the desk and carefully unzipped it. Beyond the silence, she heard the ticking of the clock and steady breaths of the kids in the front row.

'I suppose you've read the paper,' she said without raising her head.

No one said anything, but several kids murmured back and forth at each other, hoping to find someone who would speak for the class.

Lara pulled out her laptop. 'If you have any questions, now is the time to ask because once I start my lecture I'm not discussing this again.'

Tim Gregory, the big beefy football player in the back of the room, half raised his hand. 'Is it true?'

Lara's gaze met the boy's. 'The article in the paper about me? Yes, it's true.'

Annie, a girl who always wore athletic shorts, white tees, and a scrunchie in her long black hair, sat taller. 'So, like, you were strangled once?'

'Yes, I was.'

More murmurs rippled across the room.

Tim's smile looked more uncomfortable than jovial. 'This dude killed six women before you.'

'That's right.' Her gaze skimmed the astonished faces to Danni, who stared with wide-eyed understanding.

'So how did you get so lucky?' Annie said.

Lucky. Lara had never thought that luck would have a double-edged sword. 'I don't know.'

'Yeah, but aren't you afraid?' Annie said.

Lara laid her hands on her desk. 'Honestly, at this point I'm more afraid that the majority of you are going to fail my class this semester.'

That caused several kids to sit forward in their seats.

'I've tried to treat you as adults, but frankly most of you

are more worried about the next party than you are about this class.' Indignation welled, jostling aside the lingering fear of a man she could not remember. 'If you think it is an easy A you are going to be sadly mistaken. Most are going to have to hustle hard just to get a C. And for some, I know you need that C to remain on the roster for the fall sports teams.'

Tim grumbled. 'Coach said I shouldn't worry about snapping pictures when I should be doing strength conditioning.'

She smiled. 'Coach is wrong if you want to pass, Mr Gregory.'

He groaned. 'That's not right. I worked hard for my spot on that team.'

'You're not working hard in my class, Mr Gregory, and that is all I care about.'

He opened his mouth to protest.

She raised her hand to silence him. 'I don't want to hear your excuses. Do your work or fail.'

'The coach says art is just fluff.'

'It's fluff that'll get you kicked off the team.'

'You'll lose your job,' he countered.

She grinned at his attempt to threaten. 'Mr Gregory, I was nearly strangled to death seven years ago. Do you think losing a job scares me?'

He frowned but didn't speak. Several of the kids sniggered nervously.

'I can promise that you won't pass if you don't do the work. And whether I'm gone or not you'll still have an F, and you won't be playing ball in the fall.'

She hoped her big speech would prompt everyone to

sit up a little straighter and pay closer attention, but, other than the random rustling of pages, there was little change from last week.

She dismissed the group into the darkroom, where they worked for the next couple of hours. When lab ended, the students shuffled past her, some glancing at her as if they'd wanted to say more. But under Lincoln's watchful eyes, none voiced their thoughts and each left.

Danni stopped at her desk. 'Hey, if you want to shoot more pictures, I'm in.'

Lara smiled. 'Thanks, but it might be wiser if you stayed clear of me for the time being.'

'Because of the other dead women?'

'I don't want anything to happen to you.'

Danni straightened to her full five foot one inch. 'I've seen my share of shit.'

A half smile tugged at the edge of Lara's lips as she stared into the girl's world-weary eyes. 'No need to see any more. Thanks, Danni, and as soon as I get the all-clear I'll give you a call.'

'You better.'

When the last student left, she packed up her bag and breathed a sigh of relief. 'Okay, Lincoln, let's take a walk.'

His ears perked up and tail wagged, he followed her down the staircase and out the back door. The air was hot and the sky clear. This would be a good day to shoot pictures and she mentally inventoried her developing supplies.

When she reached her truck a white paper flapped under her windshield wiper on the driver's side. A glance around confirmed that the same flyer was stuck under all the wipers. An ad. She got into the car, started the A/C and waited until it had cooled a little before she let Lincoln hop up into the passenger seat. She tossed her backpack on the seat between them.

She grabbed the flyer and as she balled it up she caught sight of words scrawled in red magic marker over the advertisement. Carefully, she unfurled the paper to read: *The killer is close.*

Lara snorted her disgust as she stared at the childishly handwriting, reminiscent of Tim Gregory's. She'd nearly been strangled to death. Been on the run for seven years. And now this little creep thought he'd scare her with words.

She'd have gone to the dean, but knew she'd need more than an anonymous note before sanctions would ever be levied on a star football player. 'Nice try, Mr Gregory.' Resisting the urge to toss the note, she shoved it in her backpack as she slid behind the wheel and slammed the door behind her.

If the damn note had done anything it had solidified her decision to stand her ground. She wasn't running this time. She wasn't.

The locals kept talking about the day's milder temperatures, but Raines believed Texas was hotter than hell. He longed to return to Seattle with its cool misty days, great coffee, and familiar streets.

Staring down at his plate of fried eggs, toast, and grits he fished his cell phone out of his breast pocket and dialled his home number. He waited through the rings until he heard the answering machine featuring his wife's voice: 'You've reached the Raines residence, leave a message at the beep, and we'll get back to you.'

Raines checked his watch and realized he hadn't allowed for the time difference. It was four in Seattle and Susan had left work and was hustling over to Tara's school. He dialled Susan's number hoping to catch her before she reached the chaos of the carpool line.

After several rings, her voicemail kicked in, and he waited until he heard the beep before lowering his voice a notch. 'Susan and Tara, it's me, Mike, a.k.a. Dad. I'm still in Austin and still chasing a bad guy, but I hope to be home real soon. Call me if you get the chance.'

Loneliness knotted in his chest as he thought about his two girls. God, but he missed them.

He needed to catch this son of a bitch and fast so that he could get home to them. He'd given Beck his files and six days' time. His patience had worn thin. And his promise to stay away from Lara had officially expired.

Flipping open a weathered notebook, he checked the notes he'd scribbled on Lara. Included was a detailed sketch of her schedule. Monday. Her lab would be finished.

He glanced out the café window and stared at the bright sky. He was no artist by any stretch, but if he were a photographer, he'd haul out his camera on a day like today and shoot pictures.

He dug ten bucks out of his pocket, dropped it on the table, and glanced toward the diner's manager. 'Got to go, Mack. Money's on the table.' In just six days he had an established routine with the owner. Susan and Tara would have had great fun with that tidbit.

'Glad having you, Mr Raines. See you for dinner?' Mack said.

'Wouldn't miss it.'

He grabbed a handful of mints as he walked past the cashier and headed out toward his rental car. When he travelled he always rented the same kind of car, Toyota Camry. For the most part the models didn't change too much from year to year, which meant he didn't have to spend needless time fumbling with buttons and knobs.

Soon he was headed south out of town on I-35. When he rolled down the interstate he spotted the black truck parked on the side of the road. Lara's truck. He almost laughed. Folks said he was rote, but it was his experience that most people were just as predictable. Artists shot their pictures on somewhat of a schedule, cops stuck to old habits that had seen them through too many crime scenes, and killers stuck to patterns.

As he drove past the truck and headed for the exit and off-ramp to the access road, he knew it would be this killer's habits that tripped him up. He liked blondes. He liked dressing them in white. He liked his pennies. He had violent sexual urges. So far he'd killed three women and, Raines knew in his gut that there were going to be more. He had no reason to stop until someone made him stop.

And Raines intended to be that someone.

He pulled up behind her truck and parked. He could see in the distance that she had her big tripod bellows camera out and was preparing to shoot.

Getting out his car he could see that she had that damn dog with her. Lincoln. The thing looked more like a wolf than dog, and Raines wouldn't have been surprised if the dog was a wolf. He knew a lot about her, but he wasn't sure if she'd picked the dog up in Virginia or on her way to Maine last summer.

Careful to stay upwind of the dog, he watched Lara as she stared at her antique lens. No detail or imperfection was too small. Finally satisfied, she replaced the cap on the lens, put the negative holder in the camera, and removed the lens cap. By his count, she waited a full minute before she replaced the lens cover.

She removed the glass negative, still encased in its wooden holder and turned. When she glimpsed him for the first time, she dropped her negative and it hit the rock-hard ground. Despite the casing, glass shattered.

Her expression hardened.

She took several steps toward him. 'Detective Mike Raines.'

'Ms Lara Church. It's been a long time.' The years had been good to her, leaning out her features and adding maturity he preferred.

'Not long enough.'

'I was at your opening.'

The dog picked up on her edgy tone, and his ears slid back on his head as he stared at Raines. 'I didn't see you.'

He certainly didn't expect a grand welcome, but he also wasn't up for a fight either. 'Might want to keep a hold on that dog.'

'Why? I think I would enjoy watching him eat you up.'

'I'd hate to shoot him.'

Her gaze turned murderous. 'You'd shoot my dog?'

'If he came after me, yes.' He shoved out his frustration in a breath as he slid his hands into his pockets. 'Look, I didn't come here to stir up trouble.'

Easterly winds blew the wisps of hair in her eyes. She swatted them away like buzzing flies. 'Of course you came here to stir up trouble. That is what you do best, Detective.'

'No need to call me detective anymore. I retired six years ago. I'm a private detective now.'

'What's that mean? You're going to stir up my life on your own dime instead of Seattle's?'

'I'm still after the Strangler.' He rattled the change in his pocket. 'I knew you were in Austin within weeks of your moving here. When the cop called and said the murders were near you, I knew the Seattle Strangler was active again.'

She shifted her stance, uncomfortable now. 'You kept tabs on me?'

No hint of apology. 'I always said you were the key to this killer. It made sense to keep an eye on you.'

'Why would you care? You're retired.'

'You can take the cop out of the job, but you can't take the job out of the cop. This was the case I could never let go.'

She shook her head. 'Leave me be, Detective Raines. I don't want anything to do with you.'

'Look, I know I was a bit heavy handed with you back in Seattle.'

She knelt to pick up the negative case. Shards of glass rattled inside. 'A bit heavy handed? I tried to help you.

I tried to remember, but you wouldn't accept that I couldn't remember . . . didn't have the memories. You followed me around. You gave me no peace.'

'I still believe those memories are locked in your brain.'

'You don't know anything. And I need for you to leave me now.'

'I've met with Beck. He's got my old case files, and I studied his crime scenes. He wants you to remember as well.'

A bitter, sad smile curled her lips. 'Why doesn't it surprise me that you two are working together?'

'He's not so different than me. A case gets under his skin, and he can't let it go.'

She held up her hands. 'I have nothing else to say to you.' Lincoln growled, but she kept her hand on his collar. 'Leave.'

'I'm not leaving Austin until I crack this case, Lara. I'm not. Whoever this son of a bitch is, he is killing women, and you can bet your last dollar that he is coming after you sooner or later.'

'If I'm such a target why didn't he just kill me seven years ago? Or when he knew I'd moved to Austin? Why drag it out?' she half shouted.

'Because he's like a cat. Cats don't just kill their prey. They toy with them first. He wants to see you afraid. He wants you to suffer. And when you are completely terrified he's going to kill you.'

Colour drained from her face.

'Lara, please,' he said softly. 'I don't want to be an enemy. I want to work with you. I want to catch this guy.'

236

Dark circles smudged the skin under his eyes. He looked paler to her, but she wasn't sure if stress had taken its toll, or she'd just become accustomed to Beck's deeply tanned skin.

If he'd bullied or ranted, she'd have dug her heels in deeper. Even his trademark edge, which she remembered from their first meeting, had vanished.

'Ms Church, I am Detective Raines with the Seattle Police Department.'

Eyelids so heavy with sedatives fluttered open. Her neck ached so badly she could barely sit. She'd had no idea how many neck muscles she used just to sit up.

Raines's black jacket and turtleneck combined with slicked-back blonde hair made the lines of his face all the sharper. Dark eyes void of compassion glared at her as if she'd committed a crime.

She moistened her lips and stared at him.

A metal chair scraped across the floor as he pulled it closer to the bed. He sat and leaned close. The scent of his soap mingled with stale cigarettes. 'I've spoken to the doctors, and they told me you don't remember. But there has to be some detail about this john you remember.'

Hazy, bruised senses sharpened. 'What?'

'The john.' A lazy, knowing grin accompanied a lingering look. 'How'd you meet him? Did you hook up with him on the Internet like the others?'

'No!'

'Then how? Come on, Lara, it's just the two of us. You can tell me, and I'll keep it to myself.'

Confused thoughts rattled in her brain, making it impossible to string the right ones together. 'I'm not a prostitute.'

His grin turned bitter and mocking. 'So maybe you like to call it something else. Dating service. Escort. Massage. I really don't care how you earn your money, honey. I just want the guy that attacked you.'

The IV in her arm pulled when she tried to sit up straighter. 'I'm not a hooker.'

He tugged her sheet closer to her collarbone. 'I got nothing against whores, honey. I don't. I just want this guy.'

Tears clogged in an already raw throat and burned. 'I'm not a whore.'

'Look, if you're worried Mom, Dad, or boyfriend are going to find out about how you make your spending money, I won't tell. It will be our secret. Just tell me how you met the guy.'

The hot Texas wind couldn't erase the chill of the memory. 'You've changed your tactics, Detective. Do you remember that insulting me didn't work?'

He shook his head, his shoulders heavy with regret. The lines around his eyes were deeper and the greying around his temples was thicker. 'I was exhausted when I met you initially. I'd been chasing this guy nonstop for months. You were my first break, and I was desperate for anything that would crack the case.' He held out his hands in supplication. 'I wasn't fair to you. I'm sorry.'

The man she'd known seven years ago would never

have apologized. He'd been so hard, unyielding, and driven, she'd often joked that he'd have sold his own mother to solve the case. 'This kinder, gentler Detective Raines just doesn't ring true with me.'

A frown deepened the lines around his mouth. 'I've changed a lot in the last seven years.'

'So have I.'

His jaw tightened and relaxed. 'Why won't you work with me?'

'Because,' she said calmly, 'you're an asshole.'

His eyes widened with surprise, but instead of getting angry, he laughed. 'I won't argue that. In fact, I've been called worse.' He reached in his pocket and pulled out a card. 'I'm hoping we can put the past behind us and work together to find this guy, Lara.' He held out the card. 'This isn't just about you. Other women have died and more will die if we don't catch this guy.'

As tempted as she was to tell him to shove the card, she accepted it. Nervously, she flicked the edge with her thumb. 'I don't remember anything.'

'I've seen your exhibit. Something is locked in your mind, Lara. Something dark and scary, and it is begging to get out, otherwise you'd not be standing here.'

'I know the attack left a mark on me. I've never denied that.'

He glanced toward her camera and the distant horizon. 'It can't be safe being out here alone.'

'I've never had any trouble.'

He shook his head. 'Killers often return to their crime scenes. Did you know that?'

'Yes.'

'So are you trying to run into this guy?'

'No.' She shook her head. 'No.'

'Come on. It's the most ugly, hot, piece-of-shit land I've seen in years. No artist would give it a second look.'

She didn't respond.

'And what are you going to do if you do run into the Strangler? The dog will help, but if this guy carries a weapon the dog is going to get hurt.'

She glanced down at Lincoln, knowing she now relied on his strength.

'Do you carry a gun?' he said.

She studied the open land around him. Her shotgun was in the truck. If he were the killer and standing this close to her, she might not make it to the truck in time.

'If it's not in your hand it won't do you a bit of good out here.'

He was right. She stood in the middle of nowhere at a murder scene. What was she doing out here?

He nodded slowly. 'Help Beck and me do our jobs. We need to catch this nutcase.'

'You and Beck. The dynamic duo.'

'I am not the bad guy, Lara. I'm on your side.'

She watched him stride back toward his rental car. He moved with the quiet confidence of a man on a mission.

Lara didn't believe for one moment that he was on her side.

Cassidy was pleased with Lara's exhibit sales. Since the article had appeared, she'd had brisk traffic in the gallery.

People were curious about Lara Church and her photography. This morning's gallery visitors were simply curious. But by this afternoon, there'd been a surprising number of return visitors and real interest in several pieces. By close of business she'd had two significant sales from a couple visiting the area and a local.

She clicked on the computer and logged into her online store account. She'd been selling her art collections online for a couple of years, recognizing that her market was far larger than Austin. Her market, with the right kind of Internet buzz, was the world.

She checked her email and discovered that someone had hit the *Buy* button on an image titled *Near Death*. She had set the price high on this piece because it was the jewel of the collection. Because it had been taken in Seattle, Cassidy now realized this was the spot where Lara had almost lost her life.

Cassidy blinked and reread the screen. The image had indeed sold, and the payment had been credited to her account.

She sat back in her chair and pushed her glasses up on her nose. 'Well, hot damn. That's gonna be a nice paycheck for both of us.' She quickly emailed the seller to confirm shipping instructions. The seller immediately responded and confirmed the San Antonio address.

'I don't know who you are, Mr D. Smith, but you have made my day.'

Chapter Fifteen

Tuesday, May 29, 7 am

Lincoln's incessant barking tugged at Lara's concentration as she struggled to finish the last touches on the prints she'd been working on since three in the morning. 'Five more minutes, Lincoln. Almost done.'

The dog had an internal clock, which told him he should be walking now. She too loved the morning hikes, especially when she had finished her work for the day.

But today, she needed just five more minutes. She'd been developing the photos from the last crime scene that she'd taken yesterday. In each print, she'd searched for a trigger to make the shadows veiling the truth vanish. But as much as she printed and stared at the crisp black-and-white images, there was nothing that sparked her memories. Nothing.

Lincoln's barking grew louder and louder until the distraction became too much. Shutting off the water she grabbed a rag and dried her hands before reaching for the gun she kept propped by the door. 'What is bothering you?'

The dog's possessive growl drew her through the house toward the front door. Whatever he'd seen, it wasn't a squirrel or a rabbit. Someone was on her property.

The dog crouched in the front room staring out the window. The hair on the back of his neck was raised and his tail tucked.

She glanced past the dog out the front window to see a Lexus parked behind her truck. Beside the car stood a woman whose dark pants and a silk top spoke as much of money as the gilded clip holding back neat grey hair. Behind dark sunglasses, the woman scanned the house as if wondering if she'd made a mistake.

Lara patted the dog on the head. 'Don't worry, boy. She looks lost. We'll get her back to the main road in no time and then be off on our walk.'

The mention of a walk had the dog wagging his tail. He still barked, but the tone had changed.

Lara unlocked the front door and through the screened door said, 'Can I help you?'

The woman shifted her gaze to Lara. 'I hope so.'

She slid her hands into the back pockets of her jeans. 'Did you take a wrong turn? It happens when folks are looking for some of the smaller towns in Hill Country.' Lincoln muscled against Lara's legs and pawed at the front door. Lara tugged on the dog's collar, knowing she didn't dare let him out.

The woman, unmindful of Lincoln, approached with crisp, purposeful steps. 'I'm looking for Lara Church?'

Lara's smile faded. Few knew she lived out here as the house title and phone remained under her grandmother's name. 'Why are you looking for her?'

The woman pulled off her glasses and stared at Lara with red-rimmed eyes. 'You are Ms Church. You don't look like you did in the Sunday Entertainment picture, but then I suppose an artist dresses differently for an opening.'

Tension burned up her back. 'Who are you?'

She compressed neatly painted ruby red lips. 'My name is Monica Silver. I live in Austin.'

'Is this about Sunday's article? Because if it is I have nothing to say.'

'It's not about the article. It's about my daughter, Blair Silver.'

'I don't understand.'

'Ranger James Beck came to see me at my home. He informed me that Blair was the latest victim of the Strangler. They found her body on the side of the interstate.'

Heat rose up through Lara's cheeks. 'I'm sorry.'

'Honestly, Ms Church, sorry does not do me one bit of good.' She tapped her glasses against her thigh. 'Sorry will not bring my daughter back, and sorry will not catch her killer.'

A heavy sadness rose up in her. 'Why are you here, Mrs Silver?'

'From what I've learned, you cannot remember what happened to you seven years ago.'

She pushed Lincoln behind her and pushed through the screened door. 'That is correct.'

Mrs Silver opened a slim black purse and pulled out a crisply folded piece of paper. 'I made a few phone calls. There are experts that can help with memory loss.'

'I met with countless ones in Seattle.'

'Have you met with anybody since you moved to Austin?'

'No.' Beck's frustrated features flashed in her mind when she'd refused his offer of a forensic psychologist.

Lines creased Mrs Silver's forehead. 'Why not?'

'It didn't work before.'

'That was seven years ago.' Anger clipped her words. 'What about now?'

A knot tightened Lara's stomach. 'The memories aren't there.'

Mrs Silver pulled a photo out of her purse and held it up for Lara. The image featured a young girl of about fifteen smiling into the camera. Her blue eyes sparkled with laughter. 'This was my daughter. I spoke to her for the last time on Friday. And I used that precious time to nag her. I didn't stop to tell her how well she was doing or how proud I was. And then some monster strangled the life out of her and left her by the road.' Her hand trembled as she spoke. 'Blair was twenty-three years old. When she was younger she loved to ride horses, and she collected seashells from our family vacations. She wasn't perfect, but she was my child, and I want her killer found. You owe my girl.'

Unshed tears burned in Lara's throat. 'I have tried.'

'Seven years ago. Seven years ago means nothing to me or Blair! You must try again, now. You must.'

When the woman's voice cracked, Lara's tears broke free. 'I don't know if the memories are even there.'

Mrs Silver raised her chin. 'But you will try again?'

Lara glanced at the picture of Blair. A crushing sadness cut into her. 'Yes, ma'am. I'll try.'

Mrs Silver handed Blair's picture to Lara. 'You keep it. I want you to remember her.'

With a nod the woman got back into her car and fired up the engine, vanishing in a cloud of dust around the bend.

Lara sat down on the step and buried her face in her hands. Tears filled her eyes and spilled down her cheeks. She didn't want to turn her mind back over to the shrinks. She didn't want them poking in her brain.

But she would. Not for herself, but for Blair.

Beck, Santos, and Raines stood in the conference room at Ranger headquarters and stared at the collection of pictures divided into two categories. The first six were of the women killed in Seattle seven years ago. And the second three were of the Texas victims. An image of Lara Church straddled the two columns.

Raines nodded to Lara's picture. 'Our Seattle profilers studied the characteristics of the crime scenes. The locations were remote. The victims were not buried and were posed. There were no witnesses. From that and other details, they developed a detailed portrait of the Strangler. They theorized the killer was male, thirty or older, Caucasian, had some education, and worked in a semi-professional field. He is an organized killer and chooses his victims carefully.' Raines tapped his finger on Lara's picture. 'However, something drastic changed when he attacked Lara.'

There'd been studies done on serial killers and the dark motives that drove them. But each killer, like each person, had quirks and life experiences that changed them. Cops had bad days that affected their work routines. They had fender benders, their wives got sick or angry, or their bosses read them the riot act. Killers were no different and just as susceptible to life's ups and downs.

'We can assume whatever changed when he attacked Lara became a permanent part of his ritual.' Beck circled his finger around the local dump zone. 'He's also moving closer to Lara. First he was twenty miles away. Then he was twelve miles away and now only ten miles away.'

'He wants her to know he's coming.' Raines twisted his wedding band around his ring finger. 'He wants her to notice him.'

Beck rested his hands on his hips. Knowing a lunatic stalked Lara dug at him not only as a cop, but also as a man. From the instant he'd met Lara, the urge to protect her had been fierce. 'Santos, did you find any cold cases that might have linked to Lara?'

Santos glanced at his notes. 'Lara spent twelve summers in Austin. During those years there were murders and violent crimes, but none associated with Lara or her grandmother, Edna Bower. Except for the suicide of her aunt, Leslie.'

'Any details?' Beck said.

'One single gunshot to the head. She'd checked herself into a local Austin motel and half an hour later shot herself. Medical examiner ruled suicide and the case was closed.'

'Any notes left?'

'No. Witnesses had reported a fight between Leslie and her sister, Barbara, the day before, but the sister was across town when Leslie pulled the trigger. Case was closed within a week.'

So much violence around Lara, Beck mused as he traced the doodled letters LC on his pad. 'Anything else?'

'There was nothing else in the criminal files so I tracked down a couple of DPS officers who worked the I-35 area during those years. No murders fit, but there was a string of animal slayings during those years. Not during the summer but in September and October.'

Beck leaned forward. 'Right after she left Austin.'

'The animals started off small. Cats. Dogs. Several were found at a time, which was why a report was filed. But as the years went on, the animals got bigger. Horses. Cattle. All were cut up badly with a knife.'

Raines leaned back expelling a breath. The killer didn't like it when she left. 'What were the years of the animal slayings?'

Santos glanced at his notes. 'Ten of the twelve years Lara visited Austin.'

'And they stopped.'

'When she moved to Seattle for college.'

'Eleven years ago,' Raines said more to himself. 'The year my daughter went to kindergarten. I still remember the sick feeling I had in my gut when the school bus drove away. Wife and I cried like babies. We sent our kids off so they can learn, not so some nut can terrorize them.'

The phone on the table buzzed, and Beck moved toward it. 'James Beck.'

'Beck, there's a Ms Lara Church here to see you,' the receptionist said.

Tension coiled in the pit of his stomach. She wouldn't

have come unless something had happened. 'Send her right up.'

Santos raised a brow. 'That must be Lara Church, judging by your expression.'

He straightened, doing his best to shield fresh worries. 'She wants to see me.'

Raines stretched his shoulders as if a burden had been lifted. 'You think she wants to help?'

'It would be nice,' Beck said.

Raines nodded toward the back door. 'As much as I'd like to stay, I won't because one look at me and she's liable to lock up. Keep me posted?'

Beck drummed impatient fingers on the conference table. 'Can't make a promise I might not keep.'

Raines laughed as he opened the door. 'Fair enough.'

Santos followed Beck into his office. The men barely had thirty seconds before Lara appeared at Beck's door. Her hair was back in a long braid and her face freshly scrubbed of makeup. She wore jean shorts, a red T-shirt, and sandals. She gripped the strap of a satchel purse, which grazed her hips.

She looked so young and afraid. If he'd not known her age he'd have sworn she was barely twenty, a college student herself. He noted a slight tremble in her left hand, and he could see her breathing was shallow.

Beck, the man, wanted to pull her into his arms and tell her everything would be fine. Beck, the cop, kept his expression neutral. 'Ms Church, this is Ranger Santos. We're working with him on the recent murders along I-35.'

She glanced toward Santos and nodded. 'Ranger.'

He nodded. 'Ma'am.'

Her gaze shifted quickly back to Beck. 'Do you mind if we speak alone?'

'Does this have to do with the cases?'

She swallowed. 'Yes.'

'Then as tempted as I am to send Santos away, I can't. We're working this case together.'

Her jaw tightened, and for an instant he thought she'd bolt. 'I came here to talk to you, Ranger. This isn't easy for me.'

'I know that, Ms Church, but I need all eyes and ears on this case. I can't afford to miss any detail.' He pulled out a chair for her. 'Why don't you have a seat and we'll talk? It'll be casual, and there will be no pressure.'

She released a tense breath and took the seat. Standing behind her chair he caught the scent of fresh soap and chemicals. She'd been in her darkroom so whatever had pulled her away from the art had been serious.

Santos took a seat to her right, and Beck took the other to her left.

'Did you remember something?' Beck said.

She crossed and uncrossed her legs. 'No. I haven't remembered. I had a visit today from Monica Silver.'

He frowned. It should have occurred to him that the older woman would track Lara down after she'd referenced the paper's article. 'What did she say?'

'She told me about her daughter. She showed me a picture of the girl when she was fifteen.'

Beck noted the way Lara perched on the seat as if she'd bolt at any second. 'What else did she say?'

'Not much more. But she wants me to remember.' Absently, she tugged at a loose thread on her purse.

'We all want that,' he said carefully.

She leaned forward. 'I want to remember. I do. But I kept telling you that I don't think there are any memories there.'

'Dr Granger is the one to help you with that.'

She pursed full lips and released a sigh. 'I'll talk to her if you'll set it up.'

Suspicion overrode relief. 'Why the change?'

She shook her head as if chasing off the last bits of resistance. 'Maybe the last seven years have loosened something up.'

His gaze never leaving her, he leaned forward and picked up his phone. He punched a couple of numbers. 'This is Beck. Ms Church is in my office. Can you come down? Great.'

'She's coming?' Lara sounded surprised and a bit panicked.

'Be here in a minute. Can I get you a coffee or water?'

'No thanks, I'm fine.' She tightened her hand on her purse. 'Mr Raines found me while I was shooting yesterday.'

A muscle tensed in his jaw. He wasn't sure what pissed him off more: Raines's silence or her ignoring his command to stay away from the crime scene. 'You were at a crime scene?'

Blue eyes flashed. 'That's not the point.'

'It is the point. I thought you agreed not to go to the scenes alone right now.'

'You told me not to. I didn't agree. And again, this line of questioning is about Raines.' Her tone, peppered with sass, told him she wanted a fight.

He'd not give her one today. He needed her on his side. 'He's an asset.'

'I don't like him.'

He spoke carefully. 'I told you from the get-go that I would do whatever it took to catch this killer, Ms Church. If that means working with Raines then so be it.' To shift the conversation, he said, 'What reaction have you had to the article?'

'My answering machine is full of calls regarding it. The messages are mostly from old friends and acquaintances digging for dirt. Reporters.'

For a moment he was silent. 'No one that gave you the creeps?'

She sat straighter. 'Lots of nosey, goofy people, but no one that set off alarm bells.'

'Where's Lincoln?'

The conversation shift had her relaxing a fraction. 'I dropped him at the gallery. Cassidy is not thrilled, but she's dealing, seeing as I'm turning into a moneymaker for her.'

'You're selling prints?'

Amazed pride strengthened the tone of her voice. 'Four since the article came out. And a large online order.'

'Do you know what pieces sold?'

'I didn't ask. I was too stunned that any sold.'

'Let me know when you find out. I want to know which of your crime scenes are catching folks' attention.'

Colour drained from her face as if she fully understood the meaning behind his questions. 'Do you think he'd buy one of my prints?'

'What better memento of a crime than a print created by one of the victims?'

Her voice lost its edge. 'I didn't think about that.'

Before he could respond there was a soft rap on the door, and they turned to see Dr Granger. She wore a dark blue skirt, a white shirt, and sensible heels. Black hair twisted into a ponytail and dark framed glasses emphasized green eyes. 'Gentleman, to what do I owe the honour?'

'I was hoping you could help me to remember,' Lara said.

Beck stood beside Lara. 'Dr Granger, I'd like you to meet Lara Church. I mentioned her to you earlier.'

Dr Granger crossed the room and extended her hand to Lara. 'It's nice to meet you. I read the article in the Sunday paper and some of the case files.'

Lara cleared her throat. 'My life is an open book.'

Dr Granger shook her head. 'The facts are helpful, but they don't tell the whole story.'

'Everyone thinks key pieces are in my head.' Lara moistened her lips. 'I can't promise, but I want to try to remember.'

'Excellent,' Dr Granger said. 'We can do it now if you wish.'

Lara nibbled her bottom lip. 'Better now before I lose my nerve.'

Dr Granger knit long, slender fingers together at her waist. 'Gentlemen, Ms Church and I can go back to my office, or we can talk here. Either way you two need to leave.'

'Santos and I would like to observe,' Beck said.

'No,' Dr Granger said. 'This doesn't work so well given Ms Church's history with the police and psychiatrists.'

Lara lifted her chin. 'You'll tape whatever I say, right?'

'Yes.'

'Then they'll hear it anyway. They might as well stay. Like I said, my life is an open book.'

'We'll sit back and out of the way,' Beck said, making an effort to soften his tone.

'Sit anywhere.' She sounded resigned, beaten even.

Santos and Beck moved to seats at the end of the conference table behind her.

Dr Granger took the seat next to Lara. 'You've done this before.'

Lara nodded. 'Yes, and I remember the drill.' She closed her eyes. 'I'm to breathe deeply and clear my head.'

'That's right, Lara. Just close your eyes and try to relax.' Dr Granger's voice took on a relaxing quality that had her muscles easing. 'I just want you to let your mind float back to a time when you were truly happy, with no worries in the world.'

At first Lara could not relax her shoulders. And the more she told herself to relax the tenser she became.

'Don't try so hard,' Dr Granger said. 'May I call you Lara?'

'Sure.'

Dr Granger laid a steady hand on Lara. 'Lara, just think about a happy moment.'

Eyes closed, she shifted in her seat. She took several deep breaths. Her muscles eased, and her fisted fingers unfurled.

'Where are you?' Dr Granger said.

'I'm in Austin. I'm visiting my grandmother, and I'm hiking in the hills with Rex.'

'Who's Rex?'

'He's my grandmother's dog.'

'What kind of day is it?'

'It's warm but not hot. There is a breeze, and the sky is crystal clear.'

'Is it just you and Rex?'

'No, I'm with my friend Johnny. Grandmother doesn't let me hike alone. There was some trouble in the area last fall and she worries.'

'What kind of troubles?'

'She wouldn't tell me. Only said to be careful.'

Beck scribbled down the dog's name, Rex, his mind turning to the animal slayings. And he also wrote down the name Johnny.

'Okay. Let's not worry about the troubles. Walk along the trail with Johnny and Rex. Enjoy the day. Let your mind float and relax. You are safe. Perfectly safe.'

Lara released a sigh and smiled.

'Now I want you to go back to Seattle. What does your last apartment look like?'

'It's small – a portion of a larger house. It has high ceilings and a fireplace that works. I loved that apartment.'

'And what do you do for a living?'

'I'm an intern to a clothing buyer.'

'Are you good?'

'I'm very good. I've just been offered a full-time position in Seattle, and I've decided to stay.'

'You weren't going to stay?'

'If I didn't get the job I'd promised Gram I'd come back to Austin and work in her shop.'

'Sounds like life was good.'

Lara's smile was soft and relaxed in a way he'd never seen before. 'It was excellent.'

'When you left your job that final day, where were you going?'

'Out to drink with friends. We were celebrating my job.'

'And where did you go?'

'The marketplace downtown.'

'Were they happy for you?'

She smiled. 'They were thrilled.'

'What were you drinking?'

'White wine.' She bit her bottom lip. 'I overdid it. I had four glasses. I shouldn't have had so much to drink. . . .'

'Lara,' Dr Granger said. 'Don't worry about that now. You didn't do anything wrong. You were celebrating with friends.' She laid her hand on Lara's shoulder. 'When you left the restaurant where did you go?'

The furrow in Lara's brow eased but didn't vanish. 'I decided to hail a cab. I knew I couldn't walk home.'

'What did the outside of the cab look like?'

'Yellow. Standard city cab.'

'What was the inside like?'

'Black. Plain. Spartan. I remember seeing the cabbie's profile through the partition. I don't remember him so much. The wine had hit me hard. I remember trying to count out dollar bills when he told me the fare.'

'Did he take the money from your hand?'

She opened her palm. 'I don't remember.'

'Okay. Did you hear anything?'

'Talking. The driver talking.'

'Was he talking to you?'

'I don't think so.'

'Try to remember if you heard an answer.'

Her fingers curled into tight fists, and for several long seconds she didn't say anything. 'I don't remember.'

'It's okay. It's okay. What do you remember next?'

Beck leaned forward in his seat, his hands clasped tightly.

'The nurse in the emergency room. She was ordering a rape kit.' She was silent for a moment and then a tear slid down her cheek. 'I hurt so much. My throat. My insides. It hurt to breathe. I'd never felt that way before.'

A deep, dark rage rose up in Beck. There was nothing he could ever do to prevent that moment she'd endured alone.

Dr Granger squeezed her hand. 'Let's take a break for a moment, okay?'

Lara swiped away a tear. 'Okay.'

'Before, she only remembered her hospital room and not the emergency room,' Beck said. 'She's remembering.' He glanced at Lara. 'Let me talk to her.'

The doctor shook her head. 'I don't think that's such a good idea.'

Beck sensed the fear snapping through Lara and though he saw the necessity of it all, he didn't like seeing her upset. 'We have nothing to lose. Nothing.'

Dr Granger adjusted her glasses. 'She has serious trust issues.'

'Today, she came here to see me, and she allowed me to stay. I might not be as unredeemable in her eyes as you think.'

'Don't push her too hard.'

'Sure.' But he would push if he believed it would wrestle free the memories. Lara needed to remember not only for the sake of the case, but also for her own sanity.

Beck took the seat beside Lara.

'Lara,' Dr Granger said. 'Sergeant Beck would like to speak with you. Is that all right?'

Her fingers curled into knots again. 'Yes.'

Beck nodded to the doctor. 'Lara, think back to the cab ride. What did the driver look like?'

'I only saw the back of his head.'

'What colour was his hair?'

She pursed her lips. 'His hair was blonde and thinning. When he turned to ask me where I wanted to go I noticed he had a hooked nose.'

'Good. Good. Do you remember how long you were in the cab?'

'No. I lost track of time.'

'Did you normally drink a lot of wine?'

'No. I'm not a good drinker. But it was a special night.'

'We all like to enjoy ourselves when we're with friends.

Not a bit of harm in that.' He resisted the urge to touch her. 'Did you ever lose sight of your drink?'

'What do you mean?'

'Did you set it down and go to the ladies' room or the dance floor?'

'A couple of times.' His jaw tightened. She'd been found approximately twenty-four hours after she'd gotten into the cab, and it had been several more hours before the hospital had done a tox screen and found the date rape drug. The levels had been low, but there was no telling how much had metabolized out of her system.

'What did the cab smell like?' he said.

'Stale and it was warm. I'd only been in the rain a couple of minutes, and I felt chilled to the bone.'

They spent the next twenty minutes talking. He tried every angle he could consider, hoping for a new scrap of information, but nothing new surfaced.

Finally when the doctor brought her out of her trance, her gaze fluttered open, and she looked at him. 'Did anything new come up?'

'Some memories. None that seemed to relate to the case.'

'I'm sorry. I want to help.'

'You gave it your best.'

She sighed. 'I can try again.'

Dr Granger nodded. 'I can see you tomorrow or Thursday.'

'Thursday would be best.' She rose and moved to leave.

'We'll work out the details.'

'Thanks.'

'I'll walk you out,' Beck said.

She stiffened slightly, glanced toward Santos, who had risen and now stood stone faced. 'That's not necessary.'

'Exercise will do me good.' He came up beside her. 'After you.'

They moved to the elevators and he punched the down button.

'I was hoping this time would be different.'

'We all were.'

The doors opened, and they stepped onto a crowded car of officers. Some glanced at her with curious interest; some checked her out. He hovered close, careful to put his body between her and the other men on the car. When they arrived at the first floor, he followed her past security to her truck. She unlocked it, but he opened the door for her.

'I'm sorry.' She tucked a loose stand of hair behind her ear.

'Nothing to be sorry about.'

'Then why do I feel like such a failure?'

Tension dulled her eyes. 'Carry no shame, Ms Church. You never did anything wrong. Ever.'

'I should remember.'

He offered a smile that he hoped appeared warm. 'Keep seeing the doc. It will jog loose.'

'I wish I could believe that.' She started the engine.

'Take care of yourself. Keep your eyes open.'

'I'll be fine.'

It pained him to see her drive off. She wasn't safe, but

until they got a break in this case or she remembered, there wasn't much he could do about that.

By ten in the evening Lara was exhausted. She'd been replaying the events of Seattle over and over in her head. She knew there were critical details buried deep, but they remained veiled in shadows.

She climbed into her bed and Lincoln hopped up and settled at the bottom near his blanket. He curled in a ball and released a sigh. She lay back against the pillows, watching the play of shadows on the ceiling.

Outside the wind blew. A familiar branch scraped against the window.

Since she was emotionally drained, it felt good to lie between the sheets and let her mind drift. She wanted to shut out the day and just escape.

He reached for the buttons of her silk blouse and slowly unfastened each. His hands trembled, his touch feather soft. 'White will suit you better than black. White makes you look like a goddess.'

A cool breeze brushed her shoulders as he pushed the blouse from her shoulders. 'So pretty,' he whispered. 'So pretty.'

Her lids felt leaden, and as much as she wanted to open her eyes and look at him she couldn't manage the task. Her darkness kept tugging at her, beckoning her deeper into unconsciousness. She imagined she was at the bottom of a deep pool, glancing up through the water.

A man stood above her, his image obscured by the ripples and distortion of the pool's water.

When a smooth hand cupped her naked breast she moaned, not from pleasure but the horror of knowing what was happening.

'You like that, don't you?' he said. 'I knew you would. I knew you would.'

He pinched her nipple hard and the pain reached into the darkness and pulled her closer to the surface. His fuzzy, wavy features came closer to focus and for an instant she thought the image would clear, but it didn't.

His hand slid from her breast over her flat belly and then below the waistband of her panties. 'I've been waiting for you for a very long time, Lara. After tonight you will be a part of me forever.'

She felt the weight of his naked body and erection pressing against her body. As much as she wanted to claw and scratch and scream for him to get off of her, her limbs would not move. Her voice was silent.

Her alarm blared, shattering the image and jerking her up in her bed. She shoved trembling hands through her hair and wildly searched the room for signs of an intruder. Lincoln remained at the base of her bed, one eye open as he stared sleepily at her.

Her heart racing, she smacked her hand on the alarm and shut it off. Swinging her legs over the side of the bed she let the coolness from the wood floor rise up through her body and clear her mind. She glanced at the clock. Four a.m.

'No one was here. It was a dream. Just a dream.'

It was a dream she'd never had before. Never. And it left her with a tangible sense of filth and violation.

Lara pushed the sheets off and hurried to the bathroom. She turned on the water and pulled off the oversized T-shirt that doubled as a nightgown. She took a long hot shower, hoping the hot water and soap would wash away the lingering fears, but she couldn't shake the sense that the dream had been more than a dream.

Could it be a memory? Had today's session wrestled free something deep from the shadows of her mind?

Lara closed her eyes leaning into the spray and suddenly a memory fluttered forward.

She lay on a gurney as the emergency room nurses assembled a rape kit. A female detective stood by Lara and spoke all the right words. It's not your fault. You didn't deserve this. But the woman's clipped tone made the words sound wooden, as if read from a script. And despite a nurse's gentle coaxing, humiliation burned in Lara as she put her feet in stirrups.

And then the moment was gone.

Lara tipped her face up into the water, letting the heat and wet wash over her, hoping her subconscious might whisper its darkest secrets. But it remained silent.

No answers materialized. And her feelings of failure gained strength.

Lara shut off the hot water, towelled off, and within ten minutes had donned clean blue shorts, a simple coloured shirt, and sandals. Her blonde hair hung around her face, damp but already drying and curling at the edges.

In the kitchen she buttered bread. She glanced at the clock. Nearly 5 AM. Her afternoon class didn't begin until four, but she'd never reach the spot she'd already visited three times before sunrise. There was always work to be done in the darkroom, but she didn't want to be in the dark alone. She craved the sunshine and people.

After she ate, she grabbed her purse and called Lincoln. Though it was just around six-thirty in the morning, she decided on a visit to Cassidy. She owed her cousin after yesterday's unannounced Lincoln drop-off.

As she drove farther down the road, the window open and the morning breeze blowing, she saw the dream with a more analytical mind. Of course, the dream may have been her mind's way of sorting the facts, as she knew them. She had been taken. Raped. Dressed in white. Strangled.

Yet as terrifying as the facts were, they'd never been as emotionally charged as the nightmare. She had the sense of a floodwall cracking and springing its first leak. The more she poked and prodded the dream, the more it receded.

The drive into Austin took thirty minutes. She parked behind Cassidy's gallery, and she and Lincoln hopped out of the truck and entered through the unlocked back entrance. It was just past seven, but her cousin had been an early riser since her mother's suicide. 'Cassidy?'

'Lara?'

'Yeah.'

'How'd you get in?'

'Back door.'

'It was locked.'

Cassidy rounded the corner, frowning. She wore a peasant skirt and blouse, a big chunky silver belt, and brown cowboy boots. Dark hair was swept up into a ponytail that was meant to look casual but had likely taken her an hour. 'I thought I locked it last night.' She inspected the undamaged lock. 'Shit. That's not smart of me to leave it unlocked.'

'You've got to be careful.'

Cassidy nodded as she tossed one last look at the lock. 'Yeah.' Sighing, she rubbed Lincoln on the head. 'Hey, Cujo. Come to dump more dog hair in my apartment?'

Lara smiled. 'He's not staying.'

'The hound is growing on me. Reminds me a little of Rex.'

'Grandma's dog?'

Cassidy's expression softened. 'Big old goofy hound.'

Lara smiled at the memory of Rex begging for scraps of table food. It had been impossible to deny him when he looked at her with such doleful eyes. 'What happened to Rex?'

The nostalgia vanished. 'He ran off right after you left to go back with your mom. I think we were about fourteen. I offered to go looking for him, but Grandma said no.'

Sadness tugged at her. She patted Lincoln on the head and smiled. 'I remember asking about him when I called Grandma, but she'd always change the subject.'

Lincoln sat and then settled on the floor as if he now lived here.

Cassidy studied the dog, her expression not so stern. 'He's taking over.'

Lara laughed. 'He does that.' The two walked toward the front of the gallery. 'So you tell me you had some sales?'

Cassidy waggled her brows. 'No, darling, we had four sales. Big sales. Come and see.'

Excitement bubbled inside Lara. It had been a long time since she'd felt the thrill of victory. The last time she'd felt this good she'd been in Seattle, and she'd been offered the buyer's job. For a flash, worry tempered the excitement, and then she shrugged it off. She followed Cassidy to the front of the studio.

Each time she walked into the gallery and saw her photos on the walls, pride surged. Her life had been in shambles, but she'd rebuilt it.

'So which sold?'

Cassidy crooked her finger. 'Come and see the blank space on the wall and the sold sign in place of your picture.' They moved through the gallery past the black-and-white images. The first blank space had belonged to the piece she'd taken in Maine. The waves crashed against the rocky shore, spraying water over the rocks in an almost joyful way. The beautiful rugged coast had been the scene of the double homicide, but to look at the print you'd never know violence had marked the land.

The next to sell was a scene in Virginia. The body of a young woman had been found along the banks of the Potomac River. Again, to the unknowing eye it was the image of the rising sun and sailboats on meandering waters.

'These were the two nice sales, but the big kahuna is the picture you took in Seattle.'

Lara didn't need to see the picture to imagine it. She had been the victim of this crime. Police had found her along the twisty road that fed into the distant mountains.

It had taken Lara six years to get up the nerve to return to Seattle and shoot. She'd started trembling the instant she'd crossed into Washington state. At the scene, she'd sat in her car for almost an hour, before she'd found the courage to get out and set up her equipment.

Her hands had quaked so badly, the collodion hadn't entirely reached the edges of glass so the negative had had an uneven edge that instead of detracting had enhanced the dark, moody quality.

She'd glared at the scene countless times before the show opened, willing it to talk to her. *Who did this to me? Who?* But it had remained as stubbornly silent at her mind.

'Isn't this the one you said was the jewel and you priced it the highest?' Lara said.

Cassidy managed a smile. 'I know when a piece is going to sell for a good price.'

As she imagined the piece she could feel the cool Seattle breeze thick with rain. The ground had been wet that day and her feet had been soaked by the time she'd crawled back in the truck.

'Who bought the piece?'

'A Mr D. Smith of San Antonio. And he paid full asking

price. Which means,' she added in a singsong voice, 'you can get a new truck.'

Lara barely heard what Cassidy said. 'Did he come to the show?'

'I didn't ask. He purchased the image online.'

'Did he read the article about me?'

'Didn't ask. When someone is offering to buy it's best just to say thank you.'

Tension inched up her spine. 'I don't feel so good about selling this one.'

'What do you mean? It is the most expensive image in the collection.'

'It just feels odd selling it now. The article. The murders. It feels like I'm profiting from another death.'

She'd never expected to feel this way. The images had begun as a form of therapy for her. She wanted to see through photography what her naked eye did not.

But she'd come no closer to understanding violence.

'I don't want to sell it.'

Cassidy blinked, her tone annoyed. 'It is not about what you want anymore, Lara. It's a done deal. I processed his credit card and shipped the image. It's gone.'

Sickness twisted her belly. 'That soon?'

'He was willing to pay extra to take possession of the photo before the show closes next week. And considering your battered truck and my upcoming mortgage payment, I agreed. The money has been spent. We can't go back.'

'It doesn't feel right.'

'This is just one of those artist moments. You all get

attached to a work of art and when the sell goes through you have a moment of panic. Like surrendering a child.'

It wasn't that at all. She was happy to let the other pictures go. But not this one and not to a man who might be a killer. 'I almost didn't include the piece,' she said more to herself.

'I'm glad you did.'

'I'm not.'

He was glad to see the latest killing had finally made the paper. He'd started to think the cops would try to hide his work from the public. He wanted Lara to worry and fear. He wanted her to admire his cunning and intelligence.

Poor little Blair Silver. She'd been so full of fire and spit, like she was better than him, when in fact she was nothing more than his little plaything.

He'd kept the police guessing for almost seven years. Who was the Strangler? Why did he choose his victims? Why go dark? Why return?

Before he was finished the police would look like fools, and Lara would be a terrified mess. He would crush her hoity independence and she would never make him feel ignored again.

He glanced at the article in Sunday's paper, traced the line of her jaw in her photo image, and looked at his most recent purchase – her gallery photo.

He took pride in knowing that his actions then and now had totally shaped the course of her life. She might claim independence, but her life had been completely controlled and manipulated by him.

After he'd chosen not to kill her, he had been furious with himself. Why hadn't he killed her? He had been tempted to go after her in the hospital, but he held back, telling himself it was better to let her live in fear. Soon he'd have a second chance with her.

He held up a necklace that had belonged to Lou Ellen Fisk. The waitress/student had told him proudly she was going places. She wanted out of Texas and wanted to see the world. He'd listened quietly. Later that night, when she'd been driving home, he'd been waiting for her at her house. When he'd pinned her to the ground that first time, the shock in her gaze had been priceless. And when he'd wrapped his hands around her neck and started to squeeze, he'd imagined Lara, and had felt a sweet rush he'd not known for a long time.

Lou Ellen. Gretchen. Blair. Seeking his satisfaction with others had its own reward, but soon the games would end.

And it would be Lara's turn.

Chapter Sixteen

Danni's head pounded when she showed up for her shift at the café. Her eyes felt gritty and dry, and her muscles ached. She needed sleep but found it had been damn near impossible to nap for more than minutes at a time in her mother and stepfather's house. Her stepfather, a.k.a. Mr Creepy, had been wandering the halls last night. He'd tried her bedroom door several times, but found it locked. As she'd sat in bed and watched the handle jiggle, she'd gotten up and pushed her dresser in front of the door. Mr Creepy had laughed.

She now glanced at her reflection in the stainless door of the refrigerator and grimaced at the dark smudges under her eyes. Her blonde hair looked like a bird's nest and her cheeks sallow.

'Look what the cat dragged in,' Mack joked.

She glared at him. 'Very funny.'

He grinned as he set a stack of dishes on the wash station. 'Too much partying?'

'Too much studying. Exams coming.'

Shoving her purse in her locker, she grabbed her apron.

He laughed. 'Studying? Is that what they call it these days?'

'No. Really. Studying. Got to make the grade if I hope to win the scholarship.'

He shook his head. 'You, a scholarship?'

'Yeah, I'm going places.'

His grin faded. 'What's so wrong with here?'

She rolled her eyes. 'Everything.'

His lips flattening into a grim line, he carefully and deliberately wiped his hands on his apron. 'So what are you gonna study in college?'

'Whatever gets me out of Texas.'

He sniffed. 'Texas ain't so bad. It's been good to me.'

She didn't answer, not trusting her surly mood. Mack loved Texas, his old football days, and anything to do with the past. 'Yeah.'

Feeling his glare on her, she stepped out onto the restaurant floor one minute late. The next half hour was a buzz of people, food orders, and dishes. All the while her head pounded in the back of her skull, making her wish she'd taken five aspirins instead of two.

When she spotted Mike Raines the strain in her back eased a fraction. He had quickly established himself as a welcome regular. Not only did he tip well, but also he was nice, always wishing her a good day on the way out. Too bad they didn't make more guys like Mike.

Coffeepot in hand she moved up to his table, her smile now genuine and not forced. 'So can I get you the regular?'

He glanced up from his paper over readers. His gaze skimmed over her and he frowned. 'What happened to you?'

Danni shrugged her stiff shoulders. 'What do you mean?'

He set down his paper and removed his glasses. 'You look like you've been hit by a truck. You sick?'

'Not sick, just need a good night's sleep.'

Lines furrowed his brow. 'Why aren't you sleeping?'

His voice carried a paternal hint that made her yearn for better. 'That's kind of personal, don't you think?'

'I like you. I'm concerned. So why aren't you sleeping?'

Danni shrugged, trying to make light of a situation that grew more serious daily. 'It's not that big a deal.'

'I disagree.' He leaned toward her. 'What gives, Danni?'

'Look,' she said dropping her voice a notch. 'It's not that big a deal. I was just up late studying.' Which had been true for part of the night.

Behind the intensity radiated genuine concern. 'Spill it.'

Her guidance counsellor had been asking the same question for weeks, but now she wanted to answer. 'My step-father is a douche. But he's nothing I can't handle.'

'Is he hurting you?' All the lightness evaporated and what remained distilled to menace.

Her fears and worries rushed to the front of her mind and begged to be told. And then she caught herself. 'No, nothing like that. He's just being an ass.' She glanced toward Mack, who was staring at her. Always staring. 'Look, we better drop this, or I'm going to lose this job, which I need. So can I get you the pancakes?'

He leaned back in the booth, making a visible effort to relax. 'Pancakes sound good.'

As she moved into the kitchen, embarrassment burned

her cheeks. She'd nearly told a total stranger a nasty truth. She'd tried to tell her mother once, but she'd called Danni dramatic and selfish. Since then she'd never told anybody about her new stepfather.

When Raines's order was up she was half tempted to get another waitress to deliver it. She didn't want to see pity or sadness in his eyes when before there'd only been easy laughter. He was one of the few people she enjoyed.

'Man up, girl,' she muttered as she stared at the steaming plate of pancakes.

She grabbed the order, thrust back her shoulders, and pushed through the swinging doors. He sat at his table, just like always, reading his paper. She liked the half glasses perched on his nose. They had a way of softening the sharp edges of his face.

As she approached, he pulled off his glasses and laid them carefully on his paper before leaning back.

She set the pancakes in front of him. 'Here ya go. Can I get you anything else?'

'No, I'm all set, Danni.' As she turned to go, he said, 'Wait.'

He pulled a card from his jacket pocket and handed it to her. 'My cell number is on the card. I can be reached at any time.'

She stared at the white card with its simple embossed black lettering. *Raines Investigations*. Maybe if she could summon enough pride she could just make him forget that she'd ever spoken about her stepfather. 'Why would I need to call you?'

He pushed the card toward her. 'Take it.'

As she stood there frozen, he cut into his pancakes. Irritation and anger nipped at her heels. 'I take care of myself, Raines.'

'Take the card, Danni.' His pancake-loaded fork hung mid-air inches from his mouth. 'Take it.'

She scraped the card off the table and shoved it in her pocket. 'I can take care of myself.'

He smiled. 'I've no doubt. The card is just in case.'

Lara was grateful when class was over today. Spring fever had struck and no one was interested in listening to a review on technique when the sun shone outside. Mr Gregory hadn't shown and the cheerleaders looked as if they needed a nap. Even Danni had appeared quiet and distracted.

She'd wanted to talk to Danni after lab, but she had made a quick excuse about work and hustled out of the darkroom. Lara packed up her backpack, and she and Lincoln left the building. The semester would be over soon and she was looking forward to spending more time in her own darkroom.

She arrived at her truck and noticed a slip of paper under her windshield. Her body tensing, she tugged the paper free and glanced at the words.

The killer is close.

Her heart jackhammered against her ribs as she stared at the handwritten note that reminded her again of Mr Gregory's beefy hands gripping a pencil. Crumpling the page, she cursed. She opened her door, tossed the wadded paper on the floor, and let the dog hop up onto the seat. Slowly she got behind the wheel. Once was annoying. Twice deserved a call to Beck.

A tap on her window made her screech. Her gaze darted up to find Jonathan standing by her car. He was grinning down at her, a quizzical look on his face. Hysterical laughter bubbled in her chest as she rolled down the window. 'You startled me.'

'You look like you've seen a ghost.'

'It's just one of those days. Do you teach today?'

'No. I was looking for you. I thought you might like to grab a quick dinner. I've barely had a chance to see you in the last few weeks and thought it would be fun.' He nodded toward the dog. 'And I know a place that'll allow Lincoln if we sit outside.'

A hot meal was a welcome thought. And she could use a friendly face. 'Sounds good.'

'My car is parked two spaces over. Follow me.'

'Sounds like a plan.'

Fifteen minutes later they pulled up in front of a small restaurant that had a lovely outside garden. As promised, Jonathan had a table on reserve outside where Lincoln could sit.

She settled into her seat and savoured the day's heat. It wasn't blistering hot but warm, a welcome relief from the university's chilling air-conditioning.

'They have great vegetarian fare here,' he said as they opened the menu.

Her stomach grumbled. 'I am starving.'

'Good.'

They scanned the menu and placed their orders, and

when their drinks arrived Jonathan leaned back in his chair. 'So have you sold any pieces from your show?'

She sipped her sweet tea. 'Four, as a matter of fact.'

Brown eyes warmed with pride. 'Well, good for you. I knew you'd be a success.'

'Well, that makes one of us. I was convinced I'd be hauling all the pieces home and stashing them in the back room.'

'You never used to underestimate yourself. When you were a teenager you were ready to set the world on fire. Seattle changed you.'

She rarely referenced her life in Seattle or the days her grandmother had sent Johnny to take care of her. 'I got burned, remember?'

'I was surprised you told that reporter about Seattle.'

She shrugged. 'I am starting to feel like my old self. About time the wounds healed.'

He grinned. 'About damn time.'

'I haven't had a chance to thank you for putting the good word in for me with the university. I don't think I'd have gotten the job if you hadn't.'

'Didn't take much effort on my part at all. So how do you like the teaching?'

'Honestly, I'm still trying to figure that out. Some of the students are great. Others, well, they try my patience.'

'How so?'

'Since the article, someone has been putting notes on my windshield.'

'What kind of notes?'

'"The killer is close." That kind of crap.'

Jonathan frowned. 'That's not good at all. Do you know who's doing it?'

'Ideas, but no proof.'

'Who do you think is doing it?'

'I'd rather not say. I could be wrong.'

He leaned forward. 'Have you told the police?'

'Not yet. But I plan to.'

'It should be top priority.'

'I know.' Nervous, she realigned her fork with her plate. 'I guess learning to trust the cops again isn't so easy.'

'Lara, if you don't tell the cops, I will. This is not good.'

'I know. I will call.'

His gaze lingered on her a beat too long, but to her great relief he didn't press. 'So do you think you'll stay for another semester?'

She traced her finger down the side of the iced glass. 'I got an email today as a matter of fact. The university offered me two classes in the fall.'

'Are you going to take them?'

She ignored the faintest hint of hopefulness in his voice. 'I'm thinking about it.'

The waitress arrived with their meal. The spicy scents of cumin, peppers, and cheese rose from the enchilada.

'Smells great,' she said.

He smiled. 'Dig in.'

Since it was easier to focus on the details of the meal than his warm smile, she dropped her gaze to the steaming plate in front of her. 'I will never get tired of the food in Texas. Never.'

'There's a lot to love about the state.'

'So how has the custom furniture-building business been going these days?'

'Not the boom days we had a couple of years ago, but we're surviving. I haven't had to lay anyone off, and we just got a big order from a rich patron. That'll keep us all going for months.'

'I'm glad to hear it.'

He stabbed his fork into a plump enchilada. 'Any other issues since the article came out?'

'Most folks don't recognize me from the picture in the paper. Thankfully, I'm rarely dressed up and wearing makeup and heels.'

He smiled. 'What about the media?'

'My answering machine is managing them well enough for now. And so far no one has come up to the house. Here's hoping there are more important matters for the world to worry about than a seven-year-old case.'

'A tie-in to the current murders is newsworthy, Lara.'

'I'm still hoping there is no connection.'

He shook his head. 'Hoping won't cut it, Lara. You've got to be careful. Proactive.'

Lincoln stretched out under her feet, and she glanced down at him. She'd tell Beck about the notes.

The rest of their dinner was pleasant and Lara realized she was enjoying herself. Jonathan had been her friend since she was a kid, and he felt like family.

By the time she and Lincoln made their way back home it was nearly eight in the evening. She was feeling relaxed and at ease and ready to crawl into bed with a book.

However, the sense of goodwill vanished when she

spotted Beck's truck parked in front of her house. He was sitting on her front porch, his legs outstretched and his hat dangling from his fingers. When he saw her truck, he rose and moved with a predator's ease.

She opened her door and Lincoln bounded out of the car and ran up to Beck. He sniffed his hand then dashed off toward the brush to pee.

Lara glared after the shepherd, shaking her head. 'So much for a bodyguard.'

The dog's excited barks drifted from the woods as Beck levelled his gaze on Lara. 'When he feels a threat he'll step up. It's clear he adores you.'

From the bottom step she had to crane her neck to meet his gaze. 'What brings you out here, Sergeant Beck?'

'Came to make sure you were doing okay. You don't answer your phone much. And your message machine is full.'

'The article.'

'Do you have a cell phone?'

'Yes.'

He pulled out his own phone. 'What's the number?'

She rattled off the number as she climbed up the stairs past him to the front door and unlocked it. 'Did you come out here just to get my number?'

'Dr Granger called the house several times. When she didn't get you she called me.'

Of course, he'd come about business. That made sense. So why care? 'Hence your visit.'

'She'd like to see you tomorrow at one.'

'That works. I cancelled class tomorrow so the kids

could have extra time to work in the photo lab.' She twisted the key in the lock.

He stood close behind her. 'She said she'd make any time work. Just show up.'

'Okay.' Memories of last night's dream drifted to the forefront of her mind. 'I had a weird dream last night. I've never had it before.'

The dimming sun cast shadows across his face, deepening the lines and hard planes. 'About Seattle?'

'I think so.' She opened the door and flipped on the light. 'Come in if you like.'

He followed her inside as she turned on lights and dropped her bag on top of the kitchen table. Scanning the room for signs of trouble, he said, 'What was in the dream?'

Mindful of breakfast plates on the coffee table and the stack of coffee cups on the end table, she resisted the urge to start straightening. 'It was more like a nightmare.' She set her keys on the kitchen counter and leaned into it. Speaking about the dream gave it credence and made it uncomfortably real. 'You've read my file from Seattle. You know the Strangler . . . raped me.'

His jaw tightened. 'Yes.'

When her gaze lifted to his, the intensity made her hesitate. 'I should probably just talk to Dr Granger about this.'

'You can.' He spoke carefully as if coaxing a wild horse toward the corral. 'Or you can tell me.'

'It just feels odd.'

He nodded toward a stool by the kitchen counter. 'I could use a cup of coffee.'

'I'll make some.'

'I got it.'

She thought about him fumbling around in her kitchen, getting a better look at the dishes in the sink and the counter that she should have wiped last night. 'Let me make the coffee.'

He set his hat down on the kitchen table and rolled up his sleeves. 'I'm perfectly capable.'

'It will give me something to do.'

'Have a seat.' An order, not a request. 'My mother hates anyone in her kitchen, especially if it's not perfectly clean. I've seen dirty dishes in sinks before, Lara.' Her given name sounded rougher, wilder when he spoke it.

'I'd planned to do a big clean as soon as I submitted my grades next week.'

When he moved into the kitchen it suddenly looked tiny. 'Sit.'

She sat at the tall kitchen counter. 'The coffee is in the tin next to the machine.'

'The one marked "Coffee"?' he teased.

'Yeah. And the filters are in the tin next to it.'

'I see it.'

It felt odd to be sitting at the table having someone wait on her. She lined up the saltshaker with the peppershaker as Beck moved with ease. 'You look like you've made coffee before.'

He hit BREW and faced her, leaning against the counter and folding his arms over his chest. 'Can't be in law enforcement and not know how to make a strong cup of coffee.'

He'd invaded her life a little over a week ago – a virtual stranger – and she was about to share a personal and dis-

282

turbing dream. 'How long have you been with the Rangers?'

If he picked up on the delay tactic, he gave it no notice. 'I've been a Ranger for five years, but before that I was with DPS for eight years.'

'Long time.'

'I like to think I'm just getting warmed up.' Behind him the machine gurgled and spit out coffee. 'Cups?'

'Cabinet right behind your head.'

He selected two handmade mugs. One was a bright blue and the other yellow. Filling each, he set hers by her hands and cupped the other as he took the seat across from her.

She sipped the coffee and was amazed it tasted good. 'I thought cops made bad coffee.'

'I can only cook a handful of dishes. Number one and two on that list are steak and coffee. You much of a cook?'

'Fair. My grandmother taught me a good bit when I lived with her. I just rarely take the time these days to cook. Seems a waste to pull out all the pots and pans for just me.'

'What keeps you so busy?'

She smiled. 'I know what you're doing.'

'What's that?'

'Trying to get me to relax so that I'll feel better about talking to you.'

'I thought I was making conversation.'

She traced circles on the counter with her fingertip. 'Cops don't just make conversation. There is usually an agenda.'

He set his cup down on the counter. 'Not always true.'

She shoved aside her nervous energy. 'I need to tell you about the dream.'

'There's no rush.'

He was trying to ease her pain, and for that she was grateful. 'When I was seven and afraid to jump off the diving board my grandmother told me to just jump. Get it over with, she'd say.'

He straightened as if bracing. 'Okay.'

'In the dream, I couldn't see the man, but he kept telling me how lovely I would look in the white dress.' Recounting it made her feel dirty. 'He was touching me and I knew I was going to be raped.'

'What exactly did he say?'

'How beautiful I was. How he'd been waiting for me for a long time.'

Beck flexed his fingers. 'Did you see anything? Smell anything?'

'No.' She shook her head. 'Maybe my subconscious is just working through what I've heard.'

His gaze turned ice cold. 'Or maybe you are starting to remember.'

'Yeah, but it's been seven years. Why now?'

'I don't know. Maybe you've seen something or someone that's jogged something loose.'

Her shoulders sagged forward. 'But what?'

He raised his mug to his lips. 'That's the million-dollar question.'

She sipped her coffee. 'When I was in Seattle, Raines tried to tell me what had happened to me. He wanted me to read the medical reports, but I refused. I didn't want to remember.'

His gaze held hers. 'You suffered one hell of a trauma.'

'I talked a lot about wanting to remember, but I think deep down I thought not remembering would somehow protect me. That was pretty much how I got through my childhood. Easier to live with Mom if I didn't remember the last fight or the latest disappointment. But now I feel trapped in amber. I didn't feel pain, and I didn't feel anything else. I want to know what happened to me. I think I need to know. You've read the report.'

'Yes.'

'Can you tell me?'

He drew in a slow breath and repeated the facts as clinically as possible. 'You were raped. There was no semen present, but there was a lot of vaginal bruising. There were also bruises on your thighs and wrists. There was also skin under your fingernails. DNA was tested, but there was never a match in the CODIS system.'

'CODIS?'

'A DNA criminal database.' He turned his cup slowly from side to side, but she sensed retrained anger. 'Based on the bruising the doctors assumed he'd been on top of you when he grabbed your neck.'

'He didn't rape the other women in Seattle.'

'No. His pattern changed with you, and it is holding consistent in Austin.'

A cold chill shuddered through her body. 'Why didn't I die?'

'The theory is that he was interrupted. For the first

time he chose a spot that wasn't remote. No one knows why.'

'Do you have any leads in this case?'

He shook his head, his frustration clear. 'We know he likes the I-35 corridor. All the bodies have been dumped on the southbound side. He dresses the women in home-made white dresses and each has a penny in their hand. We also found footprints at the last two crime scenes that we believe belong to him.'

'He's getting closer to me.'

'Yes.'

She glanced around the house. 'This house was always my safe place to go. It was the eye of the storm for me. Now it feels like ground zero.'

He frowned. 'How'd you get into photography?'

'You're doing it again.'

A brow arched. 'What's that?'

'Changing the subject to make me feel better.'

'I'm interested in the photography.'

She smiled. 'Be careful about asking an artist about their work. They can bore you to tears with details.'

Amusement softened his gaze. 'Then just tell me the basics.'

'I'd been working my way across the country when I spotted my first camera at an auction. After that I was hooked.'

'Why?'

'I could make the world appear as I wanted it to appear with a camera. I could manipulate light, angle, setting, and mood. And my end product was concrete and a perfect record of my travels. For someone with a key memory missing, a solid record was appealing.'

'Where did you go?'

'All over the country. I think I put fifty thousand miles on my truck last year. But when my grandmother died, she left her house to me and her store property to my cousin, Cassidy.'

'And Cassidy offered you a show?'

'She did. And my friend Jonathan got me the gig at the university. Austin, until last week, had become the perfect fit for me.'

'You still planning to stay?'

'I've more of my mother's gypsy's blood in me than I realized. But for now, I'll stay. If this guy found me here, he'll find me in the next place.' She picked at a thread on her jeans. 'Someone has been putting notes on my car at school.'

Lethal energy radiated from him. 'What kind of notes?'

'"The killer is close."' She dug in her backpack and pulled out the crumpled note and handed it to him. 'There's another in my truck.'

Utter stillness overtook him as he studied the paper. 'Who do you think did it?'

'I'm not sure.'

His gaze darkened. 'You have ideas.'

'Sure.'

'Tell me.'

She shook her head. 'Not until I know for sure.'

'Tell me.'

'No. I don't want to ruin a college career, until I'm sure.'

'This isn't a game.'

'I know. And I know you are a pit bull and as soon as I give you the kid's name you'll be all over him.'

'Damn right.'

'The kid could just be a jerk and nothing more.'

His grin looked more feral than friendly. 'I'll play nice until I'm sure.'

She shook her head. 'No.'

He frowned his frustration. 'I want you to be vigilant, Lara. This killer changed his MO in Seattle with you, and now he's in Austin. Have you considered staying in town with your cousin?'

'She hates dogs. It was all I could do to get her to dog-sit the other day.'

'You could board Lincoln.'

'No. I'm not boarding my guy. He wouldn't understand.'

'I don't like you out here.'

'You sound like my friend Jonathan.'

He frowned as if the comparison bothered him. 'He's right.'

'I've got Lincoln.'

'Lincoln has been drugged once.' Beck shook his head. 'He can't fully protect you out here. I can't protect you out here.'

'You couldn't protect me in town. If this guy wants to kill me, he will.'

Beck's eyes darkened. 'Not on my watch.'

Beck did not like leaving Lara alone in her home. He'd checked all the windows and door locks before he'd left, and he'd asked DPS to swing by several times an hour. Still, she was out in the wind swinging virtually alone. And there wasn't a damn thing he could do about it.

His phone rang as the side road reached the interstate. 'Beck.'

'This is Steve Cannon in Seattle. Thought I'd follow up and see how your investigation is going down there.'

He rubbed a knot in the back of his neck. 'Not well. We had another murder and so far have no suspects.'

'I called Raines, but he's not answering his cell. I'm guessing he's still down there.'

'He is. He's pretty damn committed to the case.'

'That's Raines. He never quits.'

'Must have had one hell of a closure rate up there.'

'It was good. After his wife and daughter died it became great.'

Beck hesitated. 'His wife and daughter are dead?'

'Eight years ago. Car accident. Hell of a tragedy. His life became all about work after Susan and Tara died.'

Raines gave no hint of the loss. 'He still wears his band. Talks about his family as if they are alive.'

'I know. They meant everything to him. Wouldn't be surprised if he still has Susan's voice on the home answering machine.'

'How was he on the job after their deaths?'

'It was hard the first two or three months. He couldn't work. But then slowly he started to come back bit by bit. Some days I could almost believe the old Raines had returned.'

'And then he quit.'

'It tore at him that he couldn't close the Strangler cases. The brass put a lot of pressure on him. He never said what happened in that last meeting with the chief, but he gave up police work. Said it was time to start making real dough so he could retire to Fiji. Honestly, I'm sorry you got this case, but I'm glad Raines has a second chance to catch this guy. He was one hell of a cop, and he deserves to nail this bastard to the wall.'

They talked a few more minutes and Beck rang off, partly sorry for Raines and more than a little worried that he had an unstable nut on his hands. There was no denying the guy knew the case inside and out, but Beck needed to know the guy could keep his shit together.

Beck pulled up in front of Raines's motel forty minutes later and knocked on his door. Inside he heard the television and then the rustle of papers.

'Who is it?' Raines called back, his voice gruff.

'Beck.'

'Just a minute.' Beck heard him moving around the room and then back to the door before snapping it open. He wore jeans and a shirt partly buttoned, and was drying his wet hair with a towel.

'You taking the time to hide your gun?'

Raines smiled. 'It would be illegal for me to have a gun in Texas.'

'Once a cop always a cop. I feel naked without mine.'

Raines motioned for Beck to come inside. 'Why the visit? There a break in the case?'

He opted not to share what Lara had told him. Along

the way his priority had shifted to protecting her. 'Just got off the phone with Seattle.'

Raines stepped aside and allowed Beck into his room. The place was clean, organized. On a simple desk a high-tech laptop, the screen saver a family photo of a younger Raines holding a towheaded toddler with a smiling, attractive blonde woman staring at him. On the wall above the desk, a map of Austin covered in yellow and blue sticky notes.

'I'm not surprised you're working the case from your room.'

Raines chuckled and tossed the towel in the bathroom. 'If you were in my shoes would you have handled this any differently?'

Beck had worked the Misty Gray case to exhaustion. 'No. I guess I wouldn't.'

Raines's smile wilted. 'So what did Seattle say about me?'

He sensed the older cop already knew the answer. 'Told me about your wife and daughter.'

'That so?'

Beck resisted another look at the screensaver. 'Hell of a thing to happen.'

'That's putting it mildly.' He swallowed and gritted his teeth. 'It is more like having your guts ripped out and fed to you.'

'Seattle said work was all you had.'

'That's about right.' His demeanour offered no hint of apology. 'I threw myself into work, especially the Strangler case. I lived and breathed it. It was a lifeline for me.'

'I can appreciate that, but I need to make sure you're not a loose cannon, Raines. You are dangerous if this case doesn't stay impersonal.'

He shook his head. 'The case has been personal to me for seven years. A change of cities or job titles does not change that. I am going to do whatever it takes to catch this guy.'

'You break any of my laws, and I am going to arrest you.'

Raines held his gaze. 'Then I guess I better mind my manners or at least not get caught.'

Beck studied the guy, searching for any whiff of trouble. He wanted to like this guy. Wanted to see him close this case. But he didn't need a vigilante on the loose. 'Keep your nose clean. If you step out of line, I'll lock you up.'

Raines ran long fingers through his wet hair and smiled. 'You're the boss, cowboy.'

It was after ten at night when he followed her car onto the interstate. He had been watching her for days. He knew where she lived. Where she worked. Her favourite grocery store. Her favourite hairdresser.

Tonight while she'd been in the bar, in a matter of seconds, he'd punctured her back passenger-side tyre and attached a cell phone jammer to the inside of her wheel well.

The battery in the jammer was good for several hours, so he knew she'd not be able to place calls from her car. The real unknown was the tyre. He'd made the hole small, knowing she'd be on the road by nine-thirty because she had an early Pilates class on Thursdays. The air would leak slowly at first and the damage wouldn't be noticeable until much later. Of course, she could stay in the bar longer or choose a different, more populated route home. In either case, his plan would be ruined. But it was the risk, the idea that he could fail, that added a thrill to the chase. What was a hunt after all if there was no risk?

Right on schedule she sauntered out of the bar and got into her car.

By his reckoning, she'd be well outside Austin city limits when her tyre went flat.

He turned up his radio listening to his favourite Lynyrd Skynyrd song on the radio. He tapped his hand on the steering wheel in time to the music and started to whistle. This was going be a good night. Yes, sir, a good night.

He was careful to stay a couple of car lengths behind her as she worked her way out of town. Several times she hit her brakes for no apparent reason. He worried that she suspected that something was wrong with her car, but each time rationalized away what she did not want to believe. He smiled when he saw her raise her phone to her ear and then seconds later toss it in her lap. No cell phone service. She had a problem. A very big problem.

He followed her for fifteen minutes down I-35 and by the time she approached an exit, the tire started to noticeably wobble. She inched over to the side of the road and took the exit, finding herself on a deserted side road. Perfect.

He slowed, put on his blinker, and parked behind her. He waited a beat. Let the fear settle in deep. Then he walked up to her car and knocked on her window.

She jumped and dropped her lifeless phone in her lap as she cracked her window. 'Hey!'.

'You all right?'

'Yeah, great.' A tentative, nervous smile said otherwise. 'I just need to call a tow truck. My car is acting funny.'

'You have a flat. Back right tyre. I could see when I was driving. Must have picked up a nail.'

She dragged fingers through her blonde hair. 'Shit. I mean, thanks. This is just the last thing that I needed.' She punched the number for information, waited, and then frowned. 'No cell service here.'

'Yeah, this stretch is known for that. Let me try my phone. Maybe we'll get lucky.' We. He'd already established them as a team. We are in this together. He dialled 411 and pretended to hit send. The jammer should have blocked any call this close to the car, but he didn't want to take the chance that his phone would work.

After a reasonable pause he said, 'Sorry, no service. Let me walk back to my car. Sometimes just moving a little will help with the reception.

She craned her neck toward his car. 'Hey, thanks, I appreciate that.'

He walked back to his car and repeated the show. When he returned, he was shaking his head. 'I drive this stretch of road all the time. About six months ago I had car trouble near here and couldn't get a signal at all. Had to walk four miles to the first gas station.'

'Four miles. Are we that far from anywhere?' Fear hummed under the words.

'Maybe just three. Hang tight, let me try again. We'll figure this out.' He'd been careful not to ask her to open her door or come to his car. A woman alone would have clenched up at the thought.

After another pause he came back. 'Sorry. I'd offer you a ride, but I don't want to come across as weird or scary.'

She smiled, her look almost apologetic. 'Creeps out there ruin it for nice guys like you.'

'Why don't I drive into town and see if I can find a gas station or a signal and send them your way?'

'Oh, God, that is so nice. I don't know what to say.' She picked up her phone and dialled again. Again, no signal.

'By the way, I'm Dan,' he said. 'That way if a tow truck stops you'll know I sent them.'

She softened even more, and this time she unrolled her window and stuck out her hand. 'I'm Pamela.'

He clasped her cool soft fingers in his large calloused hand. How simple would it be to yank her forward, grab her throat, and strangle her until she passed out? 'Nice to meet you, Pamela.'

She smiled.

He released her hand. He wanted her to open the door. He wanted her to trust him just like the others had trusted him. 'Be sure to keep your doors locked out here while I'm gone. All kinds of odd folks out here.'

She nibbled her bottom lip. 'How long do you think you'll be gone?'

'If the gas station I have in mind is open, just twenty or thirty minutes.' He checked his watch. 'But at this time of night it's anyone's guess. Don't worry; if they are closed I'll keep looking. I won't leave you stranded, Pamela.'

She glanced down the deserted road, the worry lines in her brow deepening. 'Would you mind if I tagged along with you, Dan?'

He kept his emotions in reserve. 'I'm glad to take you, Pamela, but you don't know me.' This was part of the game. Denying what they wanted made them want it all the more.

She offered him a sure and steady smile. 'I know people, Dan, and you seem okay to me. I mean, if you were a creep, you'd have dragged me out of the window when I shook your hand.'

He took a step back and put his hands in his pockets. He understood what an innocent man should look like. 'You're the boss, Pamela.'

She rolled up her window, shut off the engine of her car, and grabbed her keys and purse. Without a second thought she opened her car door.

He grinned, trying not to let the adrenaline of the hunt make him twitch. He was getting good at this. Now that he was more skilled, he could take his time, and savour the hunt.

She locked her car and smiled. 'After you, Dan.'

He moved toward his car, relishing the idea that she was following him to her death. He reached for his car door, opened it as she approached.

As she was about to get into the car, car headlights appeared around the bend. He tensed, ducking his head ever so slightly so the passing motorist wouldn't be able to describe him if ever questioned.

But the motorist did not pass. Instead he pulled up

behind his car and shone bright lights on him, Pamela, and their two cars.

The guy got out, but hovered by his car so that the headlights and the darkness obscured his face and body. 'There a problem here?'

Dan cleared his throat. If he was clever, he could fool this one and still keep his prey. 'Her car broke down. I'm giving her a ride to the station.'

'You try to call a truck?' the man said.

Pamela moved toward the light a step farther away from him. 'No cell service out here.'

'Really? I've got bars. Let me give it a try.' The man dialled and seconds later he was on the phone with a gas station and ordering a tow truck. 'Got a truck on the way,' he said cheerfully.

'Oh, that is wonderful,' Pamela said. She moved farther away from him. With each step he could feel her slipping away.

He thought about the gun in his glove box. He could kill them both now. But that would create a mess, and there was a tow truck driver on the way. He slammed the passenger-side door a bit harder than he'd intended. 'Well, it sounds like you're all set, Pamela.'

Pamela's lips trembled as she met Dan's gaze. 'Hey, Dan, I truly appreciate your help. I would have freaked if you'd not been here. Life's been kind of a mess lately and this was the last thing I needed.'

'It takes a village, doesn't it, Dan?' the rescuer said.

'It sure does.' He moved to the driver's side, now wanting nothing more than to be gone from this place.

Pamela opened her door and slid behind the wheel. She closed her door but didn't lock it.

'Tow truck should be here any minute,' the rescuer said.

'Yeah,' Dan said.

'Want to stick around?'

He searched past the headlights, still not seeing more than a large silhouette. 'Naw. Looks like you've got it covered.'

'I sure do, Dan. I sure do.'

For the first time a cold shiver inched up his spine, and he sensed this rescuer had an agenda. What the hell would a random stranger want from him? Certainly he hadn't been followed, had he?

'I didn't catch your name,' Dan said.

'No. I didn't give it.' The rescuer's phone beeped and he glanced at a text. 'Looks like the cavalry is minutes away.'

'God, you two have been great,' Pamela said. Tears welled in her eyes and tumbled down her cheeks. 'I'd have been so lost without you.'

'Yeah. Looks like.' Dan got behind the wheel of his car and fired up the engine, not sure if he was more frustrated, angry, or scared.

Chapter Seventeen

Beck got the call minutes after he arrived at the office. Another body had been found on the side of Interstate 35. A young woman. White dress. Strangled. Immediately, he placed a call to Lara. Her home phone rang once, twice, three times. With each ring, his heartbeat quickened. He dialled her cell.

'Yes?'

The sound of her groggy voice released the tension in his back. 'I woke you. I'm sorry. But I needed to make sure you were okay.'

'Beck? What is going on? What time is it?' He imagined her pushing her blonde hair out of her eyes as she swung her bare legs over the side of the bed.

'Seven o'clock.'

'I worked in the darkroom last night until three. I didn't mean to sleep late. Why did you call?'

He hesitated, knowing he was breaking protocol. 'I can't go into detail, but there's been another murder.'

A long, heavy silence drifted through the lines.

'Are you still there?' he said.

'Yes. I'm here.' Her voice sounded soft, fragile even. 'I'm so sorry. Do you know who was killed?'

'I haven't even been to the scene. I just wanted to touch base with you before I went.' Knowing she was safe would free his mind to think about the case.

'Be careful,' she said.

Her concern touched him. 'You are coming by the office today to see Dr Granger?'

'In a couple of hours.'

'Come in now.'

'I have the student art show to set up today and tomorrow.'

Temptation told him to ignore the investigation and haul her back to headquarters with him where she'd be safe. 'Get out of that house. Surround yourself with people.'

'Okay, sure.'

'Be careful.'

He hung up and smoothed a hand over his head. As he'd dialled Lara and counted the rings, he'd not been thinking rationally like a professional. He'd reacted like a man, worried about a woman.

Beck didn't want to analyze his feeling for Lara. He cared about her safety and that was enough for now.

He redialled, this time placing a call to Santos, who picked up on the first ring. 'Santos.'

'It's Beck. We've got another body.' He was scanning his desk as he spoke, triaging the active cases. All could wait until he saw the body.

'Where?'

'Thirty miles outside of Austin.' As he gave Santos the details, he shut off his computer and moved toward the door where his coat hung, all the while cradling the phone.

'I'm a good one hundred miles from there. Got a call from a local sheriff about a drug problem. I'll be there as soon as I can.'

'Good.'

Beck closed up his office and headed down the hallway to see his commander, Captain Ryder Penn. Beck knocked. Penn glanced up, a phone cradled under his ear. He motioned Beck inside. 'You're headed to the murder scene?'

'Bad news travels fast.'

'That was the mayor of Austin chewing on my ass. Won't be long before the politicians come out of the woodwork looking for a pound of my flesh.'

'Santos and I are on it.'

Penn rose, shrugging his broad shoulders. 'Is the body Lara Church?'

The question shot through him like a bullet. 'No. I spoke to her.'

'She needs to get her ass back into these offices and speak to Dr Granger.'

'She's promised to be in within the hour.'

'If she's not I'm sending a car for her.'

Beck's hackles rose. This was his case. Lara was his witness. His. 'It's under control.'

Penn glared at him. 'It better be.'

Beck arrived at the scene as the medical examiner's inspector was photographing the body. Beck studied the rural stretch of road. A killer with a woman alone would have all the time in the world to do what he wanted to her.

He tugged his hat forward on his head, shielding the sun, and moved toward the crime scene. He stood by the site, watching as a forensics tech sketched the scene on a white pad.

As he looked at the victim he had the immediate sense that this murder was different. The blonde woman wore a white dress, but the body didn't appear so traumatized. Yes, the angry finger marks of strangulation marred her neck, but her arms and face appeared unbruised.

'What do you think?' Beck asked the technician.

The technician rose and backed away from the body. 'I don't know if he was in a hurry or what, but he doesn't appear to have . . . toyed with this one as much.'

So his impression was right. 'Explain.'

'No bruising or trauma other than the strangulation marks. And the ME will have to confirm, but there appears to be no sign of sexual trauma.'

A breeze blew across the grasslands fluttering through the victim's hair and ruffling the edges of her white dress. *Why not assault her? You had plenty of time out here.*

'Thanks.' He moved to the uniformed officer who had been the first responder to the scene. He shook the guy's hand. Beck had been with DPS nearly nine years and in that time had gotten to know a lot of the local sheriffs and deputies. 'Matt, good to see you. When they move you up from Waco?'

Deputy Matt Jerrod was six one, broad shouldered with the straight back posture that hinted to his time in the Marines. He wore his hair short. A dark shadow covered his square jaw, telling Beck the deputy had worked the night through. 'Few months back. Already miss the place. You been back lately?'

'Wish I could. Wish I could. I stay close to Austin these days.'

'City living is going to make you soft.'

'I hear ya. I do.' Beck asked Matt about his family and the politics of the local election before he asked, 'Who found the body?'

'We got a call into the sheriff's office. A motorist spotted the body and called us.'

'Do you have name of the caller?'

Deputy Jerrod arched a brow. 'The call came in on a disposable phone. No trace. But then that's not unheard of in these parts. We got lots of folks coming across the border who don't want to be traced.'

That was true, but most wouldn't have paused to call in a dead body. 'You ever have an illegal or coyote call in a murder?'

Jerrod shook his head. 'Doesn't happen every day.'

'No, it does not.'

'You thinking the killer called this in?'

'It crossed my mind.'

'Why would he do such a thing? The longer that body is out here, the less evidence we're gonna retrieve.'

Killers had motives that didn't always make sense to anyone but themselves. 'Good question.'

'He'd want to stay under the radar so he could keep doing what he's doing.'

'He likes the attention. Did you see the news last night?'

'Missed it.'

'The national news anchors are paying attention to the killer now.'

Jerrod shook his head. 'Shit.'

After Beck's call, Lara's mind buzzed with thoughts of a woman she didn't know. She imagined the woman breathing her last breaths as the killer's hands crushed her throat.

For the briefest instant, her throat closed and an overwhelming jolt of fear burned through her body. She tried to draw in air but couldn't. Panic tightened her chest, and she staggered backward to the couch and sat down. She couldn't breathe. She couldn't think. She raised her hands to her throat as if invisible fingers squeezed out her life.

'It's taken so much planning to get you here. So much work.' He drove into her with a force that made her entire body scream with pain. 'I've dreamed about this moment for years. And now I have your life in my hands. If you thought you'd ignore me, you were wrong.'

Sweat beaded on her brow and her hands shook as she drew in a shaky breath and released it slowly. Her head cleared and her heart slowed.

For several seconds she couldn't move. Frozen. Unable to stand. Call for help. Cry.

'What the hell was that?' she muttered. She'd never had a panic attack before. Could that have been a memory?

She rose and found her jean jacket hanging on the back of a chair. She fished out Dr Granger's card and dialled the number.

The line picked up immediately. *'This is Dr Granger. I'm in a meeting now, but if you'll leave your name and number I'll get back to you.'*

'Dr Granger, this is Lara Church. I think I'm starting to remember. I'm headed toward your office now.' She left her cell number and then carefully hung up the phone.

Seven years of wanting these memories and now they were cracking through the blocks in her mind. And she was terrified.

Danni entered her mother and stepfather's house just after nine. Her hope was that they were still sleeping off last night's bender. If she was super quiet, she could grab and pack enough to last her several days.

Last night, they'd both had too much to drink and had started fighting early. When she'd pulled up in the driveway, she heard the shouting and the crashing of dishes. She'd not wanted to go into the house and so had pulled down the street and slept in her car. She'd considered asking Raines for help and had gone so far as to call his phone and let it ring once before losing her nerve and hanging up. He'd offered assistance, but it had been her experience that most people truly didn't want to help.

Carefully, she cracked open the back door and snuck through the polished kitchen down the back hallway to her room. She gently opened her dresser drawers and pulled out a pair of jeans, T-shirts, and extra underwear. She also grabbed the hundred bucks she'd hidden under her mattress. As she moved back through the house she could hear her step-father's steady snoring coming from the living room.

She returned to the kitchen and opened the stainless steel fridge. It was all but empty except for a six-pack of beer, a jar of mayonnaise, stale Chinese food from three nights ago, and a jar of peanut butter. She snagged the peanut butter and turned to a breadbasket, knowing the bread was only days old. She took the softest pieces from the centre of the loaf, dug a knife out of a drawer, and smeared peanut butter on the bread. Her stomach grumbled at the smell of the peanut butter. She was about to take a bite when she heard footsteps in the living room.

'Shit.' She tossed the sandwich and grabbed her knapsack. Her hand was on the back door when she heard her stepfather.

'Where the hell were you last night?' Roger Hail wasn't a tall man, but what he lacked in height he made up from girth. He had wide shoulders, muscled tattooed arms and legs that looked like tree trunks. His white sleeveless T-shirt was stained with hot sauce and his jeans hovered below a beer belly on narrow hips.

Her spine stiffened as she turned to face him. 'I was out.'

'Your mother and I were worried.' Bloodshot eyes glared.

'You two were fighting.' Her hatred for the guy goaded her to snipe, 'It didn't seem like you missed me.'

He hiked up his pants. 'Maybe we was arguing over your bony ass and all the trouble you cause us.'

Her mother and stepfather's lives were in the shitter not because they were hopeless drunks, but because they'd been saddled with a teenager. She'd heard this from both of them before, knew it was bullshit, and still it stung.

'I guess as long as my real daddy keeps sending the child support payments, which pay for your beer, you're gonna have to deal with me. Wouldn't look good to the social workers or courts if they found out you were pissing away my money.'

'Don't you get smart with me, girl.' He moved toward her, raising his hand as he did.

She'd been hit by that hand before and remembered the bone-rattling smack that had knocked her to the floor. But as strong as he was, she was smaller and quicker. When he lunged for her she ducked out the back door and ran down the steps toward her car.

He stumbled and stubbed his toe on the threshold. 'You worthless little bitch. Get back in this house.'

She shot him the bird as she ran. The momentary sense of accomplishment quickly faded as her trembling fingers fumbled with the door lock. She tossed her clothes in the car, dug in her pocket for her keys, and hit the auto door lock just as her stepfather pounded a meaty fist into the car window.

'Open this fucking door, bitch.'

Hands trembling, she shoved her key in the ignition and turned the starter. As the car engine turned over and fired, Roger reached down and picked up a large landscaping rock and hauled it over his head, ready to toss it through the windshield.

She gripped the wheel, her heart ramming against her chest as she put the car in reverse. She knew he was a mean drunk, but she'd never figured him for a psycho-pathic killer. 'Shit.'

In that instant another car screeched up the driveway. The driver's quick jerk of the steering wheel and sudden brake landed the car beside hers. Her stepfather's attention shifted and his angry glare hardened.

To her surprise, Raines got out of the car. Without a glance toward her, Raines moved toward her stepfather, gun drawn, with deliberate slowness that suggested trouble.

'Raines, what are you doing?' she shouted.

He didn't break stride or turn. 'Stay in your car, Danni. We'll talk after I've had a chat with this gentleman.'

Her stepfather clung to the rock but lowered it a fraction. 'What the fuck do you think you're doing, pal?'

'I'm here to tell you to leave that kid alone.'

A smile curled the edge of his lips. 'Or what? You'll call the cops. I ain't left a mark on her.'

'Looks like you were about to.'

'About to don't hold shit in a court of law.'

Raines pointed his .45 at her stepfather's head. 'Didn't catch that.'

Her stepfather's grin vanished. 'Wait a minute.'

'Raines,' Danni said. 'You cannot just shoot the guy in his backyard.'

Raines grinned. 'Why not? It's easy enough to do.'

The look on her stepfather's face was priceless. Fear. Hysteria. Anger. All blinked in an instant. 'You can't just kill me.'

Raines shook his head. 'I sure can. And I promise you if you come near Danni again I will kill you.'

The old man's gaze narrowed. 'What is she to you?'

'She's a friend.'

The old man spit. 'You mean she's your whore.'

Danni had heard the word from her stepfather often enough so it only made her flinch a little.

Raines however moved several steps forward, the tip of the gun moving closer to her stepfather. 'Apologize to Danni.'

'I ain't fucking apologizing.'

When Raines spoke, his tone was calm and chilling. 'I don't have to kill you with the first shot. I can start with your kneecaps.'

The old man paled. 'Why do you care about her? She's just a damn kid.'

'I have not heard that apology yet.'

Her stepfather looked as if he were chewing on barbed wire when he said, 'Sorry, Danni.'

She had to admit it felt good to see the bastard squirm. 'I'm sorry, I didn't catch that.'

Raines lowered the barrel of his gun to her stepfather's foot. 'You heard the lady. She didn't hear you.'

'I'm sorry!'

'You get that one, Danni?' Raines said.

'I did. Thanks.'

'Now get back in your house,' Raines said to the step-father. 'And if I hear or see anything regarding this kid that makes me worry, I'm not giving you a warning. I'm going to kill you.'

Her stepfather swallowed and ran back in the house. When he was out of sight, Raines holstered his gun at the base of his back.

Danni dragged long fingers through her hair and rolled down her window. 'Man, you still got some moves.'

A smile twitched at the corner of his mouth as he glanced one last time in the stepfather's direction. 'I like to think so.'

'He's going to be pissed.' Exhilaration mingled with fear. 'And I bet he calls the cops.'

'No doubt.' Raines looked down at her.

'Where the hell did you come from, by the way? You were like a fricking ninja blowing in like that.'

'I saw your missed call on my phone last night. I came as soon as I could.'

'I didn't tell you where I lived.'

'Finding people is what I do.' He glowered at the house, with its perfect and neat exterior. 'Is there somewhere else you can stay?'

'I've got my car. I've also got one hundred bucks. That'll do. Just three days until graduation and my eighteenth birthday. I'll be coming into some money then.'

'You're going to spend the next ten days in a car?'

'Sure. I've done it before.'

Raines shook his head. 'I'm staying at the Foothills Hotel. It's not fancy, but it's clean.'

She blinked. 'What, stay with you?'

'God, no.' Genuine amusement softened his expression. 'We'd drive each other insane. I'll get you your own room.'

'And then I would be in your debt. Sorry, cowboy, no can do.'

'My business does well, and I don't have anyone to spend my money on. Might as well be you.'

'And still, I would be in debt to you.'

'No, you would not. And you will take the room.'

'Or what?'

His gaze turned serious. 'I'll call social services.'

She shook her head. 'I do not like dealing with those people.'

'Then take the room, finish school, and move on with your life.' When she didn't agree he said, 'Look at it this way, I am paying it forward. Somewhere down the road you will get to do a good deed for someone. Do that deed and consider yourself paid back to me.'

'You're an odd duck, Raines.'

'So I've been told.' He rested his hands on his hips. 'You taking the room or am I calling in social services?'

'No strings?'

He laughed. 'Like what?'

'Oh, come on, you must know.'

'Danni,' he said, laughter still dancing in his eyes. 'No strings. Now want to join me for breakfast? I am starving.'

'Not at the River Diner.'

He chuckled. 'I'm a creature of habit.'

'I know a diner. It's good. And you can get your pancakes.'

'They as good as the River Diner's?'

'Better.'

'I'll follow you.'

Beck was still at the crime scene when his cell buzzed just after twelve noon. He glanced at the caller ID and when he saw Austin City Hospital he hesitated. His mind tripped through a hundred different scenarios. A colleague shot. His mother. His grandfather. Releasing a deep breath he opened the phone. 'Sergeant James Beck.'

'Ranger Beck, this is Adele Knight at Austin City Hospital. We have your grandfather here.'

He sat back in his patrol car, letting his gaze drift beyond the crime scene. 'Is it his heart?'

'Yes. He had a mild episode early this morning. He's resting comfortably now.'

'I'll be there within the half hour.'

Beck explained his situation to the people at the scene and then drove to the hospital. The old man was tougher than rawhide, and Beck couldn't remember a time when his grandfather hadn't been in command of his life. When he'd been diagnosed with heart disease last year it had been a wakeup call for Beck. The old man wouldn't live forever. 'But another decade or two will do.'

When he arrived twenty minutes later at the emergency room, he found the nurse's station. He recognized the woman at the station, Jessie Parker. She'd worked with his mother at the hospital for at least a decade. Dressed in green scrubs, blonde hair pulled up in a topknot and glasses perched on her nose, she smiled at him. 'Beck.'

'Jessie. I hear my grandfather is here.'

She tucked a pencil in her topknot. 'He is. Been raising a fuss with the nurses.'

'How's he doing?'

'It was a serious attack, but he's hanging tough. He's in room twelve. Down the hall fifth room on the right.'

A cold knot clenched his gut. 'Is Mom with him?'

'She's been with him for the last hour, but just took a break to get a coffee. She worked the night shift and needed just a few minutes to herself.'

Beck's mother worked harder than anyone he knew. When Beck, his mother, and his brother had moved in with his grandfather, the boys had settled quickly and Henry had relished being father to his grandsons. His mother, just nineteen, had not been content. She'd dreamed of being a nurse so the old man had told her to stay put with the boys and get her degree. Soon she had enrolled in a nursing programme. By the time he was seven she had her two-year degree, and by the time he'd graduated high school she'd completed the full four-year nursing degree.

Though there'd been opportunities for his mother to find a new place for Beck and his brother, she had stayed with his grandfather. His mother had dated men, and his grandfather had a lady friend he'd been seeing for over twenty years, but his mother and grandfather had never remarried, choosing instead to keep a stable home for Beck and his brother.

Everyone had assumed that when the Beck boys moved out of the house Elaina and Henry would part ways. But Henry had suffered his first heart attack shortly after the boys had moved out, and so his mother had stayed with the father-in-law who had become just as much a father to her as he had to his grandsons.

Beck removed his hat and stepped into his grandfather's room. The old man lay on his bed, his face as pale as his sheets. Time had not thinned his white hair and thick moustache. Sun etched lines burrowed deep around his eyes and forehead. The mechanic resembled Wild Bill Hickok.

He was attached to a half dozen wires and IVs, and for the first time in Beck's memory, Henry looked fragile. Beck pulled up a chair by the old man's bed, not sure if he should take his hand, say something, or just sit.

'I'm not dead,' his grandfather said without opening his eyes.

Beck loosened his tie. 'I hear you're making life tough for the nurses.'

'I don't appreciate their fussing.' He opened his eyes and looked at Beck. 'What the hell are you doing here?'

With effort, Beck kept his voice steady and light. 'I heard you were sick, but I can see they were wrong.'

The old man nodded. 'Damn straight. I don't know what the fuss is about.'

'You had a heart attack,' said Beck's mother from the doorway. Dressed in nurse's scrubs, Elaina Beck's dark hair was pulled back in a neat ponytail. She was a petite woman who'd kept her figure trim and at fifty-one could have passed for a woman at least a decade younger. A gold cross dangled around her neck. 'And it was more serious than the last.'

'You worry too much,' Henry said. 'Don't listen to your mother. She's a woman and women worry.'

Elaina arched a brow. 'I am the most sensible woman you have ever known, Henry Beck, so watch your tone with me.'

They'd grumbled at each other like this for as long as Beck could remember. 'Has anyone spoken to Steve?'

'I called your brother,' his mother said, 'But he did not pick up. I left him a message and told him to find his way back to Austin as fast as his fanny could carry him.'

'Leave the boy alone,' grandfather said. 'He's most likely working.'

'Working,' Elaina said. 'His obligation now is to family.'

Steve Beck worked for the FBI. He rarely discussed his work, which required him to travel a great deal. Right now he could be anywhere in the world.

'I'll track him down,' Beck said.

'No,' grandfather said. 'Leave the boy be. I'm fine, and I'll be out of here by sunset.'

Elaina shook her head. 'I know my boy. He'll be here for a few days.'

Beck held his comment regarding Steve. He'd give his brother a little more time and then he would track his ass down. In the meantime, he looked at his grandfather's pale, drawn face. The doctors and nurses, including his mother, were treating him like an old man. Their intentions were good, but Henry Beck wasn't used to being babied.

'Old man,' Beck said as he stood. 'You need to stop bellyaching and do what the doctors say. You don't have to like a job to do it well.'

Henry grunted, frowning at words he'd tossed out to his grandsons often enough. 'I got enough gas in my engine to kick your ass for being disrespectful.'

'I'd let you try, but I'm in the middle of a case right now. Once it's solved and you're on your feet we'll mix it up.'

'Punk.' Henry closed his eyes, but this time there was a grin on his lips.

Beck clamped his hand over the old man's and for the briefest second the old man's fingers curled around his. 'See you soon.'

Beck and his mother left the room.

'The way you two talk to each other,' Elaina said.

He cleared his throat. 'I know you love him, Mom, but he's not a child.'

Elaina's eyes reflected her pain and worry. 'He's a sick old man.'

'Maybe, but don't talk to him like he is. Give him shit just like you used to when Steve and I were kids.'

She clutched her cross and slid it back and forth on its chain. 'Your language, Beck.'

'I'm serious, Mom. Don't treat him like he's old.'

'I got it. I got it.'

Beck softened his tone. 'So how bad is it?'

'Bad. He coded in the ambulance.'

'He called 911?'

Her intent gaze glistened with unshed tears. 'He was on the phone with me when he complained of chest pains. I sent the ambulance.'

His own chest tightened with frustration. It was his job to fix the broken, and he had no remedy for the pain in his mother's eyes or his own heart. 'Is he going to be all right?'

'They need to do more tests and see what damage has been done.'

'He's tough.' The words were meant to allay his fears as much as his mother's.

'Not so much right now. Which is why you need to track down Steve. I know your brother loves Henry and would want to see him.'

'I'll see what I can do. Last I heard he was working a case by the Mexican border.'

She removed her glasses and cleaned the lenses with the edge of her scrub top. 'Just find him.'

Beck leaned down and kissed his mother on her cheek. 'I will find him.'

Her gaze narrowed as she studied his face. 'You're not sleeping.'

'Like I told Henry, I have a case.'

'I read about the women who were strangled. Is that the case?'

'It is.'

She fingered the cross dangling over her collarbone. 'Who would do such a thing to a woman?'

'I don't know, but I plan to find out.'

She frowned. 'Be careful. If this crazy man can kill a woman, he won't think twice about taking a shot at you.'

'I will.' He'd compromise his own safety in a heartbeat for the opportunity to drop this killer.

Chapter Eighteen

Thursday, May 30, 12 pm

By the time Lara drove into town her nerves had calmed and the panic had all but gone away. She'd called Dr Granger and confirmed their one o'clock appointment. With an hour to kill, she'd swung by the school to check on the students at today's open lab, being held in lieu of a final class.

There were a half dozen kids milling around the classroom attached to the lab and more in the darkroom. She counted seven students and to her disappointment, Danni was not present.

Danni had never missed a class or a chance to work in the darkroom. The kid was always early. Work done. Good, engaged questions. And now she was MIA.

Remembering Danni's drawn features yesterday, Lara quickly scanned her student list for Danni's cell number. She dialled. It rang once and went straight to voicemail. *'This is Danni. When the tone beeps, you know the drill.'*

'Danni, this is Lara Church. Just checking to make sure you're okay. Call me.'

She's a kid, Lara reasoned. Bound to skip a class now that classes were wrapping in her high school. No doubt she had graduation practice or parties or whatever normal kids did when high school wrapped.

She was feeling edgy so everyone else could join her. 'Let's see what you've done in the last week.'

'Our projects aren't due until tomorrow,' Wally complained. He stared at a collection of drying prints. His subject matter always focused on baseballs or footballs.

'I want a final look. I might be able to offer some helpful tips.'

She moved to the first table, where three girls focused on matting their black-and-whites. The first girl, Tiffany, had taken pictures of her front porch. 'The play of shadows is nice.' The next two girls had taken pictures of their cars. Not original, but they'd put forth the effort. The next few students had completed varying degrees of work. Most were close to completing their portfolio, but all could use more work.

Tim sat at the back table where Danni usually sat. He leaned back in his chair, his posture relaxed, his demeanour telegraphing a lack of interest. 'Want to see my stuff?'

She arched a brow. 'You've been photographing?'

He grinned. 'Yeah. Working like a dog. He flipped open a portfolio to reveal a collection of stunning shots of the Texas State Capitol building.

Carefully, Lara inspected the prints. 'You took these?'

'Sure did.'

She lifted her gaze to him. 'I got the impression you hadn't done much.'

He leaned forward, the front legs of his chair hitting the ground. 'Told you, it's easy to snap a few pics.'

'Snap. A. Few. Pics?'

'Wasn't that hard.' He leaned forward. 'I mean, come on, it's photography.'

'Whoever took these is a talented photographer.'

'Why, thank you.'

'I'm having a hard time believing you took these.'

'Believe it.'

She shook her head as she gazed again at the portfolio. 'What?'

'I don't believe you took these.'

'Well, I did.' His voice, peppered with defiance and anger, raised a notch.

'I'd like to see the negatives.'

'I don't got them with me.'

'Then get them. I'd like to watch you develop one of them.'

Tim glanced around the room at the other students, who were all staring at him now. He was a hothead, but smart enough to understand that confronting a teacher publicly wasn't wise. He shrugged. 'Whatever.'

She studied him an extra beat and then shook her head. 'How about tomorrow?'

'Sure.'

She lingered another twenty minutes, answering questions and making suggestions, and then she and Lincoln headed out so she could make her one o'clock with Dr Granger.

As she got to her truck, she tossed her bag in the seat and turned it on so the AC would cool the interior. Lincoln jumped in the front seat and went to sleep.

She happened to glance back and realized that her back tyre was flat. 'Oh, you have got to be kidding me. Really?'

She strode to the tyre, squatted, and spotted the knife that had been driven into the tyre. Tim or one of his buddies came to mind. 'Damn.'

Lara rubbed the back of her neck and rose. She shrugged off her jean jacket and reached for the metal box mounted to the back of her truck bed. She spun the dial of the combination lock and opened it, yanking out a jack and wheel wrench.

If seven years on the road had taught her any lessons it was how to take care of herself and her car. She'd changed several tyres over the years, and though she did not enjoy the task, she could do it.

She moved to the cab and shut off the engine. 'Sorry, Lincoln. Let's get out and sit in the shade while I change the tyre.'

He yawned and jumped out of the truck and sauntered to a bit of shade. She pushed up her sleeves, popped off the hubcap, and placed her wheel wrench on the first lug nut, loosening it half a turn. When she'd loosened all the nuts a fine bead of sweat pooled down her back, and she could feel her temper ratcheting up.

She slipped the jack under the frame, stood, and pumped the jack with her foot. The car rose slowly.

'Looks like hot work.' Tim's gleeful voice was right behind her. 'Tough break.'

Slowly she turned around. He stood there sipping on a cold soda, grinning.

A pragmatic tone hid her anger. 'Did you do this?'

He shrugged. 'Why would I do that?'

Anger burned behind the ice. 'Because you are an immature kid.'

His brow knotted. 'You deserve every bit of grief you get.'

'Why? Because I care about doing a good job, and I don't have use for slacker kids?'

Lincoln picked up on the tone of her voice and rose. His hackles lifted and he growled.

'And if your dog comes near me,' Tim said, 'I'll jab a knife in his throat.'

The heat coupled with the flat tyre had put her temper on simmer, but a threat against Lincoln was enough. She could never take Tim physically, but she could challenge his work to the dean. She moved to the front seat of her car and dug her cell phone out of her purse.

'Who are you calling?'

'The police. And after that the dean.' She was just about to hit send when she felt a large hand clamp down on her shoulder.

He squeezed hard, forcing her to cry out and drop the phone. He twisted her arm behind her back and shoved her against the truck. 'If we had more privacy,' he breathed into her ear, 'I'd fuck you right here and now so that the next time you saw me you'd be afraid.'

Lincoln's high-pitched bark cut across the lot, garnering the some attention. When the dog lunged at Tim, the boy kicked at the dog. The intended blow skidded past the dog's head.

'Let me go.' She tried to twist around, but he increased the pressure on her arm.

'Call your dog off, or I'll break your fucking arm.'

She drove her foot into his shin, and though he flinched, the impact wasn't enough to make him release his hold. He twisted harder. She screamed. Lincoln bit at the back of Tim's leg.

Footsteps pounded behind them and in the next instant, Tim's grip was broken. Circulation immediately rushed back into her arm, and she turned her fingers already curled into a fist.

Beck stood behind her, his large hands twisting Tim's arms behind his back. 'Give me a reason, kid. Give me a reason.'

The kid tried to break free, but Beck kicked his legs out from under him and sent the kid sprawling to the ground. Beck put his knee into Tim's back and cuffed his hands behind his back.

Beck rose and opened his cell phone as he stared at Lara. 'You all right?'

'I'm good.' She rubbed her arm, aware that if this encounter had gone on a little longer Tim would have broken her arm.

Beck spoke to local police and requested a car be sent to their location. Satisfied police would soon arrive, he re-clipped his phone to his belt and hefted Tim to his feet. 'Get up.'

'Christ, man, you're hurting me.'

Beck got right on the boy's ear and whispered words she couldn't hear. Judging by the look on Tim's face, whatever

Beck said wasn't pleasant. Seconds later two police cars arrived and officers got out. Beck explained the situation and Tim was lead off in cuffs.

Lara sat under a tree with Lincoln. Against her will, her mind tripped back to the dream of the Strangler. A cold shiver slid over her body, puckering her skin with gooseflesh.

As Beck approached she rose to her feet, doing her best to shield her emotions. She didn't speak, fearing raw emotions would make her voice crack. Lincoln also rose.

Beck scratched him between the ears. 'Mind telling me what that was all about?'

'A student who can't fail my class, or he'll get kicked off the football team.'

'I trust that he is failing.'

'Hasn't done a bit of work this semester, and today he turned in a stunning portfolio. I was going to challenge his work with the dean.'

Beck glanced at the tyre that still hadn't been replaced. A chilling anger rumbled under his voice. 'How'd his hands end up on you?'

'He came up to me while I was changing the tyre. I told him I was calling the police because I'd had it with his stunts.'

Beck cursed under his breath. 'He's the one that wrote the note?'

'I thought it was his sick idea of being funny. And I didn't have strong proof it was him.' She shoved a shaking hand through her hair. 'It stopped being funny when he cut my tyre.'

He rested tense hands on his hips. 'It was never funny.'

'Come to think of it I haven't laughed much.'

She sighed. 'Now, if you'll excuse me I've got a tyre to change.' She checked her watch. 'I'm late for my appointment with Dr Granger.'

'I'll change it.' A firm, hard statement.

'I am perfectly capable. I've changed enough tyres in my day.'

He shook his head, clearly annoyed by her stubbornness. 'I'll bet you have. But no woman is going to change a tyre while I watch.'

'You don't have to stick around and watch.'

He rolled up his sleeves. 'You've not known me that long, so I'll let that comment pass.'

Fractured nerves pushed her toward rebellion. 'Meaning?'

He enunciated each word. 'I don't walk away from a job that's unfinished.'

Her smile held no humour. 'You make me sound like a project.'

Muttering unintelligible words under his breath, he tossed the flat tyre in the truck bed, pulled the spare from the wheel well, and set it on the tyre rim. Carefully he screwed the bolts on and with the wrench, tightened each bolt so securely she wasn't sure if she'd be able to get it off the next time she had to change out the tyre. He lowered the jack and put it, the flat tyre, and the wrench in the back of the truck. 'Good as new.'

'Thanks.' She couldn't begrudge him the kindness.

'Any time.'

He loomed over her, tall, so strong. His scent mingled with the heat, swirling around her and making it tough for her to think. 'I have a rag in the back of the truck so you can clean the grease from your hands.'

He glanced at his blackened fingertips. 'Thanks.'

She reached over the side of the bed and, stretching, flipped open the back hatch to retrieve wipes. She pulled several from the box and held them out to him. 'That should do the job.'

His fingers brushed hers. Calloused. Rough. 'You seem pretty self-contained.'

Carefully, she curled her tingling fingers into a fist at her side. 'I learned to be, travelling around so much.'

A frown deepened the lines around his eyes. 'It couldn't have been safe for you on the road.'

'I never thought much about safety at first. I was too busy running.'

'When did you start worrying? What changed your mind?'

'My truck broke down in Tulsa. It was night and raining. I got out of the car and opened the hood hoping and praying I'd see what was wrong. As the rain pelted I tried to think back to when I first bought the truck. The former owner had warned me about loose battery wires. In desperation, I checked the battery wires, made sure they were tight and got back behind the wheel.' She'd been sick with worry. 'It started on the first try.'

'You were lucky.'

A sigh escaped pursed lips. 'I should have put more planning into my road trips. I made a point to learn about what made my truck tick and to travel by day.'

With deliberate care he wiped the grease from his hands until no traces remained. A scowl added ferocity, as he tossed the soiled wipe in a nearby trashcan. 'A woman alone on the open road is trouble waiting to happen.'

'I saved myself before.'

A hard lingering gaze held her. 'You were lucky.'

'I was smart and skilled.'

He flexed his fingers. 'All the trouble you can dream up doesn't compare to the suffering lurking and waiting on the open road.'

'You make it sound like we're in the Middle Ages.'

The grease from his hand was gone, but he wiped it again as if trying to erase a hard memory. 'Remember I was a DPS officer for nearly a decade on the Texas roads.'

Lara didn't ask for war stories. The day's heat sent droplets of sweat between her breasts. She imagined Beck's fingers following the same path. She cleared her throat and shifted the conversation. 'Have you identified the other victim?'

'No.'

'One of my students didn't show today. I am worried about her. I know she drives I-35 a good bit. Her name is Danni Rome.'

'What does she look like?'

'She's blonde. Petite, dark eyes. Just shy of eighteen.'

'It wasn't her. The victim was blonde, but she was older and tall.'

Like the others. Like me. 'Danni's just a kid. Seventeen and finishing up high school. She is smart and great, but I get a bad vibe. Home must not be so good for her.'

'I can ask around.'

Colour rose in her face. 'The kid just missed one class. That's hardly a cause to call the cops in.'

'But you have a feeling.'

'Let me give it some time. I'll call her if I haven't heard.' He stood so close she could feel the heat and energy from his body. She wanted to lean into that strength and absorb what she could. She didn't.

His gaze lingered, darkening. He wasn't accustomed to being put off. 'Okay.'

'I have to hurry to Dr Granger's.' She checked her watch. 'In fact I'm late.'

'I'd like to tag along. Listen in.'

'Sure, why not. Maybe you'll hear something when I start babbling.'

The corner of his mouth hitched a notch. 'You don't babble.'

'You know those crazy stage shows that involve people being hypnotized?' Humour acted as a relief valve.

'I've seen a couple.'

'I picture myself barking like a dog or standing straight like a tree.'

The shadows behind his gaze lifted. 'You did just fine the last time.'

'And you'll tell me if I act like a fool?'

'Of course.' Despite the stern tone she sensed teasing.

Her guard dropped. 'I just don't like giving over control.'

'So I've noticed.'

That made her laugh. 'I didn't used to be so controlling. I used to be pretty fun loving.'

'I'd say you still are.'

'How can you tell?'

'Just a hunch.'

The warmth behind the words soothed as it unsettled. She was part of the job for him, and she'd be wise to remember that. 'Let's get going.'

'Sure.'

She and Lincoln got in her car and they drove across town to Dr Granger's office. Beck was behind her the entire way. The sentinel. The guardian.

She felt protected. It would be so easy to forget she was an asset, a witness, and embrace the sensation she'd known rarely in her life.

When she got out of her car with Lincoln, Beck was there to guide her to the front entrance. He opened the door for her, and for a moment she hesitated. It had been a long time since anyone had opened a door for her.

She walked into the offices with Lincoln and the security guard glanced sharply at her, but after Beck waved him off he stayed silent.

The ride in the elevator felt like it lasted forever. With just her, the dog, and Beck there was barely enough room to move or breathe. Beck had a way of sucking in all the space's air and energy. A human tornado. Powerful. Huge. Potentially destructive.

The doors opened to a carpeted hallway, and they moved to glass doors that opened to a reception area.

A quiet brunette with dark-rimmed glasses greeted them, and soon Lara was sitting in Dr Granger's office with a promise from the receptionist that the doctor would arrive soon.

Lincoln settled down on the floor and closed his eyes.

As Beck sat next to Lara his cell phone rang. He glanced at the number. 'I've got to take this.'

'Sure.' She smiled and moved to a bookshelf, hoping to give him a measure of privacy.

He moved toward the window and faced the city sky-line. Though his voice was low and controlled, she could not mistake his words. 'So far he's fine, but the doctors are worried, Steve. Mom wants you home to see him just in case.'

There was silence as Beck listened to the other man on the line. Tension deepened the lines around his mouth with each passing second, and she couldn't help but wonder who Steve was or what had happened. When he closed the phone and faced her she saw a menace that took her breath away. This was the face of a hunter. A warrior.

'Everything all right?' she said.

His gaze shifted to her deliberately. 'Yes.'

So tired of her own problems, she shifted her attention to his. 'That's the worst lie I've ever heard.'

'I can handle it.'

'So it is a problem.'

He exhaled. 'It's family.'

She laughed. 'Translation: problem.'

'Not always.'

'Maybe in your family. Not mine. I don't remember a

Christmas, Easter, or Thanksgiving that wasn't pure hell in the Church home.'

Grasping the sadness woven under the lightly spoken words, he frowned. 'It wasn't like that in our home.'

'Who's Steve?'

'My brother.'

'Sounds like you have an issue with Steve?'

'Since when did you get so interested in my life?'

'Since mine hit the skids a couple of weeks ago. Easier to worry over what Steve has done to piss you off than wonder if I'll be able to remember the man that tried to kill me before he kills another woman.'

Beck's face softened. 'Steve is an FBI agent. He travels a lot for work and is hard to get. He rarely gets home these days. Our grandfather is sick, and I've told Steve he needs to come home.'

'And he doesn't want to.'

'He wants to, but he says he can't. He's in the middle of a big case.'

'Where is your dad?'

'Died on the oil rigs about twenty years ago.'

'I'm sorry.'

'Hard to feel sympathy for a man I barely knew. If not for pictures in Henry's house, I couldn't tell you what he looked like.'

'Do you look like him?'

'I look like Henry. Steve looks like Dad and has his wanderlust as well.'

'And so you became the super responsible one who keeps the family together.'

'Mom and Henry did that until five or six years ago when Henry had his first heart attack. When he got sick I did step in and help with the family business.'

'Which is?'

'Beck's Garage.'

'That explains how you changed the tyre so easily.'

'I've had my head in one engine or another since I was three.'

Questions initiated as a diversion from her troubles had morphed into genuine interest. 'Why the Rangers?'

'As a kid it was easy to look up to them. Henry saw early on that that was what I wanted, so he encouraged me. Did the same for Steve. Wanted us to live our own lives. My brother took off first chance he got, but I stuck around – would have been in the garage today if my grandfather hadn't fired me.'

'Fire you? Why?'

'He was smart enough to know I'd not have left otherwise.' Beck's tone was matter-of-fact.

The door opened and Dr Granger entered. She had her hair up in a French twist and wore another dark slim skirt, a white shirt, and a discreet strand of pearls. 'Lara. I am so glad you could come.'

They shook hands. 'Thanks for seeing me.'

'I'm glad to have you.' She shook Beck's hand. 'Beck. Will you be joining us for the session?'

'Yeah.'

When Lara nodded her agreement, Dr Granger ushered the three to a small sitting area with a couch and two chairs. Lara sat on the couch. Beck sat to her right in a chair, hat in hand. Dr Granger sat to her left on the couch.

'Now I want you to relax.' Dr Granger's voice had a calming, quiet quality.

Shoving out a sigh, Lara attempted a smile. 'Easier said than done. I feel as if I'm sitting on pins and needles.'

'You're not. This is just you and me talking. No pressure.'

Lara glanced at Beck. 'Locked in my memory is the face of a killer.'

'Let's not worry about that now, okay?' Beck said. 'Let's just worry about relaxing and listening to the sound of Dr Granger's voice.'

The doctor smiled. 'Ask any of the Rangers, and they'll tell you I have a voice that can put anyone to sleep.'

Lara smiled. 'Okay.'

'Close your eyes.'

Lara closed her eyes and rested her hands on her thighs. She started to breathe deeply and release the worry and fear.

'That's exactly right,' Dr Granger said. 'Just relax.' She shifted her weight on the couch so that she was closer to Lara. 'Now I want you to imagine a crystal hanging from the rearview mirror of your truck. You are sitting on the side of the road and in the distance you see mountains and blue skies. Do you see it?'

'Yes.'

'Good. Now slowly pull your attention toward the crystal and focus on the play of the sun in the crystal. Note the colours and the way the crystal spins.'

Lara's inward gaze drew in closer and closer until all that she could see was the rainbow of colours in the crystal. The physical world melted away. Her fingers eased into the soft denim fabric covering her thighs.

'We've travelled back in time to Seattle. You've just gotten a huge job promotion, and you are on top of the world.'

Lara smiled. 'I'd been waiting and hoping for this job for months.'

'You were thrilled.'

She eased back into the couch, remembering the sense of relief she'd felt when she'd gotten the call. 'Beyond thrilled.'

'And who were you celebrating with that night? What friends did you have around you?'

'The usual suspects.' She smiled. 'Angela. My roommate. Dave who was in my marketing class with me. Kyra from yoga and Nancy from the new company. They were kidding me when I ordered my second glass of wine. I was always a little rigid and focussed on work. They'd never seen me let my hair down.'

'What was your average day like?'

'I was always up by five, to the gym by six and classes or the library by eight. I treated school like a work day.'

'You studied fashion.'

'Fashion merchandising and business.'

Beck found himself drawn in by Lara's easy smile. Since the day they'd first locked gazes, she'd been tight and guarded. At her art show opening he'd seen glimmers of this old Lara. More than ever he wanted to catch the man who had crushed the free-spirited Lara.

He pulled a notebook from his breast pocket, scribbled a note, and handed it to the doctor. She glanced at it and nodded.

'Lara,' Dr Granger said. 'Let's now fast-forward to you walking outside the club. You've had a couple of drinks, you are relaxed and you are so hopeful.' She glanced at the note. 'Do you remember who was standing outside the club? Anyone that just for an instant caught your gaze.'

A frown furrowed her brow. 'It was drizzling that night, so there weren't many people. There were several cabs out front, the drivers behind the wheel. A couple walked past. They were huddled under hooded raincoats and hurrying.' She sighed. 'There was a man standing under an awning. He was huddled under an umbrella, and his collar was turned up. He was looking in my direction.'

Beck nodded to the doctor, silently encouraging her to continue asking about this man. 'What caught your attention about this guy?'

'He had an umbrella, not a rain jacket with a hood. Tourists carried umbrellas, the locals wore jackets with hoods all the time because it rained most of the time.'

'Take a moment to focus on this man. What did he look like?'

'His face was turned down, and his jacket collar up.'

Beck scribbled a list of questions and handed it to the doctor. 'What was the colour of his jacket?'

'Black.'

'Did the jacket have a logo?'

'Something in red on the sleeve, but I didn't get a good look.'

Dr Granger nodded. 'What about his hair? Was it long or short?'

'Short. Light colour. His hands were shoved in his pockets, and he was tapping his toe. He looked like he was waiting for someone.'

You, Beck thought. *He could have been waiting for you.*

'What else was he wearing?'

'Jeans and boots.'

Dr Granger glanced at her list. 'When you got into the cab, what did he do next?'

'Once I was in the cab and settled I glanced back out at him. I guess I felt sorry for him. He was running to the cab behind mine.'

'Did you get a better look at his face?'

'He was still holding his collar up. I couldn't see his face at all.' Her head cocked and she sat up.

Beck jotted down notes. *Tourist. Blonde. Midsized. Black jacket. Red logo.*

'The cab took you back to your apartment?' Dr Granger said.

'Yes. I got out of the cab and hurried through the rain to the entryway. As the cab pulled off I was fishing my key out of my purse. I always had my key out, but I'd forgotten that night. I was pretty tipsy. Before I could get it out . . .' She stopped and her breathing grew shallow.

'What happened?' Dr Granger said.

Lara raised fingertips to her lips. 'Someone pressed a

rag to my face.' Panic sharpened her tone. 'The smell was awful. And then everything went dark. The next thing I remember is the hospital.'

Beck motioned to the doctor. He wanted to ask the next question. The doctor hesitated and then nodded.

He leaned forward, his knees nearly pressing against hers. 'Lara.'

Tension rippled through her shoulders and her breathing slowed.

'Lara, it's Sergeant Beck.'

Her frown eased.

'In the dream you had the other night, you said there was a man. The man commented on your white dress.' He didn't mention the sexual assault, fearing she'd shut down.

She smoothed her hands over her jeans as if it were the imagined white dress. 'He liked the white dress.'

'What did he like about it?'

'He said . . . he said it made me look like an angel.'

Beck met Dr Granger's gaze. The doctor nodded, prompting him to continue. 'He said you looked like an angel?'

'An angel that fell from heaven. His voice was barely a whisper.'

'What did he smell like?'

She hesitated and then wrinkled her nose. 'He smelled like lemons.'

'Lemons?'

'Yes. Very strong.'

'What else do you remember?'

'He liked hurting me.' Her brow wrinkled. 'When I

cried out, he laughed.' A tear spilled down her cheek and she quickly grew restless.

Dr Granger touched Lara gently on her knee. 'You are safe, Lara. He isn't here, and he can't hurt you.'

Lara stared out with vacant eyes. 'But he can hurt me. He can see me, but I can't see him.'

Her entire body tensed, and she leaned forward as if to get off the couch. Beck shifted to the couch and sat beside her. 'Lara, you are safe.'

Lara leaned into his warmth. 'I am not safe.' She raised her hand to her neck and tears welled in her eyes.

'I'll wake her up,' Dr Granger said.

Beck hated seeing her suffer, but if he didn't find the Strangler, more women would die. He took her hands in his. Her fingers, small and delicate, were rough with callouses. 'Did he say anything else?'

Her fingers fisted around his. 'After he got off me his mood changed. He sounded angry. Said I needed to look at him. I needed to see him.' She started to weep.

Beck nodded to the doctor, signalling her to end it.

Dr Granger immediately snapped her fingers. 'Lara, it's time to wake up. Wake up, Lara.'

Lara's lids fluttered open revealing blue eyes filled with panic and fear. Wet tears streaked.

'It's okay,' Beck said.

As she lifted her gaze toward his face, she saw that he was still holding her hands. Instead of pulling away, he held tight with surprising strength. Slowly her wild look calmed.

She closed her eyes and when she reopened them she

looked controlled. She pulled her hands free, swiped her cheek dry, and sat straighter. 'Did I help?'

'You remembered that the man from your dreams smelled of lemons and that he wore a bandage on his hand. Any ideas that could fill in more details?'

Silence, and then she frowned. 'Sorry. Not a clue. But I'll think about it.'

Dr Granger said, 'I think that's enough for today.'

'I agree,' Beck said.

Lara nodded. 'I should stop by the gallery and check in with Cassidy. She sent me an email and said I've had more sales.'

Beck made no move to ease his body away from hers. He liked the feel of her next to him. 'Maybe you should give it a rest.'

She pushed her palms over her thighs and rose. 'I'd rather keep moving. Life is simpler if I'm busy and don't have too much time to think.'

Beck also rose. 'Why is that?'

'When I'm busy I'm not worrying. When I have down-time I get a little panicked.' She kept her tone light, but it didn't lessen the punch of the words.

'Why?' Dr Granger said, standing.

'The hole in my memory stirs up all kinds of worries.'

'What are some of the common worries?' Dr Granger said.

'That he is close. That he always knows where I am. I think that is why I was on the move so much. I just wanted to stay ahead of it.'

'Were there times when it is worse than others?'

'Around the anniversary of the attack.'

June 1 had been the date on the first police report. 'That's tomorrow.' He'd been wondering why the killer had returned to Austin but had left Lara alone so far. Was he waiting for the anniversary?

'What are you thinking?' she said.

'Just tossing around ideas. It's what I do all the time.'

'It's more than tossing around ideas. You've settled on a theory.' She cocked her head. 'He's waiting for the anniversary.'

'We don't know that.'

Keen eyes assessed him. 'No, but you are thinking it.'

He smiled. 'I think a lot. Why don't I follow you over to the gallery?'

'You don't need to do that. I can handle myself.' She looked at Dr Granger. 'Am I good to go?'

The doctor smiled. 'Yes. But if you have more memories or thoughts, call me. Don't worry about the time of day.'

Lara, Lincoln, and Beck moved to her truck.

'Bring that tyre by Beck's Garage, and I'll patch it up for you.'

'You'd patch a tyre for me?'

'I can patch a tyre, fix any engine, and hit any target with just about any gun. But don't ask me to dance.'

She laughed. 'No dancing?'

The laughter made her eyes brighter. 'Two left feet. Been a few women who stumbled off the dance floor cussing and using the Lord's name in vain after we took a spin.'

'I'll keep that in mind. What else you can't do?'

'I'm not fond of chick flicks, fancy restaurants, or wearing a tie.'

'And what do you like?'

A half smile flickered at the edge of his lips. 'I like you.'

She arched a brow. 'Me? Sergeant, now I'm worried about you.'

'Why's that?'

'I'm a neurotic artist who hasn't lived anywhere for more than six months in the last seven years. I work insane hours, and I'm extremely moody when the work isn't coming together.'

'Other than the neurotic artist part you could have just described the life of a Ranger.'

She shrugged. 'Perhaps we are kindred spirits after all. And,' she said, 'I'm not so fond of dancing either.'

'What do you like?'

'I like my work. I like Lincoln. I'm starting to like my house and Austin.'

He took her hand in his and traced her palm with his calloused thumb. 'I'm going to catch this guy.' Clear. Decisive. 'You are going to be safe.'

'You sound a little like Raines. He said almost the same thing to me in Seattle. And now here he is seven years later still hunting the same killer.'

The comparison to Raines was not a comfortable one. 'Do you know much about Raines?'

'No.'

'What about his personal life?'

She cocked her head, questioning. 'I remember him

showing me a picture of his daughter and saying he did what he did for her.'

'Did he tell you that his wife and daughter died?'

Her skin paled. 'No.'

'Car accident about eight years ago.'

Her gaze softened. 'I'm so sorry. I don't like the guy, but I wouldn't wish that kind of tragedy on my worst enemy.'

'He still wears his wedding band. And I would never have known if one of his old coworkers hadn't mentioned it.' Beck hooked his thumb in his belt loop. 'You're right when you say he is a lot like me. Raines and I are both driven, and we both live for the job.'

'You're afraid you'll end up like him.'

Nail on the head. His forced vacation had made it painfully clear that he had no life outside of work. He'd never minded the long hours or his meagre social life. In the last few years the line between him and the work had blurred.

Even that realization hadn't bothered him until he'd met Lara. 'I might be a bit worried about that.'

She drew in a breath as if she was bolstering her courage. 'I try to picture myself in ten years. Will I still be tromping around the country alone taking pictures? Yes. But will I be coming home to an empty house? Lincoln will likely be gone by then, and I won't have anyone.'

She chewed her lip. 'I don't love that vision.'

He put his hand in his pocket, resisting the urge to touch her. 'Might not be that bad.'

A blush coloured her pale cheeks. 'When this is all over, Detective, why don't you come by my place for dinner?'

'A vegetarian dinner?'

She shrugged. 'Some of the mushroom dishes taste a lot like meat.'

He leaned toward her, grinning. 'But you and I would both know it wasn't the real deal.'

Lara tucked a stray strand of hair behind her ear. 'Kinda the point.'

His look was probing. 'Saying I do come over for a meal.' He spoke carefully, each word deliberate. 'How about I bring a couple of steaks to cook on the grill? You do have a grill, don't you?'

'I do. But a couple of steaks?' She shook her head. 'I don't eat steak.'

He arched a brow. 'I was thinking about Lincoln.' The dog's ears perked at the sound of his name. 'We carnivores got to stick together.'

She savoured the warmth of his hand against hers. 'I'm sure he could be talked into it.'

Beck stood just inches from her, so close he could smell the mingling of her scent with her soap. Another loose strand hung over her eyes and he wanted so much to brush it back. Instead he released her hand and stepped back. 'The difference between Raines and me is that I am going to catch this guy.'

Beck arrived at the medical examiner's office just after grabbing a quick sandwich. Santos stood by the table, watching as the doctor made his external examination. 'Sorry I'm late.'

Santos looked up. 'How is Henry?'

343

'Hanging tough, but he's going to have to watch it for a while.'

'Steve there?'

'I left word with him.'

'Good.' Santos drew in a breath. 'I called the hospital, and because I'm not family I wasn't allowed to visit.' Sadness drifted behind the words.

'Go any time. And if they give you shit, call me.' He hesitated. 'Visits should be made sooner than later.'

Santos frowned. 'Got it.'

'He'll like the visit.' Beck took a deep breath, and as he released it, he brushed his personal problems into a box and locked up tight. Later, when he had time to worry and fuss, he would, but for now it was all about the case. 'What have you found so far?'

The doctor peered through clear goggles. 'I was just inspecting the dress and noting it is different than the others.'

'How?'

'Style is simpler. Less lace. No trim.'

'I was thinking about the dresses,' Santos said. 'What if we lined the dresses up and had my aunt look at them?'

'Your aunt?'

'She's a seamstress. Made all the costumes for a lot of the bands and singers in town. She can tell a lot about the way a person sews.'

'It's worth a try. Set it up.'

The doctor carefully undressed the body and placed the dress in a paper bag. 'There are no signs of external trauma,' he said. 'Except of course for the bruising around the neck.'

'The second and third victims did show bruising.'

'Especially around the ankles and wrists. Not this one.' He continued his external exam. When he began the vaginal exam, both Beck and Santos shifted uncomfortably.

'She wasn't raped,' the doctor said.

'You're sure?' Beck said.

'I'd say it's been a while since she had intercourse.'

'Why did he change his pattern?' Beck said.

'The level of violence with men like this usually escalates,' Santos said. 'Chasing the thrill requires more and more violence to achieve an adrenaline fix.'

'So why scale back?' Santos said.

Tension clawed at the back of Beck's head. 'Hell if I know.'

Chapter Nineteen

Friday, June 1, 11 am

Collecting final portfolios and assisting with the student art show did not give Lara the luxury of hiding at home, so she'd risen early, walked Lincoln, and then the two of them had gone to the art department to assemble the works for the show. She'd called Danni several times, left messages, but had yet to speak to the girl. She thought about driving by the girl's house, but decided against it. The kid had missed one optional lab. That was it. And kids skipped classes all the time.

'Transference,' Lara muttered as she stood on a chair in the gallery, hanging a watercolour. She'd been around enough psychologists to know that transference was about redirecting her own fears and worries onto someone else. It was easier to worry over Danni's imaginary problems than her own extremely real ones.

The cell tucked in her back pocket rang. Irritated by the interruption, she finished centring the image before climbing down and checking the caller ID. It was Jonathan.

Brushing off her irritation, she smiled at Lincoln, who looked up at her mildly curious, and raised the phone to her ear. 'Jonathan.'

'I keep thinking I'll run into you at the gallery or school, but you're not frequenting your regular haunts.'

'Crunch time,' she said, cradling the phone under her ear as she straightened a picture.

'I was hoping to take you to lunch.'

She studied the photo with a critical eye one last time and then stepped back. 'What time is it?'

'It's eleven-thirty.'

'That late? I could have sworn I just ate breakfast.'

His chuckle rumbled through the phone. 'You were like that when you lived in Seattle and worked for that designer. Always forgetting to eat. Always running behind. Sounds like you've finally come back to your old self.'

Awareness jostled through Lara's mind. 'Despite it all, I guess I have.'

'You're not afraid.'

'I'm cautious, but I'm not going to stop living my life.'

'That's good. I'm glad to hear it. So does this mean I can pick you up and take you to lunch?'

Her stomach rumbled. 'I've got Lincoln and the student art show, so I'll just grab a bite quick, here at the school. Rain check?'

'Sounds like a pack of nabs and a Diet Coke.'

She turned and inspected a raku glazed pot and a watercolour, both done by senior art students. 'I've lived on both for long stretches.'

'Lara, take an hour and eat a real meal. Stop and smell the roses.'

She chuckled, and her stomach rumbled again. 'Okay, fine. Sure. What time?'

347

'Why don't we make it twelve noon? I'll pick you up at the school.'

'How about one and I meet you? It'll be easier with Lincoln.'

He hesitated. 'Sure. I thought I'd grill at my house. That would give Lincoln a chance to run around outside.'

They agreed to meet in an hour and a half, and she rang off, tucked her phone in her back pocket. She was just climbing down from the ladder when she heard footsteps behind her. A low growl rumbled in Lincoln's throat. Half expecting Beck, she turned with a slight smile on her face.

Instead of Beck she found Raines standing behind her.

'The exhibit looks nice.' He held out his hand to the dog and let him sniff, and when Lincoln's hackles eased, he moved toward a black-and-white still of a thunder-cloud. 'I'll bet Danni took this picture.'

Mention of the girl's name was unexpected and jarring. 'How do you know Danni?'

'She waitresses at the River Diner. I'm a creature of habit, and I see her a lot. We struck up a few conversations, and she told me about her work. Is that hers?'

'Yes.'

'She's good.'

Lara folded her arms over her chest. 'Yes. I hope she sticks with it.'

'Me too. The kid deserves better than she's gotten.'

Lara had sensed the darkness in Danni, so much like her own, but had never pried into her private life. 'Is she okay? She uploaded her work, but I haven't seen her in a couple of days.'

He nodded, keeping his gaze on Danni's photo. 'She is.'

Lara brushed a stray curl from her face. 'What's going on with her?'

'Trouble at home. But she's settled now.'

'You know a lot about her.' He was a detail man who missed little.

'She's a good kid. Reminds me of my daughter.'

Sadness crashed over her, washing away past resentments harboured toward the man. 'Beck told me you lost your family. I'm sorry.'

A sigh shuddered through him as he faced her. 'It was a long time ago.'

'Time doesn't erase a loss like that.'

'No, it doesn't.' Weariness hung heavy on his shoulders. For the first time she didn't see him as the enemy, but a man who had lost so much. 'Where is she?'

'I put her up in a hotel. She's safer away from home.'

'I'll check in on her. Look after her if she'll let me.'

He studied her. 'I always knew you were strong, a survivor, but I didn't appreciate how strong you were until this last week. You're not the lost soul I thought you were.'

'Thanks. I think. Did you just come to tell me about Danni?'

'That and a question.'

'Always a question.' No anger, just acceptance.

A hint of humour burned behind his gaze. 'You can take the cop out of the job, but you can't take the job out of the cop.'

'What do you want to ask?'

'One last question about Seattle, and then I'll let it go.'

Her guard rose. 'Okay.'

'If you'd not gotten the job in Seattle what would you have done?'

'I'd have come back to Austin. My grandmother owned a dress shop here, and I was going to work with her.'

'She was disappointed when you told her about the Seattle job.'

Lara folded her arms over her chest. 'No. She was thrilled.'

'You kept up with most of your friends from back in the day in Seattle?'

'No.'

'What about Austin? You spent summers here, right?'

'I only had a couple of friends from my summers here. My cousin Cassidy and Jonathan.'

'I remember a Johnny visiting you in the hospital.'

'Good memory. Johnny did come up after my attack. Grandmother couldn't travel so she asked him to come.'

He frowned. 'Okay. Thanks.'

'Odd questions.'

The tension in his shoulders eased. 'We cops are full of odd questions. Always trying to understand the facts.'

'So are you giving up on the case?'

'Not giving up, but I've got business in Seattle that I have to take care of.'

'When will you be back?'

'Don't know. You take care of yourself.'

'Sure.'

She and Lincoln watched him leave. 'I'll never understand that man.'

*

Beck had been weeding through the old case files on the animals that had been mutilated or killed for ten Septembers in a row. He'd started with the most recent and worked his way back. Nothing of note in the recent years; however, a file dating back fifteen years contained the name Edna Bower. Lara's grandmother.

'Damn,' he muttered as he sat straighter.

Lara's grandmother had filled out a report saying her hound, Rex, had been killed on her property. The old dog had been stabbed at least twenty times, and his mutilated body strung from a tree. No one had ever been arrested for the crime.

Beck sat back in his chair. Fifteen years ago. Lara would have been fourteen and in early September would have just left Austin for the year.

What had she said in her session with Dr Granger? She'd been hiking with Rex and her friend Johnny. Johnny. He dug through Raines's old police files. The cop had noted that a Johnny Matthews had visited Lara in the hospital.

Santos appeared in Beck's office just after one. The day's heat had curled the edges of his short dark hair and left a fine bead of sweat at his temples. 'We finally got the security tapes from the university parking lot.'

Beck glanced up from the files. 'Does it show the kid slicing Lara's tyres?'

Santos handed Beck the CD. 'Pop this in your computer and have a look.'

The tone of Santos's voice had Beck raising his gaze. Without a word he took the CD and pushed it into the drive on the side of his computer. The icon popped up and he double clicked on it.

'This was shot when most kids were in class. A little after noon. According to security this is when foot traffic is lowest in the lot.'

'This is the only camera on that lot?'

'There are four cameras on the lot. Three were disabled. This camera is difficult to see from the ground, and easy to miss.'

The colour image was recorded from a camera that was across the lot. Leaves blocked the bottom part of the image, but he could see Lara's dark truck parked near a shade tree about fifty yards from the camera. He kept his gaze on her truck. Seconds passed. And then there was the flicker of movement in the bottom left corner. A figure wearing a university hoodie moved toward the back tyre of her truck and squatted. The flicker of a knife blade caught the sunlight seconds before the blade sliced into the tyre.

'This isn't Tim Gregory,' Beck said. 'The frame is too slight.'

'Just wait. It gets better.'

The man twisted the knife in the tyre and carefully closed the blade into its sheath before rising. He kept his head bowed, his hands clenched into fists as he watched the tyre deflate.

Beck leaned forward, wishing he could reach into the computer, grab the guy by his jacket, and slam him into the hood of the truck. He flexed his fingers. 'Turn around, you son of a bitch.'

Santos's sharp gaze held the image. 'Wait for it.'

The man stepped back from the car and turned, his face toward the camera. The distance might have made it difficult to identify him if Beck didn't immediately recognize him. 'Son of a bitch.'

Santos's grin had a feral edge. 'Ain't that a pisser?'

Darkness and fury flared. 'Let's pay him a visit.'

The next hour and a half flew as Lara cleaned up her supplies. She managed to run a brush through her hair before hustling Lincoln into her truck and driving to Jonathan's. When she pulled up in front of Jonathan's place, she checked her watch, grimacing when she realized she was ten minutes late thanks to thick southbound traffic. She got out and Lincoln bounded out, barking, his tail perked as he sniffed and snorted at the air.

She hurried to the front door and rang it. His land was adjacent to hers, but distance between neighbours in this part of Texas was measured in miles not feet. Her house was a good ten miles from his.

His parents had built his house, but he'd completely remodelled the place. Not only had he put an addition on the back of the house, he'd gutted the kitchen, upgraded the plumbing and wiring, and added a pool to the backyard. The house's style might have been casual ranch before the remodel, but now it was sleek layers of glass, wood pieces he'd created, and marble. Too modern for her tastes, but very Jonathan.

The front door snapped open. Jonathan wore khakis, a white button-down, and loafers. A gold wristwatch winked as he leaned casually on the doorjamb. 'You look happy. Beaming almost.'

'Just glad to be working.'

He stepped aside, allowing her inside. 'Good to see the light in your eyes. Good to see it.'

She turned and called to Lincoln, who came bounding up to the front porch. 'Do you want him to stay outside?'

'I've got a nice air-conditioned utility room with a big chew stick waiting for him.'

She rubbed Lincoln between the ears. 'Those are magic words for him.'

Minutes later Lincoln was settled with his big chew in the utility room, and she was sitting out on his back patio while the grill heated, sipping wine.

'Lots of veggies for you,' he said. He leaned back in the black wrought-iron chair, pleased with himself.

'A man after my own heart.'

'And brown rice, too.'

She swirled her wine. 'You know all the summers I visited, I don't think I ever visited your home.'

He shrugged. 'I can't believe that. You must have been here at some point.'

'I don't think so. I only remember you at Grandma's house.' An old memory flashed. 'Your visits were always memorable because Grandma's dog Rex barked a lot.'

He smiled. 'That old hound never did like strangers.'

'He could bark.'

Jonathan sipped his wine. 'I haven't thought about Rex in years. Whatever happened to the dog?'

'Grandma said he ran off right after I left one summer.'

The memory made her frown. 'I always suspected that Grandma had him put down, but she swore he just ran away.'

'Happens.'

She'd spent many a summer feeding that old hound scraps from the table, walking him, and pouring out her feelings to him.

Shoving aside an abrupt sadness, she moved around the deck, which smelled of freshly cured wood. 'You're a true artisan, Jonathan. This woodwork is amazing.'

'Thanks. I do try.'

'So tell me about some of your latest projects.' Best to keep their conversation light and easy. She didn't want Jonathan to assume that they'd ever be more than friends.

'I've got several big decks. Each will keep the crews and me busy for the next six months. I've also got several custom furniture sets I'm building. After that we shall see.'

She smoothed her hand over the railing. The soft browns of the wood grains jumped out. 'So what is your secret to making the wood look so rich?'

'Tongue oil.'

'Really.'

'Takes longer to apply but well worth it.'

She leaned down and inhaled the scent of the wood. The aroma touched a dark and hidden memory. Chains rattled. A lock turned. She'd smelled this before. She inhaled again, reaching for the memory that flickered bright just beyond her fingertips.

'It smells like lemons,' she said.

'I add the scent in because it's so popular with clients.'

Her mind tripped forward into the shadows reaching, grabbing, and then it embraced the nightmare she'd had the other night. The man's heavy weight crushed the breath from her lungs. Rough hands. A bandaged hand scraped over her pulsing jugular. And he smelled of . . . lemons.

Lara's chest tightened and for a heart-pounding moment her vision went white, and she thought she'd pass out. Slowly the spots cleared, and she set down her glass. She thought about her car still parked in his driveway.

'I remember when you were a kid you liked vanilla ice cream,' he said.

She touched her temple with a trembling hand. 'Yeah, I did.'

Jonathan couldn't have been the Seattle Strangler. He had lived in Austin at the time. Slowly she turned to face him and moved toward the table.

Beaming, he held his glass to his lips. 'You'll be proud of me, I got a soy version.'

She glanced into her wineglass, her stomach curdling. 'That's sweet.'

'I'm just glad you are back in Austin. This is the city where you belong. Seattle wasn't the place for you.'

She set her glass down. 'No, I guess in the end it wasn't.'

'I have a surprise for you.'

'What's that?'

'Grab your wine and let me show you.' He turned down the grill.

She thought about her car. The front door. Getting Lincoln. Running. Even as her brain tried to reason with her terrified emotions.

A tentative smile flickered at the edge of her lips, and she slowly followed him inside. Her brain worked double time to calm her fears almost making headway.

He opened the door to a room off the den. 'This is my den. Where I work on my designs. I've gotten so good at copying everyone else's styles, but I do have ideas of my own. Have a look inside.'

And she looked up.

Hanging over his desk was the picture she'd taken in Seattle. The exact spot where she'd almost died.

'My picture,' she whispered, her chest brutally tight.

'It is a stunning piece,' he said. 'The instant I saw it I knew I had to have it.'

She stood motionless. 'I didn't think you liked Seattle.'

'It's not the city so much as the picture. It captures so many feelings.'

Her stomach churned. 'What kind of feelings?'

'Hard to put into words. Power. Life. Survival. It says a lot to me.'

She turned from him and the picture, suddenly unable to breath. 'I need to get some fresh air.'

'Are you feeling okay?'

She hurried back to the front of the house and snatched up her purse. With trembling hands she fished for her keys, which had sunk to the bottom. *Damn!*

He came up behind her and placed his hands on her shoulders. 'What's wrong, Lara?'

She flinched as if he'd touched her with fire. 'I'm not feeling well. I better get Lincoln and go.'

Strong fingers smoothed over her shoulders. 'When

I came to get you in Seattle, you were so beat up and broken.'

She jerked forward, uncaring if he read her fear or not. She had to get out of here.

He cocked his head. 'What is it?'

Lara backed toward the front door. 'I'm going to be sick.'

'I'll take care of you.' He took a step toward her. 'Remember when I picked you up from the hospital and took you to your apartment?'

At the time she'd not thought about it, but she realized now he'd had no trouble finding her place. He'd moved with quiet confidence up the staircase of her apartment building. Still dazed, bruised, and battered, she'd muttered her apartment number, but he'd not noticed. She'd simply been grateful to him.

'It just about broke me to see you like that,' he said.

He had been kind. 'You wanted me to pack a bag and come home to Austin.'

'This is the safest place for you.'

Raines had shown up at her apartment that night. He'd wanted to see how she was doing. At the time she'd resented the intrusion, but now wondered if he'd not saved her life. 'You were mad at Detective Raines.'

'The man had no sense of boundaries. I didn't like the way he hounded you about your memory.'

She dug deeper for her keys until fingertips brushed the metal key ring. She glanced back toward the utility room that held Lincoln. 'I've got to go.'

He cocked his head. 'What's going on with you, Lara? Something is bothering you.'

Accusations of horrific crimes clawed at her. Why hadn't she remembered him from Seattle? *Get out of here. Find Beck. Beck would help her with this.* 'I'm not feeling well.'

His gaze danced with glee. 'It's that picture, isn't it? It has upset you.'

'What?'

'I shouldn't have shown it to you. It's brought back bad memories.' He searched her gaze. 'Has it brought back memories?'

Her heart thumped hard and fast in her chest. She thought about the dream. Memories pounded in her brain and cracked at the barriers that had kept them caged for so long.

She remembered the stalker's rough hands on her neck. The scent of lemons. The way he kept saying she belonged to him. 'No. No it hasn't brought back anything. I was so drugged. I doubt I'll ever remember.' She swallowed. 'It's just that I'm suddenly not feeling well.'

Brown eyes darkened. 'You can lie down here.'

Jonathan had rough hands. 'I need to get Lincoln.' Again she thought about her car parked not more than fifty feet from where she stood now. 'Let me get my pup, and I'll call you in the morning and we can set up a new time.'

He studied her. 'I hate to let you go home alone when you're not feeling well.'

'I'll be fine. Being at home always makes me feel better.'

'I think you should stay.'

'I don't want to.' Without taking her eyes off Jonathan, she called, 'Lincoln!' The dog didn't make a sound. 'Lincoln!' No bark. No sound. 'Where is Lincoln?'

'In the utility room.'

She started down the hallway toward the room. 'He isn't barking. That's not like him.'

Jonathan moved in front of her, blocking her path. 'I was sure after I picked you up from the hospital in Seattle that you'd come back to live in Austin. And then you just vanished.'

Breath hitched in her throat as she worked her car keys between her fisted fingers. 'Get out of my way, Jonathan. I want my dog.'

He adjusted his stance to block her as she tried to side-step him. 'You should have let me take care of you.' His adult-to-child tone grated and terrified.

'I can take care of myself.' She sidestepped him. 'I need fresh air.

He grabbed her wrist, his hold firm and unbreakable. 'You remember, don't you?'

She tried to jerk her hand free. 'What?'

Fingers manacled tighter. 'Your memory is starting to come back.'

The now punishing grip triggered another memory flash.

Cold rough fingers on her neck, pressing, as a man said, 'You belong to me.'

'Let go of me, Jonathan.' Lincoln's silence had her imagining terrible scenarios.

360

'Not this time,' he said.

She twisted her wrist, hoping he'd let her slip free, and when he didn't, she swung her fist around, scraping his face with her car keys. 'Let go!'

He screamed and jerked her forward, sending her off balance and falling forward into his chest. Before she could pull back, he clamped his other hand on her neck. Blood oozed from the three deep scrapes on his face. He grabbed her keys from her hand and sent them skidding across the floor out of her reach. Seconds later, his hands were on her neck. 'The drugs were supposed to make you easy to handle. And they did.'

Choking for air, her hands flew up to his. She scraped and pulled but couldn't release his grip.

'But I gave you too much. You could barely focus. I needed you to see me, but you were too messed up.'

How had she not seen it was him?

He smiled. 'I've been replaying that moment for seven years. Each time I imagine it, I see it so differently.' He moved his lips close to her ears. 'Now when I relive it, I see you looking into my eyes, *seeing me*, as I choke all the life out of you.'

His hot breath against her neck made her shudder. 'Please.'

He stroked a strand of hair from her eyes. 'I've wanted you since I first saw you. All year I'd look forward to your visits. And when you were in town the world felt better. You were Persephone to my Hades. But then you'd leave, and I'd be so lost. So full of anger. Black September, I called it.' His eyes grew distant as if remembering those days. 'Your grandmother lied to you. She knew what happened to Rex.' He leaned forward and gently kissed her on the lips. 'Oh, Lara, you should have heard his screams when I killed him.'

Tears rolled down the side of her face as she tried to twist free. Hate elbowed aside fear. *Think, Lara, think!*

He loosened his hold. 'There's no reason to rush this. We have all the time in the world.'

She gripped his fingers and tried to pry them loose, but found his hold unbreakable. Shifting tactics, she managed a smile. 'Jonathan, it doesn't have to be this way.'

'There is no other way. There never has been.'

'Let me go get Lincoln. We can talk later.'

His gaze dropped to the rapid rise and fall of her breasts. 'And let you go? No. Persephone must stay.'

Keep him talking. 'You killed the others?'

'Yes.' He pulled her up and across the room until they reached the centre of the living room. He nudged her forward. 'Lift up the carpet.'

'What?'

'Do it.'

She knelt down and lifted the carpet with trembling hands and discovered a trap door. The wood of the floor looked old, but the lock and hinges were new and well oiled.

He knelt, wrapping his arms around her and whispering, 'Each time I killed them, I was killing you.'

Tears filled her eyes. 'Why not just kill me?'

'Anticipating a gift is always sweeter than the gift.' He looped his fingers through the latch and jerked open the door. Below was a dark black box. 'When I put you in there, I'm going to shut the lid and then bring out that damn dog of yours. I want you to hear me kill him bit by bit.'

Sickened, panicked, and furious, she jerked at his hold. 'Fuck you!'

He gripped a handful of her hair and jerked back until tears pooled in her eyes. He licked her cheek and then kissed her hard on the lips. 'I dream about the night I fucked you over and over again.'

Images of Beck ran through her head. How many times had he told her to be careful? Raines had warned her. And she'd repeatedly said that she could take care of herself. Her foolish bravado triggered a wave of nervous laughter.

'What is so funny?' His tone was annoyed, confused.

'Nothing is funny,' she rasped. She craned her neck trying to ease his grip and widened her smile. 'Nothing.'

His hands released her neck and cupped her face. 'Why are you laughing?' His eyes had grown black.

She kept smiling, knowing her amusement clawed at him. 'It's all so ridiculous.'

His face was inches from hers as his fingers bit deeper into her flesh. 'What's so funny?'

The tender flesh of her neck ached, and she could feel the bruises rising. 'My grandmother sending you to save me. Were you in Seattle when she called you?'

His gaze narrowed. 'Yes. I'd been at the airport ready to leave when my cell rang. She said you were panicked. Couldn't remember. So I took a chance and went to see you.'

He'd lurked in her hospital doorway when he'd first

arrived. 'I'd thought you were afraid of my bruises and the way I looked. You were afraid. Of me remembering.'

Gently, he kissed her on the lips and slid his hands back to her neck. 'And you didn't.'

But she must have remembered on some level because she'd never been able to shake the growing panic no matter how much anyone tried to soothe her. 'You are pathetic.'

His grip tightened more, and now she couldn't breathe. 'Bitch.'

Outside she heard the crunch of tyre against gravel. She didn't have the breath to call out and prayed who had shown would save her. Mere seconds remained before she passed out and her brain died.

God, save me.

The front door slammed open and she heard her name. The rough voice belonged to Raines. He moved forward quickly, ordering Jonathan to let her go.

Jonathan, his gaze locked on Lara's, squeezed tighter and tighter. 'We die together.'

Her vision blurred and then darkened. She'd be dead in seconds.

And then there was the explosion of gunfire. Blood splattered her face. Jonathan jerked up, still gripping her neck before his fingers relaxed, and his dead weight collapsed on her body, pressing out what little air remained in her lungs.

She reached for his hands and pried them free just as Raines freed her of his weight. She coughed, gagged, and sucked in air as she collapsed against the floor. She mustered what strength she could and rolled on her back to find Raines kneeling beside her.

Raines's expression was hard, unyielding. 'Are you all right?'

She raised her hands to her throat, now bruised and raw. Wild hysteria rose in her throat. 'How? How did you know?'

'I put the pieces together when we spoke last. But I had no proof so I've been following you. I knew he'd make a move soon. Today is June 1. The anniversary.'

Tears streamed down her face, and she began to tremble. 'Why not go to the cops? To Beck?'

He fished his phone out of his breast pocket. 'I had no proof. Just pieces of a puzzle.'

'Beck would have listened.'

'Not without evidence.'

He dialed 911 and waited for the operator. 'This is Mike Raines.' He gave their address and told him there'd been a shooting. 'And let Sergeant Beck know about this call. He's going to want to see this.' He hung up.

Lara clutched her throat and tried to let breath control the rising hysteria. The danger had passed and yet she wanted to scream.

'It's okay,' Raines said. 'He's gone.'

She gaped at Jonathan's face, staring sightlessly at the ceiling. Blood oozed from the holes in his chest and pooled on the floor. She looked up at Raines, who moved toward her with his hand extended.

She screamed.

Chapter Twenty

Friday, June 1, 4 pm

Beck was seconds away from Jonathan's house. Tension clawed at his gut, goading him to drive faster. Dust kicked up along the sides of the rural road.

He'd been trying to reach Lara by her cell phone for the last half hour, but she'd not answered. He channelled his thoughts to the day he'd seen Jonathan talking to Lara at her gallery opening. She'd been relaxed around him. Her eyes had been bright, and she'd laughed often. And when Cassidy had called her and she'd turned to leave, she'd kissed him on the cheek. The kiss hadn't appeared sexual in any way. In fact, his first thought had been that the guy was a relative, a cousin or brother. She might have thought of Jonathan as a brother, but he'd not seen her as a sister.

He rifled through his memory, trying to scrounge more facts on the guy. Construction. High-end. Like an artist. Successful. Paltry facts that told him little about the man who had pulled out a knife and sliced Lara's tyres. If not for today's tape, there'd have been no evidence to link him to Lara and possibly murder.

When Beck arrived at Jonathan's he found three cars in the driveway: a BMW, Lara's dark truck, and a sedan with a rental sticker. Jonathan, Lara, and . . . Raines.

Beck parked behind the BMW and hustled out of his car, unclipping his holster as he moved toward the house.

Lara's scream ricocheted from inside the house.

Heart thundering in his chest, he pushed the front door open to find her standing rigid, her face as pale as ash, her gaze darting between Jonathan's body and the gun in Raines's hand.

Beck drew his weapon, his attention one hundred percent on Raines. 'Put the gun down.'

Raines's gaze hardened for an instant, but then he nodded and slowly eased the gun to the floor. 'I shot Jonathan Matthews. Three shots to the chest. Dead before he hit the ground.'

Beck's gut twisted as he moved toward Raines and pulled cuffs from his belt. 'Lara? Are you all right?'

She looked at him, her eyes bloodshot and teary. 'Yes.'

Raines put his hands behind his back and waited patiently as Beck cuffed his hands. Ex-cop. Saviour. Vigilante killer. Beck didn't know what had driven Raines.

He guided Raines to a spot at the end of the entryway so that there was distance between them. He called DPS for backup and then for the first time he looked at Lara. She went straight to him, and he held her trembling body close as he kept a watchful eye on Raines. She clutched fistfuls of his shirt in her hands and relaxed into his body. Seconds passed and all he did was hold her.

Finally he found his voice under the emotion. 'Are you hurt?'

She shook her head. 'I'm bruised, but I'm going to be fine.'

Raines shrugged his shoulders. 'He was strangling her when I arrived.'

There'd be plenty of time later for details. For now he was simply grateful. 'Thanks.'

'I've got to get Lincoln,' Lara said. 'He's not made a sound, and I think Jonathan hurt him.'

'Where is he?'

'Utility room.'

He holstered his gun as old images of mutilated animals flashed. 'Stay here. Let me go check on the animal.'

'I want to come.'

'Stay.' It was a direct command that allowed no argument.

She stared at him, her terror-filled gaze knifing him. He turned and moved down the side hallway and opened the door. Lincoln lay on the floor as still as death. Beck crouched by the animal and touched his nose. 'Lincoln,' he said.

The dog opened a lazy eye as his big tail thumped gently against the floor.

He patted the dog. 'Looks like he drugged you both times.' And it made sense. Jonathan. Family friend. He would have known about the key under the pot at Lara's house. 'We'll get you out of here.'

Beck found Lara standing in the hallway, her arms wrapped around her waist.

Raines stood ten feet behind her, watching. 'I can hear the ambulance.'

Beck nodded, but his gaze stayed on Lara. 'Good.' He wrapped his arms around Lara, not caring if Raines or the

368

world saw. 'Lincoln is fine. He's drugged but fine. He's sleeping it off.'

She gripped his shirt with her hands. 'Jonathan drugged him.'

He rubbed her back, hoping to sooth her trembling. 'Part of his game. I'll call a vet, but he looks like he'll be fine. I want the paramedics to check you out.'

'I'm fine,' she breathed against him. 'He said he was going to kill Lincoln in front of me.'

He held her tight. His mind flashed to an image of Jonathan's fingers around her throat. Christ, he'd almost lost her. 'You'll see the paramedics when they arrive.' A statement, not a request. 'And if they say hospital, you go.'

'Fine. I'm not up for an argument.'

'Smartest thing I've ever heard you say.' The half dig was an intentional test to determine her mental state.

A cock of her eyebrow told him the command rankled. 'Watch it, pal.'

Under all the bruises and trauma Lara was still there, ready to challenge. He hugged her tighter, aware Raines watched them closely. 'Tell me what happened?'

Her bravado wavered. She explained about lunch and then seeing the picture. 'Having him so close smelling of lemons and then seeing the picture. I just knew.'

'You mentioned lemons in Dr Granger's office.'

'I asked him if he killed the others, and he said yes. He said they reminded him of me.' Her eyes were a chilling blue. 'When he started strangling me, I couldn't break his grip. I was starting to pass out when I heard the door open. It was Raines.'

It galled Beck that he'd not been fast enough to save Lara. He guided Lara to a seat by the entryway and ordered her to stay. She nodded, leaned back against the wall, and closed her eyes. 'Raines, why were you here?'

Raines leaned against the wall, staring at Jonathan's body. 'I've been watching Matthews for days.'

'How did you fit the puzzle pieces together?'

'I hacked into the gallery computer and pulled up the sale on the Seattle photo. I discovered the delivery site was a warehouse, which is where I planted a couple of cameras. I suspected the buyer was linked to the killings.'

'And you saw Jonathan.'

'He picked up his package yesterday.'

'Buying a picture doesn't make him the Strangler,' Beck said.

Raines grinned. 'I did some digging and found out he'd been flying between Austin and Seattle regularly in the months before Lara's first attack. He was in Seattle the day she was attacked. I have the flight records.'

Beck glanced back at the angry red scratches on Lara's neck. Fresh fury surged. 'I'm glad you put it together.'

Raines looked pleased. 'I've had a lot of years to think about this case. More sleepless nights than any cop should have. Knowing him now, I'd say he was in love with Lara and the dress symbolized marriage.'

'And the penny?'

Raines shrugged. 'A lucky sixpence in your shoe? The ones brides carry for luck. Hell, we might not ever have all the pieces.' He pushed away from the wall. 'The penny is the one detail that nails him. That was a detail only the killer knew.'

The explanation made sense. It wasn't often that cases were solved and all the details wrapped up in a neat bow, but then most cases didn't have a hound dog of an ex-cop sniffing after for nearly a decade.

'I've tracked cases all over the country for the last seven years and none came up with the MO of this case. For whatever reason, he did not kill after Seattle. Maybe he liked the fact that the attack had left Lara broken.'

'Lara is not broken,' Beck said with force.

'I agree. She might have left Seattle battered, but she wasn't broken. She's a woman on top.' He rubbed his wrists under the cuffs. 'And that had to eat at Jonathan's gut.'

Beck shoved out a breath. Like it or not, Raines had done him a big damn favour when he'd saved Lara. 'You're going to need a lawyer.'

Raines relaxed as if he'd just finished a final exam or found out the cancer test was negative. 'Got one.'

Beck arched a brow. 'Just in case?'

Raines grinned. 'That's right.' In the distance, sirens blared, growing louder by the second. 'Worry about Lara.'

Beck tensed, uncomfortable with the ease with which Raines read him.

Raines chuckled. 'I remember a partner saying once that I stared at my wife like a starving man ogled steak.' His voice grew rough. 'We were married eleven years and she could make me weak with just one look.' He hesitated and swallowed. 'Hell of a woman. A lot like Lara. Strong. A survivor. No lost soul there.'

The sirens stopped outside the house, and seconds later he heard uniforms coming through the front door. Beck apprised the officers of the situation and then led Lara out of the house. He took her straight to a waiting ambulance.

'I need to check on Lincoln,' she said.

'I'll check on the damn dog,' Beck said. 'Just sit.'

He found Lincoln standing on wobbly feet, trying to take a step. He grabbed the dog's collar. 'Hang tight, partner. Let's get you outside.' He led the animal to his own car, turned on the air-conditioning, and locked Lincoln inside, where he was safe.

When Beck returned to the ambulance, the paramedic glanced up at Beck. 'She needs to go to the hospital and have that throat x-rayed. I want to make sure there is no tissue damage or swelling that could get worse over time.'

'Is that actually necessary?' Lara said.

The paramedic glared at Lara. 'Well, I could send you home, your throat could swell, and then we could hope that paramedics reached you before you died.'

She sighed. 'You made your point.'

'I'll drive her to the hospital,' Beck said.

'You don't have to do that.' Lara said. 'I can drive myself.'

The medic laughed. 'Right. When pigs fly. She rides in the bay with me.'

Beck nodded. 'I'll follow.'

Colour rose over her cheeks as she stood. 'You're doing it again.'

He placed his hand on her shoulder. 'What's that?'

Her throat burned. 'Making a request that sounds like an order.'

He leaned toward her a fraction. 'It sounds like an order because it is an order.'

'I don't like orders.'

'Today you do.'

Four hours later, Lara sat on the gurney in the emergency room, teetering between boredom and irritation. There'd been no sign of Beck while she'd been with the doctors. She'd had a complete exam, an MRI, and a chest and throat X-ray. Now feeling bored, nervous, and a bit abandoned, Lara had trouble sitting still on the gurney. Her thoughts tumbled to Jonathan and the events of the day, which still just did not feel real. Jonathan. He'd killed all those women.

She dug back in her memory, trying to remember the kid who had lived on the farm by her grandmother's. He'd been quiet. He'd liked to build things. Always designing something in his sketchbook. He'd laughed a lot during those summers. He'd been her grandmother's handyman, always willing to fix anything. She'd had no idea that such evil lurked behind the smile.

Jonathan had followed her thousands of miles to Seattle, stalked her, and killed other women. As much as she replayed the facts, she couldn't make sense of them.

Purposeful footsteps clicking down the hallway had her

373

easing back onto her bed. She hopped up on the gurney and folded her hands in her lap.

The curtain slid back to reveal Dr Granger. As always, she looked buttoned up and formal. Tight bun, trim skirt, white shirt, and sensible heels. Lara wondered if the doctor was always this buttoned up. When she was home alone did she ever drop her dirty clothes on the floor or drink from the juice carton?

'How are you?' Dr Granger said.

Lara straightened and smoothed her hand over her flyaway hair. 'Hanging tough.'

Green eyes scrutinized. 'Are you? It's been quite a day.'

She rubbed the back of her neck with her hand. 'An understatement, Doctor.'

Dr Granger sat in the metal chair by her bed. 'You look restless.'

'I want to get out of here. I want go home to my dog.' *I haven't seen Beck since we arrived.*

'The police are going to take your statement.'

'I've already recited my story to Beck and Santos.' She shifted, wishing the pent-up energy in her body would ease.

'Talk to me.'

'My brain is a little jumbled right now. My good friend tried to kill me.'

Dr Granger frowned, staring but not speaking.

Lara closed her eyes, willing the images of today from her mind. 'I've not been in a hospital since Seattle. I'd forgotten the smells, the sounds, and the endless waiting.'

'The doctors want to make sure you're okay.'

She picked at the edge of the white sheet on the gurney. 'I feel fine.'

'You were attacked.'

She shook her head. 'It wasn't like last time. I remember more.'

'Including Seattle.'

'Pieces of it.'

'Such as?'

'How Jonathan's hands felt and smelled when he grabbed me.' She closed her eyes. 'I can hear his voice. He sounded exactly the same today. *You shouldn't have left me.* He said that many times seven years ago and today.'

'What are you feeling?'

'I'm shaken. Tomorrow when it really sinks in I might be a mess, but for now I'm okay.' The restlessness churned and hammered into the shield she now hid behind. 'As bad as today has been, it's a relief to know that at least *I know.* Having all the pieces, no matter how ugly, is better than having nothing. I can get on with my life.'

Dr Granger adjusted her glasses. 'Trauma doesn't just vanish, Lara.'

Her fingers curled into fists. 'I'm not carrying this. I am not. I've been running for seven years, and I am not doing it anymore.'

Dr Granger released a sigh. 'If you find letting go does not go as smoothly as you'd like, call me. I'm still happy to talk.'

'Thanks.' She forced the tension from her shoulders. 'And I'm sorry I'm such a bitch.'

A smile softened her face. 'You're stressed. You're not a bitch.'

'If I'm not a bitch I'm doing a fair imitation of one.'

Dr Granger's eyes warmed. 'No worries.'

'I don't suppose you could get them to spring me early?'

'Places like this have their own pace.' She rose. 'But I'll see what I can do.'

'Thanks.'

Dr Granger departed, and Lara was left to sit once again. After fifteen minutes she glanced at the digital clock on the wall. Her throat felt fine. She'd had no trouble breathing. Could swallow just fine. And no Beck. But then why should he be here? The case was over. Solved. He didn't need her any more.

'This is bullshit. I am out of here.'

Just as she spoke the curtain to her room snapped back and a nurse in white scrubs appeared, pushing a wheelchair with a stack of clothes on it. She took one look at Lara reaching for her jeans and frowned. Familiar green eyes studied her.

Lara's fingers tightened around the denim. 'I've been waiting for an hour. I'm about to jump out of my skin.'

'The wait is over, Ms Church. You're good to go.'

Lara stared at the woman. She was in her early fifties, had dark hair with just a hint of grey, and a slim figure much younger women would envy. 'Do I know you?'

'I don't believe we've met.'

Lara glanced at the name tag. ELAINA BECK. 'You're related to James Beck?'

The nurse inspected a chart and made a note. 'Guilty as charged.'

'Your nephew?'

She glanced up and smiled. 'My son.'

Lara lifted a brow. Then remembered Beck had said his mother had only been sixteen when he was born. 'He looks a lot like you.'

'So I've been told.' She glanced down at her clipboard again. 'All I have to do is get you in this wheelchair, and you will be free to go.'

'Thank you. Thank you. Thank you. So I can get dressed?'

'Yes.' There was a half smile, so similar to Beck's, and then she vanished outside the curtains.

Her hospital gown billowing around her, Lara rose gingerly from the bed. 'Beck said he'd check on my dog. Have you heard from him?'

'If Beck said he'd check on your dog, he will. Now as soon as you get dressed, I can get you out of here.' Mrs Beck retreated, giving her privacy.

'These aren't the clothes I was wearing,' Lara said.

'Yours were covered in blood. James got clean ones from your house.'

That would be like Beck to take care of a small but important detail. It didn't mean he thought any more of her. It just was a kindness Beck would do for anyone. 'Thanks.'

Lara slid her underwear on and dressed in the loose-fitting pants and shirt. She thought about her wallet and keys, still in her purse in her truck back at Jonathan's.

And ordering a cab would be tough without her cell phone, which was also in her purse. 'Shit.'

The word had barely hissed from her lips when the curtain drew back and Beck appeared. He stood tall and straight, and she'd never been happier to see anyone. She resisted the urge to lean into him and ask him for a hug. 'Please tell me you are busting me out of here.'

He removed his hat. 'That is exactly what I'm doing.'

'Is Lincoln okay?'

'He's at your house, and he's fine.'

'Thanks.' She had been so independent and self-reliant, and now she couldn't even get home or take care of her dog. 'I'd ask for a ride to my truck, but my keys are in my purse and that is at Jonathan's house.' Tears of frustration burned her eyes and one slid down her cheek. Annoyed she swiped it away. 'Sorry. I'm out of sorts.'

He moved toward her and took her hand in his. His palms were calloused. 'Santos followed me in your truck to your house. Everything is waiting for you there.'

She sighed. 'Thank you. I just didn't know how I was going to fix this.'

He stroked her palm with his thumb. 'All fixed.'

Warmth spread through her body. 'And you're going to take me home?'

'I am.'

She squeezed his hand, needing more than was wise.

Elaina Beck appeared, her gaze skittering to their clasped hands. 'Get in that wheelchair, Ms Church. I don't want you fainting on my watch.'

'I don't need a wheelchair.'

Mrs Beck arched a brow. 'You leave in the chair or you spend the night.'

Lara stared into eyes as determined at her son's. She sat in the chair, knowing Mrs Beck would keep her here tonight.

'Ready, Ms Church?' Beck said.

He stood tall and strong behind her, and the tension melted from her shoulders. 'More than ready.'

Beck leaned over, and kissed his mother on the cheek. 'See you tomorrow.'

His mother searched his gaze as if trying to peer into his mind. 'Don't worry about me.'

'Thank you, Mrs Beck,' Lara said.

The older woman patted her on the shoulder. 'You're very welcome.'

Beck pushed her out the emergency room exit to his waiting dark Suburban. He locked the brake and took her elbow, helping her rise.

'I'm not made of china, Beck.'

'You look fragile enough to break,' he said.

She smiled as she eased into the passenger seat. 'I'm a tough old gal.'

A chuckle rumbled in his chest. 'I'll keep that in mind.'

Minutes later he was behind the wheel, and they were heading outside of town. She leaned back in her seat. 'How is Raines doing?'

'He's answering lots of questions. He's going to be charged, but there's a chance he could make bail.'

'I'll do whatever I can for him.'

Beck's hands tightened on the wheel. 'I know.'

'How did you get to us so fast? Raines had only just called 911.'

'Santos pulled the college surveillance video of Jonathan slicing your tyres.'

'It wasn't Tim?'

'No.'

She shook her head, wondering if it was possible to honestly know anyone. 'Have you found out anything more about Jonathan?'

'We found six white dresses hanging in a closet.'

'Six dresses. Six women.'

'He also kept logs on the different women. *The Book of Blair. The Book of Gretchen.*'

'*The Book of Lara.*'

'Yes.'

She dug trembling fingers through her hair. 'He was always so nice.'

A slight smile tipped the edge of his mouth. 'Killers like him are experts at hiding their secrets and projecting to the world the right image.'

'I never saw it coming.'

'No one did until it was almost too late. Except Raines.' He pulled off the main road up the dirt driveway that wound back to her place. When they pulled up in the driveway she could hear Lincoln barking.

Immediately, she opened her door and hurried to her front door. It was locked, but Beck quickly appeared at her side with her keys.

'Thanks.' She twisted the key in the lock and opened the door. Lincoln jumped off the couch and bounded toward her, his tail wagging and his ears perked. She got down on her knees and rubbed him behind the ears as he licked her face.

'Boy, did I miss you,' she said.

She rose as Lincoln barked and wagged his tail. She moved to a cabinet where she kept chew sticks, reserved for when she was working on a deadline, and handed him one. He took the bone and immediately jumped up on the couch and settled into it.

'He should be good for at least an hour,' Lara said. 'Can I make you a coffee or a snack? I'm starving.'

'I'll make the coffee.'

'Didn't we already go through this once before?'

'We did, and as I remember you lost that fight.'

'Not tonight.'

'Lady, if you think I'm going to watch you cook after today, then you are dead wrong. Sit.'

'I thought you could only cook steak and coffee?'

He guided her to a kitchen chair. 'I can make a sandwich.'

'I've got pita bread, hummus, and veggies.'

He shook his head. 'No cold cuts?'

'Sorry.'

He shrugged off his jacket and hung it on the back of the barstool. 'The things I have to do in the line of duty.'

Humour softened his face, making him rather handsome.

'You are a brave soldier.'

With her guidance he made two sandwiches, sliced several apples, and brewed a pot of hot tea. They ate in silence. Lara had not realized how hungry she was and how the food went a long way toward settling her shaky nerves.

When they'd finished, Beck balled up his paper napkin and tossed it on his plate. 'I spoke to Dr Granger,' he said. 'She told me you two visited.'

'Did she give you the rundown on me?' No missing the hint of anger in her voice.

'She didn't repeat a word you said, nor would I ask her to. She's just worried about you.'

She fiddled with a piece of uneaten crust. 'I told her I remembered a little about Seattle. Smells. Sounds.' She ran through the meagre list of memories.

'That's a good sign.'

She picked at the crust. 'I may not remember all the details. I was so out of it. And I know I suppressed what I could have remembered because my attacker was someone I trusted.'

'Knife wounds to the back hurt the worst.'

'I think it explains why I ran after Seattle, and why I couldn't return to Austin after the attack. My grandmother asked me several times, and I couldn't say yes. If she hadn't passed away and left me her house, I doubt I'd have returned.'

Beck rose and laid his hands on her shoulders. 'He's dead. He's gone. He cannot hurt you anymore.'

She rested her hand on his. Touching him felt right. 'I know that. I do. I just don't feel it yet.'

Absently his thumb moved in circles on her shoulder. The subtle movement carried with it a world of meaning: compassion, care, and sexual attraction.

The skin where he touched her quickly warmed and the warmth spread down her arms to her fingers. Looking into a penetrating gaze that made her legs weak, she moistened her lips, letting her gaze dip to his mouth. She wanted to kiss him. The idea wasn't a new one, but now that the case was solved there were no barriers. No restraints. She could find out if he cared as much about her as the case. Rising on tiptoes, she pressed her lips to his.

Tension rippled through his body. 'The timing isn't good, Lara.'

If not for the growl of desire rumbling under his words she might have retreated. 'The case is solved. I said I'd have you over for dinner.'

He laid his hand on her shoulder. 'You are a witness. You've had a trauma.'

'I want to feel alive.' Emboldened, she rose on tiptoes and kissed his lips again. The kiss was gentle, but meant to be flame to tinder.

He traced her bottom lip with his thumb. 'Hold off.'

'I've been putting off my life for seven years. My new policy is to do what I want to do now, not later.' She traced her hands over his chest, savouring the way his hard muscles tensed under her touch.

'Really?' He captured her hands in his.

'Really.' She cupped his face with her hands and pulled it forward. She kissed him, this time sending him all the pent-up desire and dreams she'd carried inside for seven years.

Moaning, he wound his arm around her waist and

pulled her to him. He deepened the kiss, and she pushed her body against his. Desire burned through her veins and sent her heart beating faster than when she ran a country mile on a hot day.

'This is coming from raw emotion.' The smooth edges of his Texas drawl had turned rough.

'I know exactly what I want.' She kissed him again and this time his hand cupped her breast.

The sensations of desire nearly swept her away. She slid her hand over his flat belly and around to his butt. A groan rumbled in the back of his chest and he deepened the kiss.

Lincoln yawned, and she cut her eyes to her right. The dog was staring at them, ears perked. 'We do not need an audience.'

She took Beck by the hand and led him down the hallway to her bedroom. Without a word she unbuttoned her blouse and let it drop and pool at her feet. A simple white lace bra covered her breasts.

He raised his hand to her collarbone and gently touched the bruises on her neck. 'I should have been there today.'

'You were coming to save me.'

'I wasn't fast enough.'

She cupped her hand over his and kissed the fingertips. 'He fooled us all.'

His jaw tightened as if an invisible force were choking the breath from him.

'It's okay.' She kissed him on the lips, his jawline and then his neck.

He groaned as if it pained him to hold back and then

very slowly backed her up until she bumped into the edge of her bed. His hand flattened on her stomach. 'You are sure about this?'

She reached between her breasts and unfastened the clip. Her bra opened and she shrugged it free. 'Oh, so sure.'

Beck gently pushed her back so that she sat down. He shrugged off his shirt and toed off his boots. Carefully, he unholstered his gun and set it on her nightstand, which was crowded with half-read books.

She unfastened his large silver belt buckle, unzipped his pants, and carefully eased her hand over his erection. Hissing in a breath, he stared down at her, his eyes dark with desire.

'Am I doing it right?' she said, suddenly unsure. 'It's been a while.'

He loosened her braid and threaded his hand through her hair. 'You're doing it just right.'

Beck moved forward until his bulk forced her to sit on the edge of the mattress and lie back. For a moment he stood and stared at her, his hand tracing the edge of her jaw and then her lips. She took his hand in hers and pulled him forward. He followed easily, his weight pressing her down, enveloping her. He kissed her neck. 'Like riding a bike, darlin'. Once you have the basics you never forget.'

No witty comeback came to mind. In fact she doubted she could string two words together right now.

Deftly, he slid her pants over her hips and squeezed her bottom in his hands. She wriggled out of the pants and kicked them free. He kissed her again, and this time his fingers slid under the silk of her panties. When he touched her, she hissed and arched into him. She'd not felt this alive in years.

As he kissed her, she fumbled with the snap on his jeans and then unzipped his pants. Her fingers brushed hot naked skin and he gasped. She'd forgotten how good desire felt, to want a man and to touch him in ways that made them both forget.

He settled between her legs, hard, ready, and yet waiting. 'Last chance, Lara.'

Desire fogged her brain. 'For what?'

He cupped his hands around her face, as his erection pressed against her belly. 'To quit.'

She moistened her lips. 'If I quit now, I will burn up in a ball of fire.'

A smile tugged at the edges of his lips. 'That so?'

She pushed against him. 'Don't keep me waiting, cowboy.'

'Yes, ma'am.' He eased into her, his body expanding hers in a way that was uncomfortable at first. 'So tight,' he whispered against her ear.

Longing coursed through her veins as his scent covered her as he moved inside her. Gradually her muscles eased, and she accepted all of him.

Despite his deliberately careful thrusts, his body contained the coiled intensity of a tornado skimming across the prairie. So much power and so much energy, yet distant enough so there was no damage.

However, she wanted him to unleash that energy, that force of nature pent up inside of him. She wanted all of him.

Lara cupped his face in her hands, pulled his face

toward hers, and kissed him. Waves of tension rippled through his body as he deepened the kiss and filled her body with energy.

She'd given her body once before to a lover in college, but those youthful exchanges had always left her spirit and body wanting. And then after the attack, there'd been no man she'd been able to trust.

With Beck she could feel the need growing inside her belly, hot and furious, ready to erupt and wash over and into every dark corner of her body.

She moaned and pressed her hips up to his. He ground deeper inside her, planting a hand on either side of her head as he moved in and out.

In a different time, she'd have wanted this dance between them to be slow, like a waltz. But the tempo had been feverous from the outset.

The wanting in her grew until she could only think of him. He ground into her, growling her name in her ear. Within seconds their tempo peaked and exploded as their orgasms crashed over them. Silence wrapped around them, and for one blissful moment they were one heart.

Afterward, Beck lay on his side, his sun-darkened hand draped on her lily-white belly.

'Your heartbeat is still racing,' he said, pleased.

She traced her fingertips over his knuckles and down the veins in his hands. 'I'm grateful it didn't stop.'

He chuckled softly. 'We wouldn't want that to happen, now would we, darlin'?'

'It would be a shame if that was our one and only time together,' she teased.

He was silent for a moment. 'I'd like to think this isn't a one-shot deal.'

A smile curled the edges of her lips. 'I think that's the first time we've agreed.'

He traced a strand of hair away from her eyes. She drew circles on his hand. For several minutes she lay next to him, the steady beat of his heart thumping against her ear.

Finally, he squeezed her shoulder and released a resigned sigh. 'I need to head back to the office and talk to Raines. I still get the sense he's holding back.'

Perfect moments like these didn't last. 'What could he be holding back?'

'I wish I knew, darlin'. I wish I knew.'

Chapter Twenty-one

Raines did not have the home-field advantage in Texas. He was an outsider who had rolled into the state uninvited, bent some laws, and shattered a couple of others. Still he was convinced if he played it right, he'd unravel the legal tangles and walk out of Texas a free man.

He sat in the interview room waiting for his attorney, Tyler J. Monroe, to arrive. He'd known when he'd arrived in Texas he was going to kill someone, he'd just not known who. Now, it was time to clean up the mess.

The door to the other room opened to Tyler Monroe, a tall, heavyset man wearing a lightweight suit, a white shirt that stretched over a full belly, and dark loafers. He carried an expensive but well-used briefcase. Clear-framed glasses rested on the top of his head. 'Detective Raines.'

'I'm not a detective anymore, remember?' Regret coated the words.

Monroe arched a brow as he sat at the table across from Raines. 'From now on, I'll be referring to you as Detective in front of everyone. I want people to remember your honorable service to the public.'

'I am what I am. And no title is going to change that.'

'Titles do matter. They've mattered since the first man

dragged his knuckles out of the cave. So, *Detective*, did you come down to Texas to hunt down a vicious killer that savagely murdered six women in Seattle and three in Texas?'

Raines knew how the legal game was played. Give just enough. 'I came down here because I thought the Strangler was active again.'

Monroe nodded approvingly. 'And you got your man, didn't you, *Detective*? Caught him red-handed trying to strangle the life out of an innocent young woman that he'd tried to kill seven years ago.'

'Correct.'

'You saved a woman from a savage murder.'

'Yes.'

The attorney's glee didn't sit well with Raines. 'You're a hero.'

He threaded his fingers together. 'I don't feel like a hero. I did what I had to do.'

Monroe smiled. 'Just keep saying that. We love heroes down here in Texas. Especially when they are humble. Now let's see about getting you bail.'

Something about the day's events made Beck's gut twist just as it had during his interviews with child killer Matt Dial.

Like then, he had no concrete evidence, but only the gnawing sense that key puzzle pieces were missing. He reached for his phone and dialled Santos as he wound down the dark gravel road, remembering the way Lara had kissed him moments ago on the front porch. A lantern light glowing above her head, she'd told him to be careful. He'd hugged her tight, reminding her for the fifth time that she needed to lock her door. She'd laughed. Said it was nice to have someone worry over her.

Worry. It was what he did when he cared. For him love intertwined with fear, loss, and pain. His mother had often said Beck was most prickly when he loved.

Love.

That was a hell of word to cross his mind now. Love. He couldn't remember a time when love ever had connected to a lover. Shit. Had he fallen so far and so fast for Lara?

Was this worry rooted in love for a quirky artist, or was it a byproduct of a cop's intuition honed by years on the job?

He didn't have an answer, only knew worry now hung around his neck like a rattler, hissing and ready to strike. When a man was nose-to-nose with an angry rattler, he didn't stop to question where the rattler came from. He dealt with it. He needed to resolve what prodded his uneasiness.

Ten minutes later he pulled up to the entrance of the long driveway that had belonged to Jonathan Matthews. Three news vans had parked outside the property, held at bay by several uniformed officers. Beck slowed, spoke to the cops at the entrance, who waved him through. At the house the darkness was awash in the glow of floodlights. There were at least seven marked and unmarked cars and the forensics van.

He glanced at the clock on the dash. Five hours had

391

passed since he'd walked out of the crime scene and gone to the hospital to get Lara.

He got out of the car as Santos walked down the front steps, a cell phone pressed to his ear. The Ranger had taken off his white hat and rolled up his sleeves.

When Santos rang off, Beck said, 'What do we have?'

He clicked the phone back in a holster on his hip. 'Raines just made bail.'

'He's been in custody four hours.'

'Apparently, plenty of time if you got a hell of a good attorney. Fellow named Monroe represented him.'

Beck shook his head. 'Monroe is connected up the ass. How'd Raines find him?'

'He hired him just after he arrived in town.'

'Almost as if he were expecting trouble.'

'He came to Texas to kill Jonathan,' Santos said. 'He was just waiting for the right time.'

Beck rested a foot on the bottom porch step. 'Raines does what he wants.'

'Which is why I have DPS outside his hotel room.'

'Good. Keep an eye on him.'

'Will do.'

'What else have you found inside?'

'Books. Journals. Each focused on a specific victim.'

Beck stilled. 'Show me.'

As Beck stepped into the house, he accepted a pair of rubber gloves and paper booties from a forensics tech and pulled on both. As he entered the study he was struck by Lara's photograph hanging behind Jonathan's desk.

Small spot lights from the ceiling had been angled so that they shone on and accentuated the image.

Anger rolled over him as he pictured Lara lying in the thick wet Seattle woods while Jonathan closed his hands over her throat.

There are fourteen books. Six from Seattle. Lara's book. The three Austin victims. And six others.'

'Intended victims?'

'Yes. They appear to be works in progress. We've tracked down three and they are alive and well.'

Beck and Santos waited for the tech to give them the all-clear and then they removed the first six books from the shelves. All the books were bound in rich red leather with the victim's name embossed in gold lettering on the cover.

Carefully, Beck opened the first book, which appeared to be filled with news clips. He turned the pages slowly, amazed at how Matthews had collected every mention of the killings in a multitude of papers. The next four were the same. Lots of news clips. But the fifth and six's victim's books had handwritten notes in the margins. *They don't see what I see. They don't know what I know. I am smarter than all of them.*

The seventh book and by far the thickest was Lara's book. Apparently, he had started this book before the first Seattle killing when Lara was about seventeen years old. There were pictures of her outside her grandmother's house with her grandmother's dog, Rex. Playing. Laughing. There was even a snapshot of a smiling Lara standing next to Matthews, who stared down at her with a wolfish grin that unsettled Beck. Matthews had wanted Lara for a long, long time.

A cold anger slid through Beck's body, momentarily clouding his thoughts. Carefully he turned the pages in the book, which chronicled Lara's life in Seattle. There were pictures of Lara at her dorm, in class, and at a school fundraiser. How many trips had Matthews made to Seattle? Carefully, he closed the book, unable to stomach more now. Later he'd look and study the pages, but not now. Not when emotions ran raw through him.

Beck picked up Lou Ellen Fisk's book. The first page was a picture of Lou Ellen laughing as she hurried from one class to the other. There were more pictures going about her everyday life. Running. Grocery shopping. Car wash. And then there were pictures of her as she lay dead on the side of the Texas road. She lay in her white dress, her clasped hands folded over her chest. More news clips followed.

Beck set the book down and picked up the book marked *Gretchen Hart* and then the book labelled *Blair Silver*. Each featured pictures of the women alive and then finally strangled to death. 'The Austin books are different than the Seattle books.' He tapped the stack of Seattle books. 'They are just news clips. There are no pictures of the women before or after he killed them. It's secondhand information.'

'Except Lara's book.'

'Her book is different from them all. It starts twelve years ago. No, the Seattle killings were different. There is a distance between him and the crimes.'

'Killers change.'

'They do.' Unease scraped. 'They do.' But what was it about the Seattle killings that bothered him? He picked up the book marked *Pamela Davis*. The instant he opened the book he recognized the last victim murdered in Austin before Lara. 'We have an ID on the last body. Pamela Davis.'

Santos dug a notebook out of his pocket and flipped through the pages. He wrote the name down along with several statistics Matthews had chronicled.

Beck flipped through her book. 'He was tracking her for months, yet the book stops right before her murder. No shots of her after he killed her.'

'He was moving pretty quickly then. He'd killed three women in the span of ten days.'

'But the details were important to him. Why did he leave that last shot out of his book?'

Raines sat in his hotel room, perched on the edge of his bed staring at the television he'd not bothered to turn on. He'd been chasing this moment for over seven years and had never known what to expect when he'd reached it. He'd expected elation. A sense of peace that one feels when he's jumped a major hurdle in his life.

But he felt none of that. He felt oddly empty. The purpose and goal that had robbed him of sleep, driven him to distraction, and, yes, given him a reason to live for so long was gone. And all he felt now was empty and let down.

A knock on his door had him tensing. He didn't want to see anyone or talk to anyone. He wanted to be alone with his emptiness and figure out how the hell he was going to live the rest of his life.

'I know you're in there, Raines.' Danni's raspy voice cut through the door and reached him.

He lifted his head. 'Go away, kid.'

'No can do. I came to see you. You're the big damn hero according to the television.'

'Danni, go away.'

'Open the door, Raines.' If she'd demanded he'd have ignored her, but the quiet pleading in her voice was his undoing. He rose, his limbs weary with fatigue, and opened the door.

She grinned up at him, a sparkle in her dark eyes. 'You look like shit.'

A half grin tipped the edge of his mouth. 'Good to see you too.'

She held up a bottle of whiskey. 'Got some of those fancy plastic cups in there?'

'You're underage. How did you get that whiskey?'

She laughed. 'Child's play. You gonna let me in?'

He stepped aside and allowed her to pass.

'Where are your glasses?'

'You're not drinking around me, kid.'

She rolled her eyes, but there was no force behind her words. 'You're such an old lady. I've drank before.'

He took the bottle from her. 'I don't care. Not around me.'

'Fine.' She vanished into the bathroom and returned with one plastic covered cup. 'You are gonna drink.'

His back ached, and his head throbbed. 'A drink would hit the spot.'

She grinned, held out the cup, and watched as he filled the cup with the gold liquid. 'You've had a day.'

He accepted the cup and took a liberal swallow. 'Thanks.'

'How's Lara?'

'She's a little banged up, but she's going to be okay.'

'Thanks for that. I like her. She's been a good friend. You've been a good friend.'

He lifted his gaze from the bottom of the cup. 'You're a good kid.'

She arched a brow. 'Ah, shucks, Mr Raines. You're gonna make me blush.'

'Smart-ass.'

'So this Jonathan Matthews asshole was a real bad dude from what I'm hearing on the news.'

He refilled the glass and sat down on the edge of the bed. 'Yeah. A bad dude.'

She sat down beside him, close but not close enough to touch. 'I'm glad you got him. I'm glad he's dead.'

He downed the second shot. 'You're a blood-thirsty kid.'

She touched his hand with hesitant reassurance. 'He hurt women. He got what he deserved.'

'That he did.' He reached in a dresser drawer and pulled a small white box with a red bow. 'Got something for you.'

Danni accepted the envelope. 'What is this?'

'Birthday present. Turning eighteen is a big deal.'

She glanced in the box and then reached for the bow.

'No, no, no,' he said. 'You've got to wait for your birthday.'

'That's just two days away.'

'Two days is two days. Promise me you'll wait.'

She chewed her bottom lip. 'I hate waiting.'

He cocked his head. 'But . . .'

'I'll wait for you.'

'Good.'

'I'll take you out for coffee, and I'll open it in front of you.'

'Sounds good, but I might not be here. I got a trip to take and I want to make sure you are taken care of.'

'Where are you going?'

'Not far.'

'You'll be back soon?'

He grinned. 'As quick as I can.'

Chapter Twenty-two

Saturday, June 2, 8 am

Lara woke the next morning feeling more like herself than she had in years. After a quick shower and a fresh change of clothes, she let Lincoln out and brewed herself a cup of coffee. She stood by the back window, watching Lincoln rooting his nose in underbrush on a hunt for yet another rabbit. The dog had yet to catch a single animal, but that didn't stop him from hunting.

Lara checked her watch. She had to get to the school and finish setting up the student art show and turn in her final grades for the semester. Once those two tasks were finished today, she was officially free to do whatever pleased her. In years past, every free moment had gone into her photography: scouring papers for crime reports, locating the scenes, finding the right time to snap her images, and then spending hours and hours in the darkroom.

She glanced at the black-and-white stills hanging on her walls. Like all her recent work they looked like landscapes, seascapes, or random city streets. But all were places of death. She'd shot them all hoping to see something that would tell her why people killed. But all the shots, though provocative, hadn't told her anything that would have prepared her for Jonathan's second attack.

There'd been dozens of calls from the media, but she'd let the answering machine take the messages. And when the machine had filled, well, then the calls just got dropped or ignored. She didn't want to talk about Jonathan.

Cassidy had fielded dozens of calls, which she'd gladly taken. Lara had seen Cassidy on the news several times, talking grimly into the camera about the monster who had fooled them all. Of course, all her interviews had been at the gallery, in front of it or in front of one of Lara's images. Sales had gone through the roof and Lara had already decided to donate the proceeds to a victim's shelter. She considered the sales blood money, and she did not want them.

Lara and Beck had talked a couple of times, but there'd been no time to see each other. She missed him, missed being in his arms. With each passing day she wondered if whatever connection they'd shared had been real or raw need that came as quick as lightning.

Shoving out a breath, she packed her backpack for the trip into town. She thought back to the summers she'd spent with Jonathan when they'd been growing up.

When she was a kid she'd found a snake in the yard and screamed. He'd raced forward and killed the rattler. She'd been relieved. Called him her hero. He'd beamed. Later he'd proudly shown her his new snakeskin wallet he'd sewn. He'd carried the wallet for years.

His trophy for a kill. She thought about his home. What other trophies had he taken from his victims?

She shuddered and set down her cup. The need to shoot more death images still lingered. And she found herself wondering if she should shoot the latest victim's crime scene. Or perhaps she should shoot Jonathan's house. Maybe there was something there that would make sense of the madness.

'Enough. Get on with your life.'

Grabbing her purse, she whistled for the dog and minutes later the two were in the truck and headed to the school. She arrived at the school and went straight to the gallery, where the unhung pictures remained. Her hope was to avoid all questions and people and just get her work done. No more drama. No more death.

She spent the next half hour finishing up the student art exhibit. The pieces were a bright and lovely collection of potters, sculptors, painters, and collages. It was an impressive display.

After taking Lincoln for a quick walk outside, she retreated to her small office, where she found the collection of portfolios stacked on her desk. She spent the next several hours reviewing them. The portfolio collection held few surprises. Most of the kids had taken pictures of the average and ordinary and had done little to make it special. Though she hadn't been expecting great art she'd hoped to find signs that the kids were learning.

The last portfolio she examined was Danni's. She'd intentionally saved it for last. She lined up each piece on the long art table and studied the images. All in black and white, she'd taken pictures of homeless people on the streets of Austin. A man standing next to a grocery cart. He wore an old coat two sizes too large and a big hat. He was reading a book. Another image featured an old woman. She was sitting on the park bench. Danni had coaxed a bright smile from the woman. Another was of a mother and child sitting outside a homeless shelter.

Each picture, though sad and moving, held a message of hope. Life might have beaten these people down, but they'd found little ways to prevail.

Just like Danni. She reached for her cell and dialled Danni's number. Before it could ring, the phone in her office rang, startling her. She hung up her cell and picked up the landline. 'Lara Church.'

'Ms Church, this is Lieutenant Davis with Austin Fire Department.'

'Yes.'

'There's been a fire at your house.'

She gripped the telephone. 'What?'

A heavy silence followed. 'The place appears to be a loss.'

Her heart dropped into her belly. 'I'll be right there.'

Danni sat on the edge of her hotel bed staring at the white box decorated with the white bow. She had promised Raines that she wouldn't open it, but the suspense was killing her.

She shook the gift. She tried to peer under the lid. Even held it up to a lightbulb hoping to see through the box's paper sides. But as much as she tried to see inside the box without opening it, she couldn't.

Danni set the box down on the bed and reached for the TV remote. She clicked on the TV and surfed through a couple of dozen channels, all the while aware of the box sitting on the bed.

'Damn you, Raines.' Why had he given her this puzzle? Why not just wait and give her the gift? Because he knew it would drive her crazy.

Frustrated, she shut off the television and tossed the remote on the bed. She picked up the box and studied the configuration of the bow. If she were super clever, she could untie the bow, peek inside, and then retie it without Raines ever being aware. When he did come back into town, she could make a show of being surprised and he'd never be the wiser.

Nibbling her bottom lip, she tugged gently at the bow. The loop slipped a millimeter. She pulled again. It slipped more. And then unable to handle the well of anticipation, she yanked the bow and it untied and the ribbon fell away from the box.

Glancing toward the door, as if she expected Raines to walk in, she pried off the box's top. Inside was a piece of paper. Carefully, she opened it and read, *Knew you couldn't make it.*

'Shit.' Danni laughed. The old devil knew her better than she thought. When she saw him next, she'd have to come clean.

She peered inside the box and pulled out what looked like a folded photograph. She opened the photograph and for a moment, stared at the image, blinking, as her mind absorbed the details.

When she fully registered what she was looking at, she dropped the box and screamed.

Lara hustled Lincoln out of the building and into the truck. Her hands trembled as she put the key in the ignition and fired up the engine. She thought about the house that had been home to her over a dozen summers, that held all her camera equipment and all her work. Was it all gone?

She sat forward in the seat clutching the wheel as she headed out toward the interstate. If she hustled, it would take her twenty minutes. In the past she'd never minded the drive. It was a quiet interlude to a hectic day. But now the minutes stretched like years.

'Don't borrow trouble, Lara. Don't.' Lincoln's ears perked up at the sound of her voice. He whimpered. She glanced at him and tried a smile. 'It's okay, boy. We're okay so the rest is fixable. Somehow.'

A car rolled up behind her on the interstate and at first she gave it little mind. But as the vehicle continued to hover behind her, her mind tripped to Jonathan and the women he'd stalked. He'd disabled their cars and when they were alone on the side of the road he'd attacked.

'Jonathan is dead,' she muttered. 'You saw him die.'

She shrugged off the fear and kept driving. She had bigger problems on her hands now. She pressed the accelerator toward the floor and watched her speedometer nudge closer to eighty.

Her exit arrived within minutes, and she took it, braking as little as possible. She kept thinking about her house and all her belongings. Her work. Computers. Cameras. Was it all gone?

She glanced into the rearview and noticed the car she'd seen earlier was gone. Her cell phone rang and she jumped. A quick glance at the phone revealed an unrecognizable number. 'Reporter,' she muttered.

Down the last road and up the driveway she came around the last bend and discovered her house was perfectly intact. No fire damage. No trucks. The house was as she left it.

'What the hell?' She got out of her car and pulled off her sunglasses. 'This is someone's idea of a joke.'

Lincoln bounded out of the car and up to the front porch. As far as he was concerned life was good and he was ready for dinner. 'We might as well eat.' She dug her keys out of her pocket and moved to the front door. As she put the key in the lock a car pulled up her driveway. She turned, immediately tense, until she saw the driver.

'Lara,' Raines said.

Her muscles eased as relief washed over her. 'What are you doing here?'

'I got a text. You said you wanted to meet me.'

Lincoln barked and growled at Raines, the hackles on his neck rising. She grabbed his collar. 'I didn't text you.' Every nerve in her body snapped with tension. 'What are you doing out of jail?'

'I made bail.' He held up his cell phone. 'I tried to call you, but you don't have your cell phone anymore.'

'I saw the number but didn't recognize it.' Still puzzled,

she glanced at her house. 'Someone called me and told me my house had burned to the ground.'

'No shit.'

'Somebody's idea of a joke?' She patted Lincoln who stood tense and alert.

Carefully, he tucked his cell in his breast pocket. 'Someone wanted us both out here.'

'But why?'

He nodded toward the house. 'Can't say. Did you tell Beck?'

'I didn't get the chance. I was so panicked I came straight away.' She dragged trembling fingers through her hair. 'I did not need this scare.'

A half grin tipped the edge of his mouth. 'Since I'm out here how about a glass of water? This damn heat is killing me.'

'Sure.' As she leaned down to speak to Lincoln, she heard a clip unfasten. She turned and found Raines pointing a gun at her.

For a heart-stopping moment, she tried to make sense of this. Lincoln growled and barked. But instead of asking for an explanation, she released the dog. It lunged toward Raines.

The dog was fast but not fast enough. Raines shifted the tip of his gun and fired, hitting the dog in the hindquarters. Lincoln yelped wildly and dropped to the ground.

Lara screamed and dropped to her knees, skimming her hands over his body. In the midsection her hand felt the warm ooze of fresh blood.

'Get up,' Raines said.

Lincoln's blood stained her pale fingers scarlet. 'Why?'

'You'll know soon enough. Let's go.'

'Fuck you! I'm not leaving my dog.'

'He's still alive, but if you don't get up now I will put a bullet in his brain.'

She glanced up at him, and the look in Raines's eyes took her breath away. It was an absence of emotion or caring. He'd kill Lincoln now. 'Why?'

'Get up.' He pointed the gun at the dog's head.

She kissed the dog and whispered in his ear that she'd find a way to save him and then rose. He whimpered and his breathing was laboured.

'Why, Raines? You saved my life yesterday.'

Raines shook his head. 'Do you have any idea what trouble you and your private stalker Matthews were to me these last seven years?'

Her hands trembled as she scrambled to calm her mind. 'What did I do?'

With the tip of his gun he motioned for her to stand. 'You were the object of his obsession. You drove him to kill. You drove him to Seattle – to *my* town.' His calm tone was more frightening than Jonathan's ranting. 'Let's go.'

She touched Lincoln one last time and then slowly rose. 'How is that my fault? He was insane.' A breeze across the rolling hills chilled her skin.

'And then you couldn't remember.' He sounded so reasonable. 'I wanted to kill you seven years ago. I hated the idea that people thought I had raped you like some animal. The press couldn't let that detail go. They called the Strangler a pervert. They said he was warped. I needed you to remember who your attacker was so that I could catch him.'

Fear compressed her chest. 'I tried to remember!'

'God, but all I did to make you remember. And you couldn't remember one goddamned detail.'

'You got Jonathan. You killed him. You are the hero of the hour.'

'And everyone knows me as the guy who killed the Strangler.'

She thought about running into the woods. If she could get past him and into the woods, she could call for help from her cell. 'Why is that bad?'

His voice sounded like a growl. 'Because he tainted the work I did. He soiled it.'

'He killed those women!'

'He killed in Austin.' Raines shook his head. 'But he was not the Seattle Strangler.'

Energy rushed from her as if she'd been punched. 'He killed those women. I heard about the journals detailing how he stalked them.'

'He killed the ones in Austin. But not Seattle. In Seattle all his information was secondhand. From papers.'

'He attacked *me* in Seattle and Austin.'

He motioned for her move down the steps. 'Just you. No one else in Seattle. Move.'

Following his orders would only make it easier for him to kill her. 'But you found the penny in my hand. You said he was the Strangler.'

Raines smiled as if relieved to share a secret long hidden. 'That penny. Drove me insane trying to figure out how he knew.'

'What?' She tripped on the bottom step and took several hard steps before she recovered.

'When I came on your crime scene and the officer in charge told me it was another Strangler case, I was stunned. But the guy was certain. The penny. He kept talking about the penny.'

Moonlight cast heavy shadows on his face. 'Only the Strangler knew about the penny.'

'That's what I thought, but Matthews figured it out.' Raines shook his head. 'Do you know the answer turned out to be so simple? Took me a couple of years to find the answer, but I did. One of the forensic techs that'd worked several of the Strangler murders went out on a date with a guy. He got her drunk, and she talked about the case. She got drunk and talked. So stupid. I kept up with everyone who worked the case. I took her out for drinks one night and she finally told me that she'd slipped up. The guilt was eating her alive. I asked her who she told, but the name was bogus.'

'Why didn't you say anything?'

He leaned forward a fraction and dropped his voice a notch. 'Because I was the Strangler.'

'What?'

'I killed the first six women. And I didn't appreciate some poacher taking over my gig.'

Stunned, she could barely string two thoughts together. 'You were a decorated policeman, and you killed six women?'

He looked relieved to talk. 'Six that were found. Eight in all.' He muttered an oath. 'When I heard about the Austin killings I knew that son of a bitch was at it again. I knew I had a second chance to track his ass down and kill him for taking what was mine.'

'You didn't kill anyone in Austin.'

He frowned, his disgust evident. 'Just one.'

She searched for logic in the madness. 'Who?'

'The last victim. The one that was not sexually assaulted. Fitting I should steal the last act from Jonathan as he did with me.' Raines sighed. 'The last Austin victim reminded me of the women in Seattle.

They were all lost souls. Broken. Sometimes death is a kinder option than life.'

'Your wife and daughter.'

'That's right. After they died I wanted to die. But I didn't have the guts to pull the trigger. And then I saw the first woman standing on the street corner. She looked so lost. So sad. I couldn't bear to see her clinging to a life that would never improve for her. I couldn't kill myself, but I could make it better for her.'

'You strangled her.'

'I thought about her for days. Couldn't get her face out of my mind. So I decided to man up and take care of business.' His voice was soft, winsome. 'It was quick, easy, and over in minutes. The look on her face after she died made me feel good. She was at peace and in a place where she'd never hurt again. And so I dressed her in white and put the penny in her hand so that she could enter heaven right. It had been a mercy killing.' He shook his head. 'But the peace didn't last, and when I saw the next lost soul I knew I had to set her free.'

'Eight women.'

'I was better at hiding them than your boyfriend. He thought he knew me so well. But he picked a spot too close to the interstate. That's why he failed.'

She felt sick. Didn't know what to say.

'When the paramedics said you were alive, I thought it was a lucky break. You could identify the poacher for me, and I could take care of him.'

'But I didn't remember.'

A bitter smile twisted his lips. 'No, you did not.'

'Why come after me now? You killed Jonathan. You got what you wanted. Surely killing me will draw attention to you.'

'The things Jonathan did to you and those women in Texas disgusted me. I was saving broken souls; he was violating women for his own pleasure. He made good and decent work appear sick and twisted. I thought I could let him take the fall for all the killings, but in the end I couldn't let him take credit for my work. The world needs to know that the Seattle Strangler was not Jonathan Matthews.'

Hysteria bubbled inside her. 'Raines, I wasn't the one who stole from you.'

'No, you were not.' He sounded so reasonable and so sure. 'But you got him started so you are going to help me finish it.'

She clenched her fingers. 'Finish what?'

'Prove to everyone that the Seattle Strangler was a better man. A humane man. Don't worry. I'm not like Jonathan. I'll make it quick. It'll only hurt briefly, and then you will know everlasting peace.'

In that split second, she knew that to stand and obey meant certain death. Disobeying could mean death, but it offered a slim chance.

She took the chance. And ran.

No one wanted the Strangler case closed more than Beck did. His bad guy lay on a slab in the morgue. His boss had slapped him on the back. The mayor of Austin and the Texas governor were crooning over a just ending to a terrible case.

And still Beck couldn't let this case go or shake the idea that he'd missed something. Like with the Misty Gray case, he was obsessed. And like then, he couldn't walk away when nagging doubts wouldn't turn him loose. 'Why the hell is this eating at me?'

He picked up Raines's Seattle file and then glanced at Matthews's journals. All the victims had books. All the journals were covered in Matthews's fingerprints. Most had his handwritten notes scrawled inside.

Yet the first six books were different. He'd collected and scrapbooked the articles about the victims as if he were an observer.

An outsider.

A copycat.

Adrenaline shot through Beck. A copycat would explain why the first six killings were so different from Lara's attack and the first three Austin killings. The last Austin victim had been different . . . more like the Seattle cases than any of the others.

A copycat.

Shit.

Beck flipped through the Seattle case files. He needed to prove that Jonathan had been in Seattle when the initial six victims had vanished. He scanned the pages making a list of the dates on a yellow notepad.

December 20
January 2
February 6
March 11
April 9
May 1

The last Seattle victim had been Lara, who'd been attacked on June 1.

Beck then glanced at the articles Matthews had collected about the killings and himself. There were older articles about the animal killings in Austin. An article about Matthews winning contracts for furniture. Another piece about him opening his own custom furniture business twelve years ago.

Beck found an Austin article featuring a picture of a grinning Matthews surrounded by a half dozen older women. According to the caption, he had crafted and donated a cedar chest to be auctioned at the group's annual fundraiser. The photo had been snapped the day before the holiday event – December 20, the exact day the first Seattle victim had vanished.

Matthews couldn't have snatched the first victim and also attended a fundraiser.

Despite what Raines had said, none of Matthews's credit card receipts showed any flights, trains, or buses to Seattle around dates the women vanished. Private planes and cash would get the job done. And driving was an option. The trek from Austin to Seattle was over fifteen hundred miles, but doable in two days if the driver pushed himself. If Matthews had wanted to travel untraced, it was possible.

But Raines had said he had evidence of Matthews's travel during that time period.

He dug deeper, comparing the critical dates to credit card and phone receipts, and found discrepancies with two other killings.

Jonathan had killed women in Austin and attacked Lara, but Beck now had proof he could not have killed three of the first six Seattle victims. He'd either had help or he wasn't the Seattle Strangler.

Something was wrong.

Very wrong.

And until Beck could explain it away with evidence he wanted Lara somewhere safe.

His radar in overdrive, he called Lara's cell. No answer. He glanced at the clock. It was after six. It would take him twenty minutes to get her place and see for himself that she was okay. He grabbed his coat and hurried to his car.

As he pulled out of town onto the interstate, his phone rang. 'Beck.'

'Got a call from a kid named Danni Rome.'

Beck tightened his grip on the wheel. 'She's a student of Lara's. Lara has been worried about her.'

'Right. Danni's been hiding out in a hotel paid for by Mike Raines.'

'What?'

'The two met up and hit it off. According to this kid, Raines helped her out of a jam with her stepfather.'

Beck pressed the accelerator and passed a truck. 'Okay. Why did she call you?'

'Raines gave her a birthday present. He told her not to open it until her birthday, which is two days from now.'

He knew enough about inquisitive teens to know the kid had opened the present early. 'What was in the box?'

'A picture of the stepfather, Roger Hill. The guy's throat appears to be cut. We sent a cruiser to the Hill house. No sign of Roger, but lots of blood.'

Shit. 'Where is Raines?'

'He checked out of his hotel room,' Santos said. 'And the rental car agency says he turned his car in at the airport. Looks like he's skipped.'

His stomach tightened as he wove in and out of Austin city traffic and then edged toward the I-35 exit that led to Lara's house. He gave Santos the rundown on what he'd found out about Matthews and the first killing.

'He couldn't have been in two places at once,' Santos said quietly.

'No. No he could not.'

A heavy silence. 'We know Matthews killed the Austin victims.'

'He stalked them and took pictures of them after they were dead. But he had nothing personal about the Seattle victims.' His hands tightened on the wheel. 'Because he was studying the killer.'

'The penny.'

'Somehow he figured it out.' The officers might have been sworn to secrecy, but leaks happened.

'Damn.'

'What about Pamela Davis? There was no sexual assault and no postmortem pictures in Matthew's book. She fits the Seattle profile perfectly.'

'Two killers?'

'Raines was in Seattle when the first women were killed and here when Davis died. And now he is gone.' Beck punched the accelerator. 'Put out an alert on Raines. I'm headed to Lara's.'

He raced down the back roads, dirt kicking up as he barrelled toward Lara's house. When he pulled up into her driveway, he saw her car and a rental. Raines. Parking, he called for backup and then, drawing his gun, raced toward Lara's truck. A dog's whimper drew his attention to the front porch where Lincoln lay bleeding. He rushed to the dog and touched him. The dog cried and his own hand was covered in blood. Lincoln had been shot.

Beck grabbed his phone, dialled into dispatch, and

asked that a vet be dispatched. He glanced up and saw Lara's keys still dangling in the door.

Lara screams echoed out from the woods.

Raines was faster than she'd ever imagined. He raced over the ground behind her, his feet thundering fast and hot. She didn't dare look back as she felt the glance would cost her precious time. She reached for her cell phone and dialled 911, but in her rush, she tripped over a rock and dropped the phone.

Lara stopped to pick up the phone. It was just a second or two of hesitation. But enough time to allow strong arms to wrap around her waist and tackle her to the ground. She hit hard on her side and felt the air whoosh out of her lungs. Stunned by the impact, she didn't move for a second until she felt herself being rolled on her back and strong legs trapping her as her arms were pinned over her head.

Sweat dripped from Raines's brow, and he huffed and struggled to catch his breath. 'You're fast.'

He was going to kill her out here in the wilderness, and no one was going to find her body for days or weeks, if ever.

Her survival rested on her shoulders now. No one was going to save her now. She tried to pull her hands free of his grip, but his fingers only bit tighter into her flesh. She flayed her legs and thrashed her body, reasoning if they were fighting at least he wasn't strangling her. Once he got his hands on her throat and started to squeeze, she'd be dead in minutes.

A burst of energy born of desperation fuelled her struggles, which she prayed were taking their toll on him.

Sweat dampened his palms, making them slick and allowing her to pull her hand free. She balled up her fist and hit him squarely in the jaw.

He cursed and punched his fist into her belly, knocking the wind and the fight right out of her. She coughed and sputtered.

He wiped the blood from his nose. 'Fighting me is only going to make this more painful, Lara. And I don't want to hurt you.'

She coughed and sucked in hair. 'You want to kill me, you bastard.'

'Death is not the worst fate you can suffer, Lara. You know life is full of pain.'

'It's my pain, you asshole. And I'll take the good with the bad.'

He wrapped strong fingers around her neck. 'It's better this way.'

'It's not.' Tears welled in her eyes and trickled down her cheek over his hands. 'It's not.'

He smiled as he started to tighten his hold. 'There's no saving either of us.'

Gun drawn, Beck hustled to the top of the hill and immediately spotted the flicker of movement fifty feet ahead. He spotted the back of a man, hunched forward. There was no sign of Lara. He took a chance and called out, 'Raines!'

The man glanced back for an instant, then returned his attention back to where it had been. Beck raced forward another ten yards, saw Lara's body trapped under Raines. Beck didn't hesitate. He stopped, steadied himself, and fired.

The bullet struck Raines in the back, knocking him to the side. Lara rolled to her side, coughing and clutching her throat. Raines, clutching his side, rose up as he reached for his gun.

'Leave it, Raines.'

Raines's gaze sharpened and then he drew his gun.

Beck fired, this time hitting him in the chest. For an instant, Raines stood there, stunned, and then slowly lowered his gaze to the blood blossoming on his shirt. He touched the blood with his fingertips, smiled, and dropped to the ground.

Beck ran toward Raines, picked up the ex-cop's gun, and checked for a pulse. None. Raines was dead.

Lara rose up and staggered to her feet. Beck raced toward her, catching her as she lost her footing. He stared at the dark red angry marks on her neck and nearly broke. 'You're okay. I've got you.'

She tried to speak, but her voice sounded like a hoarse croak.

'You don't have to speak.' In the distance, the sound of sirens grew closer and closer.

She shook her head. 'Lic . . . Lincoln.'

'That's help on the way. He was alive when I saw him.'

Tears flowed down her face.

Beck held her close. 'I've got you. You're safe.'

Epilogue

Six weeks later

'Will the patient live?' Lara said as she glanced over her truck engine into Beck and Henry's pensive expressions.

Henry, who'd been home from the hospital for over a month, shook his head. 'Gonna take some work. This baby has been rode hard.'

Beck glanced up at her, his gaze softening a bit when he looked at her. 'Don't you think it's time for a new truck, Lara?'

A fully recovered Lincoln sat in the corner of Beck's garage gnawing on a chew stick. A low growl rumbled in his chest as he halted his chewing to scratch a shorn patch on his hindquarters. The vet had shaved nearly his entire back leg and part of his right side. The hair was growing back, but he still looked moth-eaten.

Lara's bruises had healed easily, and she appeared perfectly normal, but the attacks of Matthews and then Raines had left a mark on her. She continued to wake up in the middle of the night clutching her throat and gasping for air. Most nights Beck was at her side, holding her close until her panic eased. At Beck's urging, Lara spent more time with Dr Granger, who worked with her to unlock more buried memories from her past.

Lara stared at the engine. 'But I love this car. It was practically my home for the last seven years.' She'd even slept in it some nights.

Beck's smile was warm, gentle. 'And it served you well, but the time has come to let it go.'

Lara glanced at Henry. 'It really can't be saved?'

'It would take a great mechanic at least a week to fix all that needs fixing.' He kept his gaze on Lara, not tossing even the slightest glance at Henry. 'It would cost a fortune. You are better off, and safer for that matter, if you get a new car.'

She smoothed her hand lovingly over the car. 'God, but I hate to see her go.'

'Sometimes it's best to start fresh,' Beck said.

Henry rubbed the back of his neck. Three weeks ago he'd had open-heart surgery. He was recovering well, but without the work of the garage he had grown irritable and sometimes depressed. 'Beck's more doom and gloom than me. I might be able to fix her.'

'You think?'

When she looked at Beck she saw no doubt in his eyes as he shook his head. 'Lot of work, Henry. Think you're up to it?'

Henry straightened, hooking his thumbs in his belt just like his grandson. 'Retirement is overrated. A little stress and aggravation will do me good.'

Lara grinned. 'Take as long as you like. I've got Cassidy's old car to drive until it's ready.'

Henry winked at her. 'She'll be running like new when I'm done with her.'

Beck, stifling a grin, came around the truck, and hooked his arm around Lara. 'You're biting off a mighty big bite.'

Henry snorted. 'Get out of my garage. I've got work to do.'

Lara and Beck walked outside into the sunlight. Lincoln glanced up at her and then at Henry before lowering his attention back to the rawhide.

She hooked her arm around his waist. 'You were right,' she said. 'Henry needs a project.'

'Treating him like an old man won't help him a bit.'

For a moment, she tipped her face toward the sun, revelling in the perfection of the day. She had Beck, Lincoln, Henry, and Elaina. Her work was not only selling, but she was hungry to create more. And two very dangerous men were dead. One had wanted to save his victims and another had wanted to steal their bright futures.

She thought about Raines and the detailed notes they'd found in his briefcase. Many of the notes detailed her travels over the last seven years. Crammed in the back of the notebook were newspaper articles that described the Austin murders. In red ink, he'd scrawled *LIAR* on all. Raines couldn't stand to see credit for his 'good' work tainted by Matthews. His drive to find the imposter had become such an obsession it had halted his own killing spree.

Jonathan's books had been equally as chilling. The Seattle books had been his attempt to study the Seattle Strangler, a man who'd captured his obsession. He'd spent hours and hours fantasizing about the Strangler killing Lara, whom he felt had betrayed him when she opted not to return to Austin.

One killer saw himself as a saviour and the other a righteous thief who owned the promising futures of women so much like Lara.

'You're doing it again,' Beck said.

Eyes still closed, she said, 'What's that?'

He traced a frown line on her forehead with his fingertip. 'Remembering.'

She opened her eyes, a wry smile tipping the edge of her lips. 'I spent so many years wishing I could remember, and now I can't stop.'

'Bad memories don't go away, but they do ease with time.'

'And in the meantime?'

He grinned. 'We make some memories of our own.'